VERA'S STORY
HIDDEN SCARS OF WAR

BY
FRANCES Y. EVAN

First Published in 2022 by Blossom Spring Publishing
Vera's Story Hidden Scars of War © 2022 Frances Y. Evan
ISBN 978-1-7398866-6-0
E: admin@blossomspringpublishing.com
W: www.blossomspringpublishing.com
Published in the United Kingdom. All rights reserved under International Copyright Law. Contents and/or cover may not be reproduced in whole or in part without the express written consent of the publisher.
This work is based on true life events and the recollections of the author. In some cases, the names of people and places have been changed to protect the privacy of others. The details of events and conversations have been remembered as accurately as possible although sometimes enhanced by the author's imagination.

Dedicated to the memory of my parents

Vera and Maurice

And to all those who carry the scars of war

VERA'S STORY
CHILD OF WAR

PREFACE

The heavy branch tore through the roof of the dining room, shooting debris all over the room as the woman screamed. Memories came flooding back as the storm intensified. Vera had been in this situation before, huddled down in the dark while roaring fury erupted above. All the emotions she had felt then, she felt again: fear, anger, helplessness, panic, despair. The noise, the waiting, the anticipation of disaster grew as the storm blew closer and closer. The woman covered her ears and lowered her chin to her chest. She wanted to cry out as she had as a child, but she was so much older now and must be brave and controlled. The howling grew louder. Something flew against the house. Glass broke somewhere. A loud boom of thunder caused her to cringe and pull her body into a tight ball. The wind blew in violent bursts of power, sometimes rushing through the trees, creating an ominous whistling that reminded Vera of the rushing sound of falling bombs. Something cracked and fell with a heavy thud outside. Vera cried out involuntarily and reached for her husband's arm. It was happening all over again. How could it be? They were again in fear for their lives, this time by nature, the last time by man!

Hurricane Kate came ashore in November 1985 ravaging and battering the Florida panhandle. Mini tornadoes touched down twisting and snapping sturdy tree trunks, tearing off rooves, skipping and twirling a random dance of destruction across the landscape. Vera and Maurice had retreated to the inner hallway of their ranch-style house with the recommended supplies at hand, pillows, blankets, flashlight, radio, and a half bottle of brandy (not on the recommended list.) They had filled the bathtub with water and had brought inside or tied down anything outside in the yard that could be a flying hazard. Maurice was stoic and resigned. He patted Vera's hand offering words of comfort and encouragement, assuring her that everything would be alright. He was waiting it out wondering what the extent of the damage would be and how quickly repairs would get done. They had lost power thirty minutes ago. Who knew when it would be restored? He sighed deeply. The story of his life! One step forward, two steps back. Work hard, have some success and then...another setback. They had built the house only three years ago, a pretty house, comfortable, nice location, tidy, well-landscaped yard. A home they expected to live in as they approached retirement and beyond. Now it was being attacked, assaulted by the intensity of the hurricane outside. Oh well, he thought as his eternal optimism began to surface. No use worrying. Once the storm passed over, they would assess the damage and start the clean-up. They would work together as they always did and carry on.

Vera screamed again when an almighty crash hit the roof causing the house to vibrate with the shock. The howling of the wind became louder as rafters, plywood and chunks of sheetrock tumbled to the floor. "I CAN'T STAND IT MAURICE," she shouted. "I CAN'T BELIEVE THIS IS HAPPENING. IT'S JUST LIKE IT WAS WAITING IT OUT IN THE AIR RAID SHELTER ALL OVER AGAIN!"

CHAPTER ONE

Vera was an only child. At times throughout her life, she lamented this situation but at others, she was quite content, even grateful. She appreciated the attention and time that her parents had for her and her position at the centre of their world. She also knew that her mother and father, being good, old-fashioned British parents, were careful to hide this fact, but Vera knew how they felt and how much she meant to them. She thrived in the spotlight placed on her and tried her best to behave well and earn their praise.

Florrie and Sidney married rather later in life than most couples of their time. They met when Florrie's sister, Margaret and Sidney's brother, John, who were courting at the time, introduced them. Margaret and John had been planning the meeting for some time, thinking that they might be a good match. They were right. Florrie and Sidney married a year later in 1927. During their courtship, Florrie helped take care of Sidney's mother, who was failing in health quite rapidly. Sidney watched the way that Florrie tended to his mother's needs with such gentleness and compassion. She spent hours with her and provided such comfort and pleasant company, that Sidney would be forever grateful. The young couple managed to enjoy some time together with their large circle of family and friends. There were occasional parties and outings, nothing too extravagant, but enjoyable events where they could laugh with other couples, share a joke, and belt out a song or two. Sidney enjoyed Florrie's sense of humour. She was usually the life of the party, laughing easily and often. Friends laughed just to see Florrie laugh. If something was funny to Florrie, she laughed long and hard, sometimes bent over double, turning red and gasping for air.

Florrie and Sidney married in June 1927, a year after Sidney's mother, Elizabeth died. Sidney's father, Alfred who had died in 1912, had been quite well-to-do in his day as a hairdresser. Vera heard stories that he had been quite the gentleman about town, always so properly dressed, sporting a top hat, a walking stick, white scarf and gloves. Sidney was left a small inheritance when his mother died, which was enough to use as a deposit on a house in Chingford. It was quite a lovely house; brick, semi-detached, on a quiet street with an indoor toilet and bathroom, three bedrooms, a bright kitchen, and a large living/dining room. There was a well-established back garden and a park entrance right next to their house which led to a large field and playground. It was a home that the newlyweds expected to live in for a long time and they looked forward to raising a family there.

Florrie saw signs early in the marriage that Sidney's health was not the best. When they worked in the garden, digging and planting, there were times when he ran out of energy quite suddenly and had to rest. He had trouble walking longer distances sometimes and Florrie could see that he was quite out of breath. She tried to limit any rigorous activities and kept a close eye on him. Florrie knew that as a young man during World War I, Sidney had become ill with a cold and sore throat. He had not been excused from training exercises and had to drill in the cold and rain until he collapsed. He developed rheumatic fever and was dangerously sick for several weeks which resulted in a medical discharge. Florrie was quite sure that Sidney's weakness was a lingering effect of this severe illness. Poor Sidney also suffered from a recurring skin irritation that inhibited intimacy often. It was a cross they had to bear in their marriage. They did not talk about it much. It was the reality of their marriage, to be borne and dealt with in a kind and appropriate way. The couple was very happy with each other and contented with their life and when Florrie became pregnant, they were thrilled and amazed. Vera was born on 12th March 1929, to loving, grateful parents. Florrie always referred to Vera as her "gift from God."

Vera was a lively toddler; well cared for, well dressed, walking, and talking at a very young age. She accompanied her parents to family get-togethers and parties, delighting in the company of aunts, uncles and so many cousins (Florrie had twelve siblings and Sidney had four). There were trips to the seaside and picnics in the garden, short bus excursions, days out in the country, playtime in the park, games around the dining room table and occasionally a special shopping trip for a new toy. When Vera was a little older, the family took train trips and travelled a little further away to explore new places, abbeys, castles, palaces, historical landmarks, and the scenery and beauty of Britain. These were wonderful times for Vera. Seeing these sights was exciting and inspiring but listening to her father talk to her about them, providing background and information, passing on his appreciation and passion, listening to the flow of his words, the sound of his voice, created a bond that would last forever. They were a handsome family, Florrie with her blue-black hair, smiling, dark eyes, fair skin and rosy cheeks, Sidney, auburn-haired, blue-eyed, bespectacled, with a kind and gentle expression, and Vera, auburn too, with a round face, light-brown eyes, lively, and curious.

When Vera was about eight years old, Sidney purchased a motorcycle and side car. Now the family was free to ride anytime and go anywhere they wanted. They took weekend trips with their sturdy, canvas tent and some supplies packed on the back. Florrie sat behind Sidney, both wearing goggles and leather helmets, while Vera was happily ensconced in the side car, and off they went. These were some of the happiest days of Vera's young life. She loved these special times watching the trees and hedgerows speed by, supplied with comics and a chocolate bar to enjoy along the way; an adventurous little family enjoying life.

During one of their jaunts, they passed through Portsmouth. Sidney was keen to see the HMS Hood which was at berth there for an overhaul for several months in 1939. On a bright, warm day in July, during a time when the public was invited to board the warship, Vera and her parents stood on the deck of the huge battle cruiser. It was an extraordinary experience; the size of the main guns, and all the other armament on the ship was massive and powerful. They could not help but be proud and hopeful as the Union Jack flapped in the breeze, especially as tensions were growing in Europe and the potential of war was becoming a real threat. It was the largest warship in the world at the time, earning it the nickname, The *Mighty Hood*. Vera stood there feeling very small and in awe at the genius of man to build such a floating fortress.

Vera's favourite cousin was Yvonne. She was the younger daughter of Margaret and John Middleton and so was a double cousin, related on both sides. She was sixteen months older than Vera with almost the complete opposite personality. Whereas Vera was loquacious, expressive, and outgoing, Yvonne was reserved, quiet and shy. Yvonne's young life was unfortunately not as happy and carefree as Vera's. A year after she was born, her mother, Margaret suffered from anxiety and anger issues which developed into aggressive episodes. Fearing for the safety of his daughters, John had Margaret removed from the home and placed in an institution. Evelyn, who was seven years older than her sister Yvonne, was able to mostly take care of herself and help in the house but Yvonne was more than John could handle. So, she was placed temporarily into an orphanage. For the next several years Yvonne was bounced around from different children's care facilities and foster homes. She returned periodically to her father's home for holidays and short visits, but her life was one of strict discipline, uncertainty, loneliness, abandonment, and great sorrow. The quality of care fluctuated from place to place. She often had to suffer the indignity of lice, bruises, and rashes, as well as harsh treatment, scolding, and punishment. She was assigned rigorous, physical work such as scrubbing floors and toilets. John would become outraged at the physical signs of mistreatment and neglect when he saw her during a visit, and he promptly removed her from the institution to place her elsewhere. When Sidney and Florrie observed Yvonne's condition and heard of her mistreatment, they suggested to John that he let them adopt Yvonne so that she could have a secure home that he could visit anytime. John refused. He was uncomfortable with Yvonne's situation but could not agree to her permanent adoption, even by his brother and his wife's sister. Some years later, Yvonne was placed with a family, the Embersons, where she found some peace, contentment, and the affection of caring, nurturing people. This couple also approached John to consider allowing them to adopt Yvonne. Again, John refused. Yvonne stayed with the Embersons until she was old enough to be useful at home. Evelyn married in 1939 and so John lost his housekeeper, Yvonne returned home to take up the job.

During all this time, whenever Yvonne was home for a stay, she would visit Vera and her family. When Vera knew she was coming, she positioned herself in the front window that looked out onto the street and strained her neck to look down the road to catch the very first glimpse of her. She waited there for ages until Yvonne finally came into view. Skipping to the door, she threw it wide and greeted her enthusiastically. Those visits were such a bright spot in the lives of both girls. Vera had the company of her dear cousin and friend with whom she could whisper secrets, play games, and enjoy a large family meal. Yvonne enjoyed being with her close family, being treated like a proper little girl and being spoiled with a delicious dinner, dessert, treats, and hugs. In Vera's bedroom, they would talk about their lives, their friends, share stories and sing songs. One song they often sang was *"He's The Little Boy That Santa Claus Forgot"*.

> He's the little boy that Santa Claus forgot
> And heaven knows he didn't want a lot.
> He wrote a note to Santa for a soldier and a drum,
> It broke his little heart when he found Santa hadn't come.
> In the street he envied all the lucky girls and boys
> And wandered home to last year's broken toys.
> I feel so sorry for that laddie,
> He doesn't have a daddy.
> The little boy that Santa Claus forgot.

They would both end up sobbing and then laughing at themselves. Vera and Yvonne remained close all their lives.

Vera's own words from her "Memories" binder as she reflected on her early life with her parents.

As a small child I can remember comfortable furnishings in our home in a London suburban town named Chingford. I can vividly recall coming home from school on cold winter days and seeing the brilliant flames of the fire through the window of our living room as I approached the front door. I loved that cosy feeling, enjoyed so much sitting with my mother, and the chocolate biscuits (cookies) which I used to hold out in front of the fire and melt until the chocolate was sticky and warm before eating it and drinking my cup of tea. I was fond of those afternoons and can so clearly recall the warmth of the fire and the tidy room with the table set for the evening meal. I would curl up in our large, brown armchair with my book and crayons and listen to the radio – Children's Hour – with a Larry the Lamb episode from Toy Town. I enjoyed those early years of my life with my small family (there were three of us) and I felt very contented and secure. Our home was well-cared for, and my parents were proud of their efforts.

Memories return to me when I take a walk during an autumn evening. The air cool and some chimneys excreting whirls of smoke. Guy Fawkes Night in England races through my mind. The thrill of the bonfires, the firework explodes and then when the backyard display is over, Mum and Dad invite everyone indoors to have roasted potatoes and watch the in-house fireworks.

Roast pork aroma reminds me of my mother's kitchen where she prepared a scrumptious dinner for 1:00 p.m. with homemade sage stuffing and apples roasting in their skins topped with Demerara sugar.

CHAPTER TWO

This Sunday morning was not at all like all the others in Vera's life. This Sunday morning the people of Britain were waiting anxiously beside their radios quietly and calmly, faces grim. An announcement was coming, and most people expected the worst. Vera and her parents sat waiting in the parlour, not talking much, keeping themselves occupied with everyday tasks. Sidney focused on filling his pipe with tobacco, adding just the right amount, and gently tamping it down before touching a match to the barrel and inhaling in short, rapid draws. Florrie had picked up her knitting, needles clicking along the row as she concentrated, head bowed, a slight crease between her brows. Vera flipped through a comic; one she had already read several times but deciding not to read her book since she knew she would be unable to concentrate on the story. The Sunday roast was in the oven, filling the house with an enticing aroma and the promise of a hearty afternoon dinner.

All three heads came up when the dull, monotonous music that was being broadcast came to an end and a long pause followed. Then the calm, steady voice of the announcer for the BBC informed listeners that in two minutes the Prime Minister, Neville Chamberlain, would address the nation.

For two minutes the room was silent. Florrie and Sidney knew what was coming and their thoughts were full of speculation about what life would be like for them in the months and years ahead. They had already constructed their Anderson shelter and half buried it at the bottom of the garden, they carried their gas masks which hung from a long strap over their shoulders everywhere they went and had made their blackout curtains. They had hoped for a while that none of these preparations would be necessary but as Hitler continued to defy the warnings of the allied nations and boldly marched into neighbouring countries in Europe, hopes had begun to wane. Vera was apprehensive about how the expected news would affect her. She knew that evacuations of children had started in London and other cities that were likely targets of German bombing raids. Her main concern was that her parents would decide to send her away. She could not imagine what lay ahead and how much her life was about to change.

The familiar voice of the Prime Minister interrupted their thoughts.

"I am speaking to you from the Cabinet Room at 10 Downing Street. This morning, the British Ambassador in Berlin handed the German government a final note, stating that unless we heard from them by 11 o'clock, that they were prepared at once to withdraw their troops from Poland, a state of war would exist between us. I have to tell you now that no such undertaking has been received and that, consequently, this country is at war with Germany."

The announcement was followed by the playing of the national anthem. All three immediately rose to their feet as was the custom whenever it was played, but also as an unspoken show of support and resolve. They were in it now. War had been declared and they would all do their bit, whatever their bit may be.

The country's preparations surged into high gear. Changes began in earnest for Vera and her family and big decisions had to be made about evacuation. The government encouraged parents to send their children out of London and other large cities, and high-risk areas, to the countryside where they would be taken in by families doing their bit by accepting evacuee children into their homes. Radio broadcasts from the Home Office continuously recommended this difficult decision and propaganda posters were everywhere pushing the message. It seemed to be the right thing to do to keep Vera safe from harm. Florrie and Sidney talked at length about it, knowing that most of their friends and relatives were complying with the call, signing their children up, packing their little bags and seeing them off at the train station. The scenes at the stations were heart-wrenching, with mothers and fathers trying to stay calm while hugging and waving their children away. Children lined up and climbed into train cars carrying their bags with their gas masks across their chests and tags hanging from cords around their necks with their name, address, school, and parents' names recorded on them. Some children were brave and even excited about the adventure ahead, but most were grim or openly crying at the separation from their parents, homes, and all that was familiar.

Vera was ten years old. She was a sturdy child, bright and cheerful. She was a perfect blend of her parents with auburn hair, like her father, parted on the side and fastened with a clip. She had her mother's round face, and sense of humour. She was the centre of her parents' world, and she knew it, although Florrie and Sidney strove to treat her like a participating member of a team and not like the star player. Though her parents were certainly not wealthy, they both worked and made a good living. Vera had lovely new clothes, shoes, books, new bicycle, toys, and the cream off the top of the milk bottle. It would be a terrible wrench for all three of them to part from each other. They had built a happy life together. They certainly had not expected to have to make such a life-changing decision.

Florrie and Sidney decided that the sensible thing to do was to send Vera away. They would be able to visit one Sunday a month, provided they were not occupied with essential war work at the time or too exhausted to make the journey. It fell to Florrie to tell Vera of their decision one September evening while they were washing up the dishes after dinner. In her strong Cockney accent, which Vera secretly abhorred and consciously, determinedly, would not emulate, Florrie explained very matter-of-factly what they thought was the best choice for her.

"Yuv gotta go, ya know," she stated firmly. "Gotta be safe… an' we'll be workin' lots of hours. So, we've decided, we 'ave. Yuv gotta go." Florrie kept her head bent over the sink as she scrubbed the roasting pan. "It'll be alright. 'Spect you'll like being in the country. Yuv always enjoyed rambling. Be like another 'oliday 'an you'll 'ave lots of new friends to play with an' talk to… an' Dad and I will come to see you. You'll like that, won't you? You can show us around and we can 'ave a picnic together. Be nice to spend a day in the country…" Florrie's voice trailed off as the prospect of sending her only child away became real. Vera glanced at her mother and saw that her face was very set and controlled as she focused on the job at hand. There would be no discussion or objection. "Yes Mum," she responded in a tiny voice.

Vera spent the night tossing and turning and fretting about her future. If it were just a holiday of a week or two in the country, she would embrace it. How lovely to enjoy the open fields, lanes, and farm animals. How exciting to explore and listen to the sounds of the birds, pick wildflowers, bicycle to country shops and cafes, meet new people. But to be sent away for an undetermined time and worry about her parents left behind! Her father was not in the best of health and had not been for quite some time. She saw her mother watching him on days when he came home from work so tired and drained that he could barely get out of his easy chair to sit at the dinner table. His appetite was poor too. After being discharged during World War I, Sidney had decided that he must still contribute to the war effort in a valuable way. He became apprenticed as a mechanical engineer and became very skilled. He took considerable pride in his work, accumulating his own specialised tools, which Vera loved to examine and clean for him. She would worry about him working longer hours. But perhaps it would be better for him not to have to worry about his daughter during this unsettled time. But to leave them both was unthinkable. They were a tight knit little threesome and Vera had thought this would always be her life, forever and ever… or maybe at least until one day she fell in love herself, married and had a family of her own.

The next morning, Vera sat on the edge of the bathtub, as was her custom, while Sidney shaved. The two of them enjoyed these few minutes together and discussed all kinds of things. This morning, however, they were silent until Vera asked "When will I be leaving, Dad? Shall I pack my bag today?" Sidney's razor froze and he stood very still for a moment. Vera saw that his chin quivered ever so slightly before he answered her. "Don't pack yet, dear," he replied.

Later that day, Florrie informed her that there had been a change of plans and that she would not be evacuated after all. "Yer father and I 'ave decided that the three of us will stick it out together."

"Yes, Mum," she answered dutifully. She spun around and danced to her bedroom, a broad, bright smile spreading across her face. The subject of evacuation was never discussed or considered again throughout the war even when the bombing began in earnest.

Excerpt from Vera's notes on World War II

On the 1st of September 1939, the streets of London were being stripped of their children. Public buses, lorries, private vehicles and even ambulances were utilised to transport the school children from the city and the suburbs to a place of considered safety.

The journey for the children began very early in the morning at their usual school grounds where they were loaded onto the vehicles, each child carrying a knapsack, suitcase, and gas mask dangling on one shoulder, together with a name and address tag securely pinned on an outer garment. It was arranged that the children be loaded alphabetically... The children were taken to the main London railway stations and then conveyed by train to the smaller villages in the far-off countryside. The parents waved goodbye to their children not knowing to whom they would be going, and it was probably a week before they learned of their exact whereabouts and the name and addresses of the foster parents. Very few people had telephones and communication was therefore slowed down. The sad goodbyes were for some the last, as many children were orphaned during the air raids on London.

The local villagers selected the children they wanted. It was almost like a cattle market. Some were selected if they looked fit and strong and if the boys showed good muscles. Some of the less desirable youngsters were left waiting for hours before someone agreed to take them.

CHAPTER THREE

The first few months after war was declared did not affect Vera's life too much. Life for her carried on much the same. She continued to go to school, although there were frequent gas mask and air raid drills included in the day's instruction and sandbags were piled up in the corridors. Everyone in the country had been issued a gas mask which had to be carried everywhere in anticipation of a gas attack. The masks were contained in a pressed cardboard box connected to a long leather strap which would go over the head and across the body to be quickly accessible. This plain, unstylish accessory was unacceptable to Vera and the girls at school and indeed across the land. And so, it became a trend to decorate the gas mask boxes as gaily as possible with bright colours, painted designs, clever patterns, stripes, lace, tassels and whatever they could think of to add some style and interest. Vera played with her friends, enjoyed nice meals and family time but she noticed that her father spent longer and longer hours at work and knew that his work and skills were very much in demand for the engineering and building of munitions. She observed changes taking place in her community. Church bells stopped ringing. It was ordered that church bells would be silent for the duration of the war and would only ring in the event of an invasion so that everyone across the land would be notified immediately of the emergency. Signposts and road signs were taken down throughout the country so that invaders would not easily find their way around, barbed wire was strung along the coastline and mines were buried on the beaches. Air raid sirens were placed on rooftops in towns and cities, and air raid towers were erected strategically across the landscape. Public air raid shelters were established and prominently signed. The people of Britain were prepared for an expected invasion by Germany at any moment.

Vera had helped Florrie make blackout curtains for every window in the home. They had measured the windows, purchased heavy, black fabric, and hemmed the edges to make panels. Sidney had installed a rod behind the existing curtains so that they could be pushed back during the daytime. When they were all installed, the three of them turned on every light in the house and checked their work by standing outside at night to see if the least little chink of light showed through. They were pleased to see that they were completely blacked out. The air raid wardens took their jobs very seriously patrolling the streets at night. They shouted and knocked sharply on doors if any light showed from inside the house, even fining and arresting those who were not in compliance. It was so important that when the air raids came, no light showed anywhere to guide the German bombers to inhabited areas.

It was quite frightening to be out at night. Sometimes Vera's family would visit one of Florrie's sisters who lived nearby, and the walk home was eerie. There were no porch lights or streetlamps along the way. On nights when the skies were overcast and no moonlight or stars were visible, the darkness felt heavy and pressed down all around them. At first cars and buses had to travel at night with no headlights at all but when pedestrians were accidentally killed at an alarming rate, the government reduced speed at night to 20 mph and allowed headlights to be used, provided they were dipped to the immediate roadway in front of them and were masked so that only three horizontal slits showed. Sidney carried a torch (flashlight) that also had been carefully altered and covered to dim the light and he kept it pointed down. Vera was rather intrigued with these new restrictions. She held onto her mother's sleeve as they walked, and they spoke in a whisper. Whispering was not required but it just seemed the thing to do.

No invasion came during the first months following the declaration of war, but Britain did not let its guard down. Hitler was more concerned with considering a possible invasion into the Soviet Union to bother much with Britain right away, besides, he believed that Britain would eventually come to terms. This allowed the country to build planes, train pilots, and build up the military forces. Conscription was introduced in April 1939 and when war was declared the National Service Act required all men between the ages of 18 and 41 to register. Men were conscripted by age group. 20 – 23-year-olds were conscripted in October 1939 and then as the war progressed, conscription continued to other age groups until the last group of 40-year-olds were conscripted in June 1941.

The Home Guard (first known as the LDV – Local Defence Volunteers) was formed in May 1940 and was comprised of men too young, too old, physically or medically limited or working at a job of national importance. The men trained, drilled, carried weapons, and would courageously meet that invading army if it ever came. The idea was that they would slow down the advance, giving the regular army time to regroup. Winston Churchill spoke of The Home Guard during a BBC broadcast on 14th July 1940.
"These officers and men, a large proportion of whom

have been through the last war, have the strongest desire to attack and come to close quarters with the enemy wherever he may appear. Should the invader come to Britain, there will be no placid lying down of the people in submission before him, as we have seen alas, in other countries. We shall defend every village, every town, and every city."

The first months of relative quiet on the home front, became known as the "Phoney War." Everyone waited, watched, listened, and continued with their lives. Some of the children who had been evacuated returned home to their families, but the threat was ever present and when rationing was imposed on the British public in January 1940, everyday existence took on a whole new challenge.

Vera returned home from school one wintry day and saw her mother sitting at the dining room table with a notepad and pen.
"What are you doing Mum?"
"Look at these, Vera. I got our ration books today, look - two adult and one child. This blue one 'ere is yours. You get a bit more of some things, like fruit, meat, and milk. I'm looking them over and making a list of our week's supply of all the rationed food we are allowed so that I get an idea of what meals I can make."
"Can we still have shepherd's pie?"
"Once in a while, we can, I think," Florrie answered with a chuckle. "But we're going to 'ave to be a bit clever and try some new things."
"But why do we have to have ration books, Mum? Nothing has even happened yet?"
"Not yet," sighed Florrie. "But it's comin'. Our men are getting called up and we 'ave to be sure they 'ave what they need." Vera picked up her blue ration book and flipped

through the pages.

"Blimey!" Vera exclaimed, forgetting herself for a moment. What happens if we run out of coupons before the week is up?"

"That's why I'm doing some plannin' 'ere. And I am surprised you used that word. I know you don't like it."

"I don't but sometimes it just seems to fit the situation." She thought for a moment. "Mum, does it bother you that I try to speak so properly… that I don't talk like you and Dad do?"

"No dear. Not at all. I'm proud of you for making such an effort. 'Cos I want you to speak nicely. Makes you sound better, like yuv got more goin' on up 'ere." Florrie tapped the side of her head.

"You'll be glad of it later on in your life, you will. Now sit down 'ere and let's work on a shopping list."

Using the ration books became a chore. Each family had to register with a supplier in their vicinity and the coupons were cut out or stamped to void them after use. Most of the shops that Florrie needed were at the end of Hall Lane at the bottom of Chingford Mount. Dyson's was the green grocers, Jones was the butcher shop, Buns was the baker and Fin and Tails was the fishmonger. Florrie registered with them all and made almost daily trips with her shopping bags on her arm to buy her goods. Often there were long lines at the shops and many times the items Florrie had wanted were sold out by the time she got to the front of the line. Waiting in queues, however, did provide time for women to exchange menu ideas and share complaints as well as to have a bit of a laugh. As the war wore on, some items were rarely seen, such as oranges and bananas. When these did come in, word spread around town like wildfire and women grabbed their hats and coats and trotted off to their suppliers where they waited patiently in long queues. It was a great victory to come home with such a special treat.

Britain had always had to import a large amount of food to satisfy the nation. Less than one-third of the food consumed by the population was produced at home. Britain relied on ships to bring food, supplies and equipment, mostly from the U.S. and Canada. After war was declared, enemy ships and U-boats targeted these shipping convoys as they crossed the Atlantic Ocean. Many ships were destroyed, and many brave sailors of the British Merchant Navy and the U.S. Merchant Marine lost their lives.

The great propaganda campaign in Britain included "Dig for Victory" posters. Florrie and Sidney had a large lawn and neat flowerbeds in the backyard. In the early spring of 1940, every inch of it was dug up, sieved, turned over with manure and planted with vegetables. Potatoes, onions, runner beans, peas, carrots, tomatoes, marrow, rhubarb, lettuce, parsnips, turnips were all planted and carefully tended. Florrie already had raspberry, blackcurrant, and gooseberry bushes, as well as an established strawberry patch with which she made delicious pies and jam. Narrow pathways, laid with paving stones divided the vegetable beds and a central path led to the Anderson Shelter at the bottom of the garden.

Vera had helped her father put together the Anderson Shelter several months earlier, when it arrived one day in a heap of corrugated steel and nuts and bolts and was deposited in front of the house. She quite enjoyed the process of reading out the instructions and handing over the pieces and hardware and the tools Sidney needed. The love of tools and building stayed with Vera all her life. It always brought her such pleasure and satisfaction to organize the toolshed and clean and shine the tools. Neighbours waved and chatted quite cheerfully as they worked, first digging a large rectangular hole where the shelter would sit, half buried in the ground, and then building the shelter, fitting it in the hole, backfilling it with soil and covering the whole thing with more soil, ten inches thick.

"You did a good job, both of you," Florrie said with a smile as she inspected the finished product. "But what a gloomy looking thing it is to 'ave to look at!"

"It's very strong, Florrie. We'll all be safe inside, that's the important thing," Sidney responded. "Come on, let's build some bunks, Vera, and make it as comfy as we can."

"Ooh, yes Dad, Vera answered enthusiastically. How she had always loved working with wood, a hammer and nails and spending time with her father in his woodshed. This project would take the whole weekend. They measured and drew up a rough plan and then happily sawed away, making pieces to nail and screw together, creating bunks and shelves inside the shelter as well as a sturdy wooden door. When it was all finished, Vera begged for them all to try it out that night. Florrie scoffed at first, but when Sidney caught her eye with a childish grin, she went along with it. She scurried around the house and made make-shift mattresses out of their camping equipment, found old quilts and eiderdowns, pillows and blankets, candles, matches and hot water bottles and finally made a thermos of hot tea. The family settled in for the night. They played a few games of cards, talked in hushed voices, and drank their tea. Vera always remembered that first night in the shelter. It was early spring, cold and a bit damp, but she felt safe and happy, so close to her mother and father, a tight little unit, together, ready, prepared, brave and determined. She could not know then how many days and nights she would spend there, shivering with cold and fear, listening to the whistling sound of falling bombs and waiting for the explosions that followed.

In May 1940, the situation in Europe was very grim. Hitler invaded Holland, Belgium and the Netherlands on 10th May, which was also the day that Winston Churchill became Prime Minister of the land. Neville Chamberlain had already lost a lot of confidence in Parliament when the Germans occupied Norway in April, and this was the end of his leadership. His proud statement to the nation of "peace-in-our-time" following the signing of the Munich Agreement in September 1938 had proved to be a farce. Winston Churchill was offered the post and formally "invited" to lead by King George VI. He formed an all-party coalition, soon gaining the support of the British people, who came to admire him, put their faith in him, and depend on him to keep up the morale of the country even in the most difficult times. His news updates, addresses to the nation, patriotic speeches and absolute determination and resolve that Britain would never surrender, kept the people strong and resolute. A few days after becoming the Prime Minister, Churchill made his first speech to the House of Commons in which he declared, "I have nothing to offer but blood, toil, tears, and sweat." It was to be a long struggle especially for his first year when Britain stood alone against Germany.

At school Vera was swept up in the adulation of Winston Churchill too. She thrilled to the sound of his voice, deep, slow, steady, passionate, valiant, and absolutely unflinching. At school her fellow schoolmates were well informed and united in a strong bond of patriotism. They speculated about the news and shared their observations of all that was happening around them in their lives, large barrage balloons (inflated and tethered to discourage low-flying enemy planes), propaganda posters everywhere, victory gardens and allotments for growing vegetables, fruit and herbs, patrols of ARP wardens (Air Raid Precaution), identity cards, ration books, anti-aircraft guns (Ack-Ack guns) on rooftops and the flatbeds of lorries, and air raid siren tower installations.

While the Battle of France was taking place, Vera was attending school and carrying on with her lessons. There was a lot of talk about the war, of course, but she enjoyed learning history, geography, English and spelling. She liked science too; mathematics was her challenging subject. There were intermittent gas mask drills. The children were expected to remove their gas mask from the container and place it over their heads, covering their face in a matter of seconds following the alert. Miss Palmer also reminded them often not to speak of anything they might know or overhear about war manoeuvres.

"You must remember," she said. "There are spies everywhere just listening for information that they can pass on to the enemy. Do not speak of anything that you might know. Do not speak of it on the bus, on a train, in a shop, a restaurant or even on the playground. This is important, boys and girls. This is for the safety of our fighting troops and our sailors on the seas and our brave men in the air. I expect many of you have a family member fighting in the war or know someone who will soon be deployed. You wouldn't want to put that person at risk, would you?"

"No, Miss Palmer," the children replied in unison. Miss Palmer's warning deeply affected Vera. For weeks she studied faces, expressions, and the activities of people she encountered on the bus, in the streets or in the shops. Who could be a spy, she wondered?

The Battle of France only lasted six weeks in May and June 1940. After successfully invading Norway, Belgium and the Netherlands, German troops surrounded French and British units fighting in France and pushed them back to the sea. The French and British forces were rescued in a brilliant and brave operation which would become known forever after as "The Miracle of Dunkirk," Dunkirk being the name of the small coastal town in Northern France from where they were extricated. Between 26th May and 4th June, often while under attack from German troops and aircraft, 338,000 men were evacuated from Dunkirk beaches by hundreds of naval ships and civilian vessels, "little ships," of all shapes and sizes. France battled on for a few more weeks but surrendered officially on 25th June 1940.

For Vera, the "Phoney War" was over, Britain stood alone against the might and aggression of Germany and the Axis powers. The Battle of Britain had begun. Hitler expected that Britain would accept a negotiated peace and "realise the hopelessness of their situation." However, after waiting for several weeks and seeing that Britain had no intention of surrendering, he considered an invasion by sea. He was advised by his officers though, that Britain's naval power guarding the English Channel and North Sea would first have to be diminished and other war preparations and systems would need to be targeted for an invasion to be successful. The invasion was postponed until September and Hitler called for a major air offensive against air bases, aircraft factories and radar stations to damage vital British air support industries. The Luftwaffe, Germany's air force, began bombing raids in southeastern England.

Again, words from Winston Churchill prepared the people of their beloved land for action ahead.

"What General Weygand has called the Battle of France is over... the Battle of Britain is about to begin... Let us therefore brace ourselves to our duties, and so bear ourselves, that if the British Empire and its Commonwealth last for a thousand years, men will still say, 'This was their finest hour'".

It was an exhilarating time for youngsters in England. Enemy aircraft flew in formations across the skies above them, carrying bombs intended to destroy military facilities to weaken the resistance of Britain to future attack and invasion. Vera and her schoolmates, and anyone who heard the drone of enemy aircraft overhead, craned their necks to watch them. Some shook their fists at them as they passed over, swearing and cursing. But when the RAF intercepted them, dogfights began, and it was horrifying but thrilling to watch the battles in the sky.

One afternoon Vera and her friend, Hilda, daringly headed to the top of Chingford Mount for a clear and panoramic view of the action above. There were a few people there, some with binoculars, and Vera spotted Maurice Brown with a few of his mates. They were pointing and whooping as several planes engaged. The planes were quite high, but it was easy to tell them apart. The British Spitfires and Hawker Hurricanes had concentric circles on the underside of their wings and the German Messerschmitts had the German cross on the underside of theirs. The British planes clearly had the better of the Messerschmitts bombers and were turning more tightly which enabled them to shoot at the enemy planes as they tried to evade a Spitfire or Hurricane on their tail. When one of the Messerschmitts was hit and started to descend rapidly trailing smoke, the group on the Mount cheered. Maurice spotted Vera and gave her a wave. Hilda noticed and nudged her friend. "Ooh, look! He's waving at you, Vera."

"Yes, I see. That's Maurice Brown. He goes to our school but he's a year older than us. You know, Hilda, I think he likes me. He always waves when he sees me. But he's always with his mates and they're a loud group. Always looking for mischief too."

"Well, he's a nice-looking boy, isn't he? Got a lovely headful of curls and a nice face."

"Hmmm," Vera responded. Her gaze returned to the sky. Another German plane was hit and fell in a perpendicular descent. A Spitfire took some fire and manoeuvred to a lower altitude. Some wisps of smoke trailed from one of the wings. It flew away from the fight. The remaining two Messerschmitts turned away and headed in the direction of the coast, pursued by two Spitfires.

"That's right!" Maurice shouted after them. "Go get 'em boys!"

Vera and Hilda cheered them on and turned to leave. As they left the Mount, Vera glanced back over her shoulder. Maurice was watching her. She gave him a small smile and a flick of her hand in acknowledgement.

The Battle of Britain ended in victory for Britain but came at a high cost. So many pilots were needed, and they were rushed through training with limited flying hours in the sky. Young, inexperienced pilots were thrust into combat and of almost 3,000 pilots involved in the Battle of Britain, 544 of them never made it home. The Luftwaffe had more planes and pilots but suffered a higher number of losses in their attempt to cripple Britain's military build-up, due to the domination of the skies of the more manoeuvrable Spitfire and Hurricane.

Vera did not fully realise at the time how critical those few months of the Battle of Britain were. She was so focused on her own part of the war, living everyday life as best as she could with all the restrictions, sacrifices, and dangers that she had to deal with daily. Later in life, though, she read and researched to fill in the gaps and to fully understand the immensity of the glorious achievement that she had witnessed and lived through.

The famous words by Winston Churchill of the Battle of Britain will be long remembered.

"Never in the field of human conflict was so much owed by so many to so few."

Note in Vera's World War II notebook
Identity Cards were issued to everyone with a number and full details of birth and residential address. I remember mine – Vera Grace Middleton, I.D. number DEVN 128/3

CHAPTER FOUR

Vera sat on a wooden bunk with a book on her lap. The air raid siren had sent them scurrying yet another night down the garden path, through the vegetable garden into the grim interior of the cool, dim Anderson shelter. The small space was lit with an oil lamp hanging from a nail hammered into the wooden frame. Florrie was pouring cups of tea from a thermos which had been prepared earlier, while her father turned pages of his newspaper grunting and sighing from time to time as he read. It was mid-September 1940 in Chingford, a suburb of London, and the nighttime bombing raids on the city had begun in earnest a few weeks before.

"How bad do you think it will be tonight, Dad?" she asked.

"Oh, probably much like last night… and the night before that."

"'Ere's yer tea, luv," Florrie said, handing a cup to Vera. Never you mind about them bombs. None of them 'ave come close to us, 'ave they? We'll be alright down 'ere, won't we Sid? 'Ere Sid. 'Ere's yer tea. Come on… get yer nose out of the paper."

"I hear them! Listen. They're coming… the planes," Vera cried. The three of them held still and listened as the drone of engines grew louder and louder. "Alright," said Sidney. "Let's 'ave a song. What should it be? *Roll Out the Barrel?* Let's sing *Roll Out the Barrel*. Nice and loud now." Florrie picked up her concertina and played a few notes of introduction before the three voices joined together in the familiar, old song. The singing helped so much, as did the game of cards that followed. Only when a bomb hit close enough to rattle the shelter's framework did the family pause, as Vera cried out and Florrie and Sidney held their breath. The bombing continued all night, so after a while, Vera and Florrie stretched out on the bunk, pulled a blanket over themselves, and attempted to sleep. Sidney picked up his newspaper and resumed reading until his eyes became too tired and his focus wandered. He had worked another long shift and he knew the shifts would become longer and longer. He expected them to stretch to 24 and 36 hours. There was important work to be done. He knew the stress and lack of rest was taking its toll and that his already poor health was weakening all the more, but that had to be put aside at this desperate time for Britain. He removed his wire-rimmed glasses, rubbed his eyes and loosened his tie. He was fully clothed as always when in the air raid shelter. One never knew how long the bombing raid would be, although lately the all-clear siren had not sounded until dawn. He wanted to be dressed when he left the shelter whatever time of day or night. Sidney prided himself on being a gentleman, dressing smartly in crisply ironed clothes and a well-tailored suit. Although not tall or muscular or what would be considered a handsome man, he had a round, kind face, a full head of auburn hair and an amiable, outgoing personality. He was interested in everyone and everything, listening appreciatively to the opinions of others and enjoying a good debate. He also loved a good joke, parties, singing, and visits to the local pub. He was popular with both men and women who were attracted to his engaging personality.

Sidney looked over at his dozing wife and child. They brought him so much happiness and pride. What a threesome they were. Their life before the war was full and lively. Since he and Florrie had a large extended family, they visited and partied often. Florrie was a gifted musician who couldn't read a note of music but only had to listen once to a melody to produce it on the piano. She had a ragtime style and was at the centre of every gathering, banging out old favourites, with everyone singing in loud and imperfect harmony. Each song usually ended in howls of laughter. Vera loved these parties. Being an only child, she so enjoyed spending time with her cousins. As he watched over them, Sidney wondered how they would manage without him. He had hoped that the war would be short-lived, especially when Winston Churchill became Prime Minister a few months ago. His messages were always so encouraging and uplifting. He was remarkable and had such a knack for calming the nation, speaking of the challenges ahead and the sacrifices of all, but also, he spoke proudly of the British spirit and the strength and resolve of the people. He was able to fan the flames and ignite the fiery spirit in men, women and children, hardening them to the impact of war and uniting them in a collective effort to thwart the enemy, by whatever means they could. The home front had to remain steadfast and support the brave men fighting on foreign soil, on the seas, and in the air. Everyone was expected to contribute in their own way whether it was by managing on rations so that the fighting men would be well-provisioned, donating anything in the home that was made of aluminium to the huge piles during collection drives, mending and patching clothing, growing fruit and vegetables, taking in evacuees or families bombed out of their homes, working as an air raid warden, clearing rubble and debris, and so much more. This all passed through Sidney's mind as he sat looking at his family. *They will get through this*, he thought. *They are strong. Stronger than they think.*

The bombs fell all night. Vera slept in fits and starts waking several times to the sound of explosions that were a little too close. She glanced over at her father who had finally lain down on his own bunk. He was awake and staring at the ceiling. He was so tired but could not sleep. Vera pulled her pillow over her ears as a tear slid silently down her cheek, an eleven-year-old girl whose life had turned upside down.

The nighttime bombing raids which became known as the "Blitz" continued every night for fifty-seven consecutive nights. This period was meant to destroy the morale of the people. It became a prolonged time of great fear and deprivation, but the British were made of sterner stuff, and they became hardened to their lot, determined in their defiance and united in a great surge of patriotism.

Each morning after a raid, as the all-clear sounded, families emerged from their shelters and trudged up the garden into the house. They prepared for their day and went on their way, glancing this way and that to assess the damage that had been done to their neighbourhood by the enemy overnight. They would step over rubble and shrapnel on the street, avoid smoke and fire engines, stop and stare at a crater where a house once stood, and watch in amazement at families that were already clearing up broken glass, debris, shaking out curtains, blankets, and sweeping off steps leading up to the front door. This became everyday existence and while the horror never faded, it steadily became accepted as the new normal, and reaction to it became calmer, steady, and controlled.

This was the Blitz of London which began on 7th September 1940. On that first Saturday night, waves of German bombers flew across the English Channel to bomb the London docks. Many tons of bombs were dropped including high-explosive incendiary bombs which started raging fires. Fire fighters worked through the night to control the fires with the help of many citizens, but much was destroyed, and many were killed. Vera looked toward the city from Chingford at dawn the next day and the sky glowed red.

Vera walked to school each morning wondering if the building would still be there. She would breathe a sigh of relief when she saw it still standing. Class sizes varied each day. So many children had been evacuated that the number of students was half the number prior to the war, but many teachers had been conscripted or called into war work which reduced the number of available teachers. Older, retired teachers had been recruited to fill the need and obviously the curriculum and quality of lessons had suffered. Vera had always liked school but especially now since it gave her purpose and a schedule and something to fill her daytime hours. She enjoyed discussing her lessons with her parents and showing off what she had learned.

One day following a long night of bombing, Vera arrived at school to be told that school would be closed for the rest of the week. Several streets nearby had suffered severe damage and the families of some of the students would need to be relocated. Some of the teachers had gone there to help with the children. Hilda trotted over when she saw Vera.

"Oh, Vera. Thank goodness it wasn't you. I was worried."

"I'm glad you're alright too. It was bad last night. Some of those bombs got awfully close."

"Yes. I hardly slept at all. The shelter rattled and shook sometimes so much that I thought it might collapse."

"No. It won't collapse, Hilda. My father says we are

very safe in the Anderson shelters. Only a direct hit could… well, you know, we are quite safe inside."

"I know, I know. But sometimes in the evening when we have just finished dinner… when that air raid siren goes off, I just want to stay in the house. It is so nice and warm, and I have all my things and my nice comfy bed."

"Oh, I know! But we must go down there. Who knows if our house will be hit? Look what happened to those families near the school. It could easily be us. My mother and father are very strict about it."

"Yes, yes. You're right. But all the same…"

The girls parted at Hilda's house and Vera continued to Waverly Avenue. She had the house key around her neck since both parents worked every day. She let herself in and stood for a moment just inside the door. She hated being there alone. The house was so quiet and lonely, and she was finding herself alone there more and more as the war progressed. She understood it well enough. Everyone had to step it up, work harder, longer, and faster. However, being an only child made it more difficult especially now, today, since school was closed. A lot of hours stretched ahead of her. Maybe she should have asked Hilda to come home with her or maybe, if she was lucky, Yvonne might stop over. But Yvonne would not know that school was closed. Vera sighed deeply feeling very sorry for herself. She grabbed the strap of her gas mask and yanked it angrily over her head dropping it on the bench there in the hallway. She pulled off her coat and hung it on a peg and then charged upstairs. She would write to Yvonne, at least, and complain to her about the day.

Vera discovered that school was open again the following week but then, on that first day back, during a spelling lesson, the air raid siren sounded. Miss Palmer calmly directed the children to leave the classroom and move to the hallway, where sandbags had been stacked up along both sides. The children sat on the floor between the sandbags and Miss Palmer continued with her lesson. Vera paid attention as best she could but the drone of approaching planes and the explosions of bombs dropping in the distance, certainly distracted her. All the students were acutely aware of the blasts approaching closer and closer and they waited apprehensively for the raid to pass over. Some of the children hunkered down with their heads down and arms wrapped around their bodies. When the all-clear sounded, everyone stood up, breathed a sigh of relief and filed back into the classroom.

This was education for Vera and all Britain's city children for the next few years. Schools were temporarily closed at times, or permanently shut if bomb damage was too severe. Some schools were consolidated, class sizes grew with the lack of space and teachers. Many schools resorted to morning and afternoon sessions to accommodate the number of students. Children of the war years in Britain suffered a great setback in their education and in many cases, this affected the rest of their lives. Even at her young age, Vera was very much aware of this and took it upon herself to learn as much as she could on her own. She read profusely, listened to radio programmes, studied the newspaper, searched for articles in the family's outdated set of encyclopaedias, looked up words in her dictionary, borrowed textbooks from the library and asked questions of her parents. Florrie answered her enquiries in a matter-of-fact manner, adding her own viewpoint with moralistic overtones. Sidney enjoyed delving deeply into the subject, providing background and history if he had the knowledge. If not, he happily explored the topic with his daughter to find out more.

Life continued on throughout the Blitz which finally ended the night of 10th May 1941, with a massive raid which caused the highest number of deaths and casualties of any single night and a ring of fire around London. Bombing raids continued after the Blitz but on a smaller scale and the people of Britain had become conditioned to endure them. Hitler's goal had been to terrorise the population and break the morale. However, he had not been able to do so. When he heard reports of the indomitable spirit of ordinary folk, continuing about their business, striving in a surge of nationalism, pride, and courage to endure all hardships, of groups entertaining and singing in the Underground stations during air raids, he was enraged as well as confounded. Germany had suffered heavy losses during the Battle of Britain and during the prolonged bombing campaign and so, while continuing to keep the British people on edge with a steady bombardment of air raids, Hitler decided to turn his attention and his forces to the Soviet Union.

Vera continued to attend school following the Blitz, sometimes hunkered down in the corridor again but there was an air of optimism when the constant nighttime raids lessened. At home, though, Vera was very much aware of her father's failing health. The worry, stress and overwork were taking a heavy toll and it was obvious that he was struggling. Then, a huge decision was made.

A friend of Sidney's offered to put him in touch with an acquaintance who was looking for someone to run a small hotel and pub about an hour's drive from Chingford. The family travelled to the location, met the owner, and toured the property. There was a small staff already in place, so

Sidney and Florrie would concern themselves mostly with the pub, the accounts, and the upkeep. Florrie played the piano to demonstrate what an asset she would be, banging out all the popular songs and old pub favourites. The owner was very impressed and took an immediate liking to the family, which had already come highly recommended. The deal was made, the date was set, and everyone was happy. Sidney sold off their furniture since there would be furnished accommodation at the hotel for them, and the family moved into temporary furnished rooms for a short stay until the start date arrived. All three were very excited. They would move away to a safer location which, although it still could experience a stray bomber or the dumping of bombs following a raid, would be a calmer, less stressful life for them all. Florrie and Sidney looked forward to the social aspect of the job, Florrie playing the piano, entertaining, and getting to know the locals, Sidney enjoying many a chat, debate and laugh with the patrons, getting to know their names, greeting them with a smile, and Vera starting at a new school without all the interruptions and making new friends. She would certainly miss Hilda and other classmates and her family that lived nearby but they were not all that far away. She was old enough now to take the train by herself if she wanted to visit.

However, waiting for the weeks to pass until they could embark on their new life was difficult. Gone were the furnishings that had always been there throughout Vera's life, the grand dining set with the thick, carved legs, the handsome sofa, Sidney's comfy easy chair, her own single bed with the lemon-yellow embossed bedspread, and lamps, curtains, wardrobes, chests. All the comforts of home that were familiar and taken for granted. Sidney noticed tears in Vera's eyes as she watched a bookcase being carried out of the front door.

"I'm sorry, dear. I know it is hard to see our things go, but we must have money for our expenses and to get settled in our new place. But won't it be a lovely new life for us… and won't we enjoy decorating our new home? Just think about all the happy times we will have. What an adventure, eh?"

"Yes, Dad," Vera replied, dashing away her tears and squaring her shoulders. "A new life!"

The temporary accommodation was adequate, though the furnishings were on the shabby and well-used side. They brightened it up as much as they could with the few decorative items they had kept and reminded each other it would only be for a few weeks or a month or two at worst. Although their house was now empty, Sidney decided not to sell it. The mortgage was frozen during the war and the selling and buying of houses was difficult and just not a priority. He decided to wait for a better time to come to deal with the house. Also, it was comforting to know it was there if, for some reason, the new job did not work out. During the waiting period, Sidney continued to work long, laborious hours. He looked so grey and weary one morning that Florrie forbade him from going to work and took him to the doctor instead. Sidney's doctor recommended a long holiday in Torquay to regain his strength and reinvigorate him. "You need a rest," the doctor said. "Your heart is not strong, Sidney, and the strain you are under now, working so hard, moving, losing sleep because of the blooming bombs, is taking its toll. Take a few weeks off, *a few weeks* mind you, not a couple of days! Go to the seaside. You need some good sea air, peace, and tranquillity." The doctor's order provided Sidney and Florrie with official leaves from their jobs and the family travelled by train down to the sunny, warm shores of England's Riviera at

Torquay.

What a wonderful break it was to be in the lovely seaside resort where palm trees grew and thrived. The hillsides overlooking the ocean were dotted with beautiful houses and gardens and the broad seafront walk was still busy, even in early September, with seafront kiosks selling ice cream, cockles and mussels, colourful beach toys, flags, inflatables, kites, sweets, and souvenirs. The family checked into a charming bed and breakfast where they would spend three weeks. The weather was glorious, with plenty of sunshine and gentle breezes carrying the invigorating tang of sea. Vera gloried in this time away from the stress and strain of life at home. The three of them happily cast aside their cares and worries and relaxed, enjoying the simple pleasures of a true holiday. They started each day with a hearty breakfast in the little dining room at their bed and breakfast, the view overlooking the sea, sparkling in the sunshine.

"You know, Vera," Sidney began. "Right here in Torquay, Admiral Nelson visited for a time. His fleet was anchored just offshore in the bay and later, when Napoleon had been captured, he was held on a ship here. When the ship sailed into Torquay's Bay, Napoleon declared… now let me see if I can get this right… 'Quel bon pays,' which means what a lovely country."

Vera gazed out at the beautiful bay imagining a warship there with Napoleon gazing back at the picturesque landscape. "When was that, Dad?" she asked.

"Oh, dear me, let me think. It was around the turn of the last century, 1801, I believe."

Most of the day was spent strolling along the seafront where there were benches every few yards. Sidney could sit and smoke his pipe a while when he became tired. Sometimes, Vera skipped down the steps to the beach and searched for beach treasures or took off her sandals to wade in the waves lapping on the shore. In the wet sand she wrote their names: Florence, Sidney, Vera and encased them in a giant heart. Her parents indulged her at one of the kiosks, buying her some silly trinkets to keep as souvenirs of the holiday. One was a small leather purse with Torquay embossed into it. They also bought her a "rock" very familiar at all seaside resorts. It was a hard candy, a long rod, wrapped in cellophane with a picture of the resort inside, showing through. The length and diameter varied. Hers was about ten inches long and two inches in diameter. The word TORQUAY was printed around the circumference just inside the outer edge of the rock and it was there all the way to the end. The rock would probably last Vera for the full three weeks of the holiday. Florrie bought a few postcards to send back home and at an ice cream stall, they all enjoyed a "99," an ice cream cone with a chocolate Flake bar stuck into it.

The days passed by in sweet contentment. Every day they spent time on the seafront. Several times, they sat in deck chairs on the sand. While sitting there in the sunshine, Sidney would close his eyes, and listen to the rhythmic sound of the waves rushing onto shore, the squawking of seagulls circling above and the distant sound of children laughing and people talking. He became so relaxed that he often nodded off with a gentle smile on his face. Florrie waded in the waves with Vera sometimes. and Sidney once or twice, took off his shoes too, rolled up his trouser legs and joined them. They explored the town, walked in the many lavish gardens, played cards in the evening, and read books. There was such an assortment of cafes and restaurants for their evening meal, they usually chose a casual place and ate simply - fish and chips, liver and onions, shepherd's pie - but on their last night they chose a fancier location which advertised entertainment. There was a band and a comedian. Sidney had quietly asked if the comedian was appropriate for children and was assured that he was.

"Ooh, Dad!" exclaimed Vera. "This is nice!"

"Cor, Sid, bit of a pretty penny it is in 'ere!" Florrie noted as she perused the menu.

"Have what you want, luv." Sidney answered. "It's the end of our holiday. And hasn't it been lovely?"

"Oh yes!" Vera replied.

"It certainly 'as, Sid. I've enjoyed every minute of it, I 'ave. And you don't 'alf look the better for it too! Done you the world of good, it 'as."

"Yes, I think it has… I think it has."

The band was wonderful and played so many popular hits. The diners gaily sang along, and some took to the small dance floor. Sidney took Florrie by the hand and swayed slowly with her for one of their favourites and later he led Vera to the floor to dance with her. It was a special event for Vera. She had never danced with her father before, except as a small child standing on his feet. The comedian was very good too. He had the place laughing aloud, heartily. Some of the jokes really tickled Florrie and, as usual, many of the audience was laughing at her, the prolonged hearty laugh, and drawing in of breath followed by a whooping exhale.

Walking home, Vera basked in the glow of the evening, the fancy meal, the excitement of the live band, dancing with her father and laughing with her parents. She was twelve years old, soon to be a young woman and that special night had made her feel grown up, ready to embark on the next phase of her life. She wondered what lay ahead.

As the train chugged on carrying them home the next day, Vera's thoughts returned to the war. For three weeks she had been able to forget about it but as they travelled closer and closer to London, the signs of destruction, rubble and dreary reality brought it all rushing back. They had enjoyed a respite, her father seemed better in health and back to their lives they must all go.

Sidney received a letter notifying him that his start date at the pub would be four weeks hence. All three were glad to know of a definite date to move on to their new life. They were excited about their new venture and anxious to get started and settled in their new home. Sidney returned to work and, though the hours were long again, he was dedicated, as always, with an eye to training others to manage some of the more detailed work that he had done so well. He noticed a recurring pain low down in his belly and complained about it to Florrie. She gave him a nice hot water bottle to lay on it and gave him bicarbonate of soda. "You probably haven't been eating right, Sid," she said. "Cor, this rationing is 'ard for anyone to get enough roughage these days. I'll make extra vegetables for dinner tomorrow and a nice, big pot of porridge for breakfast." The pain diminished for a couple of days but then returned stronger than before. He began to run a fever and felt very unwell. Florrie became concerned and hurried Vera off to school one morning before running to the telephone booth at the end of the road to call the doctor. When she described the symptoms to the doctor, he told her to take Sidney directly to the hospital. "If it is what I think it may be," he said, "he needs attention immediately."

At the hospital, Florrie paced, wringing her hands waiting and wondering. Sidney had been whipped away and she had been directed to the waiting room. He had been doubled over with pain and his face was so pale. A nurse finally entered the waiting room and asked Florrie to accompany her to the attending doctor's office. Florrie entered the office warily and sat on the edge of the chair facing the doctor seated at his desk. The doctor wore a kind expression, nodding slightly to acknowledge her fears.

"It is rather serious, Mrs. Middleton. I am afraid that your husband suffered a burst appendix just after arrival here at the hospital. He has been in surgery, and we have done all that we can with the latest medicines and antibiotics to clear the bacteria which has spread throughout his abdomen. However, as you must know, Sidney is not in good health generally and his body has suffered quite a shock. To be quite honest, I am not sure that he has the strength to overcome this." Florrie slumped in the chair and covered her face with her hands. Then she lifted her head and took a deep breath to respond.

"Thank you doctor for all you 'ave done. I appreciate your tellin' me straight. Can I go and sit with my 'usband now?"

"Yes, of course. My nurse will take you to his bed on the ward."

Florrie sat beside Sidney for the rest of the day and part of the next. He regained consciousness only once giving his wife a weak smile. "It's bad, isn't it? He whispered weakly.

"Your appendix burst, Sid, but they are giving you medicine and you will feel better soon."

"Vera?"

"She's okay, luv. She's at school right now and will probably ride her bike round to one of her friends later. I will bring 'er up to see you when you are a bit better. I 'spect they will let 'er in 'ere for a quick visit." Sidney could not stop his eyes from filling with tears. "That would be lovely. You know how much I… both of you. You know how much…" He choked on the lump in his throat. Florrie grasped his hand and squeezed.

"We know, luv. We know. Don't get yourself all upset. Just get better and come 'ome."

He nodded feebly and closed his eyes. His breathing was shallow and weak, and Florrie was sure she could feel the last of his strength slowly leaving his body. She let the tears fall unchecked down her cheeks still holding his hand, silently praying, loving, despairing, until with a sudden, sharp inhale of breath, Sidney slipped away.

From Vera's war memories binder – a contribution to her creative writing class

I slowly changed from the state of excitement to growing fear each day and, like everyone else, I had to continue to function doing necessary tasks. School attendance was spasmatic and sometimes not at all, depending on damage sustained. When we were able to attend, much of the day was spent sitting in school hallways between sandbags and trying to continue a class debate. We were able to have quizzes and practised our times tables.

Another thing I can recall is how in the mornings, so many people would be sleeping on the public buses on their way to work, their heads flopping forwards or sideways. They had had no sleep during ten hours of bombing night after night.

There were wonderful times and comradeship during the war years. People showed enormous compassion and we helped and needed each other. Bravery and sacrifice were witnessed daily. Some good came out of all that bad, although heavy loss of life on the home front and the western front was a burden hard to bear.

The wail of those air raid sirens, I'll always remember, the memory of which will haunt me forever. However, I can recall such wonderful, jolly times spent in public air raid shelters where we supplied our own entertainment. Those with talent played accordion, banjo, or harmonica while we all sang with gusto to drown out the sounds of whistling bombs, our own heavy gunfire from anti-aircraft guns being propelled around the streets on trucks, and the continuous explosions of the bombs being dropped all around us.

CHAPTER FIVE

Vera cycled home late in the afternoon of the first Saturday in October. She had spent the day at Hilda's where they had spent a happy time together playing jacks and cards and making paper dolls. Vera was not too fond of making paper dolls or playing dolls of any kind really. She did not really like arts and crafts type of activities, but she knew that Hilda enjoyed it, so she did her best. Vera was much happier when they went outside to play "donkey" with a ball against the brick wall of the house. When they went back inside and she glanced at the clock, she realised she should get back home. She was hoping that her dad was home from work. He had been working such long hours again, that she had not seen him in several days. Her mother had mentioned rather off-handedly that he had left before she got up in the morning and returned long after she had gone to bed. But this was Saturday, and she was anxious to see him.

As she turned the corner on the street where they were staying, Vera noticed several cars parked in front of the house and people in various stages of leaving, saying their goodbyes to Florrie, hugging her and looking grim. All were wearing dark, formal attire. Most of the people she recognised. They were friends and relatives. Uncle John was there and Auntie Het and Auntie Lou and… she looked around for her father with a sinking feeling in her stomach. What was going on? Vera rode up to her mother, "Mum, what has happened? Where is Dad? Why is everyone here, Mum? Mum? What is it? What is this all about?" Her aunts and uncles were watching her with such sorrowful expressions. Auntie Het dabbed a handkerchief to her eye.

She knew then. She knew.

An hour later, Vera was collapsed on her bed sobbing while Florrie tried to console her. She wondered if she had done the right thing by not immediately telling Vera of her father's death and keeping her away from the funeral. She thought that the sombre occasion would be too much for her to cope with at her tender age. Her sisters had advised her that children should not attend funerals and Florrie had been too easily swayed in her distress.

"I think you are right, Florrie, said her sister Lou. "It is not a place for children. Won't do 'er any good at all. She don't need to be there and see all that."

"Yes," Edie agreed. "It will be much too distressing."

"I know. But I just thought… well, you know, Vera is quite mature for 'er age. I did wonder if she would want to be there."

"No, I think you are right to keep her away," Lou responded.

In truth she was glad of the excuse to delay the time when she would have to tell her daughter the awful news. She herself was despairing. Their situation could not be any worse. They had lost a loving husband and father, had sold all their furnishings and so many of their belongings. They were living in a few rented rooms, in the midst of a war, air raids, restrictions and rationing, and had lost the thrill of the wonderful new venture that they had planned. Florrie knew that she would have to grieve quickly and quietly. She had no time to dwell on herself. She had to focus on Vera to get her through this and to get their lives in order.

That evening, after Vera had sobbed herself to sleep, Florrie sat up thinking long into the night. They had to get out of these rooms. They were dismal and depressing and had only ever meant to be a stopgap between their old life and their new. She could move back into their house, but it would need to be refurnished and would be a terrible reminder of their happy life with Sidney. No, she thought. They needed to get away, perhaps spend time with family members who lived further away. Her sister, Lylie lived in Devon, Sid's sister, Vi, lived north of London, Edith lived in Bath, and she had some dear friends dotted around the country. It would be lovely to see them again. She jotted down names and locations and formulated a rough route, a huge loop around England that would bring them back home again. Maybe by then they could return to their own house, have a scrounge around for some essential furnishings and settle in, with Sidney's loss not being so raw and painful. She would make sure their lives were busy and full. They would go into London to see some shows, spend time with the family that lived around them, go to the cinema. It sounded like a good plan. Just what they both needed. They would leave in a week or two. Florrie was satisfied and took a deep breath but on the exhale her composure collapsed, her eyes brimmed, and her shoulders sagged. "Oh Sid," she whispered. "All our plans... I miss you so my luv. Am I doing the right thing? It's all for Vera now. She's what will keep me going... *Vera!*" She lowered her head into her arms resting on the table and allowed herself a few minutes of hearty sobs of utter misery and gloom. Then she sat up straight, wiped away her tears and added a note to her list. There was one more thing to do before they left.

Two days later, Florrie and Vera waited outside their old home. They did not go inside, knowing that it would look bare and forlorn, abandoned, and empty. Vera could not help but keep turning to look at the house and stare at the windows wishing that she could catch a glimpse of a familiar figure inside. Where was her father? Surely, he was still here somewhere. How could he be gone forever? She was trying to accept the facts, and his sudden death but had not witnessed any of the events of his final days, could not say goodbye or attend his funeral. All her life, Vera would dwell on this. She did not get the closure that she needed, and it just never felt real to her. Her eyes stung as a man turned the corner onto the street and approached them with a sorrowful smile.

"Hello, Florrie, nice to see you again," he said shaking her hand. "And this must be Vera. Cor, yer dad talked a lot about you, 'e did." Vera managed a shaky smile then looked down at her feet.

"I was so sorry to 'ear about Sid. Wonderful chap and a good friend, 'e was. Everybody liked 'im. And what a treat it was to work with 'im. Taught us a lot, 'e did. 'E'll be missed a lot, believe you me!"

"Thank you, Arthur. That's very nice to 'ear.

"Thank you for thinkin' of me… about the bike. Bin wanting one for ages and just 'earing Sid with 'is 'oliday stories…well, I know 'ow much you all enjoyed it."

"Yes… we did, we did. Er, I'll just unlock the garage for you. Perhaps you will back it out. It's all ready to go."

"Yes… yes, of course."

Arthur started the motorbike and slowly eased it out of the garage. Vera closed her eyes and held her breath when the engine revved. She could almost imagine her father sitting on it waiting for Florrie and Vera to stow their things and climb aboard.

"Do you want to take it for a run or check it over? Make sure it is what you want?"

"Not necessary. I know Sid took care of it. Engine sounds perfect and everything is clean and polished. Your price is more than fair, Florrie." He held out an envelope and Florrie handed him some documents.

"Well then. I'll be off. I 'ope we get as much pleasure out of it as I know you all did. I wish you the best of luck and please do let me know if there is anything I can ever do for you." He smiled, tipped his cap, backed onto the street, and rode away. Vera watched the vehicle travel to the corner, turn and disappear from sight. Two tears brimmed over and rolled down her cheek. The sale of the beloved motorcycle and sidecar brought home the reality of the finality of her old life. She felt numb and frozen in that moment of time. How could they go on? What future did they have? Florrie also stood unmoving as the motorcycle drove away. What happy times it represented. Their life would never be the same again. She allowed herself a moment to remember the three of them setting off on one of their adventures, smiling and waving to neighbours as they left, her arms wrapped around Sidney's waist, Vera settled contentedly in the sidecar… Then, she sighed softly and laid a hand on Vera's shoulder.

"Right! That's that taken care of." She put the envelope into her handbag and gave Vera a gentle push. "Let's 'ave our tea out tonight, shall we? Come on. We'll walk down to the café and 'ave a nice tuck in. I've made some plans I want to talk to you about. All right, luv?"

"Yes Mum. That's all right," Vera answered distractedly.

Over beans on toast, several cups of tea and Victoria sponge for dessert, Florrie explained her plan to her daughter. It sounded interesting to Vera. She always enjoyed seeing her extended family and she was anxious to be away for a while, to have a distraction from her old life. They would start at Uncle Harold and Auntie Vi's house in Watford, where they had been invited to stay for as long as they liked. Derek and Peter, their two sons, were lively, playful cousins and she was quite fond of them both. Florrie showed her the rough map she had made with the stops circled on it. The final circle was back in Chingford which would be sometime in the spring, her mother explained, where they would reside, once more, in their own house on Waverly Avenue. Vera nodded, satisfied with the arrangements.

The next day, they packed suitcases, paid the last of their rent and left their lodgings. The two walked determinedly away from the dismal, brick house with the dingy, cheerless rooms heading for the bus, which would take them to the Underground station, which would take them to the first stop on their grand tour.

Note in Vera's binder of memories
My mother decided it was in my best interest NOT to attend my father's funeral service, which was a mistake, because I was never able to have closure of his life. It took many years before I was able to fully accept his passing.

Note in Vera's binder of war memories

My mother was amazing and was able to overcome her loss. She had a remarkable talent for fighting back when the chips were down. She made sure we were always busy and put herself out to take me to the West End theatres (when they were operating) and we saw "Perchance to Dream" and the "Dancing Years" by Ivor Novello, the "Barber of Seville" by Mozart and many shows at the London Palladium with Tommy Trinder and Max Bygraves. These famous theatres were always 75% filled with servicemen dressed in their khaki, Air Force blue, and the Naval navy-blue uniforms. We could hear the guns firing and the drone of the enemy planes as we sat laughing at the comedians or being enthralled with the dance and songs of Ivor Novello, Gilbert and Sullivan etc.

CHAPTER SIX

Watford was a pleasant town with trees displaying their autumn colours and many gardens still flourishing with asters, chrysanthemums, hydrangeas, and even some roses still in bloom. It was only a short walk from the train station to Vi and Harold's house, so Florrie and Vera walked the distance carrying their suitcases. Vera looked around with more interest than when she had visited with her parents in the past. They had stopped several times when they were nearby on one of their motorcycle outings for short visits but had never stayed long enough to explore the town. Arriving at the house, Vera was reminded that there was a school directly across the street. She remembered teasing her cousins that they must only have to roll out of bed fifteen minutes before classes started. The school was small and a typical Victorian, brick building. There were some children in the playground, the sound of their voices at play caught Vera's attention and she stood watching for a while. That was me, she thought. Just two weeks ago, at school joking around in the schoolyard, not knowing that my father lay dying in the hospital.

The front door opened, and Aunt Vi stood on the threshold smiling a welcome.
"Oh, come in, come in. I'm so glad you're here. The kettle's hot so we can have a nice cup of tea. Have a good journey, did you? Hello Vera, dear. Don't you look nice? Let's go upstairs so that you can put your suitcases in your room."
"Thanks, Vi," Florrie responded. "A cup of tea sounds lovely."
All three climbed the stairs and Vi swung open one of

the bedroom doors.

"This will be your room. Now you can arrange it any way you want to. The wardrobe is empty and so are the drawers in the chest, so you just make yourselves at home. Sorry the bed's not a bit bigger, it's a three-quarter, but I expect it will do well enough. This was Derek's room, and he is now bunking in with Peter so it's all yours."

"Oh, Vi, that is so nice of him. 'Ope 'e doesn't mind being turfed out of 'is own room."

"Not at all. He and Peter often end up falling asleep in each other's rooms anyway. And they are both looking forward to having you here. Now, don't you go feeling that you are the least bit of an inconvenience."

"Thank you… for 'aving us, Vi. Just what we need right now."

"Auntie Vi, are Derek and Peter in school today?" Vera asked.

"Oh yes but they will be home in a couple of hours, so come on, let's go and have that cup of tea and then you can put your things away before they come home."

The boys came tumbling in the door, all grins, a few minutes past four in the afternoon.

"Hello Vera… hello Auntie Florrie," they called.

"Come on Vera, come and see the games we have sorted out," said Derek.

"Unless you want to walk down to the park for a while before it gets dark," Peter suggested.

Vera giggled at their enthusiasm and opted to go to the park first and play games when they got back. So off they went, trotting down the road leaving Vi and Florrie some quiet time to spend in conversation, talking about Sidney and the unfairness of his death, how much they would both miss him and the future without him. Vi, Violet, was

Sidney's younger sister and they had always been close.

Florrie and Vera spent three months in Watford. It was time well spent and soothing to their souls. Because of the length of time they stayed, Florrie enrolled Vera in the school across the street. It was beneficial for Vera to have a somewhat normal routine. The lessons were rarely interrupted. Watford had its share of bombs, but the frequency was much less and not as severe. Vera enjoyed her teachers and her classes, and she made a couple of temporary friends. She was busy all day and the evenings were relaxed and entertaining. Derek and Peter were a few years younger than Vera, but they were bright and funny. There was always a game or puzzle or project to work on together and on the weekends the three of them explored the neighbourhood to see what was new with the war. They watched the Home Guard drilling and visited bomb sites. The boys showed Vera the public bomb shelters in town in case she was ever caught out during a raid. They read propaganda posters that were on display all over town and looked at shop windows as they slowly became decorated for Christmas.

Uncle Harold was a warm, easy-going man who was very fond of Florrie and Vera. Vera was rather in awe of him because he was a professional musician who played the trumpet in the BBC Variety Band. He was usually in London on the weekends, rehearsing and playing on the radio. The radio was an important communicator of news and guidance during the war, but it was also a wonderful means of entertainment and cheer. There were children's programmes, mysteries, comedy shows and music. When the BBC band played, the volume was turned up and the family listened, tapping their feet, and singing along if a familiar tune was played. The big band music was so welcome in so many households and lifted spirits of war-weary Britons. There were a lot of new hits that were patriotic songs, British and American, to boost the morale of the people and to promote the war effort. *"We'll Meet Again"*, *"There'll Be Bluebirds Over The White Cliffs Of Dover"*, *"I'll Be Seeing You"*, *"Boogie Woogie Bugle Boy"*, *"Don't Sit Under the Apple Tree"*, were played so often that everyone knew the words and were united even more by music and song lyrics. The people were becoming strong, determined, and defiant. Uncle Harold enjoyed a live audience too and played at many venues with the band where the dancefloor would be packed with couples swaying to romantic melodies or jitterbugging to a lively number. At home, he often practised new pieces and the family would gladly be his audience, clapping and dancing in the living room while a cosy fire blazed, and dessert waited on the table.

Uncle Harold took Vera for a walk one afternoon and treated her to tea and a teacake in a little café. They had been laughing and joking as they walked but when they sat down with their tea, Harold became rather quiet and thoughtful.

"Vera," he said. "I know you have been through a terrible time, and I don't want to make you sad again, but I want you to know that your aunt and I are here for you and your Mum if ever you need us at any time."

"Thank you, Uncle Harold," Vera responded. "I have been so enjoying my time with you all that sometimes I forget… I forget that Dad is gone. Sometimes I think that when we go back home, he will be there, at our house, waiting for us. And, I have to remind myself that it happened… that he really is dead.

"I know luv. It will be that way for some time. But your

life awaits. This war will end one day, and such an exciting future will stretch before you." Vera nodded knowing this to be true and that she would have to move on and grow up and have a life and family of her own. But would the pain ever ease up? Would she ever be able to remember her father with a smile instead of tears? As if he could read her thoughts, Harold offered some kind-hearted reassurance. "Your father will always be with you. All the love and caring he gave you is with you still. He provided a strong foundation for you to grow on and he would want you to be strong and happy in your life. Remember that. And soon, when time has passed and the hurt is not so fresh, you will be able to think of him and talk about him with love and a smile, not always with tears." Vera nodded again and smiled gratefully at her uncle. She would remember Uncle Harold's words to her always.

The weeks passed pleasantly, and Christmas arrived. The weather was dull and a bit rainy but the family in Watford was determined to have a bright and merry time. Vi and Florrie worked wonders with the ration books, planning meals and saving coupons. Uncle Harold had taken the boys and Vera to choose a perfect tree and gifts were bought and hand-made so that there were a good variety of presents under the tree on Christmas morning. A lovely, bright fire burned in the grate, carols played on the radio, the dining table was ready for the traditional Christmas dinner, roast beef, roast vegetables, Yorkshire pudding and gravy. Places were set, each had a gaily coloured Christmas cracker. When the family sat at the table, the crackers were pulled, *snap, snap, snap*, and paper crowns were placed on their heads. Jokes and a little trinket were found inside each cracker so everyone in turn read their joke aloud and displayed their little prize. For dessert they enjoyed

Christmas cake, jam tarts and mince pies. Florrie played the piano after dinner and Harold accompanied her on the trumpet. Vera had received some new books, a watch, a brush and comb set, and hair ribbons. Auntie Vi had knitted her a lovely scarf with matching mittens and Uncle Harold bought her a diary.

The family welcomed in the year 1942 with hope and optimism. The United States had joined the war effort following the attack on Pearl Harbor on 7th December. Britain was no longer alone. A strong and determined ally would make all the difference. That night, in their shared bed, Florrie spoke softly to her daughter.

"It has been a lovely Christmas, hasn't it? And, it has been wonderful to stay here with Auntie Vi, Uncle Harold and the boys. But you know what our plan was. It will be time to move on soon. We will make a couple of visits for just a few days with old friends of mine and then move on to Bath where we will stay with your Aunt Edie. She may have a little job for me to do there for a couple of months. Bath is lovely, you know. We will enjoy it there. Then we will end up in Dorset, on Auntie Lylie's farm. Our last stop before going 'ome."

"Yes, Mum. It all sounds nice… but I will miss it here. We have been quite happy, haven't we?"

"We 'ave… we 'ave. We 'ave really needed this time 'ere. We are ever so grateful but now, on we go, slowly working our way 'ome."

"Yes, Mum. On we go."

Florrie revelled in the company of her friends. The first visit was with a friend who was not married and had a tiny cottage in a small town. Again, Florrie and Vera shared a bed, which was to be the norm for them for quite some time. After the initial excitement at seeing each other again and the expression of sympathy and condolences, the conversation reverted to shared memories of their youth. Vera had often seen her mother chatting and laughing heartily, but this was different. She sat transfixed as stories flowed and the two friends, giggled like schoolgirls. Vera thought some of the stories were rather silly and probably exaggerated but the ladies howled heartily at the antics of their younger days. Each incident triggered another and the two volleyed back and forth all afternoon into the evening. Florrie's friend, Jean, had a tea all prepared so they took a break to lay the table and serve the food. Jean chatted politely to Vera during tea. She was curious as to how she was coping with the war and how it was affecting her life. Vera liked Jean but she knew this visit was for her mother and was happy to take a back seat. After tea Vera sat with one of her new books and read for a while. She went up to bed early and fell asleep listening to the muffled voices and bursts of laughter downstairs. She was happy that her mother was so enjoying this reunion.

A few days later, they were off again, this time to a friend who had a family, a husband, two young girls, a toddler and a baby. This visit was different because of the activity of the household. The husband was away on war work, so Doris was happy for the company and extra hands. Florrie and Vera helped with the children during the day and Vera noticed that her mother was so pleased to be busy and helpful. She was always that way, the first to offer a hand, visit someone who needed care, run errands for someone. It seemed to satisfy a need in her to be useful and supportive. She and Doris chatted about old times also, theirs was a friendship that had begun in the workplace and was one of shared values and dreams for the future.

"Do you remember, Florrie? You always said you would have one child and you would name her Vera. Isn't it amazing that it worked out that way?"

"Yes. I must 'ave 'ad a premonition. And very glad I am too."

"I never knew that Mum," Vera remarked.

"Yes… I named you after a musician's wife. 'E was a good friend of your… of your father. I 'eard the name and always liked it. Thought if I 'ave a girl, that's what I'll call 'er. Vera."

"And you, Doris," Florrie continued, "you said you wanted a houseful of children. You have four. Is that enough or do you plan to 'ave more?"

"Oh, yes," Doris chuckled. "Got another one on the way now."

"Cor!" Florrie laughed.

They left Doris and her brood after a few days and took the train to Bath to visit Edie, another of Florrie's older sisters. There were thirteen offspring of Florrie's parents and Florrie was the eleventh. Edie was second in the birth order, so she was a good deal older. Of all her mother's siblings, Vera knew the least about Edie. She had left Chingford suddenly, under mysterious circumstances and had not seen any of them since. She had kept in touch with only Lylie and Florrie, occasionally sending a card or letter to them. Florrie had written to her older sister and asked if it would be convenient to stop and visit for a brief time. She was surprised to receive a letter back gushing with excitement and hospitality. She and Vera could certainly come and stay and would be most welcome.

Edie had a flat in Bath almost directly in the middle of the city. Florrie had given the address to the taxi driver at the train station, and they had stared in amazement when he pulled up in front of a modern apartment block, steps away from shops, restaurants, and offices. Edie and Florrie hugged tightly when the door was opened to admit them. Vera had been amazed by the ornate exterior of the building and was even more impressed with the inside. The rooms were large with lofty ceilings, and the kitchen was equipped with every modern convenience available. She was so fascinated by this handsome, confident woman who lived alone and worked locally for a well-to-do firm. This was new and different from what she had always thought was a woman's lot in life, to be a wife and mother, homemaker, cook, shopper, laundress, and nurse. Edie showed them around the flat. It was quite spacious and decorated smartly with tastefully coloured fabrics, modern furnishings and carefully chosen accent pieces. It reminded Vera of some rooms she had once seen in a magazine. It was the kitchen that caused Florrie to stop and stare. Everything shone. There was a lovely, gleaming white refrigerator, a nice oven range, bright red cabinets on the walls, red and white checked linoleum on the floor, a deep white porcelain sink and a walk-in pantry. A red kettle sat on the stove, a red clock on the wall and red checked gingham curtains at the window. There were some electronics in the pantry on the shelf. Florrie recognised a toaster, but she was not sure what the other items were.

"Crikey! Edie, what a kitchen. Cor... what a place you 'ave 'ere."

"Yes, Florrie," Edie laughed. "I'm really happy here."

"You must be doing alright for yourself, I'd say."

"I have an excellent job, Florrie. I had to work my way up and lose the Cockney but it's what I wanted to do after... well after moving away and starting a new life."

"Yes... well, we'll talk later," Florrie said, nodding her

head toward Vera who was gawking at the refrigerator.

"Can I open it, Auntie Edie?" she asked.

"Yes, of course you can." Vera pulled on the lever and swung the door open. "Oh, look Mum, there's milk and butter and cheese in here, fruit and vegetables and look, there's a freezer compartment too. Boxes of frozen vegetables, and some meat and ice cream. Goodness."

Edie laughed. "I'll give you a dish later, Vera. Come on, let's sit down and I'll put the kettle on."

Later that evening, when Vera was in bed, Florrie and Edie talked. Florrie learned why Edie had left home so abruptly and distanced herself from the family.

"That is what I thought," said Florrie. "And I don't blame you one bit! Must 'ave been so 'ard on you. Wish I could 'ave 'elped."

"Oh, Florrie, you were too young then. I had to sort it out myself. I decided then to get myself a career, so I worked hard, took some classes, and found myself a position in a good firm. In fact, Florrie, that job I mentioned would be for a month or two and it will pay quite well. We need help with someone to handle the phones and to rearrange our files. I thought it might be good for you to get back in the workplace for a while and earn a bit of money."

"Yes, Edie. I think that would be a good idea, as long as it is temporary, of course. I don't want Vera just 'anging about on 'er own though. She'd 'ave to go to school."

"There's a school just a short walk from here. We can enrol her there."

Florrie nodded, quite pleased with the arrangement. It would be another new experience for Vera, new school, a historic city to explore and some cash to take back home.

Vera accepted the plan quite gracefully and found the school to be pleasant enough. There were gas mask drills and bombing raid drills, but Bath had not been targeted yet, so she felt safe and free to wander about the area around Auntie Edie's flat. One weekend Edie took them around the city. They visited the Roman Baths, which were incredible and still in such marvellous condition. The columns and statues still stood proudly and walking around, Vera could just imagine the bathers relaxing in the warm water and socialising. She learned that men and women bathed at separate times and enjoyed the Laconicum, which was a kind of steam room. They had tea in the Pump Room Restaurant, where healthy mineral-rich water was served, before moving on to Bath Abbey. The Abbey was very near to the Roman Baths and was spectacular to see with its Gothic architecture and spires reaching up to the sky. The fan vaults inside were just amazing and the fifty-two stained glass windows took their breath away. Edie showed them the Royal Crescent and the gardens, and they walked alongside the River Avon. She also pointed out some of her favourite shops.

"This bakery has delicious sticky buns and cream tarts. That fish and chip shop is the best in Bath. Over there is a nice dress shop and that is a wonderful book shop across the street." Bath was full of museums too. Vera was excited. She would be able to fill her free time in so many ways and she looked forward to poking around on her own after school.

The visit with Aunt Edie extended to two months. Florrie enjoyed her little job and was happy to feel useful doing something new and different. She was glad to be earning some extra money too. It would be so helpful when they settled back in their own house again. She liked Bath very much and felt quite a home there, but it was time again to travel to their last stop.

The Dorset countryside was gorgeous as they peered out of the windows on the train. Vera loved Dorset. They had camped there several times while touring with Sidney on the motorcycle and had usually popped in to see Auntie Lylie and Uncle Will. Auntie Lylie was another older sister, being third in the birth order of thirteen. She had two grown children who no longer lived at home, and she lived surrounded by acres and acres of fields, hedgerows and country lanes. From the train station, they had to take a bus and then a taxi for the last two miles of the journey. When they arrived at the cottage, Auntie Lylie dashed out of the door, threw her apron up over her head and bent over laughing. Vera had seen her mother do this very thing often. This is who she must have acquired the behaviour from. Florrie began laughing too and soon Vera could not help joining in. Her mother and her aunt ended up bent over double, gasping for breath, and wiping away tears.

Lylie and Will were a delight. There were no airs and graces about them. Their home was humble but cosy and cheerfully decorated in a jumble of mismatched furnishings and fabrics. Here Florrie and Vera were at complete ease and comfort. Although they shared a bed yet again, it was large and soft and piled high with blankets and quilts. There were two hot water bottles lying on the bed, ready to be filled at night before they slipped between the covers. Uncle Will came in from tending the animals and gasped in exaggerated shock when he saw Vera.

"Well, just look. She has grown at least a foot since we saw her last! How old are you now? Eighteen? Nineteen?"

"No, Uncle Will," Vera chuckled. "I'm twelve."

"Twelve. My goodness. And what a lovely young lady

you are," he said giving her a squeeze.

Meals were simple and delicious. Vera loved them all, egg on toast with bacon and beans, liver and onions, chicken pie, rabbit stew. There was always dessert, usually a nice thick custard over rhubarb or apple pie. Living on a farm, there was more to eat without depending on coupons all the time. This was a welcome change. When the meal was done, Uncle Will would always enquire if everyone had eaten enough. When he was assured that they had, he would respond, "very well then, sufficient sufficeth!"

Water had to be drawn from the well outside and stored in a tank in the kitchen. This became Vera's job while she was there. It was such a novelty that she enjoyed the task immensely, as well as feeding the chickens and rounding up the sheep at the end of the day with Uncle Will. The novelty of the outhouse was not appreciated as much. On cold nights and mornings, it was rather a shock to the system to trot across the yard to relieve oneself of the call of nature.

The two months spent on the farm were calm and gentle. The only sign of the war was the occasional flyover of planes, sometimes British and sometimes German, but always they were on their way somewhere else. "We do have a shelter here, dug into a hillside, but so far we have not had to use it. Still, it's there just in case," Uncle Will told them. Florrie was so at ease with her older sister who could not help but fuss over her and worry about her state of mind. It was such an unusual feeling for Florrie to be cared about in a motherly way. Her own mother had not had much time for nurturing her children. She had thirteen of them and a husband who ran the home like a tyrant.

Florrie despised her father who often knocked her mother about and expected complete obedience from the members of the household. Her father had had a musical gift from whom Florrie must have inherited hers and he had a piano in the home and, although he rarely played, he forbade anyone else to touch it. It was too tempting for Florrie, and she played it when her father was away at work. He discovered a plate with some crumbs left on the piano one day and learned that Florrie had used it. His anger had erupted terrifyingly at the defiance, and he administered a sound thrashing. Florrie's mother watched in despair but was just too timid to intervene or come to her defence.

Florrie basked in the care and concern of her dear sister and the kindness of Will. She relaxed in the beauty of the landscape and the privacy of the farmhouse. She loved the stars at night, so bright and seeming to be so close, almost within reach, and the absolute silence of the countryside when she lay in bed. It was so different and refreshing and such a perfect ending to their tour. It was spring and time to go home.

Vera rambled almost every day. She walked miles in her wellies across the hills and following hiking tracks. There was a tiny hamlet two miles away where she could buy a comic and perhaps a sweet or two. There were animals, hundreds of sheep, cows and horses. The other farmers became familiar with the young girl walking on the footpath through their farms and they waved a cheery hello and tipped their hat. She breathed deeply of the fresh air, sometimes aromatic from rich, robust animal smells, enjoying the solitude and connection with nature.

It was while they were staying with Lylie and Will on 24th May 1941, that they heard awful news on the wireless one evening. In the Atlantic, the new, powerful German battleship, Bismarck had sunk the mighty Hood. It had been struck by a lucky long-range shot which had detonated the rear magazine where shells and explosives were stored. HMS Hood sank in a matter of minutes. More than 1400 men were aboard and there were only three survivors. The little group in the cosy living room were stunned. This was a great blow to the war effort. They sat speechless and despairing until Uncle Will stood up to offer a prayer for the souls of all those lost. Vera thought back to the day she had stood in the sunshine on the gleaming teak deck of the magnificent warship. It was now in pieces on the bottom of the ocean! *What horror this war has wrought!* She thought. *How much more loss would they have to endure?* The British were determined to hunt the Bismarck and destroy her. She had been damaged by HMS Prince of Wales during an exchange of fire, and as she attempted to flee to port for repairs, Bismarck was attacked by torpedoes from heavy cruisers and bombers on 27th May and slipped below the waves leaving 2,000 dead and 110 survivors, who were picked up by British ships.

Morale suffered for a while after this devastating battle at sea, but life had to continue on, and one day, Vera returned to the farm after an afternoon's ramble with rosy cheeks and sunlight in her hair to find her mother packing clothes into their suitcases. She sat down resignedly on the edge of the bed. The well-planned loop had served them well. It was time to return to Chingford and face the future.

CHAPTER SEVEN

As the train chugged closer and closer to London, Florrie thought back over the last six months. It had been a happy time and had achieved the purpose that she had intended. It had separated them both from the memories of their home and Sidney and all the plans they had as a family. It had been busy and so different, and she knew that Vera had grown from the experience and all that she had learned. She looked at her daughter who was dozing in her seat and wondered how she would cope being back home again. She had arranged the months away knowing they would be a great distraction for them both, but she wondered if they were prepared to slip back into their old life and carry on.

Signs of the war became obvious as they travelled closer to home: the craters and piles of rubble, the long queues at the shops, air raid siren towers, men in uniform, barrage balloons, air raid shelters and brightly coloured propaganda posters in the stations as they passed through. *Dig for Victory, Loose Lips Sink Ships, Fighting Fit in the Factory, We Will Beat 'Em Again, Keep on Saving Coal, Gas, Electricity, Paraffin, Join the Women's Land Army, Keep Calm and Carry On.* Florrie sighed and yet felt herself rising again to the challenge. She would return to work in the factory and work long, hard hours doing her bit for the cause. After all, a safe and bright future depended on winning the war.

A change of trains in London and a bus ride to Chingford brought them back home at last. Florrie and Vera walked the last short leg of the journey with mixed emotions. How would they feel entering their house again? It would be empty, cold, and bare. But tomorrow they would start their search for furnishings. It would all have to be second-hand or borrowed at first but soon everything would look comfortable and cosy again. It would be exciting to find things together and would keep them busy for quite a while. As they approached the house, Florrie's footsteps slowed. Something was wrong.

There was smoke rising from the chimney and lights on inside the house. Florrie placed her suitcase on the pavement beside her and stared as she recovered from the initial shock and began to realise what obviously had happened.

"Wait here, Vera," she said as she opened the garden gate and proceeded up to the front door. Vera watched her mother knock at the door, their own front door, with a sinking feeling of dread. A woman opened the door wiping her hands on a dish towel. There was a short conversation during which Vera saw the woman's expression change from surprise, to understanding, to compassion. The woman went inside and reappeared at the door with a paper of some kind which she handed to Florrie. Her mother scanned the paper and handed it back nodding to the woman with a brief thank you before she turned and walked back down the garden path. The woman watched Florrie leave and saw Vera waiting on the pavement with their suitcases beside her. Her face crumpled and she quickly stepped back inside closing the door with a gentle push.

"What's happened, Mum?" she asked. "Who is that lady? What is she doing in our house?"

"Well, dear. It seems that our 'ouse was empty for so long that the council used their authority to take it over for emergency use. They placed a family who 'ad been bombed out of their 'ome in it."

"But we are back now. Can't we tell the council that they need to put the family somewhere else now?"

"I don't know, Vera. I will 'ave to go down to the town 'all tomorrow and find out. Meantime, come on, let's go to Auntie Lou's and stop the night with 'er and the family." Florrie picked up her suitcase, her face pale and grim, and started off back down the street. Vera picked up her own suitcase and followed but she could not stop the tears when she glanced back over her shoulder at the house. She had not realised how much she had yearned for her old home, for the familiar surroundings and the settled feeling of continuity, safety, and belonging that it afforded. She turned back and saw her mother striding steadfastly ahead. Her mother's thoughts and emotions must be in turmoil too, she thought. But there she goes, onward and upward, ready to face the next challenge. And just then, the air raid siren sounded.

Florrie spent an hour at the town offices the next morning and was politely informed of the special authorities extended to various departments during this time of war. One of them concerned vacant housing which could be requisitioned at the convenience of the government for housing homeless, bombed out individuals and families. After explaining her circumstances and the reason for her absence from the home, the response was sympathetic but unchanged. Florrie was referred to another office where her name was placed on a waiting list for a suitable home, and she was given the addresses of several boarding houses that offered temporary rooms for rent. She was assured that her mortgage remained frozen, and her house would be restored to her at the end of the war. When she was given several official documents along with words of condolence and good luck, she realised there was nothing more she could do.

Louisa was Florrie's oldest sister and the firstborn of the thirteen. Her house was bustling at all times with several of their children still living at home and married children popping in to visit often. Louisa had grandchildren already and really thrived with the activity surrounding her all the time. It was lively and fun, but Florrie did not want to impose on the family for more than a few days. She checked out the addresses that had been provided for her and inquired at the most suitable location. There were two rooms available with a shared bathroom. Florrie paid two weeks in advance and proceeded from there to the factory where she had been working prior to Sidney's death. There was work available, the supervisor knew her well and was glad to have her back as an experienced worker in his department. So, Florrie had sorted things out quite well. She felt pleased with herself for her swift action, for securing a job, finding a new place to live, and taking charge of her life again. Vera would be able to return to her old school and be near her friends again. But then, as she walked back to Lou's house, the sadness returned and settled over her like a dark cloud. The reality of their new life was bleak. During the excitement of the tour with Vera, Florrie had always had the image of their house in the back of her mind and the vision of returning to their life there. They would have to continue to deal with the loss of Sidney which would come to the forefront again living with the memories in that environment, but it would have also felt comforting and warm. Florrie allowed herself to wallow in her sorrow and the unfortunate change of her plans as she walked. She had a heavy load and responsibilities to bear. But, as she drew nearer, she shrugged it off and thought about what she would do to bring pleasure and happiness into their lives. Vera must have some brightness and joy in her young life. They must endure the hardships of the war like everyone else. There were people far worse off. She had some money, a job, and a roof over their heads. They would survive.

The rooms were adequate. There was a small living room with faded wallpaper, two tired and worn easy chairs, a tiny table with two straight-back chairs, an old, threadbare rug, and a standing lamp with a heavy dark, shade. In one corner of the room there was a small waist-high storage cupboard with a single, electric hotplate on top. The bedroom had a double-sized bed with a lumpy mattress and a wardrobe with five hangers inside. The bathroom was across the hall and shared with two other tenants. Florrie had shopped before they moved in and so there was some food ready for them, tea and milk and a tiny amount of sugar, crackers and a few ounces of cheese, bread and a little butter, a tin of spam and soup, apples, potatoes, and a few vegetables. She had also bought a new kettle and teapot. She had found a frying pan and saucepan inside the cabinet. Whatever did not fit in the small cupboard, was stored under the bed. It was enough to get started.

Vera looked around disapprovingly. "It's not fair, Mum! Why do we have to live here while those people live in our house!"

"Don't expect life to be fair, Vera. The war is not fair. Losing our 'ouse is not fair. We are not the only ones living in rooms like these. It is all part of the war effort. We'll just 'ave to make the best of it. Now sit down. I bought a newspaper today. Let's see what is playing in the West End. We can go into the city and see something this weekend."

"Really? Can we? Are theatres open?"

"Yes, most of them are. A lot were closed at the beginning of the war, but most are open again now. People are desperate for entertainment and are willing to take the risk. During a heavy raid, though, everyone will 'ave to leave and go to a shelter."

"Oh, that's wonderful! Let's choose something now. Open up the paper, Mum."

Vera returned to school the next day and Florrie went to work. As Vera walked carrying her lunch, she thought about the evening before. She and her mother had read through the theatre listings, making a list of the plays that they both agreed were good possibilities. Then they each listed the plays in order of preference and laughed to see that they had both chosen the same one on the top of their list. Vera went to bed thinking of the theatre, the lights, the excitement and anticipation of the music and actors on stage, the laughter and applause and the journey home chatting about the plot and the songs and the magnificent costumes. She fell asleep smiling and Florrie's heart smiled too for the first time since they had left Dorset. Vera was excited to arrive at school and reunite with her schoolmates. Hilda ran over squealing with delight when she saw her friend. The two had so much to catch up on, talking nonstop until the school bell rang and the youngsters lined up to enter the building. An air raid interrupted class and the children moved to the corridor to continue. Vera sat amongst the sandbags again, listening as best she could to Miss Palmer talking about adjectives and adverbs while planes droned overhead, and bombs burst in the distance. When the all-clear sounded, back they went to the classroom and Miss Palmer asked Vera about her travels around the country. "Would you like to share some of your experiences with the class?" she asked.

"Yes, Miss Palmer," she answered timidly. She started off rather quietly and cautiously not sure if she could hold her schoolmates' attention, but when she saw the genuine interest in their faces, she became more confident relating her stories. The children particularly liked hearing about Bath, the Roman Baths, and the Abbey. They wanted to hear more about the schools she had attended in Bath and Watford. They also enjoyed her stories of the farm in Dorset. They looked at her with a combination of envy and admiration which made Vera feel a bit like a celebrity and quite lucky that she had been able to experience these adventures. She thought of her mother and all that she had done to give them both some breathing room and distance from their tragic loss. She would tell her about this little presentation she had given. She was sure it would make her feel so happy.

During the next few months Florrie took Vera to see quite a variety of shows in London. It was a wonderful experience for Vera and something to look forward to each month. They would enjoy the anticipation of the event, talking about the upcoming performance and the best travel plan to get there as well as where they might like to have dinner. It was a full day out and always so special. She would remember those occasions always, especially "Perchance to Dream," and the "Dancing Years" by Ivor Novello, the "Barber of Seville" by Rossini, and variety shows at the London Palladium featuring Tommy Trinder and Max Bygraves. She and Florrie laughed heartily at their jokes and antics on stage as did an audience so appreciative of a chance to relax and have a good laugh. The theatres were usually well-attended by servicemen from the full range of military units. They were dressed in khakis, Air Force blue, and navy-blue uniforms. The audience could hear guns firing and the drone of the enemy planes as all sat laughing at the comedians or appreciating the dance and songs of Ivor Novello, Gilbert and Sullivan and other great writers. Unless the air raid siren sounded, they were quite used to the sounds of war outside and could dismiss it from their consciousness quite easily and focus on the entertainment on stage. After a show, Florrie and Vera made their way home, chatting about all that they had seen. The exciting day out would lighten their mood for several days.

On several occasions they were in London when the dreaded air raid siren blasted. They hurried to the closest Underground station and rode the escalators down to the platforms where they sat on the hard, paved surface with their backs against the tiled wall if they were lucky to get a spot there and waited out the attack amongst a massive crown of Londoners. One evening, just as the show was wrapping up at the Palladium, the siren sounded, and ushers hurried down the aisles to steer people to the exits. Everyone moved quickly, purposely, but calmly to the closest exit and rushed to the Underground. Vera and Florrie exited through the main doors at the lobby entrance, walked briskly down Little Argyll Street and descended the steps into Oxford Street Underground station. The escalators were packed, passageways were bustling, and the platforms were already crowded by the time they arrived. Some people had already staked out an area and had brought pillows and blankets with them. These were families who elected to spend their nights in the Underground quite regularly rather than run for cover all hours of the night when the siren sounded. Vera and Florrie found a place to settle down and wait it out. There was hushed chatter all around them and the sounds of explosions throughout the city. The sound of falling bombs could be heard quite distinctly even in the Underground and each different type had its own identifying whistle as it fell. Some people became experts at determining the size and kind of explosive that was about to hit. The sound of emergency vehicles rushing through the streets with the clanging of bells added to the cacophony above. The people below listened quietly wondering at the damage being inflicted on their city. There were so many beloved historical landmarks as well as well-frequented local buildings, shops, churches, offices, pubs and, of course, theatres.

It soon became rather smelly, humid and stuffy with so many people squashed together and very little air flow, but it just had to be tolerated. There was no use complaining. Police and porters patrolled the platforms and during a long night often had to push back arms and legs which were hanging over the platform as people slept and a train was about to roll in. Sometimes if the platform was just too crowded, they would instruct groups to board the next train and travel to the next station or the one after that until they found one that was not so jam-packed.

However, inevitably, the mood of discomfort and gloom lifted when someone stood and started to sing a well-known song, perhaps *"Land of Hope and Glory,"* or *"Rule Britannia"* or *"God Save the King"* and everyone would join in. Someone else would start singing some popular party songs, *"Boiled Beef and Carrots," "Don't Dilly Dally on the Way," Bicycle Built for Two," "Pack up your Troubles*." A voice would call out, "something for the kiddies" and the children would sing along to some of their favourites, *"Grand Old Duke of York," "Underneath the Spreading Chestnut Tree," "Run Rabbit."* The singing might be followed by a juggling act or magic tricks or a variety of riddles and jokes. Tea and biscuits were often served by the Women's Voluntary

Services. It was always such a welcome treat and a blessing when these volunteers appeared with their carts and steaming urns, kind smiles and caring hearts. Sometimes professional musical performers made the rounds of the Underground stations and then the tube platform would really ring out with musical instruments, raised voices and laughter. At those times, the war was almost forgotten, and the sounds above were almost unheard. Vera felt very much a part of a united force, a strong civilian unit proud and resilient against Germany and that evil little man, Hitler. She and these British people randomly finding themselves sheltering together, were of one mind and purpose, to resist, to endure, to stand firm and to never, ever surrender.

When the all-clear sounded, it was almost a disappointment. This gallant assemblage began to disperse, some riding the escalators back up to ground level, some boarding trains as they came through but some remaining on the platform with their blankets and quilts, deciding to spend the entire night there. There may be more raids, there may not, but many families, especially those with little ones sound asleep clutching a favourite stuffed toy or doll were loath to disturb them.

Vera and Florrie made their way out of the city and back to Chingford. The bus brought them to the large roundabout at the bottom of Chingford Mount and from there they walked ten minutes to arrive at the boarding house where they lived in their two little rooms. It was quite late, so they hurried to bed. Vera fell asleep quite cheerfully with show tunes and songs of the Underground still echoing in her head.

CHAPTER EIGHT

The war dragged on and rationing tightened even more. Almost everything was rationed now. Food that was rationed included bacon, ham, meat, eggs, cheese, butter, milk, tea, sugar, cereals, rice and biscuits. Petrol, clothing, shoes and soap were rationed also. The rationing system adjusted as the war progressed to consider the needs of individuals. Workers doing heavy labour would require larger rations, children could manage on smaller rations but needed higher amounts of fats and proteins. Also considered were the needs of nursing mothers, the sick and people with special needs. The amounts allowed per week were very limited. Butter and cheese were rationed at 2oz per person per week, milk at three pints, tea at 2oz, sugar at 8oz and eggs at one per person plus an allowance of dried eggs. Meat was the equivalent of two chops and bacon and ham at 4oz each. Raisins, sweets, jam, and tinned goods were rationed too. Vegetables, fruits, and fish were not rationed but were usually in very limited supply.

It was a struggle for housewives to purchase food, prepare nutritious meals and make sure there was enough to last the week. The government printed cookbooks and guides with recipes and suggestions for stretching meals in creative ways. Florrie managed as best as she could, always prioritising Vera's dietary needs. Fortunately, restaurants and cafes always had meals to offer, even if choices may be quite limited, so they usually ate out once or twice a week. It was difficult also with the limitations on clothing. Vera was growing steadily and needed larger sizes and bigger shoes. Florrie was able to mend, darn and make alterations to some items which helped lengthen the time they could be worn. Vera sewed well and could patch and knit. There was usually a small pile of clothing waiting for attention. Vera did not have a lot of clothes, most people did not during the war, but she was rather fastidious in her appearance and so took good care of her wardrobe. Occasionally Florrie was able to buy some goods on the black market. There were people who specialised in obtaining rationed items or hard to find goods to offer them for sale for an inflated price but without requiring coupons. This was illegal, of course, but very much accepted, and welcomed by average folk. To get a little extra of something, or to be able to buy favourite items that were so rare and hard to find, brought such pleasure to a humdrum routine and provided a little ray of sunshine. These black-market operators were known as "Spivs" and although they might be looked down upon by some, they provided a service too, in their own dubious way.

Air raids continued quite steadily. The Anderson shelter at the rooming house where they were staying was adequate but cramped since it had to accommodate the inhabitants of the house, which was six or seven, sometimes even eight. Some evenings, when the siren sounded with its ominous undulating warning, Vera pleaded with her mother that they stay in their rooms and not be pressed tightly into the dimly lit interior of the shelter. But Florrie was firm every time and shepherded her out of the door and down the path to safety.

After a few months, the woman who owned the house approached Florrie to tell her that she would have to vacate. She was very apologetic, but her sister and her children had just lost their home in a particularly nasty raid, and they were in a terrible state. They had lost all their possessions and were quite desperate. "I'm afraid they are rather strapped for cash and will have to come here where I can help them. I am so sorry Mrs Middleton but I need you to leave by the end of the week." It was a bit of a blow to Florrie, but she soon recovered. She would find rooms somewhere else. One rooming house was much like another, and they had so little to move. Two days later and a half mile away, Florrie found another place and off they went again with their suitcases. Using a small, borrowed trolley cart from Louisa, they transported their few larger pieces and food items. When they were settled in, Vera inspected the premises. The contents included mismatched furniture, a wobbly table, ugly wallpaper, throw rugs on the floor, squeaky bed, and heavy, black-out curtains at the windows. There was, however, a sink and a tall narrow cupboard in a corner of the living room. The bathroom was shared, as was the norm in these situations. She shrugged her shoulders and looked at her mother. "Home sweet home," she said. Florrie scanned the room considering and then she burst out laughing. Vera joined in and soon the two of them were in hysterics, Florrie doubled over as usual, cheeks flaming red. "Ooooh, ooooh," she exhaled, recovering, and wiping her eyes. "Never mind. It will do us just right. Come on, dinner out tonight and then we'll stop at Auntie Lou's for a cuppa on the way 'ome. We'll buy a newspaper an' all. See what's playing next week. Did you notice there's an old wireless on the table? That'll be nice, won't it?"

"Yes Mum. It will be," Vera responded quite cheerily, buoyed by her mother's indomitable spirit.

It was a beautiful July evening, 4th July, Sidney's birthday, Florrie remembered, but she would not mention that to Vera. They had almost got through that first year without Sidney. Amazing, she thought. *Dear Sid. It's not that I've forgotten you. Never will. But I hope you are proud of us and how we are coping.* Vera had not forgotten the date and was thinking about her father also. But she would not mention it to her mother and spoil their dinner.

The war news was grim in 1942. In February, Singapore had fallen to the Japanese at a terrible cost to allied forces. The Japanese had advanced down the Malay Peninsula and attacked the British base there which consisted of British, Australian, and Indian soldiers. On 15th February, the British surrendered and 85,000 personnel were captured. Soldiers were imprisoned or transported to other Asian places to be used as forced labour. Most died in captivity due to severe hardship, brutal treatment, and starvation. Churchill spoke to the nation, calling the fall of Singapore "the worst disaster and largest capitulation in British history." He acknowledged the great loss and setback but rallied the nation, boasting of the determination and steadfastness of the British people, reminding them that they were no longer alone, that the United States was a new and strong ally. He stated that three quarters of the human race was united against the enemy and that "they shall not fail but move steadfastly together."

British ships were sunk in April, cruisers HMS Cornwall, HMS Dorsetshire, aircraft carrier HMS Hermes. A blitz on Bath took place on 25th-27th April, destroying many buildings and killing 417 people. Florrie was relieved to receive a letter from Edie, letting her know that she was not hurt. The disastrous Dieppe Raid on the German-occupied port in Northern France on 19th August cost thousands of lives. It was meant to be a show of strength to re-establish the Western Front. The RAF and the Royal Navy suffered severe losses attempting to provide ground support and tanks became stranded on the pebbly beach which jammed up the tank treads stopping them in their tracks. In October, milk rations were cut, and Canterbury was severely bombed. There were, however, victories in Africa. General Montgomery was victorious at the Battle of Alam el Halfa in Egypt in September and in November he forced a retreat of German forces in El Alamein.

Florrie took Vera to see the patriotic film, *Mrs Miniver,* which starred Greer Garson late in July. They saw it in London and watched the newsreel which preceded the film with alarm and dismay. It appeared that the enemy was well-entrenched throughout Europe and had established dominance and control of most of the countries there. The film, however, was a much-needed boost to the morale and succeeded in stirring the hearts of the spectators, bringing a tear to the eye and courage to the spirit.

Vera turned thirteen years old in March of 1942. They had still been in Dorset at the time and had enjoyed a happy celebration with Lylie and Will. Lylie had managed to bake a home-made cake for the occasion. Florrie had saved up clothing coupons so that she was able to buy her daughter a lovely, tailored dress and a pair of shoes with a little heel. As 1942 progressed, Florrie encouraged Vera to spend time with her friends, to go to the Odeon Cinema in town, have tea in the café and arrange meetings with Yvonne when she was available.

At fifteen, Yvonne was old enough now to help her father in the house. She could shop, clean, and cook for him as well as earn a wage. Florrie was worried about her niece. She was a very beautiful young lady with thick, dark hair that fell in luscious waves, striking violet eyes, lovely features, rosy cheeks and a trim, petite figure. Lately though, Florrie noticed that she looked tired, sad, and listless. When she discovered that she had to hand over most of her wages to her father for the privilege of living in his house, she was furious. She paid a call on her brother-in-law, John, and found Yvonne on her knees scrubbing the slate floor of the hallway. After giving John an unabridged piece of her mind, she tapped Yvonne on the head. "You've got to wise up, my girl," she said. "There's no future 'ere for you. Get out of 'ere." Florrie was gratified to learn that a week later, Yvonne had moved in with her sister Evelyn and Evelyn's baby, Michael. James, Evelyn's husband, was away, a soldier deployed in the army. Yvonne was able to work and help her sister with the baby. It was a much better living arrangement. Evelyn was a good housekeeper and cook so Yvonne ate well and felt appreciated. There were times when she felt a little controlled and overshadowed by her sister, since Evelyn was seven years older, rather outspoken, opinionated, and brusque, but she was able to overlook it and not take offence. She was quite happy and grew very close to Michael, spending lots of time with him, appreciating the feeling of being adored. Yvonne was able to visit Florrie and Vera often, sometimes now with Michael in tow. Life had finally begun to improve for Yvonne.

During a particularly heavy bombing raid one night, the house where Florrie and Vera had their rooms suffered some significant damage, windows were blown out, the roof needed repair and cracks appeared in the walls. They had to leave the premises since it was unsafe to live there.

"Off we go Vera," Florrie declared quite decidedly. "Enough of this! Back to Watford for a while."

"Are we going to stay with Auntie Vi and Uncle Harold again?" Vera asked.

"Only for a few days, luv. We'll find our own place somewhere nearby. 'Ow do you feel about going back to that nice school again?"

"That will be alright, Mum," Vera answered distractedly. She was considering all the feelings of being uprooted again, the changes, uncertainty, disconnectedness, insecurity. She stood in the middle of the dusty living room, looking so lost and forlorn, but Florrie was dusting off their suitcases and starting to pack. Vera felt better as she began packing her own things. What was she leaving anyway? Tired, old rooms, bombing raids, and a disrupted, substandard education. Florrie used a large shopping bag to carry her kettle and teapot and some of the food that was worth carrying. Vera had another shopping bag with food also. And off they went, hefting their loads down the road to catch the bus at the bottom of the Mount. "We'll be back again, Vera. Don't you worry. Chingford is our 'ome. We'll be back again one day."

They stayed with Auntie Vi and Uncle Harold less than a week. During that time Florrie was busy looking for new rooms, getting work for herself and enrolling Vera in school. "You don't let any moss grow under your feet, do you Florrie?" Vi said with great admiration. "Don't think I could handle things the way you do if I was in your shoes."

"'Course you would. You do what you 'ave to do. "'Specially if you 'ave someone depending on you."

"You do know that you can stay with us as long as you want, don't you?"

"Yes, I do, Vi, and I appreciate it very much. But I expect we will be 'ere in Watford for a while. We need our own place. We're very glad that we will be near you though. We'll see a lot of each other."

"That will be nice, Florrie."

Vera settled into her temporary life in Watford quite well. She especially appreciated the school and the return to more normal, structured lessons. Although there were air raids, they were less often and less severe. Their rooms were in a house on a pretty street called Spring Gardens and they were brighter and cleaner than their previous accommodations. There was a tiny kitchenette area which made meal preparation easier as well as comfy chairs and bed. Florrie found work in a large printing company in town. They moved several times while in Watford. Moving had become such a frequent occurrence that it was no longer a shock or much of an inconvenience for the two of them. If Florrie heard of accommodation that offered a better location, or nicer facilities, or closer to work, she would settle up with her landlord and move on to the new place. They never moved far, since she wanted Vera to be within easy walking distance of her school. Florrie and Vera became very practical in their lives and living conditions. If something else was more suitable, then that was where they would go, with no emotional attachments to a place, and no hesitation picking up and moving on. They stayed in Watford through the Christmas holidays and into 1943. When Vera turned fourteen in March of that year, Florrie worried again about her future. The standard education for her would be coming to an end soon and she wanted her daughter to have a skill to offer in order to secure a job with some prestige and consequence. She would need to get some advice from someone who had some professional experience. Florrie smiled to herself when the obvious person came to mind. Edie. She would write to her sister Edie in Bath.

Florrie also exchanged letters often with her sister Lou, keeping her informed of the changes of address in Watford.

Lou updated Florrie on Chingford, where the latest bombing raids had fallen, streets and homes that were affected and the sightings of American servicemen around town. *There are Yanks about now,* she wrote. *And you should see the girls when they see one. Shameless they are, chatting and flirting with them, they are, while our poor lads have been fighting the bloody war for near on three years now.* One such letter had just arrived the day before, so when Florrie heard a tap at her door one evening, she was surprised to see Louisa standing there when she opened it.

"Lou! Whatever are you doing here? Has something happened? Is everyone okay?"

"Oh, it's all right, Florrie. Good news actually. You remember that you left my name and address with the town council as your contact when they put you on the waiting list?" Florrie nodded. "Yes…"

"Well, I got a letter in the post today. A place has been found for you. Guess where? Waverley Avenue! The letter said that they knew that you 'ad been dispossessed of your house there and thought you might light to take the available space on the same street." Florrie's mouth dropped open.

"Really Lou? Oh, my gawd! 'Ow marvellous."

"It's the whole ground floor of the 'ouse, Florrie. There are tenants upstairs, an older couple, but you'll 'ave a kitchen, big living room and bedroom and … well 'ere's the letter. Read it yourself." Lou rummaged in her bag and produced a typed envelope. Florrie read it through quickly as Vera got up from her chair where she had been listening intently and stood beside her mother as she read.

"They need to know by tomorrow," Lou continued. "That's why I came 'ere. If you want it, you 'ave to come back with me tonight and go down to the town 'all tomorrow morning to accept." Florrie looked at her daughter. "Vera, we've done a lot of moving, and we like Watford, don't we? What do you think?"

"Do you really have to ask, Mum?" Vera replied. She bent down and pulled the suitcases out from under the bed. "Hurry up. Let's get packing. You said that we would go back to Chingford again one day, well, that day is today!" Florrie turned to her sister. "Thanks ever so much, Lou. Sorry you 'ad to be put out so much to come and tell us. We'll pack up. Won't take us long and I'll leave a note and the key with the money I owe the landlady on the table 'ere."

"Oh, I'm so glad you're coming 'ome, Florrie. I missed you, I did. What can I do to 'elp?

"You can put the kettle and the teapot into one of these shopping bags and our food in the other. That's all we 'ave. We travel light." Florrie chuckled after this comment and the chuckle grew into hearty laughter as she saw the humour in her words. *Oh, here we go again*, thought Vera. Lou joined in and it was the usual laughing fit, feeding off each other, revelling in a moment of utter joy.

The three of them worked quickly and in thirty minutes they were on their way walking to the train station. While Florrie and Lou chatted excitedly, Vera took special notice of all the familiar streets and shops and buildings they passed along their route. Yes, she did like Watford and her school and her new friends but the opportunity to go back home made her realise where she really wanted to be and where her heart was. With all the risk, the bombing, the disrupted and irregular school days, the scenes of destruction and debris, the opportunity to go back home and to live on the street of her childhood, was undeniable.

CHAPTER NINE

In 1943, hope and optimism returned to Britain. Although there was terrible news of twenty-seven merchant vessels sunk in the Atlantic over a four-day period in March by Germany, the German surrender at Stalingrad in the Soviet Union in February, the resignation of Mussolini in July and Italy's surrender in September boosted the morale of Britain and the Allied forces. The general feeling was that victory was becoming more of a certainty with time, with patience, persistence and continued hard work and sacrifice.

Vera and Florrie were so happy to be back in the old neighbourhood. It did not even feel too sad walking by their old house. They felt that they were back where they belonged, remembering happy times with Sidney. The house was a replica of their old one, even located on the left side of the semi-detached unit as their own house had been. It was so spacious inside and even though they only had use of the rooms downstairs, the rooms were quite large. They had forgotten how nice it was to move around in such open space, and there was a proper kitchen with cabinets, a stove, and a sink. They finally got to do their shopping for "bits and pieces," as Florrie called it. They spent a few days browsing in second-hand shops finding a table and matching chairs, a decent looking settee, and a comfortable easy chair, as well as a fairly large wardrobe for their clothes. There was a double bed already in the bedroom, but Florrie discarded the mattress and bought a new one. It was the only brand-new purchase she made. The rooms had light fixtures on the ceiling, but they picked out two standing lamps to warm up the décor and brighten the interior. Florrie arranged to have the furniture delivered and when it arrived, the empty rooms looked like a home. They walked around with delight. In the kitchen their kettle sat on the stove, the teapot on the counter and food was in the cupboard.

"Well," Florrie said. "We just need some pictures on the wall and rugs on the floor, but we can look for them later. What do you think, Vera?"

"I think it is wonderful," she said, arms outstretched, spinning around. She had not felt so happy in a very long time. "Well, it's back to work at the factory for me tomorrow and back to school for you," Florrie said. "But let's eat out tonight. It's been such a busy day, a good day, and I think we deserve a bit of a celebration, don't you?"

Youth groups began to pop-up all over London, opening in schools, church halls and other locations that lent themselves to populations of youngsters who were in desperate need of activities and opportunities to socialise. They were well organised to provide a safe place in the evenings with entertainment, education, fun, games, and music. Vera had turned fourteen in March and as daylight hours increased and the weather became warmer, Florrie encouraged her to go.

The youth group added a whole new dimension to Vera's life. She was a very social, outgoing girl and to have a place to go to mix with her peers in the evenings was just thrilling. She was able to walk to the high school, where she could enjoy table tennis, darts, card games, music, and dance as well as specialised classes on all types of interesting topics. A group of volunteers organised the programme, even offering tea and simple refreshments. On the rooftops, older boys took shifts, listening for distant bombs and sirens. When the threat got too close, they blew their whistles, and everyone headed for safety in the halls which were lined with sandbags. When the all-clear sounded, a steady one-pitch tone, the young people would dust off the tables, sweep up any glass or debris and return to their activities. Vera decided to attend a photography class. She had asked for a camera for her fourteenth birthday and Florrie had been able to find quite a good one at a pawn shop in town. Vera wanted to do it justice and create an album of her own pictures. She found the class to be very helpful with lots of suggestions about light, positioning of objects, background, and focus. The students were directed to bring a favourite photograph to the next session for sharing and analysis. She was busy jotting down instructional information and tips when she felt a tug on her hair from behind. She spun around to see an impish, grinning young man's face smiling at her. "Fancy a game of table tennis after class?" he asked.

Maurice Brown was a year older than Vera and full of fun. She remembered him from watching the dogfights on the Mount and the odd sighting around town. He always caught her eye because he was maturing into a rather handsome fellow with a kind face, confident manner, striking blue-grey eyes and a ready smile. He always seemed to be on the go and full of mischief. She was amazed that he could sit still during photography class and suspected that he was not so much interested in photography as he was, perhaps, in meeting her. Vera accepted the game of table tennis and from that day on, Maurice began to seek her out when they were at the youth group together. He always arrived with a gaggle of chums and left with them too, but in between he and Vera danced, played games, and chatted together.

Vera mentioned him to Florrie one day. She described him and told her that he was paying her a lot of attention.

"Nice boy is 'e?" she asked.

"Yes, he seems so, Mum but I don't really know him very well yet. He always comes with a bunch of friends. They are rather loud and boisterous, but they are funny too. They always have us laughing."

"Well, that's alright. Just you keep a sensible 'ead on your shoulders and 'ave yourself a good time. Don't let 'im get too familiar or comfortable with you. You're young yet. Got lots of time and lots of fellas to meet."

"Yes, I know Mum… but Mum? I do like him. He's very nice to me."

"Yes… well. So he should be!"

Florrie was thoughtful following the conversation. She pulled out a letter from Edie that she had saved with some others in a box in the wardrobe. It was the response to the letter she had sent asking for advice for Vera's future working prospects. *Consider Pitman's College in London*, Edie had written. *It is very prestigious. We have hired several shorthand typists who have successfully trained there and received certificates. I believe it is a two-year course and will put Vera in very good stead when she completes it.* Right! Thought Florrie. It was time to sign her up. It would give her another interest too… other than Maurice Brown.

Vera started at Pitman's in September 1943. She had to commute into London, but it was not really too much of an effort. Down at the roundabout at the bottom of the Mount, she caught a bus which took her right into the heart of London quite quickly. Buses left from there so often that the residents called them "banana buses" since there were always bunches of them coming and going. She jumped off the bus and walked briskly for ten minutes, and there she was at the college. She enjoyed travelling into London every weekday. She felt quite grown-up and independent. She was just one of many thousands commuting from a vast radius around the city, men in their business attire, women dressed in smart, tailored office apparel, servicemen in all sorts of uniforms. Everywhere she looked, the city was bustling with delivery vans, taxis, cars, buses, bicycles and pedestrians. It invigorated her and provided her with a new sense of purpose. The college and her classes were also most satisfying. She found shorthand so interesting, learning it quickly and easily. The sound of all the typewriters clicking away in the classroom, thrilled her. She was soon earning certificates regularly as she reached a new level of wpm (words per minute). Even the air-raid interruptions did not bother her too much. It was a chance to chat with her classmates in the shelter and compare notes on their progress. This was an enjoyable time in Vera's life. She was busy, she had purpose, she and Florrie had a nice place to live and there was the youth centre and… Maurice.

The old couple upstairs in the house on Waverley Avenue were quiet and unobtrusive. However, when Vera returned from her day in London, Ag, short for Aggie, which was probably short for Agatha, would inevitably appear at the top of the stairs as she was hanging up her coat. "And how was London today?" she would ask. "Have a nice day, did you?"

"Yes, thank you, Ag," Vera would respond. "Very nice day." Sometimes Ag would invite Vera upstairs for a cup of tea. She would usually oblige, knowing the couple was rather lonely and looking for some company. Art would put the kettle on and then sit in the parlour while Ag made the tea. He asked Vera about the college and how she was doing there. He asked about London. What was it looking like? Did she see a lot of bomb damage? Their parlour was a jumble of friendly clutter; newspapers and books lay about on tabletops, a vase of flowers was on the dining table, Art's pipe and tobacco pouch beside his easy chair, Ag's knitting on hers. There were framed photographs on the fireplace mantle and a bird cage hanging from a stand near the window. A little yellow canary whistled happily inside. "Dickie" was the pride and joy of the couple and provided them with an interest and some company. The little bird was quite tame and would sit on Art's finger chirping away. He had a small vocabulary of words which had been patiently repeated over and over by Ag and Art. "Hello," it said. "Where's Ag?" "Pretty boy" "Goodnight".

When Florrie returned home from work, the two had dinner together, which was usually something fast and easy, then they cleaned up the kitchen, did the dishes and listened to the wireless while reading the newspaper, or mending clothes, knitting, or writing letters. On weekends, there would be laundry to do, mostly in the sink, with bigger items soaking in the bathtub upstairs. The bathroom consisted of a bath and sink. The toilet was a separate small closet-like room next to it. Baths had to be scheduled with Ag and Art since hot water needed to be rationed to conserve fuel. People were asked by the government to mark the five-inch line by painting a black line around their bath so that they would not be filled beyond that point. Most people complied, including the King, who directed that the bathtubs at Buckingham Palace be marked in that way. Florrie spent some time in the garden tending the fruit and vegetables planted there and Vera would dust, sweep, and tidy their rooms. She quite liked these chores. It gave her pleasure to polish the furnishings that they had found together, and she appreciated that they were their own. It was rewarding to put things away, in their cupboards, drawers, wardrobe and enjoy the order and cleanliness that she had created. And then… on the weekends, there was the youth club!

Vera was much more contented with her young life. To be settled in her new home, to be busy with college, and to have fun with friends on the weekends were reasons to be happy despite all the wartime restrictions. The war was always there. It was part of life every day, but she would not allow it to be her only focus. She would live by the rules imposed on her, do her part conserving and sacrificing and she would be brave, helpful, and resourceful but she would keep an eye to the future as well. One day the war would end, and she would be ready. And so, the months wore on until the year drew to a close. Christmas arrived, New Year's Eve was celebrated, and it was 1944.

Soon after Vera's fifteenth birthday in March, Vera noticed that her mother had become somewhat distracted and thoughtful. She would study the living room and move things around so that an area at one end of the room was left bare. "Mum," Vera said, "whatever are you doing? We had everything set up so nicely."

"Never mind. I just wanted to see if we could fit something else down this end."

"Fit what? What else do we need in here?" Florrie sighed and sat down.

"Well, dear, I am considering letting someone stay 'ere for a while. Someone I work with was bombed out of 'is 'ome and is looking for somewhere to stay."

"*His* home? So, it's a man?"

"Yes, it is. And a very nice fella he is too. Think we could fit a single bed there," Florrie said pointing to the empty wall space. "Maybe a small dresser for 'im too."

"What! Mum, you're not serious! After everything we've... all those places we lived in... what we've been through! We finally have these nice rooms and now you're going to bring a stranger in to live with us!"

"Yes Vera! After all that! I want to 'elp this person. I've worked with 'im at the factory for a long time and I consider 'im a friend. He 'as 'ad a lot of trouble in 'is life, and I want to give 'im somewhere to lay 'is 'ead. 'E'll be paying a little rent to me and..."

"No Mum! No. You can't do this!"

"I can, my girl and you will just have to lump it!" Florrie rarely raised her voice in anger, but she was irritated now. "It is only temporary. We know what it's like to be 'omeless and desperate, don't we? I expect you to be understanding about this and treat this man with compassion and respect."

Vera was speechless. It was unusual for her mother to speak to her in that way. The impact of her words and the anger in her voice unnerved her. She said nothing more, but her eyes filled up with tears at the thought of another man moving into their home - their space - moving in where her father should be. *It should be Sidney! He should be here. He should not have died!*

It happened quickly after that. A single bed was installed along the back wall of the living room as well as a small dresser with a few drawers. Ted arrived with Florrie one day after work carrying a suitcase and duffel bag. He was there temporarily... and it would last for thirty-one years.

Vera was resentful, and remained aloof, but she was courteous and polite as her mother had demanded. It was obvious that Florrie and Ted were good friends. They spoke easily and freely with each other and shared laughs often. He was a slightly stocky man with curly, greying hair. He worked long hours and looked tired and drawn. Vera learned that he had a wife in a mental asylum, a grown son and a young daughter, Pearl, who lived with his sister in Bath. Ted did not try to engage Vera in deep conversation but inquired about her training at Pitman's from time to time. Evenings were the hardest time for Vera, after dinner had been cleared away. She had a hard time relaxing during those unscheduled hours while the wireless was on and the three of them occupied the same space. She often excused herself early and took a book into the bedroom. Ted stayed up until both Florrie and Vera had retired for the night and then he put up the folding screen that he had made around the bed. He was very handy and had made the screen as separate frames with hinges. Florrie covered the frames with fabric, and it worked perfectly to provide Ted with privacy for sleeping, and dressing. Vera begrudged the set up. The situation was awkward, uncomfortable and she hated it. He also was a heavy smoker. Florrie too had taken up smoking during the war. Vera often complained to her mother about it but Florrie responded sharply that it was a small pleasure that she was entitled to while so many other pleasures were denied.

On weekends Vera managed to be out most of the day with friends, down the shops or at the cinema. In the evening she went to the youth club. Ted kept himself busy in the garden and in the small workshop on the property. He made shelves for the kitchen, birdhouses, a useful side table for Florrie, and a small bookcase for Vera. She thanked him reservedly but graciously. It was actually a useful gift for Vera's book collection, but she was unable to display impassioned gratitude. The air raid siren was even more dreaded since now there were five of them occupying the Anderson shelter. It was sheer torture being confined to such a small space, let alone listening to the planes overhead and the descent of the bombs followed by explosions all around. Although the war news was becoming more optimistic and people were beginning to believe that victory would ultimately be achieved, the fact that bombs were still dropping most nights and rationing and hardship continued as part of their daily lives, made them realise that the end of the war was still far away.

By May 1944, Vera and Maurice were becoming a couple. They spent all their time together at the club and enjoyed each other's company. They were becoming the talk of the youth group. Maurice did not mind that at all. He took it all in stride with a wink and smile. The pair was happy, outgoing, and fun to be around. Maurice had started walking Vera home at night after the club closed. During these walks they learned a lot about each other, their likes and dislikes, their families, their wishes, and dreams for the future. Vera told Maurice about the loss of her father and of Ted moving in. She poured out all her feelings of resentment and anger. Maurice listened sympathetically and acknowledged her sentiment.

"It must be difficult for you, I'm sure. You do not want him there. He must feel like an intruder. But…" He thought carefully about how to put his next comment. "He didn't cause your father's death, did he? It wasn't his fault. What is he like, anyway? Is he unkind to you?"

"No, not at all. He is polite to me, but it is like he's treading on eggs around me, not sure how to behave or what to say. We are just not at ease with each other. He and Mum, though, they talk all the time, and laugh a lot, but they can sit quietly too, without feeling awkward, listening to the wireless, or reading. It makes me feel… oh, I don't know… it's not like it was. Mum and I were everything to each other and now… well she has another focus, another interest in her life. She says they are friends, but I think there is a little more to it. I can't help but think it's a betrayal of my father and yet I realise that Mum is entitled to enjoy male company and companionship. Oh, I'm not explaining this well at all. I'm just not ready for this!"

"Vera, it sounds like he is trying his best to be as considerate as possible. And there will probably come a time quite soon, when you will be glad that she has someone in her life."

"I do think of that. When I finish at Pitman's, I will get a respectable job, hopefully, and who knows what I'll do or where I'll go then?"

"Yes, who knows?" Maurice responded with a smile.

Maurice was a year older than Vera and lived in Chingford on Hurst Road near the Chingford Mount Cemetery. It was only three quarters of a mile from Waverley Avenue. They had noticed each other around town in passing for years. But it was the war and the youth group that had brought them together often enough for them to form an attachment. Maurice told her jokingly about his name. His birth certificate showed it as Maurice Walter Brown, Walter being his father's name, but his mother said that his full name was Maurice Walter George Thomas Lipton Brown but that it had been too much to include on the birth certificate. Thomas Lipton was a self-made man from Scotland who had eventually entered the tea trade offering tea at a low price to the poor working class. His tea became known as the Lipton brand. He also became a yachting enthusiast entering the America's Cup several times unsuccessfully. He was well thought of and well liked because of his easy, friendly manner with all types and classes of people as well as his modesty and lack of snobbery. Charlotte and Walter, Maurice's parents, admired him for his accomplishments and pleasant disposition and so added his name in tribute to his success.

"I quite like introducing myself to people using the full name," Maurice stated. "It always gets a chuckle and is a useful conversation starter."

"It *is* unusual," Vera replied. "I thought long names like that were reserved for royalty."

"Yes. Makes me feel quite special," he laughed. "It's just Mum, Dad and me at home now. I have an older sister, Eileen but she got married last year. Mum was not too happy about that; I can tell you! Eileen wasn't even twenty, but, Ray, her husband, is a very nice chap. I like him. So, I expect it will work out okay."

One evening while walking home from the youth centre, the air raid siren shrieked into the darkness. Vera and Maurice had not reached Waverley Avenue yet, so they picked up their pace. They hurried along Hall Lane and then broke into a run as planes began to appear almost directly overhead and the whistle of the bombs were nearby. "Must be unloading the rest of their bombs on their way back," Maurice shouted above the racket. Ack-Ack (anti-aircraft) guns had joined the foray and Vera was gasping with fear as the noise intensified and the danger of being caught out in an air raid filled her with dread. Maurice glanced up at the sky and saw searchlights illuminating the planes. It was a bad raid. Lots of planes and bombs raining down. The whistle of one of the bombs was too close. Maurice grabbed Vera by the shoulders. "Quick! Against this brick wall!" he shouted. As Vera bent down and pressed up against the brick half-wall of one of the gardens along the street, Maurice spread his body over her as best he could, shielding her from any wreckage or shrapnel from the blast. Vera screamed when the bomb exploded and covered her ears with her hands. Then Maurice was pulling her up, grabbing her hand and leading her into a run again. They turned onto Waverley Avenue at full pelt heading for number twenty-two. Florrie was at the door of the Anderson shelter looking out anxiously. Maurice let go of Vera's hand and watched her as she sped down the garden path. "Maurice… come on!" Vera called over her shoulder. "No. I'll be alright. Better get on home. Mum and Dad will be worried." He turned and ran back down the street. It was only three-quarters of a mile to his house, but it seemed a lot further that night.

Maurice had enrolled in a local "cadet" unit of the Home Guard that had been organised to recruit boys who wanted to participate in the war effort but were too young to enlist. He trained and drilled with the Chingford boys, was issued a well-used, bolt action World War I leftover rifle, and performed bomb damage duty. Drilling and training were thrilling for Maurice. He felt powerful, prepared, and determined to fight well if need be. He was taught how to strip down his rifle, clean it, load and unload it, and actually had to take it home with him so that it was available at all times should an invasion ever take place. He felt like "the cat's whiskers." Bomb damage duty, however, was a dreaded task. He knew he would be busy after the bombing raid that he and Vera had run through. He would be one of a crew sorting through rubble, collapsed walls, blown apart houses, listening for voices, cries, and any signs of life amongst the ruins. Following bomb damage duty, he would trudge home late in the day relieved that he had not found any bodies in the wreckage or devastated by images of death and mutilation that would remain with him forever.

On 6th June 1944, the D-Day invasion took place. The nation suspected an invasion was planned, as did Hitler, who anticipated the assault to be along the north coast of France. He ordered his General, Erwin Rommel, to defend the region and finish the 2,400-mile Atlantic Wall with beach obstacles, mines and machine gun bunkers. The Allies conducted a campaign of deception using fake radio broadcasts and double agents and leaking information about General Patton's "phantom army," to lead the Germans to believe that the invasion would take place at Pas-de-Calais. Operation Overlord was the name given to the campaign, which landed along the beaches of Normandy, commanded by General Dwight D. Eisenhower of the United States. More than 5,000 ships left England, carrying more than 156,000 American, British, and Canadian troops and supplies. Although there were many casualties during the landings, the operation was successful, and the course of the war turned against Germany. As the Allies advanced through Europe, the end looked to be in sight.

The mood in England was bright and optimistic. People began to talk of victory and think about a peaceful future. Life would soon become more normal again, free from air raids, rationing, restrictions and fear. Then Hitler punished the land for the invasion with new weapons. Weapons of terror. Weapons of revenge. The V-1 and V-2 rockets.

Maurice had travelled into the city one afternoon to meet Vera after her class. It was a lovely day in June, and they strolled leisurely along the Thames, discussing plans for the evening. Maurice stopped suddenly and pointed upriver.
"Look Vera. That's a strange looking plane there." Vera

followed his gaze and saw the low flying craft cruising above the river on a steady course. As it flew nearer, the sound of the engine was unusual too. It droned loudly and heavily.

"Wonder what that is," Maurice thought out loud. "Never seen anything like it."

"I haven't either, Maurice. But I think we ought to move along. I didn't like the looks of it."

"No…" Maurice replied. "Neither did I."

The young couple had seen one of the first unmanned V-1 flying bombs which were launched from the coast of France or Holland, directed at targets in southern England and carrying a powerful warhead. It was fuelled to reach its target and when the fuel was exhausted, it would fall and explode. The pulsejet engine caused it to have a buzzing sound and it soon became known in England as a buzz bomb or doodlebug. When the air raid siren sounded and residents waited in their shelters, they heard the doodlebug coming. The distinctive drone could not be missed. They would hear it track closer and closer and listen with great anxiety, hoping that it would pass over and move on. Often the engine would cut out, everyone would hold their breath, and then it would start up again for a while. When the engine cut out completely, the occupants of the shelter would know that it was falling. The wait and the dread were the worst fears they had faced in the war. It was unbearable, this new, inhuman form of terror. One that could only be initiated in the evil, twisted mind of Hitler. It was too much. The morale of the brave, battered, and deprived people of Britain sank to a new low.

For a while, Vera brooded. She began to wonder why she should continue at Pitman's, why she should see her friends, why she should bother with Maurice. She despaired of her future and the sense in making plans. How much longer would they have to live like this, scraping by all the time, living on reduced rations, spending half her life in an air raid shelter? And now, live with the horror of this random, senseless, soul-destroying bomb. She trudged up the stairs one evening to see Ag and Art. The old couple was pleased to see her and chatted away happily. Vera listened and smiled as best she could, but it was quite obvious to them that she was deflated.

"What is it, Vera?" Art asked. "What's bothering you, dear?"

"Oh, I've just had enough, Art. What is there to look forward to? I just don't see an end to it all."

"Don't give up now, Vera. Look at all we 'ave come through. Why these new buzz bomb that old 'Itler is throwing at us… it shows desperation on 'is part. 'E knows we won't give up. 'E's done in, 'e is. Must be feeling scared and defeated. Look what 'e's got on his doorstep. Our brave lads, the Americans and all the other allies all headed right for 'im. Don't give up now, Vera. We're almost there!"

In July Vera received a letter from Yvonne. She had taken a two-week holiday in the Midlands and was staying with Evelyn who was living near the base from which her husband, James had been deployed.

Why don't you come on up for a day if you can Vera? It is so quiet and soothing here. Such a change from London. You can meet me at Wickstead Park. Have you ever been there? It is wonderful. Evelyn said you could stay a few days if you like. My last day here is the 12th. We could travel back together. I hope you can come. Let me know as soon as you can.

Vera responded that she would come up on the twelfth and travel back with Yvonne the next day. She did not want to take any more time off her college classes, but she did relish the idea of a change of scenery and a lovely day out. They arranged a meeting place in the park and looked forward to their reunion.

It was a lovely summer day when Yvonne made her way through the park. It was her seventeenth birthday, and everything felt rather special to her. She breathed deeply of the fresh air which was scented with flowers from the gardens. She listened to the birds chirping in the trees, watched children playing on the lawns and in the playground, and strolled around the little lake as several majestic swans drifted by. She sat on a bench near the tearoom where she and Vera were to meet and pulled her knitting out of the bag that she had carried with her. She knitted contentedly away lifting her head every so often to see if Vera was approaching. After some time, she checked her watch. Vera was late. Yvonne knew that it would take some time to travel from Chingford and that it would involve a transfer or two, so she was unperturbed and happy to sit in the sunshine and knit and look around and wait. Vera was almost an hour late when a young boy approached Yvonne. His face was smeared with dirt, his clothes were grass stained and he had a grubby soccer ball tucked under his arm. She looked at him questioningly with a smile. "That Yank," he said gesturing with his thumb to a spot behind him. "He wants to meet you." Yvonne turned her gaze to the location where the boy had pointed. There stood a tall American soldier, cap in hand, smiling hopefully. She was about to tell the boy that he should report back that she was waiting for someone and did not want to be disturbed, but she hesitated before the words came out. There was something about the way the man was looking at her with obvious admiration. She saw genuine wonderment as if he had just found something that he had been seeking for a long time. In an impulsive reaction that was very much contrary to her cautious and shy nature she responded to the boy, "Yes. All right." The boy turned and nodded to the soldier and moved on along the path.

The American soldier walked up to the bench, smiling at the beautiful girl who sat there returning his gaze. He could not believe his luck that she had agreed to meet him, and he wondered for a moment what he could say to start a conversation.
"Do you know what time the park closes?" he asked.
"I believe it is just before sunset," Yvonne responded.
"Oh, okay... would you mind showing me around?"

When Vera arrived at their meeting place, there was no sign of Yvonne. She scanned the area, the other benches, and the pathways nearby and spotted her cousin in the distance walking with a soldier. An American soldier! She hurried along toward them with growing curiosity and wariness. "Yvonne?" she called as she came near enough to call out. Yvonne turned and smiled apologetically.
"Oh, Vera... er... this is Bob. I'm showing him around. I'll... er... meet up with you later."
"Where... when?"
"I'm not sure," Yvonne responded smiling up at Bob. "I'll see you back at Evelyn's if we miss each other." She turned and strolled off with her soldier. Bob offered his arm and Yvonne slipped hers through his. Vera watched them go in amazement. This was so unlike her cousin, going off like that with a stranger, a Yank, mind you! Now what was she supposed to do? She looked around noticing

that there were a sizeable number of American uniforms about. *Well,* she thought, *the first soldier who asks for my company... I am saying yes.* While she stood sulking, she felt a tap on her shoulder and a young male voice asking, "Would you like a cup of tea?"

"Yes!" she answered whirling around. An awkward looking Yank stood there, short, and pimply faced. Vera managed a smile and accompanied him to the tearoom turning over excuses in her head about why she would have to leave in a little while.

The day at Wickstead Park had been a disaster for Vera but enchanting for Yvonne. Her handsome soldier had put her at ease with pleasant conversation, kindness, and consideration. They had talked a little about themselves, their families and the war. Bob's full name was A. Robert Porter. "A" for Albert was not a name he went by at all. He was Bob; tall, dark and handsome - just what many girls wished for. He was from Connecticut in the U.S. and stationed nearby at the Army Air Corps Base. He had a large family who all lived in small apartments in his mother's large house. He hoped to attend college after the war. There was an immediate attraction between them and when they exchanged addresses, Yvonne knew that she would be hearing again from him.

At Evelyn's later that evening, Yvonne chatted happily about her day with Bob. Vera was resentful and sullen at first but thawed as she realised the obvious infatuation and did not want to spoil her happiness. Goodness, she deserved some after all! The three Middleton cousins laughed and giggled and wondered together about Connecticut. Funny name for a place. *America... wow! Imagine what it would be like, living there!*

On the train ride back to London, Yvonne was already writing a letter to Bob. Vera watched her, noticing that she wrote it with a sweet smile on her face. She thought of Maurice. Did she think of him that way? Their relationship was developing much more slowly, and they were younger too but, yes… it was becoming more serious, and they were exclusive with each other. She was always excited to see him, and they had such fun. *So, perhaps they would end up together,* she thought. *Who knows?*

Paris was liberated in August. Morale in Britain was briefly lifted with this news. Newsreels at the cinema showed Allied troops marching down the streets with French citizens greeting them, waving British and American flags, throwing flowers, cheering, hugging, and kissing. The people were ecstatic. But then, the following month, another type of rocket was unleashed on London, Norwich and Ipswich on the east coast of England. The V-2 rocket was faster, quieter, and more powerful than the V-1. It was the world's first long-range guided ballistic missile. Since the rocket flew at over 3000 miles per hour it was faster than the speed of sound. There was no warning and no sound until it hit, and due to its 2200 lb. warhead, it left large craters and terrible devastation, and loss of life with its explosive impact. The people again slipped into a period of dismay and gloom, wondering what else the Germans could throw at them. The air raid shelters were no help against the V-2s. A hit anywhere in the vicinity, would cause considerable destruction and death in a 180-metre radius. The British lived with even greater fear as part of their everyday life. *Keep Calm and Carry On!* Meanwhile, the war continued in Europe and in the Pacific and it was becoming more and more apparent that Germany was losing ground.

More and more of the launch sites of the weapons of terror were becoming overrun by Allied troops and in March 1945, the last of these weapons of terror finally fell on British soil.

CHAPTER TEN

Bob and Yvonne's courtship was restricted by the demands of the U.S. Army Air Corps, 8th Air Force Command located at Daws Hill in High Wycombe, England. While there, any time that Bob could secure a pass for a day or two's leave, he travelled to Chingford or Yvonne made her way up to Kettering to meet him. These times together were short with long intervals between but much anticipated and cherished. Several times, Bob was deployed to the European theatre but, after his talent for writing was noticed, he was selected to report on successful missions and write anecdotes for publishing in military newsletters and magazines. This assignment fortunately put him at lower risk and allowed him to hone his literary skills. During their times apart, the young couple relied on letters back and forth. They were devoted, committed, and knew they were destined to be together forever.

As 1944 drew to a close, a great battle took place in Europe, Hitler's last major offensive. On 16th December 1944, Germany initiated a surprise attack on the Allied line in Belgium, France, and Luxembourg. German forces numbered 450,000 troops and committed heavy support of equipment, tanks, and the Luftwaffe. The Allied line took the form of a large bulge and so this offensive, called the Ardennes Counteroffensive, since it surged through the Ardennes Forest region, became known as the Battle of the Bulge. The advance was halted by the U.S. 2nd Armored Division, whereupon Allied air attacks on German forces and supply lines weakened the enemy. However, the battle continued until 25th January 1945, when Germany retreated to its original position. There were high losses of life on both sides. Germany lost between 63,000 and 98,000 troops killed, wounded, missing, or captured. 19,000 U.S. troops were killed, 1500 British and Canadians. For the United States it was the deadliest campaign in American history. Churchill referred to it as "undoubtedly the greatest American battle of the war". This last unsuccessful campaign by the enemy followed by the advance of Allied troops, led to the defeat of Hitler, who promptly committed suicide, and resulted in Germany's surrender on 7th May 1945. On 8th May 1945, the Allies accepted the official, unconditional surrender. The date became known as V-E Day (Victory in Europe) and the victors celebrated.

Vera and Maurice travelled into the heart of the city with Eileen and Ray in Ray's car to join in the huge celebration there. The car broke down for a short time, right in the middle of Tower Bridge, overheating with all the stops and starts navigating through the throng of pedestrians. They pushed it to the side of the road for a while to let it cool down. Normally people would honk and jeer at someone who created an obstacle on such a vital roadway, but the mood was so gay and joyful that people waved in sympathy, and many offered to help. When they got going again and parked, they found themselves shoulder to shoulder with a mass of humanity and they joined the surge of revellers making their way to the famous landmarks all around London. Everywhere was so crowded that Vera almost felt that her feet never touched the ground. At only five feet two inches tall, she felt herself to be wedged in the crowd and swept along like a stick in a raging river current. She held onto Maurice's hand for dear life. But the sights were amazing and never to be forgotten. There were men and women atop lampposts and climbing all over statues and monuments. Traffic was as a crawl. People boarded buses, waving from windows, upper decks and swinging from the poles. Taxis and cars beeped continuously to add to the glorious jubilation. Trafalgar Square was swarming, Piccadilly Circus was a joyous street party, Buckingham Palace and the Mall were a sea of humanity. The King and Queen made eight appearances on the balcony of Buckingham Palace during the day, waving to the crowd, acknowledging their cheers. Six times they were joined by their daughters, Princess Elizabeth (wearing her Home Guard uniform) and Princess Margaret, and one time by Winston Churchill.

Churchill also displayed his famous "V" for victory hand salute from the balcony of the Ministry of Health in London. "God bless you all," he told the crowd and the nation. "This is your victory! It is the victory of the cause of freedom in every land. In all our long history we have never seen a greater day than this."

Church bells, which had been silent throughout the war, were ringing all over London. Vera, Maurice, Eileen, and Ray ended up on Westminster Bridge, serenaded by the loud, bells of Big Ben. The crowd burst into song; their voices joined with others lined up all along the Thames. Vera sang loudly and heartily, belting out patriotic favourites, *Rule Britannia, Land of Hope and Glory, God Save the King.* The people joined hands, danced and laughed together, one family in joyous celebration. The crowds were so dense that the foursome had to physically force themselves through to their next location. They stayed until well into the night, watching the fireworks from London Bridge, able to enjoy the festive flashes and booms so different from the fires and explosions of the last several years. It was the early hours of the morning, as dawn was breaking, before they arrived back at home. Many revellers stayed on into the next day or two, unwilling to detach from the feeling of euphoria and unbridled happiness. Back in Chingford, the celebrations continued in neighbourhoods across the town. As in cities, towns, and villages all across the land, the long-suffering citizens needed to fully acknowledge the victory; the end of war and bombs, the end of loss and death. Tables were set up in the middle of the street and food which had been in such short supply and so carefully managed, appeared from all households, meat pies, stews, soups, cakes and fruit pies. Decorations were made; banners, garlands, and paper chains were stretched across the road from roof to roof. There was music, dance, and merriment for days. A conga line formed on Waverley Avenue. The line danced its way down the street, entering houses, making its way through the rooms and out of the back door into the next house, all the way down the street and back up the other side. The national parties across the land lasted for a week and then, satisfied that the end of the war had been properly recognised, people returned to their lives and duties and responsibilities once more. There was another party to be had, though. V-J Day (Victory over Japan), 15th August 1945, was the day of celebration following the surrender of Japan, bringing an end to World War II.

Vera again travelled into the city to celebrate, this time with Yvonne and a friend. The three young ladies danced through the streets, carefree and joyous. Their futures lay ahead of them, now full of hope and promise. Yvonne looked down at her engagement ring. Her future would take her to America and a whole new life. Bob would soon return, and they would make their plans. She would be leaving England and her family and friends. She felt a twinge of nerves and regret as she thought about this amidst the celebrations of her countrymen and then Vera was pulling her arm. "Come on Yvonne. We're going to St. James's and then to the river." Yvonne nodded and smiled at her cousin. She thought she would probably miss Vera most of all.

Vera was finished at Pitman's. She had excelled there and received many awards and certificates of achievement. She secured her first job in London, working for the Bank of Australia as a short-hand typist and secretary. She was a wage earner at last and able to contribute financially to the household.

"Thank you, luv," Florrie said when Vera handed over some of her pay packet. "I can manage without it… really. I'd rather you keep it. Enjoy yourself, spend some money on yourself. Save some and 'ave a bit put by."

"Oh, but Mum. I'd like you to have some. Please take it. You need to enjoy yourself a bit too. Buy something for yourself or something for the house. We were going to get some pictures for the walls, remember?"

"Yes, alright. I will do that," Florrie replied, realising that it meant a lot to Vera to be able to provide a little extra and lighten the load for her mother. "I'll accept a bit from you each week for a little while. Be nice to get a few new things and some extra food. Suppose it will take time before we 'ave more in the shops to buy. But I will only accept it for little while. Then you manage your own money and save some for the future."

The future. It took some time for Vera to change her mindset from surviving on a daily basis, having her activities and plans dictated by the air raid siren, to the freedom, spontaneity and fearlessness of this new life every day. When she awoke in the morning, she felt blessed, full of life and energy and ready to live life fully again. There was still a lot of work to be done removing bomb damage, pulling down destroyed buildings, clearing the streets, restoring schools and rebuilding. It would take years, but work had started. It was uplifting to see the number of work crews toiling away, slowly making progress. There were vans and lorries and equipment everywhere in towns and cities across the land. No one minded the noise or the dust or the heavy equipment on their streets. It was the country bouncing back, building up again and moving on.

The summer and autumn of 1945 were wonderful for Vera and Maurice. They spent days together on the weekends riding bikes, playing tennis, visiting with friends. Sometimes, Maurice was able to borrow a car and they would pack a lunch and travel to the countryside for a day out. Maurice had left school at age fourteen as the war was raging. He had managed to attend a polytechnic academy for a couple of terms, picking up some useful skills and then had worked alongside his father, Walter, in the construction trade. He had also learned paperhanging from Walter. It was a skill that he was to fall back on several times in his life.

Maurice and Vera were away on a weekend jaunt in October when Bob was suddenly granted a leave to get married and have a few days honeymoon. He and Yvonne married quickly in a local registrar's office, Yvonne in a borrowed blue dress and Bob in his uniform. They were a stunning couple standing on the steps outside the building for a photograph to commemorate the day. Florrie was able to arrange a modest wedding reception in the back garden at Waverley Avenue. Yvonne's father, John, her sister Evelyn, and little Michael were there, a couple of aunts and cousins and friends, and the Embersons. Yvonne was so disappointed that Vera was not there, but the plans had been made so fast and unexpectedly that she was not able to get in touch with her. She kept looking down at her left hand which had only recently been adorned with an engagement ring and now displayed an accompanying wedding band. She was married to her Wickstead Park soldier. She was Mrs. A. Robert Porter and a new unimaginable life stretched before her.

When Vera returned, Bob and Yvonne were away on their honeymoon in Eastbourne.
"I can't believe I missed her wedding, Mum!"
"Yes, I know. Of course, Yvonne wanted you there, but Bob's pass came through unexpectedly. You should 'ave seen her pedalling around town on her bicycle picking up flowers, borrowing a dress, and letting people know about the occasion. Bob will have to report back to 'is base in a few days so you will be able to see Yvonne and ask her all about it. We took some photos which I will pick up in a day or two so you will see how beautiful she looked and 'ow 'andsome her new 'usband was in his uniform."
"What happens now? Where will they live together?"
"Shouldn't think they will see much more of each other before Bob ships off back 'ome."
"Oh, Mum. That's horrible, isn't it?"
"Yes. The United States military will make all the arrangements for Yvonne now. But, if you could 'ave seen their faces and 'ow they were lookin' at each other… well I think they are just so 'appy that they tied the knot. They will be patient and will soon be together in their own 'ome."
"In America," Vera mused. "So far away, Mum. When do you suppose Yvonne will go there?"
"Don't know, luv. Sometime next year, I should think."

Bob was shipped out in November with a small, framed wedding photograph carefully packed amongst his belongings. The joy of returning home was dulled by his dismay of leaving Yvonne behind. He prayed that it would not be too long before they were reunited.

It would be five months. Yvonne was informed in March that she would be leaving from Southampton at the end of the month. She would have to spend two weeks in a "bride's camp" prior to departure, where her credentials would be checked as well as her physical condition. This was difficult for Yvonne, since it had a similar feel to the years she had spent in homes and orphanages during her childhood, but she was friendly with some of the other brides, commiserating and talking about the places they were going in America. During her time at the camp, her engagement ring was stolen when she took it off to wash one day. Absentmindedly, she placed it on the side of the sink and walked away without it. She had only walked a few steps when she realised she had left it behind but when she returned, it was gone. She was devastated and dreaded having to tell Bob of her unfortunate mistake. When she was finally assigned to a ship, she had to endure a ten-day journey during quite changeable conditions. There were times when she and many others were seasick and miserable. In the cabin she shared she hung one of her dresses up to wear later and it was admired by one of the brides. Yvonne slipped it off the hanger and gave it to the young lady. A very generous gift indeed. The ship docked in New York on 6th April. The "brides" were labelled with tags as if they were packages or luggage and had to be claimed with the appropriate paperwork by their spouses. Bob was waiting for her, claimed her, and presented her with a lovely gardenia which he pinned to her jacket.

Grinning broadly and clasping hands, they boarded a train which would take them to her new home in Bridgeport, Connecticut. On the train, Yvonne noticed a small boy looking at her curiously and twisting his head while he stared at her. When she looked down, she chuckled as she realised that the boy had been trying to read the tags which were still attached to her clothing. She gazed out of the windows at the strangeness of her new country and read the names of the towns of the stations through which they passed, Harlem, New Rochelle, Larchmont, Mamaroneck, Rye, Port Chester, Greenwich, Stamford, Norwalk, Westport, Fairfield and finally, Bridgeport. One of Bob's friends waited at the station with his car to take them both home. Bob introduced Yvonne to his friend, who was dazzled at the sight of her. He picked up the luggage to place in the trunk and gave Bob a quick wink of approval.

They drove to Cottage Street where Bob's mother owned a very large house which was divided into several small apartments. Several of Bob's siblings and their families lived in the house and they were all waiting anxiously to meet Bob's English bride. Whereas Bob was quite reserved and calm in his demeanour, his siblings were not! They greeted her boldly, loudly, and enthusiastically. She was even picked up and twirled around during the introductions. The family members who lived at the house were Bud and Lois, Bob's brother and his wife; Edna and Larry, Bob's sister and husband, as well their two daughters, Pam and Gail; Rosalie, Bob's half-sister and Goldie, Bob's mother. Bob had another sister, Myrtle, whose husband was Stuart; a sister, Dorothy and a brother, Clint, who were also there to greet Yvonne. It was quite a crowd for a young timid English girl to meet all at once but the obvious joy and enthusiasm of the family and the genuine welcome and kindness extended to her endeared them to her immediately. Yvonne had a lot to learn about her new home, country, traditions and culture and she had many willing teachers. The little apartment that she and Bob shared was small but private. It consisted of a large sitting room/bedroom with a big bathroom on the first floor. The hallway off the room led to the nearby kitchen and big communal living room and to a wraparound porch. Bob worked while he attended the University of Bridgeport, ultimately graduating with a Bachelor of Arts degree in English. They would live there for five years before buying a small house of their own.

Yvonne worked locally also and was very supportive of her husband and his long hours at his job, attending university and studying. At times she became very homesick for England and longed for the familiarity of country and her sense of belonging as well as for the family that she had left behind.

She wrote letters often and was so happy to receive them in return, wondering how life was for them all in the aftermath of the war. She dreamed of returning to see everyone again, but she discovered that she was pregnant early in 1947 and her focus changed with the exciting news. It would be twelve years before she visited England and saw her family again.

Note in her Vera's memories binder
I reminisced about my young working years in London, racing across the city to the Bank of Australia (my first job.) How exciting were those days when life was full of great expectations and ambition!

CHAPTER ELEVEN

Vera was loving life in 1947. She and Maurice were together as much as they could be and starting to talk about the future together. One Friday, Maurice met Vera in London after her workday was done and walked with her toward St. Paul's Cathedral.

"Where are we going, Maurice?" she asked.

"Never mind. You'll see. There is something we need to do."

"What is it? What do we need to do?"

"Just wait, Vera. This is a lovely walk, isn't it? What a lovely day for January."

And it was a nice day. The temperature was mild, the sky was blue and there was that Friday feel in the air. The workweek was over and the people on the streets were more relaxed as they made their way home. The huge cathedral loomed as they approached. It was stunning in the winter light with the magnificent dome silhouetted against the brilliant sky. Maurice led Vera to the western side of the beloved landmark to a pedestrian only area where there were shops and restaurants.

"Are we going to have dinner here tonight?" Vera asked.

"Yes, we are. But first we are going in here." Maurice pulled open the door of a jewellery shop. "'bout time we picked out a ring, don't you think?"

"Do you mean…"

"Yes, an engagement ring," Maurice said, finishing her thought. "I had a look in here last week and there is quite a variety. Some are new, some are vintage, and some are second-hand. I thought you would find one that you liked here."

"I… I'm sure I will."

"It is all right with you, isn't it? I mean I thought we had an understanding of where things were going with us."

"Well, yes, of course," she replied, as her excitement mounted. So, this was the proposal she had been waiting for, no formal, mushy episode, no romantic, embarrassing declaration. The ring would confirm their "understanding." She smiled. That suited her just fine.

Vera selected a vintage ring. It was in a platinum setting with two larger diamonds side by side in the centre and several smaller ones in descending tiers on each side. It was brilliant and elegant and just to her taste. The jeweller took Vera's finger measurement and assured her it would be sized to fit. Maurice presented a down payment and agreed with the jeweller on weekly payments until it was paid off. Thereafter, Maurice travelled into the city every Friday to make a payment and then travelled back home with Vera. The ring was paid off in three months, just in time for Vera's seventeenth birthday. The day it was paid off, they celebrated with a nice dinner in a nearby restaurant before heading home. Maurice had not yet told his parents because he knew they would disapprove of such a serious commitment at his young age. They had met Vera a few times and had been polite but reserved. Maurice's sister had married at age eighteen and they would certainly not want their son to do the same. Vera had, however, shared the news with Florrie, who was quite accepting but with a firm condition.

"Lovely! I like Maurice. He's an 'ard working lad and very nice too. I don't mind you getting engaged but, I want you to wait until you are twenty-one before you marry. That's a long time from now, I know, but it will give you both a chance to change your mind if it doesn't feel right.

Not sayin' you will," she added quickly as Vera started to protest. "If it is meant to be, you will last that long. So, if you agree to that, I'll be 'appy for you."

"Yes, Mum. I will agree to that. It will give us time to save up too. Maurice wants to buy some land and build us a bungalow when we are married."

"And very nice too! I'm sure 'e will."

For a few months Charlotte and Walter Brown, Maurice's parents, remained unaware of their son's engagement. But soon after Vera received the ring, she and Maurice proudly showed it off around town to their friends. The ring flashed and sparkled on Vera's finger and the young couple were excited to share their news. What a delightful couple they were. Everyone liked them and was happy for them. Unfortunately, word of the engagement found its way to Auntie Julie, and she dutifully reported the news to her sister, Charlotte, who was most dismayed. Her beloved son had tied himself to this girl at such a young age. She also disapproved of Vera's mother's living arrangement. Maurice had mentioned that Ted moved into Florrie's house during the war when his own house had been destroyed. She thought that it was quite inappropriate to live unmarried in such close quarters with a man, war, or no war! The war was over now, and the arrangement had not changed, and there had been no marriage to make the relationship officially acceptable.

"Wole!" she commanded her husband. "You will have to go over to speak to Vera's mother. We can't have this. Maurice is just so smitten with this girl and hasn't thought it through. He is going to make his life so hard. War just over and now he's going to take on all the responsibility of marriage. And her *mother*! Living with that man! Well, how is that going to look? Whatever will people think? I just can't bear it Wole. You'll have to go over there and forbid it! First Eileen… and now Maurice…" She worked herself up until she had to sit down and take a deep breath.

"Now, May," Walter replied, using his pet name for his wife whose middle name was Mahala, "don't get all bothered. Let's talk to Maurice first and find out what 'is plans are. Can't go running off in a fret. And… who cares what people think? None of their business anyway!"

"Oh, Wole! I care… I care." She collapsed on the settee, her face crumpled and despairing.

They confronted Maurice that evening. He apologised for not informing them sooner but explained that he was not sure how the news would be received. He was only waiting for a good time to let them know about it. Charlotte poured out her objections, but Maurice would not be swayed.

"Vera is the girl for me, Mum. We have been together now for quite a long time. We only want to be with each other. We just want to plan our lives together. Is that really so bad?"

"It's too soon and you're too young… and how did you afford an engagement ring anyway? No, Maurice! I won't allow it. Your father is going over to speak to Vera's mother to get this sorted out."

"Now Maurice, my boy," Walter interjected realising he needed to support his distraught wife, "your mother does 'ave some reasonable objections. Perhaps the engagement is a bit premature. Why don't wait a year or two and we can discuss it again then?"

"No Dad. Our minds are made up. Go and have your talk with Mrs. Middleton. See what she says. She's a genuinely nice person, by the way." Maurice was angry now. "And Mum," he said turning to face her. "I paid the ring off each week from my pay packet. We are very happy that Vera can wear it now!"

Maurice stormed up to his bedroom as Walter sighed, put on his hat and coat, and headed out to speak with Mrs. Middleton.

Vera gasped when she saw Walter on the doorstep. She let him in, calling to her mother. Florrie came into the hall from the kitchen, wiping her hands on a dish towel. "Mum, this is Mr. Brown… Maurice's father, come to talk to you." Vera then went swiftly out of the back door to the garden and paced anxiously along the garden path. Ted watched her from the workshop and wondered what had made her so distressed. He hesitated, unsure if he should interfere. He always trod very carefully around Vera, being quite understanding of her continued resentment of him and not wanting to make it worse. Although their interaction had become a little easier since Maurice had come on the scene, he was loath to upset the applecart. However, taking a deep breath, he called her over.

"Look what I've been working on Vera. What do you think? Will Mum like it?" Vera glanced at the footstool which she observed was well made and attractive. "I will pad it and upholster the top when I'm finished. It will give your Mum a chance to put her feet up." He paused.

"What's the matter then? Has something upset you?" Ordinarily, Vera would not disclose anything of a personal nature to Ted, but she was too upset to remain aloof.

"It's Mr. Brown. He's here to talk to Mum. I think they have found out about our engagement, and I'm worried about… I mean I don't know what may be said and what will happen."

"Ah. Well, I don't think your mother is one to be bullied, do you? She'll stand up for you, don't you fret. It will all be sorted out."

Vera nodded. "Thank you, Ted. Er… mind if I stay and watch you work for a while? Don't want to go back inside just yet."

"No, not at all. Pass me that sandpaper over there, will you?"

In Florrie's living room Walter stood, hat in hand, while Florrie waited for him to begin.

"Now Mrs. Middleton. We just can't 'ave this. My wife is very upset. We don't want the young couple to go off planning and talking about a weddin'. They are inexperienced, 'avn't 'ad time, either of them, to know what kind of person they want as a lifetime mate and partner in life. We want this engagement called off. It's too sudden, too soon and they are too young."

"Well, Mr. Brown, I don't see it that way. Youngsters 'ave been short-changed during the war. They 'ave 'ad to grow up faster than usual. I am not going to be the one to deny them their dreams and plans for the future. I 'ave Vera's promise that they won't marry until she is twenty-one. That gives us four years, Mr. Brown. If they are still together by then, good luck to 'em, I say."

Walter nodded slowly and thought for a moment. "Ah, yes. Well, that certainly put's a different face on it, Mrs. Middleton. Think we can go along with that. Might take May, my wife, a bit longer to come to terms but, all right then. I'm satisfied with that."

"Good. And just call me Florrie. I 'ope we can be friends."

"Call me Walter… or Wole would be better. Cor, this was a bit of a bother, wasn't it? But I know we all just want what's best for the youngsters."

"Yes, that's right, we do. Fancy a cuppa tea before you go… Wole?"

"Certainly would, Mrs… er, Florrie. Thank you."

Vera heard the door close when Walter left, and she got the full report from her mother. When she saw Maurice the next day, he informed her that she was banned from coming to the house. May was still unwilling to accept the situation. Walter had taken Maurice aside and told him that he was sure it would not last long and to be a little patient. Vera felt rejected and hurt but Maurice encouraged her, telling her that his mother would come around. Sure enough, after two months, Vera was again invited there for tea. Charlotte had come to terms with the fact that there would be no marriage for years and she wanted to be on good terms with her son, whom she adored in her own reservedly affectionate way. The strained and tense episode was over. Vera came to really like May and Walter over the months and years before their marriage. May was very prim and proper and ran the house on a fixed schedule but she looked forward to family gatherings and enjoyed cooking up a good meal. She had rather a significant sweet tooth so there were always luscious, creamy cakes and buns, and she enjoyed a game of cards in the evening. Walter was very laid back and happy with his pipe and newspaper, a good joke and a lively argument. Vera noticed that he liked to gamble, sometimes coming home exuberant with his pockets stuffed with winnings. He shared the money around very casually. It seemed that Walter was excited by the thrill of the win, not so much the actual pay-out.

Vera also met Maurice's grandparents, Charlotte's parents, Elizabeth and Herbert How. They lived in Chingford also, on Hurst Avenue, just down the street from Charlotte and Walter. Their daughter, Julie, actually owned the house. She was unmarried and had worked her way up to a good, steady job. The youngest sister, Lily and her husband, Stan, also lived in the house and the five of them cohabitated very well together. Stan was a bus driver who worked nights. He slept part of the day, and everyone very considerately tiptoed around and spoke in lowered voices. When Vera and Maurice came to visit, they were usually greeted at the door by one of the occupants with their finger pressed to their lips, silently informing them that Stan was sleeping upstairs. The house was a large, terraced, brick home, with the typical wrought-iron gate, garden wall and a well-tended front garden. The back garden was long and narrow and still had the air raid shelter at the bottom. It had been bricked over when it was installed to make it less unsightly. Plants and flowers were planted around it for now, although Herbert often said, "one of these days, Stan will take it down."

Vera and Maurice were expected to make a Friday evening visit with the family there each week. They were served a nice dinner followed by a game of cards. Dinner was served by way of a sliding panel pass-through between the kitchen and the living room. A large dining table was on the living room side of the handy opening. The door would be slid open, the dinner passed through with a brief comment, "this one's for you, Wole," then the door would be promptly slid shut again until the next plate was ready. It was a ritual that was repeated week after week. After dinner, Charlotte, Julie and Lily did the dishes while grandmother, Elizabeth sat by the fire. She nodded off for a little while, waking up in perfect time for cards. Stan would usually appear in time for his dinner and to chat for a while before leaving for work. Vera saw that Maurice was obviously fond of his family, though a little in awe of his grandmother. She was strict and so prim and proper and

Victorian in her ways. She was a small, thin lady who always seemed to be wearing black. The hem of her dress reached almost to her ankles, and she wore black leather, lace-up shoes. She was addressed as "mother" or "grandmother" except by Herbert who called her "Lizzie." Although she was always pleasant and polite, Vera had the feeling she was being studied and evaluated much of the time while she was there.

Maurice loved his grandfather, Herbert, whom he called Grandpops. He had an easy, happy personality and enjoyed the company of his grandchildren. He used a cane to get around and was limited with his activities, but he chatted happily with Maurice on many different topics. Stan was very pleasant too, but Maurice thought that he had life a bit too comfortable and was catered to rather too much. Lily, the youngest sister, was a lot of fun. She was lively, cheerful, and funny. She joked and laughed a lot. There were times when the other three ladies thought she had overstepped the mark and she would be admonished with, "Oh, Lily, really!" or "Lily… please…" or "Oh, Lily, for heaven's sake!" Maurice and Vera thought she was wonderful and chuckled quietly to themselves at her bold comments. When they had stayed an acceptable period of time, the young couple would take their leave and dash off to the cinema or to visit with friends to enjoy the rest of the evening. With few exceptions, this was how Friday nights were spent for the rest of their courtship.

Following the banished period when Charlotte finally accepted the engagement, she and Walter held a big engagement party at Julie's house. Charlotte, Julie, and Lily prepared food for days and the spread of food was most impressive. Off the living room was a doorway leading to a glass conservatory. This was the perfect place for tables and chairs and plenty of extra garden chairs were placed on the lawn in the garden. There were about fifty people in attendance including Florrie and Ted, Eileen and Ray and baby Christine who had arrived in January 1945, several aunts, uncles, cousins and friends. It was a happy celebration and confirmation to the young couple that there were no lasting bad feelings, only wishes of love, good fortune, and happiness.

Maurice was often able to borrow a car or sometimes, Walter's van to take Vera to seaside towns and resorts in southern England, Cornwall, and Wales. Beaches had been completely off limits during the war due to the anticipated invasion and they had been strung with walls of barbed wire as well as with buried mines and mines at sea just offshore. There were spiked barriers at the tideline to deter landing crafts, as well as anti-aircraft guns and concrete pillboxes for machine gun positions. Quite quickly after the end of the war, the beaches had been cleared and returned to the people for their enjoyment. Some beaches were signed with warnings that they were still off limits if there was concern that undetected mines may still be on the beach, or the beach was in a location where unexploded mines from the sea could wash up during a storm. The courting couple were anxious to enjoy the beach and the sand and the waves again. Over the course of the next few years, they took numerous holidays, spending time at seaside resorts along the English and Welsh coastline. In Cornwall, they relaxed on the beaches of Penzance, and toured St Michael's Mount, as well as the geographical landmark known as Land's End. They drove along the Jurassic Coast in southern England, popping in for a brief visit with Auntie Lylie and Uncle Will while in Dorset. In

Wales they travelled to the island of Anglesey to Llanfairpwllgwyngyllgogerychwyrndrobwllllantysiliogogogoch. This small village was a popular tourist destination for its natural beauty and for its name, which was the second longest one-word name of a town in the world. The railway station boldly displayed the full name across the platform. The English translation is as follows; St. Mary's Church in the Hollow of the White Hazel Near to the Rapid Whirlpool of Llantysilio of the Red Cave.

In Llandudno they stayed at a bed and breakfast that had been a favourite destination of Maurice's parents for family holidays in the past. Mrs. Morgan was the proprietor. She was happy to see Maurice again and welcomed Vera, informing her of breakfast hours and the time of day when hot water would be available for washing or baths. She showed them to their reserved rooms across the hall from each other and the large, shared bathroom a few doors down.

"Thank you, Mrs. Morgan," Maurice responded. "I am looking forward to your scrumptious breakfasts. I told Vera that they will last us all day until dinner. She is my fiancée, by the way although we will not be getting married for a few years."

"Well, that is very wise of you, I must say. Give yourselves a little time to grow and experience life without all the responsibilities and worries of marriage and family before you settle down. Let me take a look at your ring, dear." Vera proudly extended her hand smiling at the kindly, slightly greying, older woman. "Perfectly lovely, dear. My best wishes to you both."

Llandudno was a place to relax and enjoy the natural beauty of the town on the northern coast of Wales overlooking the Irish Sea. Mrs. Morgan's establishment was part of a terraced stretch of homes, hotels and restaurants along the two-mile promenade facing the ocean. Vera's room faced the sea and Maurice's faced inland with a view of the rolling hills and distant villages in a breathtaking landscape. The weather during the summer of 1947 was warmer and drier than usual. The young couple spent all day outside, on the beach, walking along the promenade, taking boat tours, cycling all over the area, and perusing the shops and local craft stalls. They took the tram to the summit of Great Orme. It was a bright sunny day but as they ascended, the temperature dropped markedly. Vera wished she had brought her jacket and nestled close to Maurice for a little more warmth. The views however were spectacular, and they marvelled at the herds of wild goats, the variety of sea birds and the colourful wildflowers clinging to the rock face on their way up to the top. On the lower elevation of the mountain, there were charming little homes nestled in the hillside accessed by steep, narrow tracks that wound their way around the rugged terrain. The homes all had names which Vera read out to Maurice as they passed them by. They agreed that the views were magnificent, and the houses were so quaint but decided that it would be too much of an inconvenience living on the side of the mountain. At the summit, the wind was strong, but Vera was delighted to catch some stunning panoramic landscapes with her camera. The entire town of Llandudno, the coastline, the bay and the hills stretched before them.

On the last day of their holiday, they decided to drive out from Llandudno to explore the surrounding countryside as well as Conwy Castle. The castle was built by King Edward I between 1283 and 1289 as a grand fortress during his conquest of Wales. The ruins of the original structure were still powerful-looking, impressive, and imposing. Maurice told Mrs. Morgan of their plans for the next day and that they planned to leave early, so they would not be having breakfast. The next morning Maurice dressed quickly and tapped on Vera's door to be sure she was awake and getting ready.

"Yes," Vera responded. "Come in Maurice. I'm almost ready." Maurice entered, quietly opening, and closing the door so as not to disturb any of the other boarders. Vera was brushing her hair in front of the mirror. She wore a floral print cotton dress and strappy sandals. Maurice smiled at her. "You look nice," he said. "Fresh as a daisy."

"Thank you. It looks like such a lovely day outside. I'll just bring my cardigan in case it turns cool while we are out." She stepped over to the wardrobe to retrieve the cardigan when they heard a gentle tapping on Maurice's door across the hall. "Maurice…" a voice whispered. "Maurice, it's Mrs. Morgan. Just wanted to be sure you were awake. I know you wanted to get an early start this morning."

Vera and Maurice stared at each other paralysed for the moment. Mrs. Morgan was being so thoughtful and kind, but the situation was not salvageable. Vera covered her mouth with her hand and her eyes were wide with horror. Mrs. Morgan tapped again, "Maurice?" There was nothing for it. Maurice would have to respond.

"Er… I'm in here, Mrs. Morgan," he called timidly. There was silence for a long moment.

"Oh… yes… alright then." And then the sound of hurried, retreating footsteps down the hall.

"Oh, dear!" said Vera. "Whatever must she think!"

"And we are completely innocent," Maurice responded with an amused grin.

"Should we go down and explain?"

"No, I don't think so. No need to explain. We will just behave as normal and wave to her as we leave."

"Oh dear. What bad luck that she should come and knock on your door right after you came over here."

"Now Vera, don't let it spoil the day. Come on, let's get going." He crossed the room to the door and held it open. "You know… I should have just opened the door and stepped into the hall. Mrs. Morgan would have seen that I was fully dressed and realised that I had just popped over to make sure you were ready to go."

"Yes, of course. It's just that we were caught off-guard and didn't have time to think."

"Come on then. Let's go." Maurice followed Vera down the hall with another uncomfortable thought. But he did not think it was the right time to tell Vera that his parents were coming to stay for a week next month, even though he felt quite sure that Mrs. Morgan would not say anything about the incident to them.

The years following the war were so exciting for Vera. She loved her work in London, being engaged to Maurice, saving diligently for their future together, visiting with family and friends and spending holidays touring the country. She had even come to terms with Ted. Although there was some residual resentment, she realised that her mother was content with him and that, as Maurice had predicted some time ago, she was glad he was there for her mother as her own life was filling with plans and a future with Maurice. There was some sadness in the family in 1949 when Lily, Maurice's fun-loving aunt, was diagnosed with a brain tumour. The family was saddened when it was apparent, following surgery, that there would be no recovery and that it would be a rapid, downhill journey. Elizabeth How and Herbert had lost two sons in childhood and did not expect to lose another child during their lifetime. Elizabeth became even more solemn and quiet as the year progressed and Herbert busied himself in the garden for hours on end. Friday evenings continued with dinner and cards. Lily insisted that they should.

In November of 1949, Vera and Maurice decided that they had waited long enough. Although Vera had promised to wait until she was twenty-one before she got married, the couple hoped that she was now close enough to that requirement that the family would approve their getting married a few months early. They talked with Charlotte and Walter first.

"Alright by me!" Walter declared. "You two 'ave proved your devotion, I would say. What do you think, May?"

"Weell…" she began. And then she thought of Lily. Wouldn't it be nice to have a wedding and a happy occasion before she died? And it was only a few months short of the commitment they had made. "Well, yes. I think it will be alright. But have you thought about where you will live? I know you have been saving to buy a building lot but where will you live in the meantime?"

"Well, Mum, Dad. We thought we could move in here for a while. Would you mind that? There is a lot of room here and just the two of you. Perhaps we could have my bedroom and the spare room as a sitting room. What do you think? Walter put down his newspaper and took out his tobacco pouch. As he rolled himself a cigarette he nodded thoughtfully. "Yes. Very sensible. What do you think, May?" Charlotte sighed with relief. This would give her more time with her son before he left her home for good. Eileen had been so young and left so abruptly. She was not ready yet for a completely empty nest.

"I think we can make the rooms upstairs very

comfortable for you both."

When they sat down with Florrie, she chuckled and nodded to herself. "I was expecting this conversation now that your twenty-first is not that far off. We ought to start making some plans, I suppose."

"Well, Mum… you see… we thought, Maurice and I, that we might make the date sooner rather than later. Could we make it as soon as possible? We feel like we have waited long enough."

"Yes, Mrs. Midd," continued Maurice. "Do we have to wait until Vera's birthday? I know she made you that promise but, what do you think, have we proved ourselves to you by now?"

"Yes, you 'ave. And very well done, too! You're quite a pair and I'm mighty proud of you both. All right then. Vera and I will put our 'eads together and check into some places to 'ave a nice weddin' reception. Got to check with the church too. 'Ow much do you want to be involved in the plannin', Maurice? Got any ideas in mind?"

"No. I'll leave it all up to the two of you. Just tell me where and when to show up," he said with a laugh.

Vera and Florrie soon had the church date, Saturday, 21st January at St. Edmund's Church in South Chingford, not far from the Mount. They secured a location for a wedding breakfast following the ceremony in a private upstairs room of a local restaurant. Florrie suggested that close family and friends be invited back to Waverley Avenue following breakfast for a continuation of the celebration, where she would provide hors d'oeuvres, sandwiches, wine, tea, and coffee. Vera loved the idea and was even more excited when Uncle Harold offered to play music with a couple of his band mates at the house. The plans came together quickly. Vera had her wedding gown made for her by a friend of Florrie's, she chose the dresses for her bridesmaids, two close friends, Joy and Joan, and little Christine, and she asked Uncle Harold to walk her down the aisle. Ted was an invited guest, but she had made up her mind a long time ago that he would not have a role in her wedding or be in any way, a surrogate father. Florrie accepted this with complete understanding and in a rare, sentimental comment told her daughter, "Dad'll be with us that day, you know. 'E'll be with us in spirit."

The day dawned bright, sunny, and crisp. A large, shiny, hired car drove Vera and Uncle Harold the short ride to the church, where a large congregation waited inside. Since Vera and Maurice were so popular in town, word had spread during the previous few months of the upcoming nuptials. Florrie waited by the church gate to straighten, fluff and smooth Vera's dress and veil where it may have become crushed or twisted in the car. "Alright luv," she said. "You look a picture!" She then entered the church, walking to the front row to sit beside Ted. She nodded and smiled at Maurice who was waiting in front of the altar. Maurice looked very dapper in a dark, pinstriped, double-breasted suit. He had a crisp, white shirt and silk tie and he carried leather gloves. His hair had been recently cut and shaped and the mass of curls on top had been trimmed down to a more mature sweep of waves. *Here Comes the Bride* began to play on the organ and the congregation stood and turned to witness the procession of the bridesmaids and the entrance of the bride. Everyone was all smiles as Vera approached on her uncle's arm, stunning in a flowing satin dress. The gown had full, puff sleeves and a sweetheart neckline. She wore long gloves of lace that reached to her elbow and two strands of pearls adorned her neck. Her shining, auburn hair had been carefully curled and pinned back from her face with a garland of orange blossom from which trailed a long lace-edged veil. She carried a dramatic spray of pink carnations that reached almost to the floor. The ceremony proceeded with the usual prayers and vows, signing of the marriage registry, and the Wedding March by Mendelssohn for the recessional. When the newly married couple exited the church, the bells in the church tower were ringing and the people gathered outside were waving and cheering. There were congratulations all around with hugs and kisses until the photographer organised the group into a series of photographs staged along the beautiful exterior of the church. The lovely stone walls and dramatic, stained-glass windows provided a perfect backdrop to the bridal groupings. He took several family shots as well as a large group picture including all the attendees. The photographer then directed Vera and Maurice to the heavy, studded, wooden doors at the entrance to the sanctuary where he caught them in a striking pose, gazing happily at each other. As they proceeded to the car which would carry them to the wedding breakfast, a cascade of colourful confetti showered them, thrown with giggles and wishes of good luck from many of the onlookers.

At the wedding breakfast there was champagne and toasts and the reading of telegrams from people who could not attend. Music played softly as the guests ate and when dishes were cleared away, a beautiful two-tiered wedding cake was brought out to the table. Vera looked to survey all the dear faces around her. Her mother, aunts and uncles, some cousins, close friends, Maurice's parents, grandparents, Auntie Julie, Stan, Eileen and Ray, little Christine and baby Gillian. One person missing was Lily.

Her health had deteriorated, and she was now confined to hospital. Vera had suggested that her bouquet be taken to her there. When it was time to leave, Stan picked up the bouquet from the table, congratulated the couple again, and left to visit his wife and tell her all the detail of the wedding that he knew she would want to hear.

The party at Waverley Avenue continued well into the evening. After the war, Florrie had been able to sell her former house on Waverley Avenue and had been able to purchase number 22. She had decided to have a long conservatory added which ran the full width of the house off the back and created so much additional living space. It was a perfect spot for the party to spill into. A couple of paraffin heaters warmed the area, and chairs were arranged along the perimeter. Uncle Harold and his bandmates positioned themselves at one end and music filled the house for all to enjoy. Vera and Maurice waltzed for the first time as a married couple, there in the conservatory, under a star-filled sky. Early in the evening, Vera slipped away and changed out of her wedding dress into her "going away" suit. It was a finely tailored, fitted, two-piece set in jade green. She and Maurice mingled a little longer, thanking everyone for coming and then waved farewell and departed. They had a borrowed car which was waiting with their suitcases already inside. They drove off into the night, hearing the music fading slowly behind them.

There was no big honeymoon planned. The young couple did not want to spend a lot of money on a big trip in January. They just desired a few days of privacy to relax with no agenda at all. They had not even booked anywhere. They drove out of town until they had gone as far as they wanted and then they looked for a nice, cosy accommodation. They headed northwest and found a cheerfully lighted inn, *The Farmer's Rest*, in Saffron Walden about fifty-two miles from Chingford. There, they stopped, tired, excited, nervous and happy and were finally able to sleep in bed together, at last.

Vera's contribution to her creative writing class – Comparing Grandparents

My husband's grandparents lived in a new house in northern London (Chingford.) They didn't own their house – it belonged to their middle daughter, Julie, who shared it with them. The kitchen was nicely equipped with a grey-mottled gas cooker, white porcelain sink, and draining board, and a glass-panelled cupboard for the china. It had a sliding serving hatch door through which food and dishes could be passed into the dining room. Once a week the grandchildren and their parents sat around the table and played family games. The house was bright with colourful furnishings and decorations. A large Airedale dog lived with them and there was a beaded privacy curtain hung between the dining room French door and the small, glass sunroom beyond. They were not wealthy but had a comfortable lifestyle, well clothed, well fed, and no debts.

Grandpops went to the British Legion once a week to play dominoes and have a pint of beer, and that was the extent of his outside interests. He had spent his whole life fitting piano keys to grand and upright pianos, and even had the honour of installing the keys to the organ in St. Paul's Cathedral. His right hand third and fourth fingers were permanently bent from holding the tools of his trade.

Grandma was a fanatical housekeeper, dusting, polishing, cleaning, and cooking for the family. She was very prim and proper and sat always with the back of her hand under her chin in case it drooped. Auntie Julie, their daughter, was an office superintendent in the offices of the Caribonum Company, manufacturer of typewriter ribbons and carbon paper. She never married and cared for her parents until they died in their nineties.

On the other hand, my grandparents lived in an old Victorian house, dingy, with little light. It had a long, narrow passageway and steps down to the kitchen and scullery. The kitchen had a large wooden table on which meals for the thirteen children had been served over the years. Adjoining this room was the scullery, housing a blacktop range and oven which was coal or anthracite fuelled, and a brown earthenware sink with one brass cold water tap. A galvanized bath was still used by them as it had been for their children.

I remember my grandparents as elderly, my mother, being one of their youngest children. My grandfather did not work for years, depending mainly on the income of his working sons and daughters. He made their shoes when they were little and in later years, he repaired clocks. I can recall entering the dim house and hearing dozens of clocks ticking in a stifling, musty atmosphere. He would be sitting in the rocking chair, grunting and coughing with a pipe in his mouth. He had a large stomach and always wore a waistcoat with a striped shirt. His snow-white hair and bushy moustache would have made him an excellent Father Christmas, but his personality would not have matched as he regularly beat his wife and children, a very common Victorian habit. He didn't drink alcohol and was a gifted musician, so he had two qualities to his credit.

My grandmother (Gran), despite her husband's beatings, survived until she was seventy-three when she died of a worn-out heart. I was seven years old. She had been the typical meek and timid wife who had taken great punishment from her husband and if at all possible, was always careful to hide her injuries from the family – she dared not anger him further. This sounds like a terribly morbid household but in fact, the children had their own fun and games and deceived my grandfather in every way imaginable as that was their only method of revenge.

Notation in one of Vera's notebooks
Many homes repaired and rebuilt by Maurice operating with his

father, W.G. Brown & Son, Ltd. Building Contractors, specialising in war damage.

CHAPTER TWELVE

Vera settled happily into her rooms in Walter and Charlotte's home. She shared a nice bedroom with Maurice that looked out onto the back garden. A slightly larger room next to it was converted into their sitting room, which she furnished with a small, second-hand settee and easy chair that she had found at the same used furniture shop where she and Florrie had shopped together years ago. She added side tables, lamps, and colourful cushions. They had a wireless and gramophone and an assortment of 78 records, and some attractive wedding presents to decorate the room. A set of hand-painted, silver floral plates adorned the walls as well as a shiny, new mirror hanging from a silver chain. She had changed the curtains to attractive drawable drapes in a blue-green colour to match the cushions. There was a lovely glass bowl filled with fruit and a bone-handled biscuit caddy by the window, on a small table which had two matching wooden chairs. Under the bed, she stored some food, just as she and Florrie had done over the years, to keep it separate from Charlotte's. Rationing was still in effect at this time, even almost five years after the end of the war. Charlotte was a master of managing the coupon books and menu planning, so she offered to prepare dinners a few times during the week for all four of them. Vera was grateful for this since she was still working in London every day. Charlotte did most of the shopping too, so Vera provided her with a list of items that she needed and paid her each week for her purchases, as well as the small rent that she and Maurice owed. She shared the kitchen with Charlotte to make tea and when she needed to prepare simple meals for herself and Maurice. It was a very pleasant and suitable arrangement.

Some evenings after work, Vera walked to Florrie's with Maurice for dinner and on weekends she often popped in for a cup of tea and a chat. Maurice still worked mostly with his father, but he was itching to move on to something of his own. He managed to get some private jobs, wallpapering and painting, sometimes demolition, foundation work and the like. It was all physical labour, but he toiled at it happily and earnestly, excited to learn anything new along the way. He and Vera were able to continue saving and were able to augment their bank account when Walter, who continued to gamble, came home with a big win. As usual, the cash was spread on the table. Charlotte took a portion to put away in a private account so that there was always a protected balance that Walter could not touch to gamble away. Maurice took some with mixed feelings. He was grateful for the chance to add to his building lot fund but concerned about his father's continuing gambling addiction. He spoke to him about it on several occasions, but Walter downplayed the behaviour. "Nothing to worry about, my boy! Just a bit of fun, is all."

Later in the year, Vera discovered that she was pregnant. She was filled with a mixture of emotions; happy but nervous, excited but fearful, and disappointed that it had happened so quickly. She would have much preferred to have bought their land and built their little bungalow before starting a family. Maurice was tickled with the news. "Imagine that!" he exclaimed.

"Oh dear," Vera replied. "This is not what we had planned. We wanted a little more time before a baby came along."

"Don't fret, dear. We'll manage. Might take a little

longer to get our own house, but won't it be lovely? A little boy or girl of our own. It will certainly liven up the house."

"What will your parents think, Maurice? Will they be upset about it?"

"Shouldn't think so. Mum especially will be thrilled, I expect."

Charlotte was indeed excited, just as Maurice had predicted. She was all smiles and giggles when she was told. Walter put his pipe and paper down and stood up to give Vera a hug and to shake hands with Maurice. "Congratulations, my boy. When is the little nipper expected?"

"The doctor at the clinic said end of April," Vera responded.

"Ah, lovely timing. Just as the weather is warming up. The baby can sleep outside in its pram while I work in my garden. Going to try peas and beans next year, Maurice. Did I tell you?"

Vera suffered quite badly with morning sickness, so it was not long before it became too difficult to continue the commute into London and she had to resign from her job. This was difficult for Vera since she so enjoyed her work and being part of the bustling big city. It took a while for her to adjust to her new situation and cope with the inconveniences that came along with pregnancy. She became caught up in Charlotte's rigid schedule of housekeeping, shopping, and cooking. Charlotte had a schedule for all her tasks. Monday was wash day, no matter the weather. It was an arduous day of dreary work. Charlotte had a laundry copper on wheels with a wringer on top. This was quite typical for a lot of households, although Florrie still used a wash tub, scrub brush and washboard. The copper was rolled into the centre of the kitchen, where both women had room to work. The tub was filled with water and heated to boiling point by a coal burner located beneath the tub. Soap flakes were added and when the water was hot, whites were added first. A copper stick was used to stir and plunge the clothes down and around in the tub. When the whites had sufficiently boiled, they were lifted out with the copper stick and placed in a large basin to cool. They were then rinsed thoroughly in fresh water several times and fed through the wringer which turned with a crank to squeeze the water out before being placed in a basket to be hung up to dry. Meanwhile, another batch had been added to the copper, perhaps sheets, towels, dishcloths and finally coloured clothing would be washed. If Monday's weather was fine, the loads would be taken out to the back garden and pegged to the line. If not, Charlotte would stretch lines across the kitchen and peg them there and drape them over drying racks. Vera dreaded Mondays.

The rest of the week was easier. Each day there were set housekeeping tasks to do. Ironing was Tuesday; vacuuming, sweeping, dusting, was Wednesday; polishing, stairs, and windows was Thursday; and baking was Friday. Although milk was delivered daily to the doorstep and the baker's van came around once or twice a week, shopping had to be done six days a week to purchase food for meals. There was no refrigerator, so everything had to be bought fresh. Vera learned a lot from Charlotte's organised schedule and though she would not be so rigid in her own home, she was grateful for Charlotte's guidance and discipline. Florrie had not been very regimented with her housework. She worked full time, after all, and she did not want to burden Vera with too many menial tasks. Vera helped her, of course, but it was with a much more casual attitude. "You get a chance to go out and do something nice, leave it! The housework.

Leave it and you go! It will be 'ere waitin' for you when you get back. Remember that when you 'ave your own 'ouse one day," Florrie would say. Charlotte, on the other hand, would not be able to enjoy herself *unless* the work was done.

Vera quite liked the shopping outings. It was a chance to stretch her legs and interact with people. She trailed around mostly with her mother-in-law but sometimes went off for a while on her own to make a few personal selections. When they returned home and put the food away, Charlotte would put the kettle on, and they would enjoy a nice cup of tea together, perhaps with a chocolate biscuit or maybe a jam tart.

The building lot fund grew slowly but steadily with a few setbacks relating to purchases for the expected baby: nappies, rubber pants, baby clothes, blankets, a small cot and bedding. Florrie and Ted bought a lovely pram with spring suspension and Charlotte and Walter bought a soft leather carry cot as well as a highchair. Vera grew slowly but steadily and began to feel the strain of the daily shopping trips with Charlotte. April came and went without the infant's arrival. During a shopping trip in May, Vera could not keep pace with her mother-in-law and had to stop repeatedly. She was obviously feeling uncomfortable and bent over frequently with her hand pressed to her extended belly. Charlotte looked at Vera with a worried frown and decided that they had better return home right away. It appeared that labour had indeed begun.

Maurice was located at his jobsite, and he drove her to the hospital in Walthamstow, the neighbouring town. There Vera was admitted and Maurice was dismissed. He was told that he could telephone during the day and night to inquire about Vera's progress. This was the norm for the maternity ward in 1951. There was a waiting room, but he was advised to go home. A first baby's labour was usually quite lengthy. Maurice went home to wait, stopping at Florrie's on his way to push a note through her letterbox for her to read when she returned home from work, informing her of the situation. It was indeed a lengthy labour. The baby was in the breech position and could not be turned. Vera was placed in a ward with other women in various stages of labour, where she was monitored at regular intervals by the nurses on duty. She laboured all night and into the next day and was becoming exhausted, moaning with the ineffective contractions that racked her body. In the bed beside her a woman was in labour with her fifth child and she tried to comfort Vera as best she could.

"It's alright, luv," she said. "Take some deep breaths and try to relax between pains. It will soon be all over. Next baby will be much easier."

Next one! Vera thought. *Next one! Let me get through this one first!* As the pain began to peak, she reached down and could feel that two tiny feet had emerged. She gasped in alarm and stretched her arm toward the call button on the wall behind her, but it was located just beyond her reach. In desperation she grasped a Coca-Cola bottle on her side table and was able to push the button with it. When a nurse arrived, she was whisked quickly away to the delivery room, and finally, at 3:30 p.m. on 10th May, the baby was born. The little girl weighed five pounds and appeared to be healthy, but she was placed in an incubator as a precaution due to the prolonged labour and breech birth. Vera would not be allowed to hold her baby for two days.

Frances Yvette was brought home to Hurst Avenue ten days later. Florrie spent the day with Vera, delighted with her first grandchild and helping with her care, as well as easing her daughter's discomfort and recovery. Family members, including Maurice's grandparents, Auntie Julie, Uncle Stan, Eileen and Ray, stopped by for visits during the week. The weather was becoming warm so that Vera could take the baby out in the pram for the daily trek to the shops with Charlotte and, as Walter had wished, the baby slept in her pram in the garden as he prepared the vegetable beds. Charlotte kept to her strict schedule but eased expectations for Vera, allowing some discretion and accommodation due to the needs of the infant. She did not interfere in the handling of the child, the feeding times, nap schedule or crying at night. She did not pick up the child without asking Vera's permission. She was a perfect mother-in-law in that regard. If the baby cried heartily, she would ask Vera, "Can I pick her up now, Vera?"

"Not just yet. Let her cry a little longer. We shouldn't jump up immediately whenever she cries." After a few minutes more Charlotte would ask again, "Is it alright now?"

"No. Not yet." And a little bit later, "Now?"

"Yes, alright, now."

Frances thrived, grew, and became the focus of the household. She was a fairly easy baby, happy and content to study her surroundings, manipulate her toys and laugh and smile at the antics of the adults around her, especially Maurice, who picked her up, whirled her around and made funny faces. She perhaps showed a tendency for patience and persistence when she would spend an hour pushing crumbs around on the tray of her highchair in an attempt to grasp them in her little fingers. Florrie visited often to cuddle and play with her granddaughter and Vera often pushed Frances in the pram over to Waverley Avenue to spend time there. Vera loved the walk on a bright sunny day pushing the beautiful, dark green pram with the shiny wheels and the gently bouncing spring suspension. It felt so luxurious. Ag and Art were always thrilled to hear her arrival and popped downstairs to coo and admire the baby.

A year passed and Maurice was becoming impatient to move on from construction work. He wanted a business of his own. One that he could run himself and grow. He knew that he had the ability to learn new skills, take on new tasks, to work long hours and to accept the risk of a new venture. He had that outgoing, amiable personality that drew people to him. He was young and ambitious, alert to new opportunities and anxious to succeed. But first he intended to build that house that he and Vera had been saving for and he began the search for a nice building lot. Through fellow construction associates, Maurice heard that the town of Romford, which was only eleven miles south-east of Chingford, was developing quite rapidly and that building lots were quite affordable there. He and Vera and Walter drove there to have a look around. They found it to be a pleasant, growing town with a busy shopping centre, a railway station, and many bus routes. In the Collier Row section of town, they found a corner lot on Hamlet Road. The "For Sale" sign had a reasonable price that the couple could afford. Vera jotted down the contact information and the three of them walked the property. It was large, flat with heavy, clay soil and an abundance of grass, weeds, and wildflowers. Walter bent down to pick up a handful of the compact dirt. "Yeees," he acknowledged. Just like my garden. Heavy to dig and bad drainage. When you plant flower beds or vegetables, you'll 'ave to add compost and maybe a bit of lime." Maurice winked at Vera as he thought, *digging planting beds seems a long way off.*

"What do you think, Dad? Seems a nice bit of land in a nice area. Collier Row. Must have been charcoal burners here once upon a time, don't you think? I like this lot, backs onto open fields, quiet, in a nice sized town but just like being in the country right here."

"I think it's a nice spot, 'ere. Course all that open land will get built up slowly but surely, but the location is very good, and the price is right too."

"Do you like it, Vera?" Vera was all smiles.

"Oh, yes. Not too far from Chingford but so much quieter and look at the houses that have already been built. They are mostly brick bungalows. Just what we wanted. Think our plans will fit in here very well."

"Alright then," Maurice replied. "Suppose we should go into town and find the estate office."

Maurice had been able to pay for the land outright but needed a "new build" mortgage for the construction of the house. Work began on the site early in 1952 when Maurice had secured a heavily regulated construction loan. The plans called for a spacious three-bedroom bungalow with a modern kitchen and pantry, a wide, stately entry hall, and a large front room which was a combination dining and sitting room. At the end of the hall was a shiny new bathroom and a separate toilet. Maurice had studied the blueprints so much that he knew every measurement, doorway, and window by heart. He worked during the day at his contracted jobsite and finished the day at his own property, clearing the land and digging the footings. On the weekends, he worked there half a day Saturday and all day Sunday, when Walter would lend a hand. When the footings and the slab were poured it was a day of great celebration. Vera was giddy with excitement as the project progressed. It was a dream come true. A home of her own at last. She could not help but think back to the years when she and Florrie had moved so frequently and made do with such shabby, depressing rooms. In her mind she positioned furniture in her new house, thought about curtains, and paint colours, and wallpaper. She talked to Frances about it and the baby listened without understanding but smiled at the joy and excitement in her mother's voice and clapped when her mother twirled and whirled with pure pleasure.

As the framing went up, the house began to take shape. Maurice had to have professionals install the electrical and plumbing, of course, and he had roofers tile the roof, but almost everything else he did himself, with some help from his father and friends when he installed windows and tackled heavier tasks. Supplies were often difficult to find and the cost of much of the materials was quite high. The early 50s following the war was still a time of reconstruction. Damage and ruins from bombing raids were still visible everywhere and the clearing away and rebuilding took time and a lot of bureaucratic oversight. Maurice usually had to hunt for building supplies, and often used salvaged materials from demolished structures. He continued to save earnestly to be able to afford a few upscale selections. The windows in the two rooms facing the street fell into this category. They were especially stunning with their diamond glass panels providing a classy, elegant façade. The exterior he had planned to be all brick, but it was in such short supply that he bricked only a third of the way up the structure and finished the rest with stone-encrusted stucco. The finished appearance was rather pleasing to the eye with the contrast of the warm orange of the brick and the multi-tones of the stone in the pale stucco. He framed the front entrance with an arch of brick which added dramatic architectural detail. Slowly, slowly, the bungalow took shape. With the exterior completed, Maurice could turn his attention inside. This was his area of greatest skill. He wallpapered the bedrooms and sitting room, painted the kitchen, bathroom, and hallway. He added trim, doors, cabinets, light fixtures and finished the floors with slate in the hall, linoleum in the kitchen and bathroom, and wood everywhere else. In the late spring, Walter started work on the garden. He dug flower beds, turning over the heavy clay, and adding compost and manure, laid paving stones, raked and sowed grass seed and planted rose bushes and small shrubs. His wheelbarrow rolled miles around the garden as he worked. He was in his element planning the layout, moving soil from one project to another, building a low wall and walkway in the front of the house, planting bulbs and decorative flowering shrubs all the way up the garden path to the front door. On sunny, warm days, Vera often brought Frances with her and sat her on a blanket while she worked on Walter's flowerbeds, tidying, edging, and adding some of her particular favourite perennials. She breathed in the rich, earthy smell of the soil while the bright sunshine warmed her back as she knelt there. The garden became quite a showcase. The plants thrived and flowers grew in a multitude of colours. It was a pretty landscape with fields and trees beyond, a lovely setting for a charming new home.

In the summer of that year, 1952, the house was complete. Vera and Maurice left Hurst Avenue and moved with Frances, now over a year old, into their own bungalow on Hamlet Road. They were thrilled. The long wait and all the hard work had been worth it.

CHAPTER THIRTEEN

Vera was so happy in her new home. For the first few days, she often walked from room to room spreading her arms and gliding across the floor, glorifying in the space. She could not help but think back, remembering everywhere that she had lived in her life. Memories of the war years, all the moving, resettling and insecurity of that time lingered prominently in her memory and the contrast of those years to her new life loomed large. She realised that the last time she had lived in a family home with a traditional family unit was 21 Waverley Avenue with her mother and father. So long ago, half her lifetime, and yet only twelve years had passed. She thought of her father, dear Sidney. How she wished he could see this house, and know Maurice and his granddaughter, Frances. He would love them all. He had missed so much by dying so young. The familiar dark cloud began to descend as it always did when she thought of her dad, but she shook it off as she heard sounds from Frances waking from her nap.

A month after the move, Maurice returned home one day in an old truck. Vera heard a rumbling engine sound outside followed by a loud bang and hiss. She hurried outside to find Maurice stepping down from the driving seat of an old, 1932 Dennis truck. It was a battered old banger with a steel-hoop structure covering the truck bed which was covered with a heavy canvas. It looked much like a covered wagon from the wagon trains she had seen in Western films in the cinema. She stood bewildered and apprehensive, but Maurice was all smiles and bursting with excitement.

"Vera, look! I am now in business for myself! I bought

this for £50. Couldn't resist such a good deal. It's a mobile shop, Vera. Look." He lifted the canvas to reveal low, wooden-slatted sidewalls stretching the length of the sides of the truck bed. Shelves and bins and storage boxes were fastened along both sides with a centre walkway for access. A set of scales was fixed to a wooden orange box at one end next to an ancient cash register. "I am going to begin right away. Tomorrow I will drive to Covent Garden to buy my fruits and vegetables and then I can start a round."

Vera opened her mouth to comment but shut it again. She was unsure what to say. This was the first time Maurice had done something so impulsively. She knew he was anxious to start his own venture and was open to all types of work, but this was something completely new and unexpected. His exuberance however, caused her to smile. As he talked about establishing a round, she began to warm up to the idea.

"Look, Vera. All these new streets and houses around here, and quite a long walk to the shops. Don't you think housewives will be grateful not to have to trudge into town so much? Nice fresh fruit and vegetables to choose from every day."

"Well… yes, but I quite like a walk into town. I…"

"Oh, you will still have to shop in town for so many other things but not for fruit and vegetables anymore. It will lighten your load, won't it? Maybe I will expand after a while… maybe carry eggs, sausages, and bread."

"Won't you need a licence or a permit or something?"

"Oh, I'll find out about all that," Maurice replied, with a dismissive wave of his hand. "Don't worry. Now, come on let's have our tea. I will need to get to bed early tonight. I'll need to be on the road early tomorrow around 4 o'clock in the morning to get into London and load it up." He patted the side of the cab affectionately.

"What about cash, Maurice? You will need a fair amount, I would think."

"Not a problem. I took enough out of the bank when I went there to get the cash to buy the truck."

"Oh," said Vera. "Yes. All right then. Looks like we are in business." She squashed her concern that he had so boldly decided on this new endeavour on his own without discussing it with her first. She knew he was hard-working and would put his all into making a success of the business. She decided that she just could not dampen his adventurous spirit. She would support him through this.

The following morning, well before dawn, Maurice started the truck by turning the crank. It coughed and sputtered and rumbled noisily into life. Vera cringed and slid down under the bed covers, hoping that the neighbours had not been disturbed She listened to the sound of the truck door slamming shut, the gears grinding and the rough, old engine chugging its way down the street, the sound slowly fading as it began its journey into the heart of London town.

Maurice learned a lot about the fruit and vegetable trade over the next few months. He was correct that the mobile greengrocer shop would be well-received. He soon established a route and time schedule so that shoppers knew when to expect him and they greeted him cheerfully and gratefully when he rolled up the canvas to show his produce. He received requests for other items from his customers too and thought about how he could expand his merchandise to satisfy their needs. Rainy days, though, were a problem. When he rolled up the canvas, the produce got wet, potatoes became muddy with the dirt and dust covering them and business was a lot slower those days. The business did well enough for a year until the old truck's engine gave up and caught fire in the middle of town one day. Maurice decided to move on to a different vehicle. He bought a yellow, 1937 Dodge bus which he modified by stripping out the seats and installing the shelves, cupboards, bins and display counters that he needed. He fitted two new sets of scales, and an updated cash till. The luggage storage compartment underneath the seating area of the bus was perfect for storing extra merchandise and specially ordered items. He bought an order book with carbon paper for special orders and a supply of paper bags. Bad weather would no longer be a problem with the enclosed bus, and customers could enter at the front and exit through a back door. Perfect for perusing all the wares and making their selections. Maurice added popular goods to the bus including washing powder, soaps, eggs, sausages, pies, cakes, canned foods, tea, sugar and flour. The bus became a travelling shop and began to turn a healthy profit. It was hard work, though. Maurice worked long hours acquiring his merchandise, loading the bus, stocking the shelves and bins, and making his rounds. He was very pleased, however, with the success of his new business and looking over the books and accounts which Vera kept meticulously for him. She kept files for easy reference, banked the takings, and typed letters, reports, notifications, and recorded special orders.

As Christmas approached in 1953, Maurice took orders for chickens, turkeys, geese, chocolates, nuts, and flowers. It was an exciting time organising the bus and making it look festive for the holiday. The evening before Christmas Eve, the meat orders, plucked, tied, and labelled, were kept on tarpaulins in the cooler parts of the house, away from the fireplace and any heaters. The hallway, bathroom and third bedroom were perfect for storing them overnight.

The bungalow resembled a meat market. On Christmas Eve morning, Maurice rose early, at 3:00 a.m. to load up the bus in the correct order of delivery. The bus was tightly packed by the time he finished and at 7:00 a.m. he was ready to set out. He started the bus, waved to his wife and daughter who stood at the front door to see him off, and put it into gear. A sudden, ominous clunking noise emanated from underneath the bus followed by the grinding of metal on metal and the vehicle listed hopelessly to one side. Something important had obviously broken. Vera stood aghast while Maurice climbed down from the driver's seat and peered under the chassis.

"I'm going to get help, Vera," he called and then took off at a sprint. He returned with a mechanic from his local vehicle repair garage. Frank was a friend of Maurice's. He had done work for him on the old truck, managing to keep it running for a year. Now, he bent to examine the problem with the bus. He saw right away that the half-shaft had snapped.

"You will need a new half-shaft which will be hard to find for this old bus, I'm afraid, Maurice."

"Where should I try, Frank? Anywhere around here at all?"

"No hope around here. You will have to go into London to the Dodge manufacturer on the south side of the city. Even there, though, they may not have the part."

"Well, Frank. I have to try. I'm all loaded up with Christmas orders. Can't let my customers down."

"No. You can't. My wife is one of them!" he chuckled. "Here, I'll write down the address of the manufacturer and the part number that you need."

"How much will it cost?"

"Should be about £25, but you had better take extra. You don't know how much it may be marked up. I'll install it as fast as I can when you get back. Good luck to you, Maurice."

"Thank you, Frank." He dashed into the house to get some cash. Vera followed with Frances in her arms. "Oh, Maurice! Why did this have to happen? Today of all days. Oh dear, oh dear, oh dear…"

"Now Vera, don't start fretting. That won't do us any good. I've got to go right now dear, right now!"

Maurice took off at a jog into town to the railway station. He boarded a train to Liverpool Street where he asked at the information booth for the Underground line that he needed to get to the address Frank had given him. He tried to relax as the Tube train sped along, but there were so many stops to be made along the way, and he squirmed and fidgeted in his seat with frustration as the minutes ticked by. When he finally arrived at his station, he hurried through the crowd, up the escalator and out onto the street. He asked some passers-by for directions to his destination, but they shrugged and apologised for not being able to help. He dashed back inside the station to check the map on the wall and was able to get himself pointed in the right direction. He alternated between speed walking and jogging as he made his way and when he reckoned that he was close, he was relieved to spot a friendly Bobby on his beat who directed him to the manufacturer. He glanced at his watch. It was 11:45 a.m.

There was a guard at the gate also checking his watch. In fifteen minutes, he would be locking up for a nice long Christmas holiday. Employees were departing, smiling, waving, and wishing each other "Happy Christmas!" Maurice rushed up to him explaining his emergency and the all-important part that he needed so desperately.

"Cor, mate. Everyone is leaving now. We're closing

early for Christmas. Don't know if there is anyone back there who can 'elp you."

"I've got to get that part. Do you mind if I go back there and see if there is anyone who will look for me?"

"Alright, mate. You've got fifteen minutes. Good luck!"

Maurice rushed through the gate heading in the direction of a building to which the guard was pointing. It was a long, windowless warehouse. Not many people remained on the premises, but he headed for an employee who was just rising from his desk and reaching for his coat. He was wearing a blue shirt with his name embroidered above the pocket, *Jim Sullivan, Supervisor*. Maurice quickly explained his situation and the urgency of getting the part for the bus while he handed him the paper with the part number on it. The man nodded sympathetically.

"Well, let's see if I can help you," he said. He looked down at the part number and frowned. "Oh, now, this is an old part. No, I know that we don't have this in stock." Maurice's shoulders sagged as disappointment and despair swept over him. "But I do have something that came off a very similar model, just a year newer than your bus. You might be able to make it work. Hold on a minute." The supervisor walked away and disappeared down one of the aisles in the warehouse. Maurice waited hopefully and breathlessly until he returned carrying a long, steel shaft almost four feet long.

"Best I can do. If you've got a good mechanic, mate, he should be able to get this fitted. If you want it, I'll only charge you £8."

"Yes!" Maurice replied. "I'll take it! And thank you very much, Jim. You have just saved Christmas for a lot of people, most of all…*me*!"

Maurice made the return journey carrying his precious half-shaft. He stood for most of the time on the

Underground since the train was cramped with passengers; London workers and shoppers departing the city for their homes in the suburbs. Many were carrying large bags and wrapped presents and there were plenty of pushchairs squeezing on board as well as children of all ages and sizes being shepherded by busy mothers. He stood the half-shaft on end and wedged it between his knees to keep it secure and protected. The trip home seemed to take twice as long as the inbound journey. When he finally arrived home, Frank and the garage crew were waiting and set to work immediately. It was 4:00 p.m. As supervisor Jim had predicted, the shaft was not an exact fit. The flange had to be ground down, in order for the end piece to fit into the socket on one end. It took two hours to make the modification and even then, the piece only held in place by a half inch. Frank told Maurice to drive as if the bus were made of glass! It was 6:00 p.m.

Maurice drove slowly and cautiously, avoiding bumps and dips in the road as he went. He was so relieved to be moving with his Christmas deliveries but concerned that his customers may have despaired of him showing up with their orders. Had they made other plans? Had they shopped at the last minute before the stores closed to be sure they had what they needed for Christmas dinner? At his first few stops, his customers were relieved and pleased to see him and so it continued until late in the evening. All of his customers expected him and had waited for him to arrive. Many women came out to the bus late in the evening in their robes, slippers and with curlers in their hair. No one grumbled. Everyone was happy to have their supplies. At midnight, Maurice was making his last stops, weary, but cheerful as he apologized to his faithful customers and wished them all a very happy Christmas. He chuckled to himself as he drove home, realising that he had been making special deliveries to lots of families on Christmas Eve, just like Father Christmas. He surveyed his empty bus with a deep feeling of gratitude and satisfaction and with thoughts showering blessings on Jim, the supervisor, and Frank, his friend, the mechanic. He whistled Christmas Carols all the way back to his bungalow. Vera was awake when he got home. She had paced most of the night wondering if the shaft had held up. She was so relieved to see the bus pull into the drive and her husband emerge all smiles. She ran a hot bath for him to ease his aches and the stress of the day. They could now relax and enjoy a happy Christmas after all.

The half-shaft stayed in place and secure while Maurice operated the travelling food market for two more years.

CHAPTER FOURTEEN

The house in Romford was located on a corner lot and was situated at a slightly higher elevation than the other properties in the area. On the right side of the property, a street ran perpendicular to Hamlet Road and on the left another house was built. The new neighbour, Mr. Conway was not a very friendly soul, and he began complaining to Maurice immediately, insisting that Maurice's garage encroached on his property by about one foot. Maurice maintained that a survey had, of course, been conducted prior to building and that he had built within the boundaries. The neighbour did not believe him and contracted for another survey to be done. He was irritated when the survey proved that Maurice had indeed built within his own boundary line. Mr. Conway then complained that the water shed from Maurice's garage roof flooded his property on that side and he insisted that Maurice attend to the problem. In an effort to oblige and satisfy the bothersome neighbour, Maurice installed larger gutters and redirected the flow of runoff by changing the angle of the downspouts. However, the problem flooding continued. Mr. Conway decided to bring the matter to the County Court. The matter was decided quickly. The case was decided in Mr. Conway's favour with a penalty assessed against Maurice in the amount of one shilling (twelve pence) to be paid annually to his neighbour. Maurice chuckled that evening with Vera.

"Well dear, I think we can afford that, don't you?"

"Yes. Let's give him a pound. Then we'll be paid up for twenty years!"

Mr. Conway was furious with the unsatisfactory decision

and immediately appealed the decision to a higher court. He took to standing outside with an umbrella, glaring as he watched the water accumulate every time there was a heavy rain. Vera and Maurice ignored him and his strange behaviour. They had exciting news to focus on when they discovered that Vera was expecting again.

"Perhaps it will be a boy this time," Maurice speculated.
"I expect you would like to have a boy, wouldn't you?"
"Well… yes, I suppose so. One of each would be nice."
"We'll just have to wait and see."

The appeal process moved slowly as the pregnancy progressed and on the very day that labour started for Vera, a summons was delivered for Maurice to appear at the Old Bailey, the highest court in the land. The case was to be heard in thirty days by a panel of three judges. Vera was appalled that the minor grievance had been elevated to such an extreme level, but her immediate concern was the intensifying pains of labour which demanded her attention. Charlotte had come to collect Frances the day before, to keep her until the baby was born and Maurice had cut his rounds short so that he could be available, if needed. Vera thought that she had better call for the midwife right away. This labour seemed to be progressing faster than her first, so she lumbered to the telephone box around the corner and called the clinic. She was told that a midwife would be on her way directly. In less than fifteen minutes, the midwife arrived, pedalling her bicycle, and ringing the bell as she pulled into the drive. She removed her medical bag from the basket and marched into the house confident and ready to take charge.

"Where can I get towels, a basin of warm water, soap and an ashtray?" she asked. *Ashtray?* Vera wondered.

"You can find all of that in the bathroom at the end of

the hall," Vera responded, slightly bent over, and rubbing her belly. "There's an... er... ashtray in the front room. Through there." She pointed to the door across the hall from the front bedroom.

"Right! Let's get you comfortable now. Is this your bedroom here? Come on then, off with your clothes and get a nightie on. Get yourself into bed and I will be back in just a tick." The midwife returned with the items she needed and had already lit a cigarette which dangled from the side of her mouth. She set everything down and propped Vera up with pillows before beginning her examination.

"Hmmm. Yes, well, looks like we have some time to go yet." She glanced at her watch. "Let's see if we can move things along a bit."

Vera felt the midwife prodding and pushing and amazingly felt relief from the waves of contractions and pain. She followed the instructions from the midwife as she told her to relax, rest and, as time progressed, to push. The woman smoked continuously, lighting a new cigarette soon after one was smoked down to a stub. A blue haze began to hang in the air. When Maurice returned home with his customary honk, honk, on the horn, the midwife met him at the door.

"Vera is in labour," she informed him. "It won't be much longer now. I suggest you pop down your local and have a pint or two. Come back in an hour." Maurice hesitated on the doorstep. He was anxious to see Vera but not interested in being witness to her discomfort or the business of childbirth at all. It was not the place for a husband to be. So, he pivoted, thanked the woman, and walked away.

The baby was born about a half hour later. When Maurice returned, he found the bedroom to be in good order with his wife sitting up in bed holding a tiny, little bundle. The midwife was packing up her bag and giving her parting instructions.

"Now, you stay in that bed for a few days. No housework. Drink plenty of fluids. I will be back next week to check on you." Turning to Maurice she added, "She could do with a nice cup of tea."

"Yes, ma'am. Right away."

Maurice sat cautiously on the edge of the bed after the midwife had let herself out. "He peered at the baby sleeping in Vera's arms and leaned over to kiss it gently on the cheek. He kissed Vera and asked, "Well? Is it Jeffrey or Ruth?"

"It's Ruth. Another little girl."

"Imagine that! Won't Frances be happy?"

"Yes. And I have saved all Frances's baby clothes. We shouldn't have to buy much."

"Isn't she beautiful?" Maurice gazed at his new daughter in amazement. "How do you feel, Vera?"

"I really feel quite good, Maurice. I didn't have much pain at all. I can't believe how easy it was this time."

"Wonderful! Well… I'd better get that cup of tea."

"That will be lovely, thank you. Oh, before you go," she added gazing up at the haze hanging in the air, "would you mind opening a window?"

Ruth did not appear to be a very content baby. She cried long and hard throughout the day and night. Vera and Maurice took turns pacing with her, comforting her trying to settle her without much success. After a few days, they were worn out and frustrated. A visiting neighbour, Susan, with whom Vera had become quite friendly, stopped by to take a peek at the baby and Vera told her about the constant crying.

"Are you breast feeding?" she asked.

"Yes."

"Any problems with it?"

"Well, my breasts are rather painful and swollen and the baby stops and starts during a feeding and cries then too."

"Hmmm," said Susan. "Just a moment. I'll be right back." The neighbour dashed out of the door and returned ten minutes later with a baby bottle of warm National Dried Milk. "Try this." Vera took the bottle and put it to the baby's mouth. Ruth sucked on the nipple greedily. She drank down the entire bottle without stopping and promptly fell asleep. Vera laid her down in the soft pink carry cot with a grateful sigh.

"I don't think you are producing milk, Vera. At least not enough to satisfy the baby and I think you had better call the doctor about your nursing problem. You could have an infection that needs attention."

"I think you must be right. I have been feeling rather feverish. Thought I was overtired, but I will have the doctor round. Thank you ever so much, Susan. I expect she will be a bottle-fed baby from now on."

Later that day, Charlotte brought Frances home. Ruth was still fast asleep in the cot. Frances peered over the side at her sister, a tiny little person wrapped up nice and warm, sleeping contentedly. Charlotte smiled down at her fifth granddaughter and chuckled to herself when she remembered Walter's exclamation when he was informed of her birth. "What! Another girl. Would have liked to get at least one grandson!" Charlotte walked down to the telephone box for Vera, to call the doctor and she returned to inform Vera that he would be stopping by later in the afternoon. "Thank goodness!" Vera answered with relief. "I should have realised that something was wrong."

Vera gave the baby another bottle that night, which Ruth sucked down as eagerly as she had the first. They all slept well, especially Vera who was quite sleep deprived, until Maurice was awakened by the sounds of choking from his baby daughter. He leapt out of bed, picked up the infant and held her upside down by her legs before placing her over his shoulder and patting her on her back. The baby's throat cleared, and she breathed comfortably again. Her little stomach had not been able to handle the large quantity of milk that she had gulped down. Vera woke as Maurice was tending to Ruth.

"Is she all right Maurice? What happened?"

"She's all right now, dear. She was choking. I think we need to put a little less milk in her bottles from now on. It was just too much for her to handle." Maurice would remind Ruth many times in the future that he had indeed, saved her life that night.

Thirty days later, Maurice drove the bus into London to answer the summons to a sub-court of The Old Bailey. He had consulted with a solicitor who reviewed the case and agreed to represent Maurice in court and was quite confident that the case would be decided quickly and favourably. Before he departed, Maurice told his wife that if they won the day, he would honk his horn as he turned onto Hamlet Road to declare the victory. Vera kept busy in the house to keep from fretting too much, but she could not help worrying about the outcome if they should lose. What would the judgement be? What reparations would they have to pay to Mr. Conway? How big a setback would it be to their finances and the business? Ruth was thriving on the National Dried Milk and she, herself, was completely recovered so all was in good order in her private world. If only she did not have the court case to worry about.

Vera had just settled Frances down for her nap and fed a warm bottle to Ruth when the doorbell rang. She laid the baby in her cot and answered the door. Mrs. Robinson stood on the doorstep holding an envelope. "Oh, hello, Mrs. Brown, sorry to disturb you. I know you must be busy with the new baby and all, but I am collecting for poor Mrs. Shea… you must have known her, she lived at number 6, and she was always pottering around in her garden… well, I'm sorry to say she died two days ago and …" Just then the bus turned the corner onto the street and a loud honking commenced. Vera clasped her hands together joyfully as she watched the bus approach. "Oh, *wonderful*! How wonderful!" she said. "Oh, I'm so happy! What a relief!" Mrs. Robinson stood frozen in place watching the young woman in the throes of joy. "Oh dear, I'm sorry Mrs. Robinson. Poor Mrs. Shea… er… just a minute." Vera hurried from the door to find her purse and returned to drop a contribution into the envelope. Mrs. Robinson, suitable dressed all in black, frowned as the bus pulled into the drive and Vera danced over to greet her husband. *Really!* She thought. *Young people today!*

The news could not have been better. Not only had the higher court found in their favour but the award of one shilling per year to be paid to Mr. Conway had been rescinded in the judgement. According to the judges after hearing all the testimony, they noted that Mr. Brown had done everything in his power to remedy the situation and that Mr. Conway had done nothing to change the contours of his property to alleviate the problem. They declared that rain is an "act of God," and the matter was dismissed.

"You should have seen Conway's face, Vera. He was fuming. The judgement was not what he expected at all."

"He's a miserable so and so. I shan't even look his way if I see him outside."

"Oh, not me, Vera," Maurice chuckled. "I will go out of my way to smile, wave, and wish him a cheerful good day every single time I see him."

The young family enjoyed living in their lovely bungalow for another year. Florrie and Ted visited often on weekends as did Charlotte and Walter. The two sets of grandparents became differentiated with the names, Nana Ted and Uncle Ted, and Nana Bindle and Grandad and would be called as such by their granddaughters for the rest of their lives. "Bindle" was a nickname given to Charlotte by Walter. It was based on a fictitious literary character. Walter thought it was funny and the name stuck. Charlotte was never called Charlotte by Walter. He always called her Bindle or May. Vera had finally come to terms with Ted. She realised that her mother was happy to have him in her life and that they had become quite devoted. She still felt some pangs of regret that her father could not know and enjoy his grandchildren, but Ted was pleasant and sociable, and the two older couples were becoming quite good friends. That last year living on Hamlet Road was a most happy one for Vera.

CHAPTER FIFTEEN

Maurice came home one day in in the spring of 1955 with a new venture in mind. When the children had been put to bed that evening, he sat with Vera to discuss the idea.

"I think perhaps it is time to move on from the mobile shop on wheels, Vera. It has been quite profitable for us, but I am thinking that having a traditional shop is now what we need. I've heard about one that is available, and I have been to take a look at it."

"Oh? Is it here in Romford? That *would* be nice, wouldn't it? You would still have to make a weekly journey to Covent Garden, I suppose, but customers would come to you so it would eliminate the rounds."

"Well… no, it's not in Romford. It is an established greengrocer shop available for lease in Aveley.

"Aveley? I have heard of it. Where is it?"

"It's about twenty miles away. South of here."

"Oh. I suppose that's not too bad, but you will spend a lot of time on the road, what with going to Covent Garden once a week and going to the shop and back and forth every day. Don't you think we should look for a shop closer to home?"

"Well… you see, this one is available now. Dad had a look at it with me and will help me get it going. It is in a parade of shops and so it will draw a lot of shoppers. We drove around the area. Not another greengrocers in the vicinity. We think it will do well."

"I don't know… it seems just too far away."

"Yes, well… there is a flat above the shop as part of the lease. We would live there."

Vera was taken aback. A horrible thought occurred to her. "Live there! Are you saying…?"

"Yes. We would move there and live in the flat. It is a nice flat, big and spacious."

"*Leave our house*! Leave here? Oh, Maurice, how could we? This is our home. We saved for so long for the plot and you practically built the house yourself… oh, I just couldn't."

"Now dear. Come with me tomorrow. We'll go and look at it together. I think it is a fantastic opportunity. Dad and I are quite excited about it."

"Oh dear, oh dear, oh dear." Vera moaned. "I just can't believe this."

"Never mind. Don't fret. We'll go and have a look and then talk about it some more. We must be willing to take a bit of a chance sometimes, make a move, try something new."

"Yes… but leave our home, our new house."

"Yes. Perhaps we must."

Vera knew that Maurice had already made up his mind. He picked up the key from an agency office and showed her the shop and the shelves and storage bins for display. He showed her the serving counter, scales and cash register and the storage room in back complete with washing facilities and toilet. They walked along the parade of shops: a fish mongers, butcher shop, bakery, shoe shop, toy store and chemist. Then, he showed her the flat. It was indeed quite large and in good condition, but Vera could only think of her beloved bungalow with the nicely landscaped garden now in full bloom. The flat had a concrete balcony off the kitchen which overlooked a small grassy area, rutted with tracks where delivery vans and lorries supplied the parade of shops. This would be her daughters' play area. She could see a small group of scruffy looking boys kicking a ball around, raising dust as they raced across the bare earth.

Maurice was excited and eager to move onto his new endeavour. Vera decided, with great sadness and trepidation, that she could not possibly thwart his ambitions, and would give him her complete support. So, the bungalow on Hamlet Road was put up for sale, sold quickly, and the move was made to the shop with the flat above in Aveley, Essex.

Walter helped his son for several months. They remodelled the interior of the shop to improve the displays, cleaned and swept and painted to brighten it up. They carefully selected the fruit and vegetables and arranged them appealingly in colourful displays. There was already a good customer base. The parade of stores serviced an extensive area, so the foot traffic was quite steady, and the shop was busy. Some weeks Maurice or Walter had to make a second trip into London to keep up with demand. They came up with the idea of featuring an eye-catching display when they got special produce: "Oranges from Spain," "Bananas from Colombia," "Cherries from Turkey." They tacked a world map on the wall and tacked a picture of the featured produce in the country of origin. Maurice's friendly, outgoing personality was a definite asset. He chatted easily with his customers, kidded them, and remembered their names. The business did very well. When it was obvious that the shop would be successful and that Maurice no longer needed his help, Walter decided to get a greengrocer shop of his own. He and Charlotte drove around for several weeks to check out listings of vacant shopfronts. Walter was surprised at the willingness of his wife to consider moving from Chingford, but she had already been thinking about moving from Hurst Avenue.

The house was now too big for the two of them. She had so loved the bungalow that Maurice had built on Hamlet Road and wanted one like it. There was a parade of shops in Hockley that appealed to Walter. It was a bigger parade than the one in Aveley with shops on both sides of the street and buses that stopped there on their routes steadily throughout the day. They looked around the little town and were impressed with its beauty, peace, and charm. It was not too far from Chingford, about thirty-eight miles east, nearer to the coast and the resort town of Southend-on-Sea. This is where they decided to go. Within a few months, Walter was up and running in his own shop and he and Charlotte had bought a lovely, small bungalow nearby. It did not take long for Walter to redesign the garden to make it a showplace of colourful blooms. Since he did not need to bother growing vegetables anymore, he focused on perennials, planting bulbs and shrubs that would yield flowers at all different times of the year. It was a happy move for both.

Vera tried her best to settle into the flat. She was busy enough with the two girls but could not stop comparing her new surroundings with her beloved bungalow. She just did not feel at home and was quite hesitant getting to know the town and the residents. She thought that perhaps she should have put up more resistance to Maurice's decision to move from Romford. She would have been content to stay there and take more time to find a shop location close by. But Maurice was as happy as a lark, whistling as he went about his work. She brought his lunch downstairs each day and watched him for a while. He greeted his customers like old friends, bantering back and forth with them as he served them, ringing up the purchases on the cash register with complete satisfaction. Vera heard the clicking and the ringing of the till as the chimes of his success and the knell of her loss.

While dusting one day when the girls were sleeping, feeling melancholy, but with her mind clear of any thoughts other than the task at hand, Vera felt a presence over her right shoulder. She turned and gasped to see her father's face watching her with a concerned expression. She stepped back in shock and fear and the apparition disappeared with a soundless pop leaving her standing there breathing raggedly and trembling. Vera dashed down the stairs to the shop calling out to Maurice. She rushed up to him white faced and panting.

"Vera! Whatever is the matter?"

"I've just seen my father! He was right beside me… looking at me. He looked so real, Maurice. So real."

"Oh, now dear," Maurice said taking her into his arms and patting her back comfortingly, "the mind can play amazing tricks on us. Calm down. You just imagined him. It's all right. It's all right."

"He was so real… looking at me with such a worried look. I stepped back from him, Maurice. I was so startled, and he just disappeared in an instant."

"Must have been a daydream, dear. Try not to fret about it. Now, why don't you make us a nice cup of tea and maybe a biscuit, eh?"

Vera thought a lot about the episode during the following few days. She found herself glancing over her shoulder often and remembering his anxiety as he regarded her. Although it must have been her subconscious bringing Sidney's visage to her so clearly, she was thoughtful of his expression. He was worried about her. Why? The only possible reason was because she was so miserable. She *was* miserable. She was consumed with resentment, sadness, lethargy, and displacement. All the insecurities of the war years, the moving, resettling, adjusting again and again, had returned to her with this move to Aveley. She thought of her mother and how much she had faced, endured, and suffered during those years. However, Florrie had never succumbed to misery. She must have had her moments of great sorrow and frustration, but she carried on without complaint, making the best of things for herself and her daughter. Vera felt a degree of shame and thought perhaps, that her father was looking at her with concern but maybe also with puzzlement. Was he wondering why his daughter was so unmotivated, so unwilling to be venturesome in her life, allowing herself to wallow in gloom? She felt that she owed it to him, to his memory, to his love for her, to buck up! She would shake off her despondency and move on. Though she would often think back on her father's apparition in the future and would struggle again through hard times, he never again reappeared to her.

Frances turned five years old in 1956 and started school. The brick, Victorian building was not far from the flat and Vera walked with her on her first day, navigating the route along the surrounding streets. She chatted cheerfully to her nervous daughter, introduced Frances to the teacher and departed. Frances settled in with no difficulty. She already was a good reader, rather shy and eager to please. The classroom, though, was austere with heavy wooden desks arranged in rows facing the front of the classroom. At such a young age, students were placed at the desks in order of their ranking according to the quality of their marks and ability. Each week the teacher stood at the front of the room and announced the new order. Students had to gather their belongings and shuffle around the room to their new position. Frances dreaded these days and the visual statement of successes and failures.

Frances soon discovered that there was a shortcut back and forth to school, behind the parade, across the field, and down a short trail. She tagged along with other children from the parade and began playing with the local children more and more. Maurice bought her a pair of roller skates and helped her get her balance and learn the technique. She took to it quickly and was soon speeding up and down the parade. Ruth was rather put out, however. She was confined to her pram outside the store as Frances enjoyed her new-found freedom and friends.

"*Sarsee! Sarsee!*" she would call, loudly and indignantly, demanding the attention of her sister. *Sarsee* was as close as she could get to pronouncing "Frances."

Vera noticed that Frances's interaction with the local children had caused her to pick up a bit of a cockney accent and slang. She had been so careful to speak to her with clear, accurate pronunciation and encourage her to use the correct grammar and words with an elegant accent. She continued this effort, cringing silently whenever she heard a crude word or pronunciation and correcting her daughter every time that she uttered an offensive word or phrase within her hearing. She knew that she was a bit of a snob in this regard, but she could not help herself.

Some of the regular, repeat customers at the shop would see Vera from time to time and would chat for a while. They often had young children in tow and the young mothers would have a lot to talk about and share with each other. One family became quite friendly, and they began to meet socially. Vera was happy to have a friend nearby, especially since the children got along together so well. They even went camping together a few times. The family had a little girl Frances' age who came over to play. In the summer, Vera discovered that she could make a fun wading pool on the veranda. It was made of concrete and had a six-inch lip around the perimeter to which the surrounding railing was fastened. The drain in the centre could be blocked up and Vera could fill the veranda with water. The children were delighted with it and played for hours in the water.

In 1958 Maurice heard from his father that a shop was available in Leigh-on-Sea, Essex. The location was not far from Hockley. He also heard that a new development of houses in a town called Rayleigh, which bordered Hockley, were nearing completion. He mentioned it to Vera.

"Fancy going to have a look?" he asked.

"Well… yes… but I can't believe you are thinking of another location. I thought you were happy with the way things were going here. The shop has done quite well."

"It has but this isn't the only place where we can be successful. Might be a new opportunity for us and I didn't think you wanted to live over a shop forever."

"No… I really don't." Vera's hopes began to rise. "When can we go?"

The move happened quickly. The lease on the Aveley shop was coming up for renewal and Maurice informed the owner that he would not be continuing on. Their shop and home in Aveley had lasted for three years. He leased the shop in Leigh-on-Sea and he and Vera bought a semi-detached house on Woodlands Avenue in Rayleigh. As it happened, Maurice's sister, Eileen and her husband, Ray, were looking for a house in the same area. The two couples approached the builder informing him that they planned to buy two of the new houses and he offered them a modest discount. The street was a dead-end "banjo" with a raised grassy island at the end around which the road circled. One side of the street was completely built up and the other side was partly finished. There was a large open field where the last of the houses would be constructed. Maurice and Eileen's houses were not next door, there were several semi-detached units between and a lot of young families moving in. It was early in the year 1958.

Vera was immediately at home in her new house. It was reminiscent of the bungalow in that it was built of brick, had a low, brick wall across the front garden with a wrought iron gate, and a path leading up to the front door. There was a large entry hall with stairs leading up to the second floor. The formal, front room was on the left of the entry hall. At the back of the hall a door opened into the dining/sitting room where there were double doors opening onto the back garden. The kitchen was through a door on the left. Upstairs there were three bedrooms a bathroom and separate toilet, as well as a large storage room at the top of the stairs. There was a fireplace in the front room and the dining room, and a small electric heater built into a wall in the master bedroom. Central heating had not become a standard feature in most homes at that time. The kitchen was modern and equipped with a deep sink, many cabinets, a large gas range, a long countertop, a coal stove in the corner for heat and a walk-in pantry. A door off the kitchen opened to a side yard which was wide enough to be a driveway. The back garden was deep and grassy and full of potential. In the spring, Vera planted roses along the front path and created flower beds in the front and back of the house. She loved the house and the neighbourhood and soon became friendly with many of the families on the street. She bought a second-hand piano which looked grand against a wall in the front room. She had hopes that one of her daughters had inherited Florrie's gift of music. Both girls took piano lessons from Mrs. Talmadge on Eastwood Road in Rayleigh for a couple of years. Although Frances earned a certificate, taking an examination in London at the Royal Academy of Music, neither girl had a natural gift nor were not interested in continuing lessons so eventually the piano was sold.

Frances was seven years old, and Ruth was four when they moved in, and they soon discovered that there was a vast assortment of playmates with whom to play. It was a quiet, safe little dead-end street, a perfect playground for young children. Vera and Maurice's semi-detached house was attached on the right side to a mirror image home where the Halls lived, Ken and Eileen Hall and their daughters, Janet and Diane. Janet was a year younger than Frances, and Diane was Ruth's age. On the left of the house, on the other side of the driveway area, was the right side of another semi-detached unit. The Lundbechs, Ray, Hazel, Deborah, and Nicholas had moved in shortly after Maurice and Vera. On the left side of their unit, lived the Coxes, Ted, Lil, Gillian, and Pauline.

Woodlands Avenue was idyllic. The house was attractive, bright, spacious, and comfortable. The neighbours were mostly young and friendly and a happy community. Great friendships began, especially between the Brown family, Lundbech family, and Cox family. The children played outside during all seasons and weather. They played in small groups quietly with dolls, skipping ropes, marbles, and board games, and in large groups organizing games such as "Capture the Flag," "What's your Shop, Mr. Pop," "Simon Says" and "Spud". Often the girls would stretch a rope across the road from one pavement to the other for group skipping. They had to take turns turning the rope because it took a significant effort to keep the long rope circling. The empty field across the street was a wonderful playground for exploring and adventure games. There was a large earth mound perfect for "King of the Castle" and far in the back, there was a dense thicket of blackberry bushes. In August, the children filled containers with the berries for their mothers who baked tarts and pies.

Pauline Cox was a year older than Frances and she started a club. It met once or twice a week in the shed at the end of her garden. There were games and arts and crafts and special events. She organised a special May Day with a king and queen of the May, a parade around the neighbourhood, and a maypole dance. Everyone dressed up in costume. Deborah Lundbech was Queen of the May, Tony Smith was King, and the rest of the children were all members of the royal court.

Maurice was disappointed with the shop at Leigh-on-Sea. He worked hard at it buying the produce that his customers requested, organising his displays using the tactics that had worked so well in Aveley, but the location just did not generate enough business. He realised it had been poorly chosen and after nine months he sold the business off. Luckily, he had secured a sales position with Wall's Sausage and Pie Company, working in the Essex area around Rayleigh. This was a perfect position for him, and he built up sales significantly, earning a respectable salary.

Vera was very content at this time in her life. With Maurice's new job at Wall's, she felt settled and secure and found Rayleigh to be a delightful town. Both girls were now in school. They attended Love Lane School, walking the twenty minutes there and back every day with the group from Woodlands Avenue. It was a short walk into town also. Vera walked down Woodlands Avenue to Daws Heath Road and then crossed the road to a narrow alleyway that cut through to Eastwood Road. There were shops there, but most were on High Street further along. High Street was a long road on a slight incline. At the top of the road the historic and magnificent Trinity Church stood with its impressive, crenelated tower. High Street became especially wide in the centre of town because centuries before it had been on a route for drovers moving cattle and livestock. Rayleigh was a stop on the route and became a market town requiring pens and corrals for the animals. Inevitably, Vera would bump into neighbours and friends while shopping and would stop for a chat or maybe pop into the little café with the red and white checked curtains on the windows, for a cup of tea and a quick bite. As the friendship grew with Hazel and Ray Lundbech and Lil and Ted Cox, the three couples enjoyed spending time together and would often get together for a singsong. Ray played the piano by ear and had a deep, pleasant singing voice, so the gathering was often at the Lundbechs' house with hours of music, song, and laughter. The children would play in another room usually around the table with a board game, a bag of crisps and fizzy drinks and the inevitable arguments and squabble. Once or twice, for whatever reason, the piano was moved from the Lundbechs to one of the other homes. There was a big production of creating a ramp for it to roll down over the front steps and then it was pushed down the garden path and up the garden path of one of the neighbours, on the ramp again over the steps into the front room. Several more neighbours joined the parties as they came to know each other better and as the children's play group expanded.

Hazel and Vera joined the Women's Institute which was held in town at the church on Crown Hill. There, they met more women in Rayleigh of all ages, backgrounds, interests, and abilities. It met once a week and was a wonderful opportunity to learn from each other, share stories, live up to their mission to be of help in the community, learn how to become an efficient housewife and plan some special events. They planned teas and games and children's activities, Christmas parties and jumble sales. They baked and cooked to feed the needy, made arts and crafts and donated any proceeds to a charitable organisation. One event planned by the group was square dancing lessons to which husbands were invited. Maurice and Ray were coerced into attending and the two couples attempted to follow the steps. They were hopeless, ending up collapsing in laughter as they turned the wrong way, bumped into each other, and completely disrupted their square. The other members of their square were not amused and glared at them for making such a mess of it. The two couples exited early to have a good long laugh at the pub.

It was not long before the husbands of the ladies of the Women's Institute decided that a Men's Club would be a good idea and so Maurice and Ray headed up the effort with many husbands joining eagerly. The meetings were usually held in a pub in town and became a fun night out providing a chance to relax, enjoy a pint or two and share a joke. The club focused on organising outings for the families in the summer, hiring a coach (bus) for the day and selecting a seaside location. What fun the outings were! The children were ready with their buckets and spades, bathing costumes, and inflatable toys early that day. Mums packed picnics and towels and Dads brought sport equipment for the beach: cricket sets, soccer balls and rounders bats and balls. Everyone prayed for a warm, bright, sunny day. On the coach, there and back, there was a constant stream of singing. People called out titles and everyone joined in. Children's favourites were, *"One Man Went to Mow," "Ten Green Bottles," "There Was an Old Woman Who Swallowed a Fly," "Old MacDonald," "Cockles and Mussels,"* and *"How Much is That Doggie in the Window."* Adults enjoyed *"My Old Man's a Dustman," "Any Old Iron," "Boiled Beef and Carrots," "Men of Harlech,"* and *"I Do Like to Be Beside the Seaside."* Some of the destinations were Clacton-on-Sea, Walton-on-the-Naze, Margate, and Ramsgate. Upon arrival, the group would survey the beach and pick out a suitable location for the large group. And then everyone settled in for a wonderful day. It was a day of merriment and fun. The children were jubilant racing into the waves, digging in the sand and searching for beach treasures. Before long, Maurice organized a game of rounders on the beach and many joined in, adults and children, as the group was divided into teams and the competition began. When it was time to eat, sandwiches, crisps and drinks were produced. There were booths along the seafront selling tea, ice cream, cockles and all sorts of souvenirs and beach toys. The adults bought themselves tea, coffee, and beer while the children enjoyed an ice cream cone with a swirl of soft ice cream slowly dripping down their hands onto the sand. More games followed in the afternoon, swimming and splashing in the waves and floating on the inflatables, followed by a sand sculpture competition. The children divided into groups and worked excitedly on their design, hoping to win a prize. It was not until the sun was sinking low on the horizon that the group began to gather their belongings, brush off the sand from their children's legs and feet and trudge over to the meeting point where the coach waited to take them home. The busload sang all the way home and then walked home from Rayleigh town centre through the soft, dark night. The outing excursions were the perfect summer days and provided a lifetime of memories.

On Fridays, after school, in the late afternoon, Vera walked with the girls into town where they caught the eastbound bus. There was a bus stop in Hockley not far from Charlotte and Walter's home. Maurice would meet them there after work and they would spend the evening. Charlotte always prepared a delicious tea, usually a hot meal, salad, fruit, cheese and crackers, and cream horns or cream meringues from the bakery. Tea would be followed by card games, "Chase the Ace" or "Newmarket." Pennies would be added to the kitty and regardless of who won, the winnings would be divided up at the end of the game between Frances and Ruth. After cards, Charlotte made another pot of tea and produced a box of chocolates which was passed around while they watched television for an hour or so. There was usually a *game show, "Take Your Pick" or "Twenty Questions" or an American western, "Rawhide" or "Wagon Train."*

Florrie and Ted came to visit at Woodlands Avenue quite often. Ted had recently splurged on the purchase of a car, allowing the couple to become very mobile. Both still worked, so visits were restricted to weekends once a month or so. The older couple became a favourite with Ray and Hazel as well at Lil and Ted Cox and it was always a lively, fun-filled visit. They were also able to visit Lylie, Hettie, and Grace as well as Ted's sister in Bath who was bringing up his daughter, Pearl. Sometimes Vera took Frances and Ruth to Chingford on the bus to spend the afternoon and evening with Florrie and Ted. The girls enjoyed rummaging through a large wooden bench, which served also as a storage chest, in Florrie's foyer. Florrie kept toys, books and dress up clothes in it for their visits. Ag's head would loom over the banister upstairs when she heard the children arrive. Florrie would whisper to them, "Go on. Go up and visit for a little while." The girls climbed the stairs hesitantly. Ag was pleasant enough, but she was rather tall and willowy, and the children were quite intimidated by her when she appeared so suddenly from on high. The girls also enjoyed playing darts in the conservatory and playing in the back garden, skipping, and hiding on the narrow paths that wound around the property and behind the black currant bushes at the back. Florrie and Vera indulged in a long "chinwag" catching up on all their news while Florrie prepared a nice, big meal and a fruit tart for dessert.

One Guy Fawkes night the men's club decided to have a communal celebration. The plan was to build a large bonfire in the empty field on Woodlands Avenue and have a huge firework display with all the families contributing their collection of fireworks to the pot. Prior to the big event, the assortment of "guys" made by the children, were lined up in Mr. Hall's garage for judging. A judge was selected, and he went about the business of inspecting the stuffed creations most seriously. Frances was the winner and received a large box of chocolates as her prize. The "guys" were then carried over to the field. When the bonfire was lit that 5th November, it burned big and bright and everyone cheered as, one by one, the "guys" were committed to the flames. When the fireworks started, the dads were in their element setting off bottle rockets, roman candles, crackers, coloured smoke bombs, squealers, Roman Candles, and Catherine Wheels. Maurice had built the wooden frame for the Catherine Wheels and there were several spinning at the same time. The children waved sparklers while watching the spectacular illuminations and they gasped at the loud bangs, crackles, and booms. Potatoes in their jackets were wrapped in foil and cooked at the base of the bonfire, as well as chestnuts, and hot chocolate was passed around to everyone. During the evening, while Maurice was holding a firework waiting to light it, a spark set it off in his hand. His middle finger was burned quite badly causing it to be open and raw. He rushed home and it was Frances who removed the paper and debris from the wound with a pair of tweezers. Vera and Ruth felt faint at the sight of it. After antiseptic cream was applied, it was wrapped up in gauze and tape. Maurice was impatient during the whole process.

"Come on... hurry up. That's enough! Wrap it up now. Let's get back across the road."

The celebration was continued at The Weir, a large pub within walking distance, where a separate room was reserved for the occasion. Pauline had organised her club members to develop a variety show to perform at The Weir as a thank you to their parents for the special event. She created several acts including singing, skits, comedy and dance. The club members participated in several rehearsals during the weeks prior and Pauline created a program to hand out before the show started, listing the acts and the names of all the children as well as a statement, "*We should like to say a very big thank you to our parents for this evening.*" The show started off with "The Toyshop - What Happens After Dark in the Toyshop." All the children were involved and in costume for the act. Several other acts followed, entertaining the adults who laughed and applauded at all the antics.

The following day the neighbourhood children scoured

the field for the remains of the fireworks and to see how far the rockets had travelled. They read out any names that were distinguishable on the wrappers and casings, reliving the glory of the night. 5th November 1962 was the best Guy Fawkes night ever!

One Man Went to Mow

One man went to mow,
Went to mow a meadow,
One man and his dog (Spot)
Went to mow a meadow.

Two men went to mow,
Went to mow a meadow,
Two men, one man and his dog (Spot)
Went to mow a meadow.

Three men went to mow,
Went to mow a meadow,
Three men, two men, one man and his dog, (Spot),
Went to mow a meadow.

Four men went to mow,
Went to mow a meadow,
Four men, three men, two men, one man and his dog, (Spot),
Went to mow a meadow.

Five men went to mow,
Went to mow a meadow,
Five men, four men, three men, two men, one man and his dog, (Spot),
Went to mow a meadow.

(Continue on to ten men.)

Oh, I Do Like to be Beside the Seaside

Oh! I do like to be beside the seaside
I do like to be beside the sea!
I do like to stroll upon the Prom, Prom, Prom!
While the brass bands play: "Tiddely-om-pom-pom!"

So just let me be beside he seaside
I'll be beside myself with glee
For there's lot of girls besides,
I should like to be beside
Beside the seaside! Beside the sea!

CHAPTER SIXTEEN

The job at Wall's Sausage and Pie Company was going well for Maurice. For two years he built up the sales in his territory while supporting and servicing his customers efficiently. As always, his cheerful, friendly disposition created a pleasant working relationship. Store owners and managers appreciated his visits and deliveries and looked forward to seeing him. The company was very satisfied with the increase in sales which reflected in his wage packet. And then one day he was approached by the district supervisor with unwelcome news. The supervisor had decided to cut Maurice's territory in half. Maurice discovered later that a friend of the supervisor had been assigned the half that he had been required to forfeit. It was difficult for him to reconcile himself with this turn of events. He had performed well for the company, grown sales, maintained a healthy, professional relationship with his customers, provided outstanding service, and represented the company and its products proudly. He vented his frustration to Vera.

"I just don't understand this, Vera! After all the work I have done building up my route and making sure my customers are taken care of and satisfied! Now, I am expected to hand it over to this other fellow and have my wages cut in half! This is what happens when you work for other people and companies! *This is the thanks you get?* No! I won't accept it. *I just won't!*"

He felt terribly betrayed and was unable to continue in his diminished role. He decided that it was time to move on and gave his notice.

Vera was disappointed and shaken with the decision.

Her world wobbled again. She had so appreciated the calm and security that the job at Wall's had provided. She discussed it with her husband, suggesting that perhaps he would be able to grow his reduced territory in time or that there might be other opportunities to pursue in the company, but Maurice had already moved on in his mind and was looking for new opportunities. He was excited again about the prospects of a new venture and decided that he would like to own his own business again. He was disheartened with the time and effort he had expended for another company only to be unappreciated and treated so indifferently.

Maurice named the new venture "Dock to Shop." Vera, again, would manage the billing, expenses, records and bookkeeping. The business was a hauling operation which meant that a truck needed to be purchased and a telephone needed to be available in the home for incoming work calls. The day that it was installed in the entry hallway, Frances and Ruth stared at it apprehensively. They would walk by it, giving it a wide berth, so fearful that it might actually ring. Even Vera was unsettled by it. She was anxious that it was there, not wanting the intrusion, but at the same time, knowing that the calls meant contacts, work, and income.

However, work was slow. The business needed time and patience to get going which was not Maurice's strong point. He was always in a hurry for success and to reap the rewards of hard work and dedication. Maurice did not so easily charm the dock workers, and it was hard to break into the well-established hauling trade. The jobs he managed to obtain were not enough to support the house and family. The phone did ring, but Vera began to suspect that Maurice was taking on something more than just a load of potatoes or sacks of grain. He kept his voice low and there was no sign of his usual chattiness and cheer. This was serious, secretive business. He was gone for long periods of time, sometimes hauling from the London docks to Wales and to the far north of England. He became frustrated with road delays and the licences that were required for particular goods. Vera was unhappy and worried. What kind of a business was this? Maurice did not discuss much with his wife when he returned from a run. He was exhausted and sombre. Something was not right.

"I want you to give up this work," she said to him when he dragged through the door one day. He slumped in a chair, and she put a cup of tea on the table in front of him.

"Yes dear, I know. It's not working out, is it? I have one more job to do, that's all. Then I'll give it up."

"Don't do one more job. Finish with it now."

"Well… I have a commitment, dear. I really can't let these people down."

"*These people*… who are these people that you can't let down?"

"Now, never mind. Nothing you need to worry about. Just one more run, that's all."

"Oh, Maurice! I think you are up to your neck in something. Whatever it is, get out of it. No more "Dock to Shop" or whatever it has become!"

Maurice made his last run and ended the business. He had the telephone removed from the house and began his search for a new opportunity. The British economy was in a bit of a slump and in the throes of a recession, so it was a bad time to be out of work. In desperation, Maurice took a job as a coalman. He had to shovel coal into bags and make deliveries as the company advertised, "To Your Own Back Yard." Most everyone at that time had a coal bunker in the back garden and another bunker for coke. Coal was used in fireplaces to heat the home. Coke was more expensive but burned hotter and cleaner than coal and was preferable in stoves. After the coalman had prepared sacks for delivery, he had to drive to the customers and carry the sacks on his back to the coal bunkers. The sharp edges of the coal dug into the coalman's back and the coal dust became embedded in the wrinkles and creases of the face and around the nails of the hands. When Maurice arrived home after a day's work, he had to soak in the bath and Vera scrubbed his hands in an effort to remove the remnants of coal. She could never get his hands fully clean. Even wearing gloves, the dust and grit would find its way inside. Maurice was demoralised in the job. He felt that he had sunk to a personal low. There was no satisfaction, no chance to excel, no pride in a job well done. The menial work was purely so that he could earn money to pay his bills and feed the family.

Maurice continuously perused the job listings and applied to anything he thought that he was remotely qualified for. He was amazed when he was contacted by Jacob's Bakery Limited, inviting him for an interview for a merchandising position at their headquarters in Liverpool. The company provided train tickets and two nights' accommodation. It was January with heavy snow falling when Maurice boarded the train to Liverpool. He had little cash due to his recent struggles with employment. The soles of his shoes here worn through, allowing water and snow to seep in. Vera had covered his feet and socks with plastic bags in an attempt to keep his feet dry and comfortable. She had ironed two shirts, packed a small suitcase, brushed off his suit, and made him sandwiches for the journey. She wished him luck and waited anxiously for him to return. They were in desperate straits. The job was sorely needed.

Maurice had a very pleasant trip on the train. He was traveling first class and had the good fortune to meet Sir John Gielgud, renowned British actor, who was seated in his compartment. They struck up a conversation during which Sir John discussed his career and Maurice told him of the job interview. Before they went their separate ways, Sir John handed Maurice a ticket to his next evening's performance. The following day Maurice reported to the Jacob's office for his interview. As always, his easy, friendly manner impressed the interview team as well as his experience in retail and sales. He was then taken to a room which was stocked with boxes of the full range of Jacob's products and was asked to make an eye-catching window display using them. He was given a time limit and then left alone to create his presentation. Maurice studied the assorted packages of biscuits, crackers, and snacks and laid a package of each shape on the table to spark an idea. Most of the packets were long rectangles but some were long cylinders and shorter snack-size tubes and squares. The long cylinders reminded him of something and soon he was busy building on the table. He used almost all the product that was available to him and finished just before his time was up. When the interviewers returned, they were stunned. Maurice had created an impressive battleship. It was instantly recognizable with its long cannons made from the cylindrical packets, the shape of the hull made from the rectangular cream cracker packets and the detail above deck made from the smaller snack packets. He had even created a flag from a wrapper proudly displaying the product name, *Jacob's*. It flew from the superstructure. He got the job on the spot.

Maurice was assigned a company van and given a

territory in the west end of London. He was delighted with the work, considering it to be quite prestigious and finding it interesting and creative. He was comfortable again, working a route, getting to know his customers, making new contacts, more sales and merchandising the product. His only complaint was that the salary was less than he had hoped for, but he expected that in time, he would earn increases.

A shiny red Jacob's van was at Maurice's disposal and was parked each evening in the garage which he had built when he had briefly owned a used Ford Zephyr during his time at Wall's Sausage and Pie Company. There was never any shortage of crackers or biscuits during the time at Jacob's and Maurice was able to pick up Vera and the girls in Chingford on his way home if they were there visiting Florrie. The salary, though, made it a struggle to live comfortably. The failed shop in Leigh-on-Sea and the "Dock to Shop" business had taken a toll and Maurice was still paying off debts that had accumulated from both ventures. They were living from hand to mouth.

Vera began to think about returning to work. She spoke to Hazel and asked her if she would mind keeping an eye on the girls when they returned home from school.
"Frances is eleven now so I think they will be alright alone for an hour or two before I get home from work, but if you could just check on them once or twice and help if they have any problems?"
"Of course I will, Vera. They can stay over here until you get home. The girls are usually playing together after school anyway. Where are you thinking of working?"
"Oh, somewhere in town. In an office hopefully. I haven't talked to Maurice about it yet, but honestly, Hazel, I

hardly think he can refuse. We need extra income."

"You have had a run of bad luck lately but, I'm sure it will work out. With your skill and experience, you should have no trouble getting an excellent job."

Maurice was reluctant. He was stuck in the mindset that a wife and mother should remain at home and that it reflected badly somehow on a man if his wife went out to work.

"I don't want you to work, Vera. I like to think of you at home taking care of the girls and managing the house. With my hours and working so far away, I would worry if you were at work too."

"I have already spoken to Hazel. She would be happy to keep an eye on the girls until I got home."

"That's very nice of her. But no, let's not make that decision. I have actually been thinking of another way out of our situation."

"Yes?"

"Well… I don't think you are going to like it, but it would put us right quickly and…"

"Oh, no Maurice. Oh no! Don't say it… please don't!"

"Now, Vera," Maurice chuckled, taking hold of her hand. "It is the sensible thing to do. The one place we have funds is in this house. We've lived here almost five years now and the value has increased quite a bit. We'll sell this house and find an older, less expensive house or maybe rent for a while. Don't worry… we'll stay right here in Rayleigh." Vera's eyes filled up with tears at the thought of leaving Woodlands Avenue, the neighbourhood, her friends and the house which she had come to cherish and love.

"I'd rather work and be able to stay here," she replied as her voice trembled. Maurice pulled her into his arms. "I know you would, dear, but we need to get out from under our debt more quickly that your working would allow us to do. Now, won't it be a relief? Aren't you tired of scrimping and worrying? We would be more comfortable and able to enjoy life more. We need to move on."

"Oh Maurice, I just don't think I can. I am very happy here. I thought we would stay here a long, long time and the girls, they will be so…" She gulped back a sob. "They will be heartbroken."

"They will get over it. They will still be going to the same schools, seeing their friends. They will be fine, dear. Besides, it's good for them to experience change and adjustment. That is life after all."

Vera stepped back from Maurice in anger. "Don't lecture me about change and adjustment. I've had just about all I care to have of that in my life. I may be convinced that your plan is necessary but do not use change and adjustment being good for them as part of your argument!" Maurice realised he had touched a nerve as Vera stormed off to the bedroom to have a good cry. He would leave her alone for a while. He knew she would come around eventually. She always supported him in the end.

Although Vera supported him in the move, it was indeed, time for her to get a job. This would be the compromise that Maurice would have to make. She discovered that the GPO, General Post Office, was hiring in London, and she applied. She was contacted for an interview. When she travelled into the city by train, and walked to the grand, imposing General Post Office building near St. Paul's Cathedral, she was reminded of those times, years ago, when she was part of the working crowd, and the feelings of excitement and purpose returned to her. The interview went well, and she was told that she would be contacted about a secretarial position. She did not know at the time, but the political backgrounds of herself and her close family were investigated because she would actually be working for three engineers who would be involved in secret work. When she started work, she was sworn to secrecy and took that oath very seriously. No details of what she learned were ever discussed with family or friends. The engineers worked at the Post Office building to conceal their special mission. They were involved in a project to put Britain's first satellite into orbit. These engineers collaborated with the United States, whose rockets would launch the satellite and the whole enterprise was kept confidential because the Russians were working on satellites of their own. The "space race" was in full swing. Vera enjoyed her work as a "secret writer" as well as the people she worked with. The Post Office employed a number of blind and disabled individuals. She struck up a friendship with a particular group of them. They were very competent in their work utilising Braille machines and typewriters and she was fascinated. They all had beautiful Labrador guide dogs who were so well-trained, sitting at their feet obediently and alert to their needs but also calm, placid, and affectionate.

Vera's income was helpful, but the house went up for sale and the girls had to be told. They were indeed devastated. Vera told them as gently as she could and emphasised that they would be staying in Rayleigh and that they would be able to walk over to Woodlands Avenue as often as they wanted to. It did no good. Their world was shaken and forever changed; the sweetness, the comfortable feeling of belonging, being part of the neighbourhood play group, waving and chatting to the adults who knew them so well, the house so much their own now, the garden, the red swing, everything so familiar and dear. The house sold quickly to the Sinclairs. It was not an outright sale. The deal was an exchange of houses. Mr. Sinclair lived on Brocksford Avenue, about a mile away. He had a small, tight bungalow with a value much less than the house on Woodlands Avenue, so Maurice received a cash amount as part of the deal. Mr. Sinclair came to the house for the final time before the closing with his large dog on a leash. Frances and Ruth stood in the entryway intimidated by the dog and resentful of the sale. Just as Mr. Sinclair was about to leave, the dog urinated on the welcome mat.

Vera tried not to compare her new home with the house on Woodlands Avenue. There was no comparison except that it was also a semi-detached unit. The rooms were small and pokey. The kitchen was not well equipped or comfortable in which to work. The linoleum floor was in poor shape, so Maurice pulled it up to reveal old newspapers spread out underneath. Vera washed the subfloor well as there was a lingering smell of dog and Maurice laid a new linoleum floor. He refreshed the interior with a new coat of paint and some nicer wallpaper. The wallpaper in one of the bedrooms was especially strange, depicting crying teddy bears. The little bungalow was improved but nothing could make up for less space. The feeling was tight and cramped. Vera and Maurice's bedroom had been added on as a dormer. The stairs leading up to it were accessed in the second bedroom downstairs. Not an ideal arrangement. It was also very cold in the upstairs room as three sides of the structure were exposed. A small paraffin heater was all that provided any warmth. The living room was small and doubled as a dining room. It had a fireplace; the only one in the house. The back garden was also small. There was a hedge bordering the property of the other semi-detached unit. An unfriendly elderly lady lived there. She looked over the hedge, scowling if the children were noisy playing outside. Vera did nothing to enhance the front or back garden. She just did not feel motivated. Maurice mowed and she only clipped and weeded the already established plantings to keep it looking tidy.

Frances moved up to high school where she made new friends and joined the netball team, and she became best friends with Hilary who lived on Bull Lane. She was enjoying more freedom now that she was a little older. She and Hilary often walked into town after school and had tea and a teacake at the little café or they went to Hilary's house to listen to records. They also rode their bikes around town and once, all the way out to Hockley to pop in and surprise Nana Bindle (Charlotte.) Ruth ended up having to change schools after all due to the relocation. At first, she was upset. She would not be in classes with Deborah at Love Lane but when she began attending Grove Road School, she quite liked it. It was a much more modern school than the old Victorian building that was Love Lane. She also liked her new teachers and their teaching style.

Visits continued with the families on Woodlands Avenue and Brocksford Avenue and the friendships remained strong, but it was bittersweet to return there for Vera. She could not bear to look at her old house or hear anything about the family living there. She was keen to invite her new blind friends to stay for occasional weekends in Rayleigh and introduce them all to the Lundbechs and Coxes. What a squeeze it was! The girls slept on quilts and cushions on the floor so that their two bedrooms were freed up for the visitors. There was Keith, Maureen, Rita, Rhoda, and George all around thirty years old and just delightful guests. They were such fun-loving people, very intelligent, with a keen sense of humour. Vera was constantly amazed at how they fully accepted their disability, not complaining about it at all, but living with it and enjoying life. They loved music, parties, puzzles and games. They attended concerts and fairs and travelled. They participated in anything they possibly could. Maurice was happy to have them. They were just his kind of people. When Ray, Hazel, Lil, and Ted came over to meet them it was a joyful evening of banter, games and song, and interesting discussion and debate on such a variety of topics. Sometimes, the whole group walked into town to a pub. The children were happily situated in the pub garden with the guide dogs to play and were treated to a steady supply of fizzy drinks and crisps while the adults enjoyed some drinks inside.

Keith amazed Vera most of all. When he arrived at the house, he walked slowly around for a while, feeling for doorways, furniture, and the layout of the rooms. Then, he was able to remember where everything was and walk around comfortably. He also wanted to try roller skating when the girls were playing outside. He strapped them on and took some time to get familiar with the new sensation of movement. Then, as the girls called out directions and warned of bumps and dips in the pavement as they ran along side, he skated off at good speed and with his usual confidence. The exciting job in the city and the new-found friends helped Vera cope with the disappointment of leaving Woodlands Avenue and the setback of her new home.

It was during a visit with the Lundbechs that a subject was first raised that would change all their lives significantly forever. Frances, Ruth, Deborah and Nicholas were occupied with a game outside while the adults chatted together. Vera mentioned that she had received a letter from her cousin Yvonne in the States. Yvonne had come for a visit to England back in 1958 with her oldest daughter, Barbara. She had come for the whole summer, spending time with her father, John Middleton, and visiting Florrie, Hettie and the Embersons, who had fostered her as a child. She had also stayed a week with Vera and Maurice and by extension, with Hazel and Ray. Maurice had enjoyed making fun of her American accent and colloquialisms and they had all been interested to hear about her life in America and how it compared with life in Britain. Yvonne had impressed them with the seemingly easier lifestyle, the plentiful jobs, the streamlined cars that most people seemed to have, the big refrigerators, the central heating and schools that continued to age eighteen, the prospect of college or university following. Vera told them that in her recent letter, Yvonne wrote that the summer weather was lovely and that she spent many days at the beach with the children. In the back "yard" they played badminton and volleyball and had "cookouts" on their charcoal grill. Barbara was thinking of attending the University of Connecticut when she graduated from high school, and they were contemplating where they would go on vacation. They would travel by car, maybe to Washington, D.C., or Boston or maybe up to a lake in New Hampshire. It all sounded so appealing to the two couples who could not help but compare it to their own lives.

"Good Lord!" exclaimed Ray. "What a life. Sounds wonderful, doesn't it?"

"Yes," replied Maurice. "Makes you wonder…"

"Wonder what?" Hazel laughed. "How we could all have a life like that?"

"Well... yes."

"My goodness, Maurice," said Ray. "Can you just imagine all that would be involved in moving to the States?"

"I don't know," Maurice laughed. "Other people have done it."

Vera felt a cold tingle rising up her spine. A dreadful thought began to take shape. She stood up quickly and said she would put the kettle on. "Maurice, get the cards out. What do we want to play? Sevensies? Newmarket?"

Nothing more was mentioned for a while about America. Vera was careful not to mention Yvonne or anything that could lead her husband's thoughts back to the letter and its description of life across the Atlantic. But she knew that a seed had been planted in Maurice's mind; a thought, an adventure, an opportunity, a new beginning. She knew the subject would come up again.

In July 1963, Maureen, one of the blind friends, wanted to take Frances and Ruth to see a ballet on the stage in London. She had grown close to the girls and talked to them at length about their hobbies and interests and wanted to do something special for them. Vera discussed it with Maurice, and they decided that the girls could travel into London on the train themselves. Arrangements were made that Maureen would meet them when they arrived at Liverpool Street Station under the big clock in the large concourse. Frances and Ruth had a wonderful day out. When they met Maureen, she took them on the Underground to Covent Garden and they enjoyed a lovely tea in a pretty, little tearoom including a large pot of tea, finger sandwiches and scones with butter, jam and clotted cream. The ballet was a matinee at the Royal Opera House in Covent Garden. The theatre was so impressive for the girls; the façade was glorious with its dramatic columns and the interior was so large and open with an ornate ceiling, several tiers of sweeping balconies and plush red seats. Swan Lake was performed, starring Margot Fonteyn and Rudolph Nureyev and it kept Frances and Ruth spellbound. Maureen went back with them to Liverpool Street Station and saw them onto their train. Frances felt very grown up, travelling back and forth to London in charge of her younger sister. At Rayleigh Station, the Jacob's van was waiting for them, and all the way home they related the details of the grand event to their parents. It was a day never to be forgotten.

A few weeks later, the Browns went over to the Lundbechs on Woodlands Avenue for a visit. While the children played together, the adults chatted, and the subject of America was raised again.

"The more I think about it," said Maurice, "the more I think we should look into it to find out what is required to emigrate."

"Oh, now wait just a minute…" Vera responded. "I didn't realise you have been seriously considering the idea."

"Good Lord, Maurice!" said Ray. "Are you actually thinking about it?"

"Well… maybe it's not such a crazy idea. Lots of people emigrate, after all. What motivates them? A better life, more opportunities, getting out of a rut? I just don't see much of a future for us here. We seem to have settled into our particular lot in life, we fit in a certain slot and that's where we are expected to stay. I would be excited to give it a try. Maybe set a five-year time frame. Come back after five years with new experiences and a fresh outlook and more to offer."

"Maurice, don't you like your job at Jacob's?" Hazel asked. "I thought you were quite happy with it."

"It's a nice job. I like the work, but the wages are just not enough, Hazel. It is going to be hard to get ahead there and I feel just so stuck not being able to anticipate advancement in spite of my best efforts."

"I know about the feeling of being stuck," Ray responded.

"But you have an excellent job, Ray," said Vera. "You are lucky to have a government job at The Inland Revenue. You are so secure there."

"Secure… yes, but I am bloody bored with it!"

"Oh, Ray!" said Hazel.

"Well, I am! I've been doing it for years."

"Look, let's just find out what is involved if we should ever want to emigrate. No decisions. Just information," Maurice suggested.

"Have you thought of everyone we would be leaving behind?" Vera was becoming agitated. "What about your parents, Maurice, and my Mum and Ted? What about our friends… and the girls… how will they feel about it? Leaving their friends, their schools, their grandparents? Everything they have ever known."

"Yes… yes, I know. But let's not get ahead of ourselves. Don't fret, Vera. We'll just find out what the procedure is, so we know what we are talking about. We won't say anything to the kiddies about it."

Vera knew that the seed was taking root. Maurice went to various agencies in London to ask questions and gather information, pamphlets, guides, and forms. He became more and more excited about the prospect of living in America. Ray made enquiries also and suggested that he and Maurice should apply for passports. "Not a bad idea to get them now, Maurice… just in case." It was when the passports arrived that Vera knew her life would change drastically. Looking at the official pages and the smiling photograph of her husband confirmed to her that the decision was final. They were moving on.

The next few months were unbearable for Vera. There were many meetings with Ray and Hazel discussing all the arrangements. Hazel seemed to be taking it in her stride. She was very matter-of-fact. "If it doesn't work out Vera… we can always come back." She was also happy to see Ray's enthusiasm and excitement of new prospects. She knew he had been unhappy in his job for a long time and just going through the motions every day. At this point in their lives, as they entered their forties, it was now or never. But Vera dreaded telling the girls and Florrie. She privately hoped something would occur to change Maurice's mind. Perhaps a huge promotion at work which would make him loath to leave the job. She talked to him about all the negative aspects that she could think of to no avail. It came down to resigning herself to a new life in America or refusing to go. When she thought about it in those terms, she decided, as always, to support her husband. She could not bear to force him to give up his dream and continue in his struggle to be successful in England. She would then have to live with the unspoken blame of their unsatisfactory existence. The only thing that she appreciated about the move was the fact that she would be leaving the pokey, little bungalow on Brocksford Avenue.

Florrie and Ted were coming for a visit and Vera decided that it was time to tell them of the plans. "We had better let the family know now. After all, Christmas is coming. It may be our last Christmas together and they should probably know before..." Her voice trailed off as she fought back tears. "Oh, Maurice, my poor Mum! How on earth will she handle this news?" Maurice comforted his wife and for the first time felt a twinge of doubt about his decision. It *would* be a huge wrench for Vera and Florrie, he knew, but surely it was for the best. "Mum and Ted will come and visit us. Just imagine how nice that will be. We'll tell them it's a five-year trial plan. Come on now, let's be positive about it."

Florrie and Ted sat stunned while Vera poured tea with a shaky hand. "Mum," said Vera. "We will probably be back. Don't know if we will like it there. We are hoping that you and Ted will come visit us soon after we are settled."

"Never flown in me life," Florrie responded, looking down at her lap.

"Then it's about time you did," Maurice chuckled. "The world is getting smaller, you know. People fly all over the place nowadays."

"What are you going to do over there for work, Maurice?" Ted asked.

"I've written to Bob, Yvonne's husband, and asked him if he could send me any job opportunities that he sees. Bob is in the advertising business and is a good writer. He is going to help me put together something he calls a "resume" which lists my credentials and experience. I expect I will find something quite quickly. Ray and I have been invited to stay with James and Evelyn for a while until we get jobs and places to live." James and Evelyn and their children had emigrated some years ago having been sponsored by Bob Porter.

"Sounds like you've got it all worked out, Maurice," Florrie said, dully. "Can't fault you for your courage and ambition, that's for sure. But... are you really going to give up on England?"

"Well, it's not that I am giving up, so to speak. It's just that the States is the place to be right now. It's thriving, growing and full of opportunity. We're going to try it for five years."

"I understand. I do. I don't blame you at all. It's just that…" The words caught in her throat, and she could not continue.

"Oh, Mum. I know… I know," Vera panted. But it's not for a while yet and you will come to see us there right away." The side door opened. "Oh, here come the girls. We haven't told them yet."

The visit continued calmly but without the usual easy banter and Florrie's ready laughter. However, the girls did not notice any undertone. They chatted away about school and friends and funny stories unaware of the bombshell that had just been dropped in their grandmother's lap.

The following week it was Charlotte and Walter's turn.

"You're bonkers, Maurice! Leaving dear old England?" said Walter.

"Oh… oh…" Charlotte gasped, dropping into a chair. Another round of explanation, assurances and attempted pacification of the "five-year plan" followed. Walter would not be mollified. "Well, that's it then! Maurice, your impulsiveness has no bounds. Think the grass is greener, eh? Well good luck to you!"

"Dad, now, I know this is a surprise, but I want to have a go over there. You'll come and see us."

"Not so likely!"

"Come on Dad… Mum? You will come, won't you?"

"I… oh… I can't take this in. I can't believe you want to do this. Oh, dear! Eileen and Ray have just moved down to Devon. We will have none of our family living near us anymore."

"Mum, Eileen and Ray are just a train ride away and soon you will be preparing to visit us in America. Imagine that!"

"I can't! I just can't imagine it!" Charlotte cried. Vera squirmed in her seat. She understood her mother-in-law's shock and dismay. Maurice was being so nonchalant about it, so offhand, like it was not a massive trauma to their lives. All he could see were the possibilities that waited for him and the prospects for a new and exciting life ahead. He was already halfway there in his own mind. He did not have much thought for who and what he was leaving behind.

"You will come and see us… lots of times," Maurice repeated, and then in a gentler tone, "I've got to try it, Mum. I'm getting nowhere here, and it has been a constant struggle. I am very optimistic that things will go well for me in America.

"Don't know what I would rather hope for," replied Charlotte quietly, almost to herself. "That you fail over there so that you come back, or that you succeed and live a better life all those miles away."

Maurice and Ray had interviews in London at the United States Embassy early in December. They were approved and issued their "green cards." They went to a travel agency to get quotes for travel to the U.S. and discovered that it was a good deal cheaper to travel by boat, so passage was booked on the SS Rotterdam for 22nd February 1964. They told Vera and Hazel that they would also travel by boat with the children when it was time for them to depart. With the plans and arrangements made, it was time to tell the girls.

Ruth was stunned and confused with the news. "But I

don't know anything about America!" she declared. "What is it like there? Where are we going to live?"

"Well, I am going to Connecticut where Auntie Yvonne lives, to a town called Fairfield. I will probably find a house somewhere near them. And I think you will find that America is a wonderful place. The country is so big and the roads and houses and gardens and cars... everything is bigger in America."

"The Lundbechs are emigrating too," Vera quickly added. "So, you will still have Deborah... and Nicholas to play with."

"Oh, really? Oh, do they know about it yet?"

"They are being told today too. But this is a secret between our two families at the moment. We don't want you to talk about it with anyone else," Maurice instructed.

"*I don't want to go!*" Frances declared. "How can we leave England? It is where we belong. And... oh, how can we leave Nana Bindle and Grandad and Nana and Uncle Ted! I've got my school, my friends... *no, I won't go!* You can all go! I will stay here. I'm not going!" Tears began to roll down Frances's impassioned face.

"Now Frances..." Maurice responded soothingly. "I know this is a bit of a shock to you. It will take some time to get used to the idea. Your grandparents will come out for some lovely, long visits and you will make lots of new friends. It will be a wonderful new life for us all."

"*I don't want a new life! I want to stay in this one!*" It was unusual for Frances to bark at her father or stand up to him, but she was so distraught and frightened at the prospect of the big move, that she could not help herself.

"I think you had better go down to your room and get hold of yourself," Maurice stated firmly. Frances spun around, flew out of the room, down the little hall to her bedroom. She flung herself onto her bed and sobbed into the pillow. Some time later, Vera entered the bedroom and spoke to her daughter with words of sympathy and understanding. She explained that she knew it would be hard for her to accept and adjust to the idea, but she justified the decision, maybe more to herself than to Frances, by talking about all the advantages of living in America and how lucky she was that her father had such an adventurous spirit. "A lot of people would just love to go there. Once you are there, you will soon settle in. Believe me… I know. I have had to do it many times." Frances was rather surprised by her mother's attention and effort to comfort her. It was unusual. Her parents were loving but not pandering or coddling in any way with their children. Their style was the typical strict British ideology of the time, "Get on with it!" "Stiff upper lip!" "You think you are so special!" Displays of emotion were rarely seen or tolerated. Those few moments of empathy from her mother would always be remembered.

A few days later, there was a meeting of both families, this time including the children. Deborah and Nicholas had been informed also of the future plans, and it could now be openly discussed with the reminder that all that was talked about was to remain private and to stay just between the two families. Maurice and Ray were scheduled to leave in February. In the meantime, Hazel and Ray would put their house up for sale. When the house sold, Hazel and the children would squeeze into Brocksford Avenue, and they would share the expenses of the home. Hazel had been working for a while in the Love Lane Primary School kitchen. When the men were established and ready for their families to join them, the Brocksford Avenue house would be sold. It was all worked out. Frances could barely stand to sit there and listen. Nicholas was almost eight years old and was rather accepting of the idea, Ruth and Deborah were quite tickled by the big secret that had to be kept and the excitement of living together for a while.

"We will go to America by boat too, won't we Daddy?" Deborah asked.

"Yes, dear. And you will have a wonderful time." The two girls giggled together.

"Now one thing," said Maurice. "We have to stop calling Frances "Fanny." That has a very different meaning in America." Fanny had lately become a nickname for Frances that they all used often.

"Oh… what does it mean in America?" Nicholas asked.

When they were told, the children burst into giggles, except for Frances, who was *not* amused. The evening continued with discussions of American accents, television programmes, food, housing, central heating, weather, schools and the massive size and dramatic features of the geography of the country.

"It's a young country, you know," said Maurice. "Not even two hundred years old."

"I don't know anything about it," Frances moaned. "Nothing about America has been taught to us in school, at least not yet."

"Well… we'll all learn together," Maurice responded cheerfully.

As Christmas approached, Vera and Maurice were mindful of the importance of this last Christmas together with their parents. Eileen and Ray invited the family and Charlotte and Walter down to Devon where they had moved several years previously. They would stay for a few days over the holiday and arrangements were made to stop at Chingford on the way back for the weekend following. The visit in Devon was special. Frances and Ruth enjoyed spending time with their cousins. Christine was eighteen and the girls were in awe of her. She played records on her phonograph and did the "twist" in the living room. She was so grown up and already working as a hairdresser. Gillian was fifteen and a favourite of Frances. She was funny and liked to show the girls around the countryside. The house and property were large. Ray operated his own businesses. He and Eileen had dog kennels and bred pedigree Pekinese dogs as well as owning and running a hardware store. Both businesses prospered. The family was happy in the country, appreciating the wide-open spaces, rolling hills and easy lifestyle. They had two ponies in a spacious paddock where Gillian and ten-year-old Rosemary offered to let Frances and Ruth ride. Unfortunately, it was a case of the town cousins visiting the country cousins. They watched Rosemary trotting around on the back of one of the ponies so easily and confidently, but the girls were not comfortable in the saddle and were happier walking alongside. They went for a long hike, over hills and dales and along country roads. The countryside was breathtakingly beautiful, even in the winter.

Christmas Day was great fun with the family all together, opening presents. Little five-year-old Rosalind could hardly contain her excitement and it was a joy to watch her. There was a splendid Christmas feast in the afternoon. Frances had made a traditional Christmas pudding in her cooking class at school in which she had hidden a sixpence for good luck. There were Christmas crackers, paper hats, jokes and laughter around the table and card games to follow. It was a Christmas to remember, and the last one they would spend together. The holiday continued in Chingford with Florrie and Ted; more gifts, more lovely dinners and a spectacular Christmas cake complete with a fringed cake skirt and tiny figurines placed on top.

With the holidays behind them, the weeks passed quickly. Vera dreaded the day when Maurice would leave. The full realisation of her situation and all that she would be left to do, began to set in. She would be left with so much responsibility and so much to manage before she and the girls would be sailing the Atlantic, hopefully sometime in the summer. Maurice on the other hand was giddy with anticipation. For him, it was an adventure, a fresh start and he could not wait to get going. But first, there would be some goodbyes. The two families planned two farewell parties. One for friends and one for family.

The little house was full for the friends' party. Fortunately, the invited guests were all friends of both families. There were the Coxes from Woodlands Avenue, friends from the men's club and Women's Institute, and the blind group from the Post Office. Although it was winter, it soon became quite warm inside, so a couple of windows were opened a little bit. The party got into full swing. Voices were raised in song and conversations became interspersed with loud laughter. There were plates of finger food passed around and plenty of things to drink. Halfway during the evening, there was a knock at the door. Two young policemen stood outside, straddling their bicycles.

"Sorry sir," one said to Maurice. "Sounds like you are having a nice party, but we have had a noise complaint. Your neighbour is bothered by the noise you are making. Can you tone it down a bit, please?"

"Yes, of course," replied a tipsy Maurice. "Sorry to be a bother. It's a farewell party. Going to America you know. Sorry you had to come out."

"No problem, sir. Not far from our beat. We were just

about to clock off from our shift anyway."

"Well then, come on back and join us if you've nothing else to do tonight." Ray joined Maurice at the door.

"What's this, Maurice?" he laughed. "You in trouble?"

"Well, we have to quiet down a bit, Ray. I've invited these nice lads to come back after their shift."

"Yes! Come back. Have a little fun at the end of your day. We are going to play some funny games later."

"The two young men looked at each other and nodded. "Might just do that sir."

"And no more "sir." I'm Maurice and… oh, here's Vera, my wife. Vera these fellas have come by to ask us to quiet down a bit. There has been a complaint."

"Oh, yes, alright. We'll do what we can."

"They are clocking off now. I've asked them to come back when they are off duty."

"Oh, yes. Join us! Do!"

In half an hour the young Bobbies returned, leaned their bicycles against the side of the house and joined the party. They were accepted happily into the group and became the subject of some friendly teasing and jokes. They were offered food and drink, and soon joined in the joviality, singing, and chatting away in their uniforms. Their police helmets became fun to pass around and try on. The noise level which had diminished somewhat for a while, increased again. There was another knock at the door. Ray answered this time. The grumpy woman from next door stood on the doorstep in her dressing gown, slippers and with curlers in her hair. She was frowning, annoyed and angry.

"I live next door," she declared, "and I am…"

"*Come in!*" said Ray. "Come on in and have a drink."

"I wouldn't step foot in *there!*" she replied indignantly. Maurice came to the door and added his invitation to the woman.

"Come on," he coaxed. "A nice drink before bed would do you good." Over his shoulder, the woman caught a glimpse of two policemen in uniform partying with the guests. They were missing their police hats which were circulating about the room. She was aghast! "*Come on…* this is a farewell party. We are leaving for America in a few weeks."

"Well!" she responded. "That's the *best* news I have heard in a long time!" She turned on her heels and departed while Ray and Maurice laughed heartily.

"Poor old dear," Maurice chuckled. "She will be happy to see the back of us!"

The family party was much more subdued. Florrie and Ted were there, as well as Charlotte and Walter, Will and Ann, Hazel's parents, Auntie Julie, and old Mrs. Grotia from Woodlands Avenue who was a favourite in the neighbourhood. The children sang a few songs and passed out the hors d'oeuvres. There was a game of charades which was fun and entertaining for everyone. There was an accusation of cheating, and a mock trial took place with Walter officiating as the judge. It was very amusing and entertaining. A farewell, good luck toast to Maurice and Ray was an emotional moment but given heartily and sincerely.

The final days approached. Maurice gave his notice at Jacob's, bought traveller's cheques and U.S. currency, and packed his suitcases. Ray and Eileen came up from Devon with their girls to say goodbye. It seemed that all was in readiness. It was decided that they would all go to Woodlands and have lunch at the Coxes on the date of departure. Following lunch there were group photographs taken and lots of hugs and kisses all around. A taxi was called, and everyone stood waiting, each absorbed with their own emotions; sadness, excitement, anxiety, resignation and regret. The weather was bright and sunny. There were children playing on the street and a few neighbours in their gardens waving. The taxi pulled up and the last hugs and squeezes were shared as the suitcases were loaded. As the taxi pulled away and headed down the street, Maurice and Ray twisted in their seats to look out of the back window. The four children, Frances, Ruth, Deborah and Nicholas were chasing after the car singing "Rule Britannia" and waving little Union Jacks.

Excerpts from a diary kept by Maurice during his beginning days with Jacob's
Dec. 20, 1962
Went for first interview with Jacob's Biscuit Company at Bedford Row, London. 9:30 a.m. – Mr. Hall.
Have good news. I have to report to Liverpool office for second interview on 28th December.

Dec. 28
Wonderful news. After long interview with six other applicants, I got the job. Start on Jan. 7, 1963. £750 per year, plus expenses and company van.

January 7, 1963
Left home at 6:00a.m. by train to Liverpool. First day at Jacob's.

Jan. 10
In Sales Office all day. Still very cold, not sign of snow now. Have been told I'm here for three weeks.

Jan. 24
Running very low on money. Hope I'll get through. Drove home in new van. Terrible journey – freezing fog all the way.

Jan. 27
Heard today that Grandma How is very ill indeed and has not very long to live.

Jan. 31
Last day of January. Thank goodness, I shall be glad to see the back of it. Camden Town and the City today. Try to meet Vera for lunch at 12:30.

Excerpt from Vera's recollections of the 1960s
I had been contemplating returning to work for some time but lacked the confidence to re-enter the business world. My two daughters were seven and ten years of age in 1961, and I felt a little more at ease about leaving them for half an hour each morning and then a short time after school with my good friend, Hazel. I applied to the G.P.O. (General Post Office,) Engineering Branch in London, and managed to find employment with suitable hours.

CHAPTER SEVENTEEN

The Lundbechs' house soon had a buyer, and the closing date was set. Hazel became immersed in sorting, packing, discarding and selling the contents of the home. Ray's piano was sold as well as most of the furniture. Deborah and Nicholas's beds would be moved to Brocksford Avenue as well as a chest of drawers for clothing but little else was needed or would fit in the bungalow. Some boxes containing toys, books, toiletries and personal items would be stacked up in the second bedroom which would be used by Deborah and Nicholas. Ruth's bed was relocated to Frances's bedroom. Hazel would share the larger bed with Vera in the dormer bedroom upstairs. Moving-in day was during the second week of March. It was a busy day but thrilling to set up the house and anticipate the time that they would all spend living together. A neighbour on Woodlands Avenue brought the boxes and few furnishings over in his van and the rest of the day was spent setting up beds, opening boxes, organising and settling in.

There was a steady stream of letters going back and forth across the Atlantic. The news was mostly good. The sea voyage had been a wonderful experience even though Maurice became seasick quite quickly. He was told to eat to calm it, which he did… in earnest, especially since the food aboard ship was delicious and plentiful. The winter crossing was rough at times and above decks ice covered the decks and rails with an impressive thick coating. The two men became friendly with several of the passengers and took part with them in the entertainment and activities provided. There were several young women travelling to spend time in the States as au pairs. Maurice and Ray enjoyed their company, joked and teased them and indulged in a little innocent flirtation. They sent photographs back to Rayleigh; smiling faces, smartly dressed, tables laden with food, beer and wine, glasses raised. They included the names of the passengers at their table and a little about them.

"Well," Hazel noted. "They certainly seem to have had an enjoyable time!"

"Yes, Vera responded. "We'll have to make sure we do too when it's our turn!"

Maurice wrote from Fairfield with news. He had found work with a well-established, family-owned construction company as a painter and wallpaper hanger and Ray got a job as a piano player in a lounge at the Mermaid Tavern, a prestigious hotel, restaurant, and bar. They were comfortably settled in at Evelyn and James's home which was located very close to the beach. As the weather began to improve, it was a lovely spot for a stroll to get some air and exercise. James had a pool table, so the men enjoyed many a game together. Evelyn was happy to have them and cooked up a storm to keep them all well-fed. The couple had five children, four boys and one girl ranging in age from twenty-three to eleven It was a busy household with a lot of coming and going, to work and to school. However, it was not long before Evelyn and Ray began to tangle. Evelyn did not appreciate Ray's outspokenness and the time he spent drinking with James in the local bars. She thought that his comings and goings were selfish without thought or consideration of anyone else in the household. Ray could not abide the control she tried to exert and the scoldings that were directed at him. They just rubbed each other the wrong way. Ray bought himself a used car and moved out. He made friends with a British couple at the Mermaid Tavern who owned a three-unit apartment house in New Haven, which was not too far away. They told him that the second-floor unit had just become available if he would like to take a look at it. Ray found it to be quite spacious and comfortable. It was just too convenient. He agreed to rent it without checking into the schools or the area much at all. He was delighted to discover that the family on the first floor were British also. Harry and Irene Jamieson, their daughter Irene and son Keith lived there and would become lifetime friends. Ray was all set. He wrote to Hazel that he would save money from his job at the Mermaid and soon he would be ready for them all to travel over.

Maurice worked as hard and as many hours as he could for the Benways, who owned the construction business. He dutifully saved as much as he could, allowing himself a small amount for necessary personal expenditures. He bought a used station wagon and started to scout around for reasonable house rentals in Fairfield. Through a contact he made on a construction site, he learned of an old farmhouse going for rent near the Merritt Parkway and the Easton border. He made arrangements to take a look. It was a grand old colonial style house that had once been a farmhouse. It needed a lot of fixing up and decorating but Maurice was up for the job. The owner agreed to rent the house to Maurice with option to buy. It was a wonderful deal and very exciting for him to work on it, decorate it and furnish it for his family. The house stood on an acre of land, set back from the street on a slight rise. There was a long driveway leading up to the house and a waterfall at the end of it which flowed from a pond on a higher level and flowed away through pipes under the driveway. The setting was absolutely stunning. The home had a large kitchen and dining area, a den, a formal living room, four bedrooms and two bathrooms. It also had a long, screened-in porch along the side of the house off the den. To Maurice, it felt like a palace. He had never been afraid of work. He spent long hours each day working for the Benways and then evenings at the house on Weeping Willow Lane. He constructed a built-in bar in the den, panelled the walls and refinished the floor. In the formal living room, he wallpapered the walls, painted the trim including the beams which ran the length of the room, and installed carpeting. The kitchen needed a new floor and appliances. Upstairs he wallpapered each room, choosing patterns that he thought would appeal to the girls. He had left over wallpaper from a high-end job that had gold leaf in the pattern and there was just enough to paper the master bedroom. When it was ready for furniture, he was amazed at how many of his recent contacts and friends had pieces to offer and with visits to a few estate sales and used furniture shops, he soon had all the necessary pieces. He purchased two unfinished wood kidney-shaped dressing tables for each of the girls' bedrooms and he painted them colours to coordinate with the wallpaper. Evelyn was an excellent seamstress, so she sewed pretty, ruffled skirts for them as well as curtains for some of the windows. The house was ready. Now he had to save up for the fares for his family to join him.

Meanwhile, on Brocksford Avenue, the two families were blending well together with a few rules and procedures put in place by Vera and Hazel that the children were expected to abide by. Everyone was busy with work and school. The mornings were a rush of activity with everyone getting ready. Vera was the first to leave to catch the train into London, Frances then left to walk to the high school, Hazel, Deborah and Nicholas walked to Love Lane and Ruth to Grove Road school. On Monday mornings, comics arrived in the early post, and it became difficult to keep the children focused as they kept gravitating to them to read a page or two. Soon they had to be confiscated by the women to be read after school. Deborah and Ruth spent hours together playing with their paper dolls and Frances kept busy with her books and sketch pad. Nicholas was the only male in the house and was only eight years old, so he was left out of a lot of the girls' activities, but he enjoyed reading and played alone with his own toys. Sometimes though, he did join in with a game of pickup sticks which sometimes got heated with accusations, "Your turn's over. That one moved!"

"No, it didn't!" Also jacks appealed to him. But when he dove for the ball and the jacks went flying, the girls got annoyed.

The back garden was a play area on dry days. Nicholas received a chemistry set for his birthday with strict instructions that it could only be used outside. The four children were intrigued, mixing up all sorts of concoctions, creating solutions of various colours and smells. No one read the information booklet or instructions included with the set. Nicholas was shaking his test tube when he exclaimed, "This is getting… very… *HOT!*" He threw the test tube in the air; the cork blew out and the glass tube exploded. It was all very exciting.

Another time, Frances organised a backyard horror house. One of the children was blindfolded and then pushed around the yard in a wheelbarrow by one of the others while Frances assailed them with a variety of sounds, growls, screeches, howls, ghostly moans. She also swept fabric over them, and wet string. The blindfolded victim squealed and cried out in exaggerated terror. It was a silly game but lively and fun for the children. The neighbour on the right side of the house, however, did not find it to his liking at all. He threw open his back door and shouted at the children to stop the game and the noise immediately. He continued scolding, telling them they were a bunch of hooligans and a menace to the neighbourhood. His raised voice brought Hazel and Vera out of the house. He turned on the women telling them that his baby was trying to sleep, and the noise was unacceptable. Hazel defended the children and told him that it was innocent play.

"Your little boy will play like that one day," she said.

"*Never!*"

"Course he will. Don't be so silly," Vera scoffed.

"You're calling *me* silly while you are all living together in that house like rabbits!"

"That's our business, isn't it! Meanwhile, our children will continue to play in the garden however they wish, and you will have to lump it!"

The four children stood frozen in place watching the exchange. It was rare for them to witness this kind of confrontation. The angry neighbour headed back to his door but threw one last remark over his shoulder before going inside. "The next time they make that kind of noise, I will drench them with my garden hose!"

"*Well!*" exclaimed Hazel. "What a charming fellow!"

"I think we'll come inside now, Mummy," said Deborah in a timid voice.

"No," Hazel responded. "Stay out for a while. I don't want *him* to think he can tell us what to do."

"Yes," Vera agreed readily. "Carry on with your game."

The children stayed outside for a while, but quietly and nervously, and then crept back in the house to find another pastime.

Walter stopped at the house on Sundays to see if there

was anything that needed doing. He always carried a large white bag which contained sweets for the kiddies. He was a welcome sight to the children as well as the two women. It was a comfort to know that he would be there if they needed his help with something. Vera told him about the incident with the neighbour during one of their visits to Hockley.

"I'll 'ave 'is guts for garters if he dares turn the 'ose on the children!" he declared.

There were woods within a short walk of the house and the ground was a carpet of bluebells in late April. The girls went to pick a large bunch for their mothers. Nicholas trailed along too. There had been rumours that there was a nudist colony in the woods and, wondering if it was true, the foursome followed the trails for a while looking for evidence of a camp. They did actually find the remnants of campfires and some discarded tin cans and so were satisfied that they had proven that the rumour was indeed fact. They had walked deep into the woods, further than they were supposed to go and turned back just a little bit spooked, checking over their shoulders, hoping not to catch a glimpse of a stray nudist. They returned home with armloads of bluebells and a secret to be kept between them.

Vera and Hazel received letters from their husbands. It was time to put the house on the market and prepare to come to America. It was an exciting time for the household, even for Frances, who still dreaded the thought of leaving England. Vera arranged for the house to be listed for sale right away. Everyone was recruited to keep their rooms and belongings tidy and not to make a mess anywhere. Everything was cleaned thoroughly, polished and decluttered as much as possible. On the rear, outside wall there was a significant crack. The children were told that when viewers came to look at the house, not to mention it or point it out in any way. Nicholas understood and followed directions, but he could not stop himself from standing wide-eyed, staring at it silently whenever potential buyers were inspecting the building.

Appointments were made at the American Embassy for interviews and medical examinations. Vera took Frances and Ruth into London on the scheduled date. She had filled out all the required forms and remembered laughing with Maurice and Ray at some of the questions. *Have you ever been a Communist? Is anyone in your family a Communist? Have you ever murdered anyone?* The medical examination was thorough and embarrassing, but all went well, and they were approved. She applied for passports and began to make inquiries about the disposal of the furnishings.

The house sold quickly. Rayleigh was a pretty town, convenient for commuting to London, near the seaside, and becoming a growing, popular, active community. The bungalow was a perfect starter home for the young couple who made Vera a good offer. The moving date was set for 23rd June. Vera and Hazel acquired tea chests for shipping their belongings. Decisions had to be made about what should be packed. The expense of shipping the chests meant that selections were limited, with much remaining behind. Just two large tea chests each held all their cherished possessions. Eileen's daughter, Christine, had recently become engaged, so she was glad to take the dining set and a wardrobe. The young couple moving in were pleased of the offer of some of the beds. All the rest was to be picked up on moving day by a charity. Vera arranged to spend a week with Walter and Charlotte and the last week before departure with her mother and Ted. Hazel was going to spend time in Ireland with relatives and the last week with her parents. All was in readiness and then came disappointing news.

Maurice sent a letter with tickets enclosed for the journey. However, they were not ocean liner tickets. He sent airline tickets instead. Hazel got a similar letter with airline tickets also. It was quite obvious that the two men had recalled the wonderful voyage they had enjoyed, meeting so many exciting, worldly people, and were hesitant for their families to be exposed to any flirtation or be taken advantage of in any way by charming, smooth talkers. The airline tickets were for the same day but for different flights, so they would not even be all flying together.

The children were quite put out. They had been promised an ocean voyage and had anticipated a touch of luxury and splendour. Vera and Hazel were miffed too, but their disappointment was dulled by the excitement of flying and finally making it to America. They were exhausted and were looking forward to not carrying such heavy responsibilities alone anymore. Hazel, Deborah and Nicholas said their goodbyes with lots of hugs and kisses and excited expectations of meeting again soon in America.

Vera and the girls stayed in Hockley with Charlotte and Walter. Vera had a meeting with her solicitor, where final contracts were signed and the solicitor arranged for the proceeds of the sale of the house to be sent to Maurice, with a small cheque payable to Vera for expenses for her final two weeks in England. It was done. Everything was tied up and all that was left was the dreaded parting and emotional farewells with family.

Eileen came up from Devon for a couple of days with Gillian, Rosemary and Rosalind. The younger girls spent a lot of time in the playhouse at the bottom of the garden that Walter had built years ago. It was very sweet with windows and curtains and a wooden table and chairs. Frances was happy to walk to the shops with Gillian to have a look around and pick things up for Nana. At tea that evening, the talk was all about America. Gillian teased that they would soon all be talking like true Yankees. Frances scowled, *"No, I won't!"* she retorted.

"I expect you will marry a nice American man, one day," Nana Bindle said to her with a chuckle.

"Oh, no, Nana. *I won't!* I will come back and marry an English man."

"I wonder if you will see cowboys on horseback," said Rosemary.

"Shouldn't think so," Walter commented. "They're all in the wild west."

The weather that week was warm and sunny. Walter had planted strawberries in his garden, and they were ripe and luscious. Frances and Ruth picked some each day to have with their tea. They played with Nana and Grandad's little Corgi, Nicky, and walked on the stilts that Grandad had made for them. The week came to an end when Florrie and Ted drove to Hockley to collect them. Charlotte made a final meal for them all, suitcases were packed, and it was time to part ways. Big hugs and cuddles and the promise to write often were shared, and they climbed into the backseat of Ted's car. As he drove away down the street, Frances turned and looked out of the back window. Walter had his arm around Charlotte as they stood at the gate in the front garden waving sorrowfully. Tears sprang to her eyes uncontrollably and coursed down her cheeks. Vera hissed at her, "Stop that!" she whispered. Frances gulped, blinked, and sat quiet for the rest of the journey, holding back her distress and heartache as she stared glumly ahead.

Florrie had taken a week off from work to spend with her family. Ted went to work each day, so the ladies had a lot of time together. The weather continued to be sunny, warm and dry so a lot of time was spent out in the garden. The blackcurrants were ready to start picking and gooseberries were also beginning to ripen. There were tomato plants growing, a full, hearty mint patch and the scent of flowers wafting on the warm breeze. Florrie and Vera worked together in the kitchen, chatting happily and asked the girls to pick some mint for the leg of lamb which would be for dinner as well as some blackcurrants for their favourite blackcurrant tart. Frances and Ruth popped upstairs to visit Ag while they were there. Sadly, old Art had passed away a year ago, so Ag was happy for their company. Frances showed Florrie a magazine she had featuring a group of young lads who had soared to great success over the last few years, "The Beatles." She pointed to each one telling her grandmother their names.

"Oh, *crikey*," she said. "*Look at the hair!*"

"It's all right Nana. A lot of the bands are wearing their hair like that nowadays." For some reason, Florrie found that remark funny and she double over with laughter in her typical fashion.

On the last day of the visit, Frances was sitting alone in the conservatory, listening to the radio. A dedication was announced on the program. "This dedication goes out to Vera, Frances and Ruth, Hazel, Deborah and Nicholas, who are emigrating to the United States in two days. It is from their friends, Lil and Ted Cox in Rayleigh, Essex. The song began. It was "You Make Me Feel So Young," a favourite of Vera's and one that was played at so many of their parties. Frances called out to her mother, "Come and listen, Mummy. Auntie Lil has dedicated this song to us."

The following day, 5th July, after an early dinner, suitcases were loaded into Ted's car, and they all drove into London. Vera had booked a bed and breakfast in west London and would take a taxi the next morning to London airport. Ted pulled up in front of the building, opened the boot and removed the suitcases. "I'll take these up to the door," he said. He knew this would be a difficult parting for Vera and Florrie and did not want it prolonged. Florrie stood stoically on the pavement as the girls approached her say their goodbyes. Florrie hugged each one tightly. "Cheerio loves," she said brightly. "Have a lovely journey and write to me all about it soon." She turned to Vera, who was struggling to maintain her composure. "Goodbye Mum," she managed. "Thank you for everything." Then they were hugging, and tears were streaming. "Goodbye luv," Florrie choked. "Best of luck to you!" Ted steered Florrie into the car. "Goodbye dear," he said to Vera with a quick squeeze.

"Thank you, Ted," she responded. "I… I'm so glad… and grateful that she has you." She turned abruptly and walked to the door of the bed and breakfast where the girls were waiting with the suitcases. She did not look back.

Frances woke the next morning to the chimes of Big Ben. She lay listening and thinking it was England saying its goodbye to her. Tears leaked from her eyes again, but she dashed them away when she heard her mother rising from her bed. Vera switched on the light and said brightly, "Time to get up, you two. Come on, let's get washed and dressed and go down for some breakfast." Vera had hung their travelling clothes in the wardrobe the night before. They were all dressing very smartly for their flight, as was the custom of the time. Ruth had a light blue two-piece suit with a matching hat. Funnily enough, Deborah had chosen the very same outfit when she went shopping with Hazel for her travel clothes. Frances wore a burgundy pleated skirt with matching vest beneath which she wore a white ruffled blouse with a velvet, burgundy bow at the neck. She also wore her first pair of nylons and shoes with a tiny heel. Vera had chosen a green and white plaid suit with a matching hat. All three had white gloves as part of their ensemble.

After breakfast, the proprietor of the B&B telephoned for a taxi, and they were on their way to the airport. It was all a new experience for the three of them. Vera asked for help and information each step of the way, and all went smoothly. As they entered the departure lounge, a young woman with a clipboard approached. She asked Frances if she would mind answering a question for a survey. "What is the purpose of your flight today?"

"I am going to join my father in America," she said.

"Don't just say *that*," Vera corrected her. "It is for a better life, better education and more opportunities," she told the researcher.

The flight was amazing for the three of them. They marvelled at the size of the plane, the thrill of lift off, and they watched the stewardesses in awe. The girls received BOAC "passports" and their "wings," metal pins to wear proudly as an accredited flyer and were also invited to visit the cockpit to meet the pilots.

As the plane descended into JFK airport, Vera felt butterflies in her stomach. She would soon be reunited with her husband and would go to her new home. Maurice had written about it but had not sent any pictures. He said he wanted it to be a surprise. She could not wait to see it and settle in. Oh, she hoped she would like it. She had left an awful lot behind.

In the arrivals lounge, Maurice waited, watching for his wife and daughters to appear. When he caught sight of them, dressed to the nines, he waved happily, smiling broadly. Vera was excited to see him but at the same time, rather taken aback. There he stood in shorts, a casual shirt and wearing a straw hat on his head. He kissed her and held her tightly in his arms. "Welcome to America!" he exclaimed.

CHAPTER EIGHTEEN

Vera realised why Maurice had dressed so casually when they exited the airport building and the heat and humidity set them back on their heels. "Oh, my goodness, Maurice, isn't it hot!"

"Sure is. Over ninety degrees today." All the way home, they chatted, with Maurice pointing out landmarks and things of interest to them all. Frances and Ruth were squeezed in the back seat with two boys, Evelyn, and James's youngest sons, who Maurice had brought with him, thinking that the girls would be happy to meet their cousins and enjoy their company during the ride to Fairfield. This was not the case. The girls had been startled to see their father dressed as he was and felt a little shy seeing him again. Having the boys along did not help. It was obvious that they had an easy, friendly relationship with Maurice, and his daughters could not help but be resentful. They wanted to be the centre of his attention after such a long separation. Kevin pulled a dollar bill from his pocket and began to educate his cousins about the images and symbols on it. The girls were not particularly interested but politely gave it their attention. When Ruth addressed Vera as "Mummy," the boys were in stitches and made fun of her accent. "Oh "Mummay… Mummay!" they laughed.

"We are not going straight to the house, Vera," Maurice explained. "I have to drop these two cheeky guys off at Evelyn and James's, and Evelyn is preparing a nice dinner for us all."

"Oh?" Vera replied, trying not to sound disappointed.

"Well, I thought it would be nice for you to see the family. They all want to welcome you and we won't have to worry about making a meal tonight."

"Yes... of course. That will be nice."

The whole family was waiting to greet Vera, Frances and Ruth. A long table was set for dinner and Evelyn was rushing back and forth to the kitchen. Vera was interested to see everyone. There was James, Michael, with his fiancé, Anita, Janet, Robert, as well as Kevin and Brian who had driven back with them from the airport. Everyone was in shorts and tee shirts except for Anita and Evelyn, who wore sundresses and sandals. Frances and Ruth sat down feeling very out of place. "Mummy?" Frances asked. "Can I get something else to wear out of the suitcase?"

"*Mummay*!" Kevin teased, collapsing with giggles.

"No dear. I don't want you rummaging through the suitcases now."

"I'll get you all a cold drink," said Evelyn.

So, Ruth and Frances, Miss Prim and Miss Proper, sat awkwardly and uncomfortably through the ordeal of a big dinner with their American cousins until, at last, Maurice said it was time to go.

It was such a relief to be on their own again, just the four of them. It had been many months since the last time. Vera looked out of the car window, observing her new hometown, Fairfield. The houses were predominantly covered with wood shingles, not brick as they were back home, and were painted in so many different colours. The properties were so spread out and the gardens, or yards, were spacious and mostly open to their neighbours. She thought it was odd that there were not many bordered with hedges or fences. The roads were wide and busy, the cars large and plentiful. Maurice was pointing out shops and stores, homes of acquaintances and friends that he had made, telling her about the magnificent Merritt Parkway, a picturesque high-speed road that had been built as part of President Franklin Roosevelt's New Deal program. She was listening but not really taking it all in, feeling overwhelmed and so displaced. And then Maurice turned onto a street, Weeping Willow Lane, which did indeed have a few weeping willows at the beginning of the road dramatically cascading their ground-sweeping branches as a formal welcome. He drove slowly past some impressive, wide, ranch-style homes and then turned into a driveway on the right-hand side. The driveway was long, leading up to a magnificent white, two-storey house with black shutters at the windows. There was a lot of property, lush lawn, established trees and a waterfall directly ahead. The setting was beautiful. Vera and the girls stared in amazement.

"Is this our house?" Ruth asked incredulously.

"It sure is!" Maurice replied, beaming.

"It's smashing!" said Frances.

"Oh, Maurice! It's so big. Can we really afford this?"

"We sure can. I told you in my letter about renting with option to buy. I anticipate being able to get a mortgage in a year or two. Come on, let's go around to the backdoor. That leads right into the kitchen. It's where I want to start the tour."

Around the back of the house, the property rose quite steeply. There was a retaining wall with stone steps to get up to the higher level. To the right side and far back beyond the waterfall was a natural pond. There were shrubs and trees at the top of the incline, so no one overlooked. The telephone was ringing as they entered the back door.

"Go on, Frances. You answer it." Maurice said.

"Me?"

"Yes, go on."

"Alright… hello?" she said, in a timid voice.

"It's Auntie Evelyn," a bold, authoritative voice

responded. "Just leave the phone off the hook so I can listen."

"Oh, yes… alright," Frances responded and let the receiver dangle from the wall phone by its cord.

"It's Auntie Evelyn. She wants me to leave the phone off the hook so that she can hear us."

Maurice whispered to his wife, "She wanted to be here when I showed you all the house, but I told her no. She did put a lot of work into the house, cleaning and making curtains, locating furniture. I know she wants to hear some of your reaction." Vera nodded, feeling irritated at the intrusion for a moment but then forgot about it in her excitement and joy viewing her new home.

Each room was a new discovery. The space and openness felt opulent and luxurious. Maurice had painted and papered the rooms so tastefully. Over the bar in the den, he had hung a mural depicting a mountain scene with a lake and pine trees. There was a full downstairs bathroom off the den with a new washer and dryer; such a luxury when Vera remembered the crude, heavy machine on wheels that she had used in England. The long living room was divided with two half-walls and columns. Beams on the ceiling stretched the length of the space. The smaller end of the room was set up as an office with a desk and the other end was the living room space. A console television stood in the corner and a long wooden stereo console housing a radio and turntable was on the back wall. A couch and two easy chairs were placed on the front wall.

"Maurice! How did you manage to get all this furniture? It is all so wonderful, so perfect!"

"I'm glad you like it. It was remarkable really. Some of the pieces came from people I just recently met who wanted to help. Yvonne helped me find the stereo console at an estate sale, as well as the kitchen table and chairs and the beds upstairs. We can replace and update the furnishings when we can as we go along."

"Can I see my room now, Daddy?" Ruth asked.

"Yes. Let's go upstairs now," he said.

Upstairs there were four bedrooms and another full bathroom.

"Go down the end of the hall, girls," Maurice said. There are two bedrooms there. You can decide whose is whose." The girls raced down the hall. One of the bedrooms was papered in a pink silk stripe and the other in a subtle pattern of swans and trees. Ruth loved the pink room and Frances preferred the other, so the choice was made quickly and easily. Between the two bedrooms at the end of the hall was an alcove with a few stairs leading to a rustic, old door with a heavy metal drop latch. The girls could not resist having a look behind the door. There were more stairs behind the door which turned to the left and led to a large attic which extended the full length of the house with an attic window at each end. It was appealingly spooky. Frances was enthralled and could not help but imagine all the secrets and mysteries that the space held.

Vera was delighting in the master bedroom with the gold wallpaper. The curtains matched so well and the bedspread had been carefully chosen.

"Evelyn made the curtains and chose the bedspread in here," Maurice told her.

"She did a lovely job," Vera responded a little grudgingly. She appreciated all that had been prepared for her in the home, but she would have to make some changes soon and put her mark on it.

"This is the spare room where our visitors will stay," Maurice said as he opened another door.

"Oh, Maurice, how nice. A separate room of their own. It's lovely." The girls called from the end of the hall. "Come down here, Mummy. We have chosen our bedrooms. Come and look. And there are stairs to the attic too!" Ruth called.

Vera was amazed at all that Maurice had been able to accomplish in five months. She was thrilled with the house and the beautiful setting and grounds, but it would take some time to feel at home. She could not help but feel like it was all a dream. Maybe when the tea chests arrived with their belongings, it would feel more real and more like hers.

"Come on dear, said Maurice, taking her hand. "Let's go downstairs and make a nice cup of tea." When they entered the kitchen, they noticed the phone receiver where it hung forgotten. Vera picked it up and spoke into it. "Hello… hello… Evelyn?" But it was silent. Evelyn had hung up.

It was a time of such mixed emotions. Vera would swing from the joy of her new surroundings and the excitement of discovery, exploring the neighbourhood and the town of Fairfield, to melancholy, missing her mother and Ted and Charlotte and Walter, Auntie Julie, dear friends and neighbours and the security of the familiar. The distance between them, an ocean separating them, communication reduced to letters, bothered her to the extreme. Although she now had a telephone in the home, none of the family in England had one and overseas telephone rates were prohibitive.

During the afternoon of the day after arrival, there was a knock at the back door. Vera opened it to a smiling lady holding a pitcher of juice and a cake.

"Hello. I just wanted to welcome you and introduce myself. I am your next-door neighbour, Diedre Hope-Ross."

"Oh, hello. Come in, please. So nice to meet you. I'm Vera."

"So nice to meet you too. Maurice has told us about you all. I'm so glad you are finally here. He has been working so hard getting everything ready. I won't stay, I'm sure you are very busy, but if I can be of any help please don't hesitate to ask. I can show you around, take you to stores and places around town, show you the schools, that kind of thing."

"Thank you very much. That's so kind of you. I will appreciate some help getting familiar with the area. And thank you for the juice and cake. What a nice treat." Diedre became a good friend. She had come from Ireland several years ago as a practicing physician and had married a doctor she met in the States. She had five children and would soon be expecting her sixth. She was fun, outgoing, kind, and generous. Vera was grateful to have her as a neighbour and friend.

Yvonne popped over soon after the family arrived. She brought Barbara, Gary and Debbie with her. It was a happy reunion for Vera and Yvonne. They hugged and laughed, so tickled that they would be living near each other again. Frances and Ruth hung back, shy and timid to see "Auntie" Yvonne and Barbara again and to meet Gary and Debbie for the first time. Gary had a bag full of comics for the girls to read and soon they were chatting quite easily, getting to know each other. Barbara was seventeen and driving so she suggested that she take Frances for a ride around town and show her the school that she would be attending in September.

Another friend Vera made quickly was Yvonne Fraczek who lived up on the hill. She had come to the U.S. as a war bride just as the other Yvonne, Vera's cousin, had done. The two had lots to talk about. Unfortunately, Yvonne was not in the best of health. She had suffered from rheumatic fever as a child and her heart had been affected. She was very limited in her mobility, becoming breathless and tired very easily. Then there were the Clarks who lived on the corner and the Roths next door to the Clarks who both had daughters Ruth's age so, Ruth had neighbourhood friends right away. Frances would have to wait until she attended school to meet girls of her own age.

The first week was all about getting settled into the house, meeting people and beginning the learning process which would continue for quite some time. It was all so new and different, as Vera described in a letter to Florrie, telling her in detail about the house, her experiences, and the people she had met. She promised photographs soon. Writing to Florrie brought tears to Vera's eyes again. The distance between them was vast and she wondered how her mother was coping. She was still working, which was a blessing. She was busy and active, and she had Ted but there must be a terrific void in her life where her daughter and grandchildren used to be. Letters went back and forth regularly, at least once a week, sometimes more. Mailing letters in an envelope was rather expensive so they usually used airletters which consisted of a sheet of thin, blue paper that was folded along dotted lines to form a square-shaped envelope and sealed on two sides. Florrie filled the entire page with tiny words to tell all her news and respond to the news she had received from her daughter. She was a wonderful writer. Her personality and sense of humour jumped from the page, so much so that Vera was often reduced to tears, missing her so.

Vera was amazed at how many women drove and how many families had not just one car, but two. It was necessary in America in the suburbs where everything was so spaced out and the town centre was miles away. She realised that soon she would need to learn to drive. In the meantime, Maurice took her to the supermarket. What a remarkable place it was. The supermarket, Waldbaums, was located on the lower level at one end of a two-storey enclosed mall. She had never seen anything like this Trumbull Shopping Park. It was a long building full of stores, a Woolworths, Super X (a pharmacy), many clothing stores, shoe stores, Korvette's department store, Mooney's Sporting Goods, Buster Brown. Vera wrote to Florrie that at the Trumbull Shopping Park she could buy everything from a pin to a kayak.

During the summer, the girls had to be registered at their schools. Ruth was registered at a new school, North Stratfield School, where she would be entering fifth grade and Frances would enter eighth grade at Fairfield Woods Middle School. A school bus would pick them up at the end of the street where it intersected with Jefferson Street. Frances had to take a test during the summer to determine proper placement according to her scores. Both girls dreaded attending new schools which they knew would be so different from ones they had left behind. The summer rolled on. Long sunny, hot days full of promise and discovery but also homesickness and regret.

The Lundbechs came to visit from New Haven. It was wonderful to spend time together again and exciting to show them all the house.

"Good Lord, Maurice, you've done a lot to this place

since I last saw it," Ray declared.

"Oh, it is just lovely!" said Hazel. "Well done, Maurice!"

Deborah and Nicholas looked around in awe.

"We live in an apartment," said Nicholas.

"It's nice but nothing like this." Deborah added.

"I can't wait to see it," Ruth replied.

"Yes… well it's in a city. There is no garden to play in. We are on the second floor. There's a small porch in the back that I like to sit in sometimes," Deborah continued.

"Did you see the wishing well when you came in?" Frances asked. "It's boarded up so no one will fall in, but there is still water down there. And let's show them the cellar, Ruth. It's quite creepy. We have to go outside and open the Bilco doors to go down there." The cellar had a dirt floor and several passageways containing wooden racks. "They must have stored things down here years ago," said Frances. "It was a farmhouse so this must have been used as cold storage." They peered around with a flashlight and found some interesting objects on the wooden shelves: old jars, long, iron nails, a cement ball the size of a baseball.

The Lundbechs stayed for the weekend, as they would many times in the future. It was so much fun to exchange stories and laugh at the differences in the common language used by Britain and America. There were so many words that had different meanings and expressions that were unfamiliar. They would all be learning and adjusting for quite some time. The friendship between the two families was unusual. The adults were really quite different. Whereas Vera was a worrier and planner, Hazel was calmer and more laid back, whereas Maurice was a physical labourer and fan of sports, Ray was intellectual and an avid reader. What they had in common, though, was the joy of camaraderie, music, singing, parties, a good hearty discussion, personal stories, jokes, exchange of viewpoints, even a friendly argument.

School started and the girls coped well enough even though they stood out like sore thumbs at first. Everyone was captivated by their strong English accents. Even the teachers called on them often to hear them speak and brought other teachers into the classroom to meet them. They had a lot to catch up on, especially American history. They really knew nothing about the history of their new country. It was during another visit of the Lundbechs that Frances, Ruth, and Deborah ventured up to the attic to find a board game that they all could play. While searching the boxes, one box was pushed against a knee wall that sealed off the attic eaves causing a section of the wall to come loose and pull away from the upright. Peering into the darkness behind the wall, the girls could see an old mirror and a wooden chair and something hanging from the rafter. When they reached in and retrieved it, they were surprised and intrigued to discover that it was a crumpled, old flag. This was a find that must be shared immediately so they hurried downstairs to show Vera.

"*Well, I never!*" she said. "It's got the stars and stripes of the American flag, but not many stars at all. I don't know anything about it. It certainly looks old, look how stained and stiff it is. I wonder how long it has been up there."

"What should we do with it, Mum?" Frances asked.

"I will find out if there is somewhere I can take it to get some information. It is so *dirty* though!"

Unfortunately, the flag would remain a mystery. Vera decided that it needed to be washed before it could be brought anywhere. She tossed it in the washing machine where it was destroyed, reduced to a frayed, unravelled rag.

Maurice began the process of teaching his wife to drive.

Unfortunately, they soon came to the realisation that it was not going to work. Maurice did not have the patience for it and the sessions would end with a quarrel and hurt feelings. Diedre was the one who took over the task and taught Vera, calmly and pleasantly, the technique and rules of the road. She passed the test and became a driver at age thirty-six. Although they still only had one car, it gave Vera a sense of independence and freedom. She could take the car when it was available and shop on her own, visit Yvonne and go to the library. She also began to think about getting a job.

Christmas 1964 was spent with the Lundbechs. It was a happy time and since Christmas Day fell on a Friday, they had a long weekend to celebrate together. The weather was unusually mild so the children could play outside and the adults could take a stroll. There were the usual presents, big Christmas dinner, games and cheer. When it was over, Vera sat down to write all about it to Florrie and could not help but feel guilty and sad. *How was your Christmas?* she wrote. *I hope you enjoyed it. Did you spend it with Pearl?*

Then came some unpleasantness. James and Evelyn's troubled marriage was crumbling. Maurice had been witness to tension and the lack of affection between the two when he had stayed there after arriving in the U.S. He had been very grateful for their generosity, however, appreciating the offer of their home as a base while he got himself established. He did not want to impose any longer than necessary and was gone a lot of the time working for the Benways and then later, on the farmhouse. While at James and Evelyn's, he was upbeat, pleasant, and grateful. He enjoyed the company of the boys and Janet, kidded them, played games, and learned from them about baseball and American football. He was especially grateful to Evelyn who took on extra work and meal preparation for him (and Ray while he was there) and reorganised bedrooms to accommodate him. He praised her on her cooking and housekeeping and flattered her with compliments often on her ability to manage it all. He strove to be an easy, thoughtful guest, contributing some rent and helping around the house. Since Vera and the girls had arrived, the two families had visited each other regularly. Vera, Evelyn and Yvonne had spent a delightful day together in New York City to show Vera some of the sights, and Maurice met James from time to time for a drink and a chat. It all seemed like a pleasant extended family situation until Maurice suddenly and unbelievably discovered that Evelyn had been telling some in the circle of friends that he and Vera was establishing that Maurice had made passes at her while he lived in her house and had attempted to seduce her. When he was informed of this by one of his friends, he was livid. He told his wife immediately.

"Vera, I just can't believe she said this! Whatever is she thinking?" Vera was angry too. She knew that Evelyn and James's marriage was not happy and that her cousin was desperate for attention. She had always been wary of her cousin as a young girl, never feeling completely comfortable around her but she had admired her too. She was seven years older, clever, and talented in many ways. However, Evelyn had overstepped the line here. Spreading rumours like this, could have caused considerable damage to Maurice's reputation.

"I don't know. She is unhappy with James and maybe resents us in some way."

"I've got to talk to James. He is bound to hear these rumours."

"I feel sorry for James. In spite of everything, I think he still loves Evelyn. But he knows her well. I think you will find that he will not believe her accusations."

"I certainly hope so. He has been a good friend. I wouldn't want him to think that I would repay his kindness so disloyally."

Vera was truly disappointed with Evelyn. When she thought about her behaviour, she became so agitated. Was Evelyn jealous of Vera and Maurice and their relationship? Was she so unhappy that she wanted them to be unhappy too? Was she trying to make herself desirable to others by speaking of an imagined affair? Vera tried to justify her actions to herself. Evelyn had an unhappy childhood, she married too young, she possessed unfulfilled talent and ability. She felt stuck, unappreciated, and frustrated. Vera understood all this and was grateful for all that Evelyn had done getting the house ready, but she could not reconcile herself with the nasty, mean-spirited allegations that could have escalated and cause a real rift in her marriage. Perhaps that was her motive. She decided that it would be better that she had nothing more to do with her. It would be decades before there was contact between them again.

The next summer, in 1965, the Browns and Lundbechs decided that they should venture out and explore their new country a little. Their funds were still limited so they decided to camp. Each family rented a pop-up camper which was pulled behind their car. They decided to head for Lake Sherando in the Blue Ridge Mountains of Virginia. It was an exciting drive with lots to see along the way. They marvelled at the New York skyline, George Washington Bridge and caught a glimpse of the Capitol dome and the Washington Monument from the highway. When they reached the Blue Ridge Parkway, they were amazed. The mountains were majestic and beautiful and rolled on for miles and miles. Sometimes, the parkway narrowed and curved with a low guard rail bordering a steep cliff face which fell away ominously from the road surface. The drivers in their cars with their campers in tow, slowed significantly, navigating the route with a white-knuckled grip on the steering wheel.

The campgrounds were spacious, peaceful and smelled strongly of pine, wood fires and earth. The families enjoyed the feeling of freedom and communing with nature. It would be a week of casual living and exploration. There were activities down by the lodge where the children learned camp songs around a blazing campfire and walked the trails with a guide who pointed out plants and trees, forest creatures and birds along the way. The adults had rarely felt so relaxed with no plans, no expectations, no schedule. Meals were cooked on the campfire and tasted wonderful in the open air. There was swimming in the lake and boating, so several languid afternoons were spent on the beach with coolers and beach chairs. One afternoon Maurice decided to take a drive along the Parkway to see more of the mountains and the landscape. Deborah and Ruth decided that they would rather stay at the campsite together, so it was Maurice, Vera, Frances and Ray, Hazel and Nicholas who clambered into Maurice's copper-coloured station wagon for the excursion. Maurice was able to better manoeuvre without pulling the camper behind but even so, the steep rises and falls were a challenge. Often, he had to pull hard on the wheel on the sharp curves and press long and hard on the brake. They pulled over into some scenic overlooks and snapped some photos along the way. It was breathtaking.

There were two mishaps during the week away. One was

the loss of Ray's wallet which he had put in the glove compartment of his car for safe keeping. However, at some point, the car was left unlocked, and the wallet was stolen. The other was on the way home. At a stoplight, Maurice's station wagon would not stop. Although he was pumping the brakes furiously, the car just drifted across the intersection and finally came to rest against the curb further down the road. The brakes had been worked too hard in the mountains and just suddenly failed. Repairs had to be made, creating an expense and delay to their return home, but all agreed that they were so lucky that the brakes had not failed on the twisting, perilous road. It was a holiday that had been much enjoyed and would be long remembered.

Vera turned her attention to the big yard. There was a lot of lawn to mow but she did not mind because the house was so pretty, set back from the road with a sweeping lawn stretching up to it. But there needed to be flowers. She dug a flowerbed along the front façade and in the back on either side of the kitchen's back door. She filled them with perennials and annuals and a few low-growing shrubs. She enjoyed stepping out to be greeted with the pleasing aromas and colours of the blooms. Just around the corner on the left side of the backdoor, Vera kept her trash barrels. She was annoyed to find them tipped over many mornings with garbage strewn about on the grass. She could not have this in her lovely yard, so she tied down the lids of the barrels with pieces of clothesline to discourage the nighttime critters and prevent them from leaving such a mess. The house and the garden looked lovely and gave Vera so much satisfaction and pride. This was her home in America! She could never have dreamed of such a beautiful homestead.

There were parties in the big, old farmhouse. Vera and

Maurice invited their new friends, neighbours, the Lundbechs, of course, Yvonne and Bob and Bob's brother Bud and his wife, Lois. Bud's hobby was photography and he had elaborate equipment and accessories with which he took stunning photographs of the parties, recording the fun and activities as well as candid portraits of the attendees. There was the usual singing and room enough for dancing too. There were silly games. "Let's see who can make the best expression of shock, worry, fear, joy, sorrow, boredom."

"How about a game of charades?" "Best joke!" "Twenty Questions." One time, Maurice prepared a spoof, "The Rising Sun." The guests, one by one, were invited into another room where two people held a sheet stretched vertically between them. Maurice ducked down behind it and held a flashlight pressed against it. He slowly swept the light across the sheet as it ascended to the top. The participant was instructed to follow the rising sun with his nose all the way to the top where Maurice promptly doused the guest's face with a wet, dripping sponge. Silly but fun and causing the merry partiers to collapse in hysterics.

Later that year, Vera was not feeling well. While shopping at Waldbaums with Diedre one day, she was dragging round the store tired, lethargic and feeling sick. Diedre looked at her with concern. "Vera, your face is as green as that cabbage you are holding."

"Oh, dear," Vera replied. "I'm afraid I will have to go home. I feel awful."

"Has this been happening for a while?"

"Yes, it has. It comes and goes."

"When we get you home, give me a urine sample. Peter can test it in the lab."

"Test it? For what?"

"To rule out the obvious. You could be pregnant."

"*Pregnant*! Oh, no. Surely not."

"Let's just check and see."

Two days later, Diedre tapped on the back door. Vera opened it to see her friend smiling broadly. "Congratulations, Vera! You are going to have a baby," she said. Vera stepped back in a daze reaching for one of the kitchen chairs. "Oh, my goodness! Oh, dear! I can't believe it!"

"Yes. I'm sure it's a bit of a shock. It will take you a little time to get used to the idea. I can recommend a wonderful obstetrician. He delivered Eric last year." Diedre's family now consisted of six children, three girls and three boys. She chatted on for a while excitedly while Vera tried to process the revelation. She was going to have a baby. She would be thirty-seven years old when it was born, Frances would be fifteen and Ruth, twelve. This was certainly unplanned and unexpected. She wondered how they would react and how Maurice would take the news.

Ruth was giddy with excitement; Frances was embarrassed and Maurice was elated. He was puffed up with pride. "You know, don't you… this baby will be an American citizen. Imagine that!"

"I'll help, Mummy!" Ruth cried. "I'll help take care of the baby. I hope it's a little girl. I'd like it to be a girl."

"Not me!" said Frances. "If you're going to have a baby, it might as well be a boy… for Dad."

"Well, we'll just have to wait and see, won't we?" Maurice remarked.

Vera wrote to Florrie about the news. *I know you have been thinking about when to come over,* she wrote. *Perhaps next summer would be best. The baby is due in June so how about July or August. Stay for as long as you can.* Florrie was beside herself with joy. *What an unexpected turn of events. Another grandchild, how wonderful!* she thought. Florrie and Ted went to the travel agent immediately to make arrangements for a summertime visit. It perked Florrie up tremendously, filling months with excitement, anticipation and delight.

Vera also wrote to Charlotte and Walter with a note included from Maurice. *Dad, after six granddaughters, perhaps this will be the grandson you always wanted. You had better start thinking of a visit. I know you and Mum are a bit nervous to fly, but now you will have to. Come on! How about it?*

As the pregnancy progressed, Vera slowed down. She realised that she did not have as much energy as she had with her earlier pregnancies. Her ankles swelled and the varicose veins that had worsened with each pregnancy ached. Frances and Ruth pitched in more at home after school. They made tea, vacuumed and helped with dinner and washing up. Yvonne visited often, telephoning first to see if there was anything she could pick up on the way. She made sure Vera put her feet up and drove her to help with some of her errands and appointments.

The family was invited for an evening at Bud and Lois's house. It was a large, old house with many rooms, interesting hallways, mysterious doors and filled with bookshelves, cabinets, and knickknacks. Vera was happy to see Yvonne, Bob, and their family, as well as Bob's mother, Goldie and some of Bob's brothers and sisters. The dining table was full of food, buffet style. When everyone had made themselves a plate, a baby carriage was wheeled in piled with presents. Vera was confused. She did not know what was going on. "It's a baby shower!" Lois announced laughing. "It's a baby shower for you, Vera."

"A baby shower? I've never heard of a baby shower," Vera responded. "All this is not for me, surely!"

"Of course, it is. Gifts for you and the new baby," said Bud.

"Oh, my goodness!"

"My word!" said Maurice.

"Come on Vera," said Yvonne, taking her by the arm. Sit over here where we can all see you. I'll bring your plate and a drink."

"Yvonne," Vera whispered. "This is such a surprise. I am just overwhelmed."

"It's an American custom, Vera," Yvonne said with a chuckle. "A way to stock you up with baby gear. Just enjoy it."

Vera was so delighted with all the new baby clothes, diapers, toys, sheets, blankets etc. Some of her new friends and neighbours had baby items stored in cupboards and attics that they were only too happy to pass on. She was well-equipped as the due date approached. There was a discussion of names around the dining room table. The tubular steel kitchen table with Formica top and vinyl upholstered chairs had recently been replaced with a formal wooden double-pedestal dining table and chairs that Maurice had seen at an estate sale. He bought it for $50 and restored it to its former glory by sanding, staining and coating with polyurethane. "We like Helen for a girl, Helen Myra," Vera said.

"And Clive for a boy," Maurice added.

"*Clive!*" Frances exclaimed with a look of disbelief. "You can't call him Clive."

"Why not?"

"He'll be made fun of at school," Ruth chuckled.

"Dad, it's just too English and not a common name here in America. Don't call him Clive!" Frances explained.

"Well, we quite like it." Maurice stated.

Maurice decided to leave the Benway company and strike out on his own again. He had learned a lot about home decorating and the building trade in the United States during his two years with the firm and was confident that he would do well operating his own business. He was determined to be successful doing everything that he was able to on his building projects himself, from preparing foundations for concrete, framing, roofing, hanging sheet rock, fitting cabinets, mouldings, flooring, painting and wallpapering. He had to hire plumbers and electricians and helpers sometimes for heavy work and to move the project along faster. He knew about permits, inspections, insurance and the various requirements to build to the accepted code, and with his usual optimism, he forged ahead. He applied for construction loans and worked hard at the site every day. He also took on work in the evenings hanging wallpaper, driving himself to the limit as he often did. When the first house was completed and put up for sale, Maurice felt proud of his accomplishment and hoped for a good return on his labour. Costs had risen higher than he expected building his first house so when he finally accepted the best price, paid back his loan and interest, paid the attorney and fees, he ended up with rather less than he had anticipated. However, it was his first effort, and he was anxious to get started right away with another build. He had made a few more contacts, learned the best places to buy his materials, and felt comfortable with his sub-contractors and bank representative who gave him tips on building lots that were available for sale. Soon the next project was under way.

Vera's labour began one afternoon in June. When Frances and Ruth returned home from school, they found their mother in discomfort with her neighbour and friend, Trudy Clark in attendance. Trudy had been a nurse, so she was calmly monitoring the time between contractions as they waited for Maurice to come home.

"Don't worry, Vera," she said. "If the contractions get too close together, I will drive you to the hospital and Maurice can meet you there."

"Does Daddy know?" Ruth asked anxiously.

"Yeees," Vera panted as another contraction gripped her. "He called to check in just a little while ago. He's on his way."

"Oh, thank goodness," said Frances who was watching her mother's straining face uneasily. Everyone was relieved when they heard Maurice's car pull up outside and he came in upon the scene of three anxious faces and a smiling Trudy.

"Well, so this is it. Today's the day. Thank you, Trudy for being here with Vera." He picked up the small, packed suitcase at Vera's feet and took his wife's arm as she stood up. "Alright dear? Off we go then. I'll call you later, girls, as soon as the baby arrives."

It was a long afternoon and evening for Frances and Ruth. They made themselves some dinner, watched television, and looked at the clock frequently. When it got late, they got ready for bed and were about to attempt to sleep when the phone rang. Frances dashed downstairs to answer it.

"The baby is here!" Maurice informed her.

"Oh, *good!* Is it a boy?"

"No, it's a little girl."

"Oh, Dad, oh…" Frances sighed with obvious

disappointment.

"Wait 'til you see her! She is so beautiful!"

"How's Mum?"

"She's just fine. She is settled in her room now. I'll stay with her a little while and then come home. You get to bed now, and I'll see you in the morning."

Frances ran upstairs to give the news to Ruth who was sitting up in bed waiting.

"It's a girl."

"Oh wow! That's great. I can't wait to see her."

"Dad says that she is beautiful."

"I'm sure she is. A little sister… Helen."

"Dad never said, but I think he was hoping for a boy."

"I'm glad it is a girl. Won't it be fun to dress her up, play with her, take her for walks?" Frances smiled weakly. She had been hoping for a boy too.

"At least it's not *Clive!*" she said.

Excerpt from Florrie's first letter to Vera after emigrating- July 7, 1964

Hello My Dears

Have just left work and on my way to Auntie Het's for dinner. Well, I'm just beginning to see properly after yet another battle which was so hard to fight, but never mind. It's all for the best for you, I pray. I feel completely lost, but I shall, I know, pull through as time goes on and as that goes, I know I shall be getting nearer to seeing you all again. What a wonderful foursome you are. I'm mighty proud of you and nobody on this earth will or can say anything against you. I love you all so dearly.

Well Vera, I do hope you had a happy journey and was okay when you landed. I guess you were all bubbling over with excitement. What a wonderful greeting you must have had. Well, look after yourselves and I wish you prosperity and happiness. God bless you all and keep you safe. Your Mum, Mum-in-law, and Nana. Proud of the lot. All my love to you Vera, Maurice, Frances, and Ruth

Excerpt from a letter from Florrie to Frances – dated June 16, 1965

I hope you enjoy your graduation dance and I hope you do well. You will have all the pleasure you want when you have finished schooling, years and years and years of it. Being brainy and to have a good sense of humour, and able to cook a good meal, is a wonderful combination to acquire.

Excerpt from Vera's memories binder – a contribution to her creative writing class.

We headed to the Blue Ridge Mountains to a beautiful campsite called Sherando Lake. It was breathtakingly gorgeous with crystal clear water, a grocery cabin, immaculate showers and laundry facilities, and a picturesque campsite layout. We wallowed in the pleasures of warm bathing with fun and games on the sandy lakeside. We watched spectacular sunsets and had marvellous cookouts, sing-a-longs and in general, great family activities. One of our final days in this delightful spot was spent mountain climbing to reach the top of a very high peak and survey the scenery.

CHAPTER NINETEEN

Helen Myra Brown was born on Monday, 6th June 1966, which was 6/6/66 or "clickety click," as Vera would say. She was indeed a beautiful baby and the first in the family to be an American citizen. The household revolved around her that summer. The timing was perfect. The girls only had a few more weeks of school before the school year was over and summer vacation began. Ruth was particularly enamoured of the baby. She was twelve years old and happy to help out and fill the summer taking care of her as much as she could. It was wonderful for Vera who was able to put her feet up during the day taking care of her varicose veins which had worsened during the pregnancy. Frances doted on the baby too but was happy to let Ruth handle most of baby Helen's needs.

Maurice was proud of his new daughter. She was a delightful babe in arms, content, smiling early, and sleeping well at night. He continued to work long hours, building another house in Fairfield, and wallpapering at night. He sometimes went days without seeing his family except for a morning cup of tea, and a little playtime with Helen during a nighttime feeding. He wanted to earn as much as he could because Florrie and Ted were coming to visit at the end of July for two months, and he wanted to make it as special as possible for them.

The household fell into a regular routine as the weeks passed by. One morning, Vera rose early to tend to Helen who was crying for her early bottle. Vera had chosen not to nurse the baby, as it was the trend at that time to use formula. She also remembered the awful time she had experienced with Ruth twelve years ago when she had suffered with mastitis. It had been a hot, humid night so she left the bed in a sheer, light-weight nightgown, hurrying downstairs to prepare a bottle in the kitchen. While warming the bottle, she heard a rattling of the trash cans on the side of the house around the corner from the back door of the kitchen. *Aha!* She thought to herself. *Those animals are trying to get into the trash cans.* Here was a chance to teach those animals a lesson. Vera filled a big pot with water and quietly opened the back door tiptoeing toward the corner. With a loud "Whoop!" she jumped out beyond the edge of the house and tossed the contents of the pot toward the cans.

"*OH!*" She cried. "*Oh no!*" There stood a drenched trash collector who had been patiently working to untie her knots. He was staring at her utterly dumbfounded as the water dripped from his cap and soaked into his clothes. Vera was horrified, but realizing that she was standing there, outside, in her flimsy, summer, nightgown, she could only spin around and retreat as quickly as she could. She flew upstairs and into her bedroom. Maurice looked at her questioningly noticing her breathless, agitated state. "*I've just thrown water all over the garbage man!* I heard a rattling and thought it was animals trying to get inside the cans."

"*You didn't!*" When she explained what had happened, he laughed aloud. "Oh Vera! Only *you* would do that!"

He raised the shade on the window and the two of them watched the garbage truck move off down the street. Two men hanging off the back of the truck and the driver were looking in the direction of the house where one of them was pointing earnestly. Maurice laughed again as Vera crumpled on the bed consumed with embarrassment. "Bet they draw straws the next time they come to collect our garbage!" he chuckled.

As the weeks passed, Vera became more and more excited. Florrie and Ted were coming at the end of July for a nice long two-month visit. She had written at length about the birth and the first weeks of Helen's arrival and was anxious for her mother to meet her new granddaughter in person. Florrie too was ecstatic. She had shopped for special baby clothing and gifts and started packing weeks before the trip. What a joy to be seeing her family again. It had been a long two years since they had left and now she had a new baby to cuddle. Vera was especially grateful to Ruth's attention and help with Helen. She wanted the house to look at its best for her mother. She cleaned and fussed, polished and shone and set up the back bedroom to make it pretty and comfortable for Florrie and Ted. It had not yet been set up with a crib, so Vera rented two single beds, bought new curtains for the window, emptied the closet for them and set up bedside tables and lamps. She was thrilled with the way it looked and revelled in the anticipation of their arrival. The baby would sleep in her bassinet in the master bedroom with her mother and father.

The day that Florrie and Ted arrived, they took Helen to Yvonne's before traveling to JFK airport. It was an extremely sweltering day, expected to reach one hundred degrees. This was a time when most cars and homes did not have air conditioning. Yvonne borrowed a little portable crib for the baby and set up fans to circulate the air. She had bottles and formula and would so enjoy taking care of Helen for a few hours. She would also prepare a dinner for everyone to enjoy when they returned. Bob would cook out on the grill, and she would make salad and vegetables, and serve fresh, crusty rolls as well as pie and ice cream for dessert. She was so excited to see her Auntie Flo too! Florrie had met Barbara during the trip back to

England in 1958, but she had not met Gary or Debbie yet.

The traffic was bad getting to the airport. There was congestion and backups along the way. It was so hot that cars were overheating and pulling to the side. On one road, a man stood at the end of his property with a hose offering to top up radiators and cool down engines. At the airport, Vera, Maurice, Frances and Ruth waited in the arrivals lounge where they were grateful for the air conditioning. They stood in their light-weight clothes, shorts, cotton tops, sandals and straw hats, ready to welcome Florrie and Ted to America in typical casual, summer attire. All had butterflies and excited anticipation as they strained to glimpse their Florrie and Ted amongst the arriving passengers. And suddenly, there they were, Florrie in a stylish, tailored, white suit and Ted in his dark suit and tie both scanning the waiting crowd for their family. When Florrie spotted them, she took one look and bent over with laughter. She had not known what to expect but the contrast was so comical compared to the last time she had seen them, all done up in their travelling outfits when they left England, so formally decked out and respectably British. What a greeting it was! Everyone talking at once, hugging, kissing and laughing until Maurice finally led them over to baggage claim to retrieve their bags. All the way back to Fairfield there was non-stop chatter, questions, and commentary on the sights they passed along the way.

The dramatic greeting commenced all over again at Yvonne's. Yvonne hugged her aunt as they both giggled with delight. Barbara took her turn and then Gary and Debbie were introduced although they felt that they knew Florrie and Ted already, having heard so much about them over the years. And then, Florrie met Helen. This time, tears sprang to her eyes as she held her in her arms for the first time. All eyes were on them until Bob rescued Maurice and Ted, inviting them outside to have a beer. Florrie checked out her new granddaughter from head to toe. "Isn't she lovely! Feel 'er skin. Smooth as silk, she said. "'Allo *Helen*!" she said, rarely emphasizing the "H" sound because it was her granddaughter's name. "I'm your old Nana come to see you all the way from England."

There was so much to see and talk about. Yvonne showed Florrie around the house and then took her into the back yard where it was shady and the worst of the heat of the day had abated. Dinner was casual, on the picnic table and tray tables with plenty of cold drinks to keep them cool. As the afternoon wore on to early evening, Maurice thanked Yvonne and Bob for the lovely time. "I want to get Mum and Ted home before it's dark to show them the house. We will be seeing each other a lot in the next couple of months so never fear, there will be plenty of time to spend together."

"Thanks, Yvonne," said Vera. I'm so glad we didn't take Helen with us to the airport. It was so hot in the car. She was much more comfortable here."

"I was happy to have her. We all were. See you soon."

Florrie held the baby in the car. "How far is it to your house, Maurice?" she asked.

"Not far. Only about fifteen minutes."

"Lovely 'ouses!" Ted remarked looking out the window.

"She's sound asleep, she is," said Florrie. Vera looked across the backseat to observe her mother gazing down at her baby granddaughter. It was a touching moment.

The house stood majestically in the golden sunset.

Florrie and Ted were amazed as the car turned onto the long driveway and Maurice drove slowly so that they could take it in. As Maurice took their bags out of the car, Florrie handed the baby to Vera and wandered around the grounds. She circled the house and ended up in front of the waterfall which was cascading dramatically in the evening light. Vera came up to stand beside her. "It's gorgeous, luv," said Florrie. "'ard to take it all in. What a beautiful setting. I will be able to imagine you 'ere now and I'll be 'appy that you live in such a place." Vera swallowed back the lump in her throat. "I know, Mum. We are very lucky to be here. Come on, let's go inside. So much to show you. We'll put Helen in her bassinet and make a nice cup of tea."

It was a visit long to be remembered by all. The first few days were all about the house, the baby, catching up on all the news, meeting some of the neighbours and relaxing in the sunshine. Ted enjoyed stretching out on a lounger in the side yard with a cold drink, his cigarettes and a good book. Florrie needed plenty of time to reconnect with Frances and Ruth. She loved to sit with them and listen to them talk about their friends and schools and all the funny things that had happened to them fitting in to a new country and lifestyle.

"Cor! This is lovely, isn't it?" she said, looking around Frances's room. "What a nice big room. Your dad outdid 'imself, 'e did!"

"It is nice, of course… and I know Dad worked so hard getting everything ready for us," Frances replied. "But Nana, I still miss England so much. Everything is big and beautiful here, but life is so different. I don't know how to explain it, I think it's because I still don't feel that I really belong here. I still feel a strong connection to England. I love the history, the towns, and villages. I miss the lifestyle and, of course, I miss my family there."

"Ah... yes. I understand 'ow you feel. Believe me. England is a country to be proud of. We 'ave fought for it, suffered for it, sacrificed for it and loved it. But your mum and dad 'ave 'ad their share of 'ard times and struggles and it 'as been 'ard for them to make a living back 'ome. Can't blame them for wanting to try a new life somewhere else!"

"Oh, I know. It's just that it may not be for me, Nana. Dad told us it would be for a five-year trial, but I don't see him ever going back. He loves it here. And now there's Helen, this house, and he's talking about becoming an American citizen as soon as he can."

"Well, luv, you will make your own life soon enough. Be 'appy in the meantime. Be 'elpful to your mum and work 'ard at school."

"Oh, yes, Nana. Of course, I will."

Florrie's chats with Ruth were so different. Ruth was completely enamoured with Helen, taking care of her, feeding her, dressing her, taking her for walks, playing with her. Florrie loved to watch her, the little mother, taking such a load off Vera.

"She's a lucky baby, she is, to 'ave a sister like you."

"I love taking care of her, Nana. I can't wait until she crawls and walks, and I can read to her."

"Don't rush it!" Florrie chuckled. "So, 'ow do you like your new school?"

"Oh, I liked North Stratfield. It was brand new when I started there, and I have made lots of friends. I go to Junior High School this year in September. I'm a bit nervous about that and I will miss being with Helen all day."

"Yes, well, I expect she will be 'appy to see you when you come 'ome. Got to get that education and 'ave time with your friends too."

"Mmmm... I know."

There were many gatherings during Florrie's visit. The Lundbechs came often, Yvonne and Bob, Diedre popped in a few times, Bud and Lois, neighbours and friends. Florrie was as happy as she had ever been, so glad to be with her family and to become part of their new world for a while. She appreciated every day, every event, every new friend and acquaintance, every place she went. She marvelled at the Trumbull Shopping Park. "Cor! What a place!" Vera took them to the beach where they basked in the sun and sat in the waves. "This salt water…" Florrie remarked. "This seawater is so good for our legs!" Both Florrie and Ted had problems with ulcers on their legs which were the result of random knocks and thumps against them. Sure enough, the sores cleared up completely during their stay. They ate on the picnic table outside, had cocktails on the porch, sang pub songs with Ray and Hazel, sat outside in the evening watching the sunset and the fireflies.

A few weeks into the visit, Evelyn drove over to pick up Florrie for the day. Yvonne had been the intermediary when Evelyn said that she would like to spend some time with her aunt during her stay. Florrie had thought about it for a while and decided that she would agree. She had thought back about the sad childhood Evelyn had endured, the early marriage to escape from her father's domination, the difficulties she had endured with James away during the war and the changed man who came back to her. She also thought of her poor sister, Margaret. She thought she owed it to her.

Evelyn was now separated from James and beginning divorce proceedings. She took Florrie to meet Al, the new man in her life whom she planned to marry after the divorce. They had a nice lunch together. Florrie quite liked him. The conversation was very safe with a lot of reminiscing and questions from Al about her life in England, what she thought of America and where she would be going while she was here. Evelyn then took Florrie to meet a few more friends where she played the piano for them for a while. It was a pleasant time, but Florrie was glad when Evelyn drove her back home. She had done her duty.

Vera and Maurice had planned a special trip for Florrie and Ted. As a young man, Maurice had enjoyed joking and teasing Florrie. When Vera and Maurice were married, they had not enjoyed a traditional honeymoon to a special destination, and Maurice had announced that one day he would take his wife and Florrie to see Niagara Falls to make up for it. Florrie had laughed and kidded him back. "Just be careful what you promise, cheeky lad!" Well, this was his chance. Especially since an old friend of Florrie's, Jean, had moved to Canada after marrying a Canadian soldier she had met during the war. She did not live too far from the Falls. She and Florrie had been remarkably close, and Florrie had missed her terribly when she moved away. Jean was one of over 40,000 British women who became war brides and moved to Canada after the war. Maurice rented another pop-up trailer and off they all went, Maurice, Vera, Florrie, Ted, Frances, Ruth and Helen. At a rest stop along the way, everyone used the facilities, stretched their legs and ate some sandwiches that Vera had packed. Vera pulled the car bed from the back of the station wagon, placed it on the hitch connecting the trailer to the car and lay Helen in it while they all ate and enjoyed the sunshine. She went into the rest stop to ask for some warm water to make up Helen's bottle. Florrie already had the baby in her arms when she returned.

"I'll feed 'er, Vera."

"Alright, Mum. Here you are," she said testing the formula on her arm. "Just the right temperature."

Everyone took their seats again, Maurice driving, Frances between him and Ted in the front bench seat and Vera, Ruth and Florrie with the baby in the rear. There were a few more hours of driving to go until they would reach the campsite near the Falls. As they drove along, a car passed them with passengers waving and pointing. Another beeped as it went by. Several other cars passed looking over, gesturing, and mouthing words.

"What's going on?" Maurice said when another car drove alongside keeping pace with Maurice's speed. The passenger rolled the window down and was calling across pointing behind the car. Maurice slowed and pulled over to the side of the highway. "Maybe something is wrong with the trailer," Vera suggested. Maurice walked behind the car, put his hands on his hips and grimaced. He dropped down the rear door of the station wagon and set the baby's car bed in the cargo area. "Oh, no!" exclaimed Vera. "We forgot the car bed!"

"Those people waving at us must have thought we left the baby in it," said Frances.

"What a stupid mistake," Maurice lamented. "Oh, dear me!"

"Never mind," Florrie commented. "No 'arm done. We would never leave you be'ind, would we?" she soothed, as the baby sucked happily on her bottle.

The campground was large, and the campsites were spread far apart with plenty of tall trees providing shade. There was a firepit for a campfire, grill for cooking and a water spigot. It was just a short walk to the facilities and showers and there was an ice machine.

"Oh, isn't it lovely 'ere!" Florrie declared. "Vera… remember our camping days with your dad?"

"Yes, Mum. I loved those times."

"Yeees," Florrie nodded lost in thought for a moment. Maurice and Ted were setting up the pop-up. It was a larger model than the one they had used in Virginia. There were two double size beds on both ends, a table on a hinge that could be raised up and secured in the middle and a bench on each side with foam cushions. Vera had packed pillows, bedding, towels, toiletries, plenty of food and an ice chest for meat, milk, beer, and soda. She had also brought a transistor radio, playing cards, a battery-operated lantern and flashlights. It was wonderful camping under the stars with a nice, big campfire and burgers cooking on the grill, plenty of time to relax gazing into the flames and chatting happily together. Vera had brought an old kettle for heating water on the grill. She made tea and warmed water for Helen's bottles. Ted and Maurice enjoyed a beer or two while Maurice attempted to explain to him how American football and baseball was played. When everyone was drowsy, the adults settled into the beds on each end of the camper, the girls spread the foam cushions on the floor and curled up in sleeping bags, and Helen slept in her little car bed.

The following day Maurice drove them all to Niagara Falls. It was a magnificent sight. The size of the Falls and the sound and the power of the water falling and roaring amazed them all. They marvelled at the rapids as the water churned and sped along before descending so dramatically, and at the mist that rose from the depths, displaying rainbow arcs which formed in the sunlight. They stood in awe witnessing the wonder and glory of nature. Vera and Florrie snapped photographs of different angles and perspectives as well as group shots standing at various locations with the magnificent backdrop behind them. Maurice put his arm around his wife and mother-in-law at one point. "There you are! Told you I would bring you here one day, didn't I?"

"Yes, you did! I never would 'ave believed it!" Florrie declared. "Nice to know you keep your promises, Maurice."

As they made their way to visit Jean the next day, Florrie read out the directions that Jean had sent her in a letter while Maurice drove. She had included route numbers and road names and landmarks which made it easy to find. When they turned onto Jean's road, Florrie checked the house numbers as the car slowly passed each one. "This is it!" she announced. "This one on the end. And that's Jean… look, sitting in that garden chair!" Florrie hurried from the car and rushed up to Jean who had risen from her chair to greet her old friend. They both burst into laughter as they hugged. It had been twenty years since they last saw each other but the years fell away with their happy reunion. There were introductions all around. Jean's husband and some of the family members were there for the event and soon tea was made, food set out and several conversations were taking place at the same time. It was a day of sheer joy for Florrie with so much to catch up on and reminisce about. She had never expected to see Jean again. Photographs were passed around. Jean had a few of Florrie and other friends of theirs during their younger days and Florrie had brought some too. There was a lot of "Remember this?" "Who's that?" "Vera, look at this photo, I've told you about this person." "Do you know whatever happened to…?"

As evening approached, Maurice announced that it was

time to go. "Got to be able to find my way back to the campgrounds before it gets dark," he declared. And so there followed the sorrowful parting, the promises to keep in touch, the hugs and handshakes, the tears and the final waves goodbye. "Thank you very much, Maurice," Florrie said with a sniff on the ride back. "Thank you for taking me to see my friend."

In September, the hot days began to cool down and there was a touch of autumn in the air. Florrie's birthday was on 16th September, just before she and Ted were scheduled to fly back home. Vera knew that the house in Chingford could be quite cold during the winter, so she bought her mother a warm one-piece head-to-toe sleeper. Florrie put it on up in her room and then came downstairs. She danced around the den up on her toes, making exaggerated arm movements turning this way and that. The family was in stitches as Florrie continued to play to her audience. Finally, Vera pointed out to her that the flap in the back which was there for the convenience of the call of nature, was unbuttoned and revealed a particular part of her anatomy. Florrie stopped in her tracks, turned around to look and then collapsed in her usual spasms of laughter while Vera hurriedly buttoned her up.

Vera and Maurice drove Florrie and Ted to JFK with Helen on the date of departure. The girls were back in school and arrived home to a still, quiet house. Everything was neat and tidy, but it felt empty and lonely. Frances peeked into the spare bedroom where Nana and Uncle Ted had slept. There was no sign of them having been there. She sat on the bed and wept. She would miss them. Her grandmother's personality was unique, bringing her own special expression of humour, happiness and wisdom into her life as well as beloved memories of England.

Vera was sombre and thoughtful for a while following the visit. It was back to writing letters again and remembering how much she had enjoyed her mother's company. At least now when she wrote, her mother would be able to picture the surroundings and know what her daily life was like and of course, she had met her new granddaughter. Perhaps it would not be too long before she and Ted visited again. Meanwhile, she had a busy household and lots to do.

Christmas of 1966 was cold and snowy. Christmas Day fell on Sunday that year so the Lundbechs arrived on Friday afternoon and would stay all weekend. Helen was six months old and the centre of a lot of attention. There was always someone fussing over her, playing with her and taking care of her needs. Deborah and Ruth loved to dress her up, bathe her, brush her little head of blond hair, feed her and bundle her up to play in the snow. On Christmas Eve a nor'easter arrived. It started to snow and continued into Christmas Day, delivering over a foot of snow. But what a special feeling of Christmas it provided, with snowflakes falling steadily outside every window, the landscape covered with a thick white blanket and a warm, cosiness inside. There were the usual games and jokes and silly conversations and the anticipation of Christmas morning with plenty of packages under the tree. Helen was wide-eyed with the lights and decorations and all the excitement of the holiday. She was sitting up by herself now and was placed in front of the tree with her little sparkly plastic ball with a spinning butterfly inside and all the brightly wrapped packages behind her, for a photo session.

Everyone had everything they needed so there was no need to go out into the storm... except when Ray discovered that he did not have many cigarettes left.

"Oh, crumbs Maurice! I can't go the whole weekend without cigarettes!"

"Oh, dear," Maurice replied. He had been a heavy smoker in his younger days too but had given it up five years ago. He remembered the craving and addiction well.

"Come on. Ray, get yourself bundled up and we can walk over to the gas station on Stratfield Road before the snow gets too deep."

"What, go out in this!" Ray exclaimed.

"Well... the alternative is to go without cigarettes. Up to you."

"How far away is it?"

"Oh, about a mile, maybe a bit less." Ray hesitated just for a moment. "Right then. Let's go."

It was like being in a different world. The snow fell steadily and heavily, covering every tree, bush and surface, turning the landscape into a winter wonderland. It was so quiet with no one outside and almost no cars on the road. The snow muffled their footsteps and any other sounds, creating a surreal experience. In the quietness, the men found themselves chatting quietly, instinctively blending into the changed environment.

"My God, Maurice! I hope the place is open!"

"Yes, Ray. I suppose it would have been a good idea to call first." Maurice chuckled.

"Bit hard going, isn't it? Seems like it's all uphill."

"Never really noticed it driving, but yes... it is a bit steep."

"How much further now, Maurice?" Ray asked beginning to puff a bit.

"Not very far now. And don't worry, Ray. It's all downhill on the way back!"

"Ha! Very funny!"

The station was open. Ray purchased multiple packs and they trudged back home. The trip had taken just under an hour. They came into the porch and shook off the snow from their coats, hats and gloves and hung the wet clothes in the bathroom to dry. Their cheeks were rosy and numb but they felt a bit like returning explorers. Maurice poured them both a brandy while Vera put the kettle on.

"Well, that was quite an adventure!" Maurice laughed. "Ray, you might want to think about giving those things up!"

Christmas morning was an exciting, noisy cacophony of cups of tea, wrapping paper, ribbons and bows, exclamations of surprise and thanks, playing with Helen and her new toys and finally, an all-hands clean-up followed by breakfast. Frances had received the gift of a portable electric organ from Vera and Maurice and was eager to try some of her old sheet music on it. Later in the day, Ray played some carols which they all sang together. Before dinner Maurice and Ray, Frances, Ruth, Deborah and Nicholas all went sledding and tobogganing on the golf course which could be accessed at the end of Weeping Willow Lane and across Jefferson Street. There were several families there. The snow was perfect, deep and compact, and the hills nice and steep. It was hard work trudging back up the hill after the long slide down but so much fun. The children laughed when Maurice and Ray tobogganed down together, ending up tipping over and landing half buried in a snowbank. The snow was tapering off as the afternoon wore on and the group headed back to the house, the smell of roasting meat greeting them, and a table set for dinner decorated with brightly coloured Christmas crackers. It was a sumptuous Christmas feast, ending with a traditional flaming Christmas pudding. Maurice had to have his Christmas "pud," Christmas was just not complete without it. Not everyone was fond of it, so Hazel had made a chocolate cream log cake which was perfect with a side of ice cream. The evening was quieter with the adults chatting contentedly enjoying beer and wine and the children playing some of their new games together. It was a Christmas forever remembered nostalgically and recounted over the years.

Excerpt from a letter from Charlotte – dated December 26, 1967
Do hope you have had a really good Christmas. Dad and I have been very quiet but have enjoyed it in our own way. I have really missed the children and thought of them a lot. Eileen wanted us to go for Christmas, but it was so far to travel for a short time, (why did all our family go so far away from us.) Still, they must make their own life. We hope to go to Devon in the spring to see them all.

CHAPTER TWENTY

When Helen turned one year old, she was walking and beginning to talk. She was very much the centre of attention especially now that she could speak and make everyone laugh at her words and antics. She already exuded confidence and was comfortable in the company of adults. She would grow up to love parties, music, fun and games and a enjoy a wide circle of friends. Vera spent a lot of time with her young daughter while the girls were in school, taking her to the beach in the summer, to the zoo and to story time at the library. Yvonne came over often during the day. She enjoyed watching and listening to Helen who was chatting away and singing a wide assortment of songs.

Frances was growing up. At sixteen she was quite involved at activities at school, she played girls' basketball and joined the field hockey team. It had taken her three years to begin to feel comfortable at school and decide to participate. She had a small group of friends who encouraged her to attend the football games and accept invitations to parties. Vera urged her to go to these events. She felt that it was time for her to blossom as a young lady and mingle more with her peers, especially boys. "These are the best years of your life, Frances," she would say. "You'll never know who you like and who you don't unless you meet people and interact. You've got to get out there. Have fun." Frances sighed. It was hard for her. She was naturally shy and self-conscious and had been set back in overcoming these characteristics with the move and uprooting from England. But she *had* been noticing members off the other sex. There were several young men who attracted her, but she kept her feelings to herself. She succumbed to her friends' constant urging and attended some of the parties. They were very low-key, usually in a basement playroom or den, with a record player, soda and chips and a nice group of boys and girls she knew from school. She enjoyed the parties and began to bring along some of her own records, dancing and joking and feeling more comfortable with high school boys. Vera was happy to see Frances getting out and socialising but she and Maurice announced another expectation now that she was sixteen.

"You need to get a part-time job after school," Maurice stated.

"It will be good for you to get a taste of the working world and to earn some money," added Vera.

"Oh, but what about the field hockey team, and my gym teacher wants me to come out for track. She said that my sprinting speed is close to the state record."

"All that is very good," Vera acknowledged. "But it won't help you much in life, will it? A job is more important. You want to go to college when you graduate, you need to save some money. That's only two years away."

"When I was your age, I had already been working for two years. You've had it pretty easy up 'til now," Maurice added.

"Well, I have worked hard at school and got good grades."

"Your grades are very good. We are very proud of you, but you should be able to manage schoolwork and a little job at the same time," her father explained.

"Anyway," said Vera, "See what you can find."

Frances felt rather discouraged with the mandate presented to her, but she knew her parents would expect her to comply. There were still strong influences from their upbringing, the hardships of the war and their no-nonsense approach to raising responsible children. She gave up field hockey, did not go out for track and got a job at a nursing home within walking distance, just up the hill on Jefferson Street. She worked from 4:00 to 8:00 after school and an occasional day on the weekend.

As Frances's junior year came to an end, she was asked out on a date and then to the junior prom by one of the young men who was in a few of her classes. Vera was just as excited as Frances when the day arrived. Hazel had kindly offered to make the dress and it was so stunning, an A-line style with ice-green satin skirt and lace bodice. When the young man arrived and came to the door, Vera had her camera ready. There were introductions and handshakes and then Frances stood stiffly next to her date who stood awkwardly beside her for a few snaps. Vera was gratified that the grand event had been properly recorded and watched them drive away with satisfaction.

Vera was looking forward to visitors again soon. This time it was to be Charlotte and Walter. They had applied for their passports and were soon going to book a flight. Maurice was so looking forward to them coming. They would meet Helen, who would be two years old, and he was anxious for them to see the house and the area. He was beginning to make plans for their visit. Perhaps they would prefer to come in the autumn to see the beautiful colours of the foliage and not come in the heat of the summer. He would mention that in his next letter. All his thoughts and plans, however, did not come to fruition. He received a letter from Auntie Julie informing him that his mother was in the hospital. She had not been feeling well for some time and was often confined to her bed with migraine headaches. She was weak and fatigued and was thought to have suffered a heart attack and perhaps a stroke. Auntie Julie wrote that she seemed to be doing a little better with treatment and that Eileen would soon be arriving from Devon to see her and help when she came home. But another letter followed soon after with sad news. Eileen wrote that Charlotte had suffered another stroke a few days later. She died at age sixty-nine. Maurice read the letter to himself, standing in the kitchen. By the look on his face, Vera knew what information it contained. Her husband put the letter down and walked slowly over to the stove to put the kettle on.

The next morning Maurice telephoned his father's next-door neighbour who popped next door to bring Walter to the phone and they chatted for a while.

"Don't know what I am going to do, Maurice. I can't believe she has gone. May took care of everything. I suppose I will have to make some decisions but… now Maurice, don't bother making the big journey home, don't want you spending all that money. Eileen is here with me, and we'll make the arrangements." When Maurice hung up, he turned to Vera, "I'm going back," he stated.

Frances and Ruth were devastated. They had been happily anticipating their grandparents' visit and suddenly, in a brief letter, they were told that their grandmother was gone. Frances sobbed into her pillow unable to get the image of her grandmother's despairing face out of her mind, as she stood at the bottom of the garden watching them drive away four years ago. Maurice left for England, arriving on the doorstep with his suitcase, unannounced and unexpected. Eileen opened the door and gasped, grabbing him in a tight hug, tears spilling down her cheeks. There were four of them in the house, Walter, Julie, Eileen and Maurice. They spent a lot of time talking together. The funeral arrangements had been made and there was time to chat together as a family, to start to come to terms with the loss and make some preliminary plans for the future. The house must be sold. Neither Walter nor Julie wanted to stay there together without Charlotte, and it seemed inappropriate to them both to live in the same house. Julie would look for a small place for herself. She wanted to stay in or near Hockley where she was comfortable and had friends and acquaintances. Walter would go down to Devon to live with Eileen and Ray. "Dad," said Maurice. "I want you to still think about coming over to visit us. Not right away, of course, but it might do you good to plan a trip sometime in the future."

"I don't know Maurice. Don't see myself coming without May."

"Well, just keep it open as a possibility."

Vera and the girls went about their daily lives while Maurice was gone. Vera was lost in thought a lot of the time, wondering about Maurice and the family in England. Florrie and Ted would be going to the funeral. They had remained quite close to Walter and Charlotte, visiting a few times throughout the year. When they returned from their visit after Helen was born, they visited with photographs and told them all about the trip describing Connecticut, the house, the lifestyle, and all their happy times. Vera was grateful that they had done that. She could just imagine them all sitting around, chatting and laughing together. Now, there had been a break. The first one. The first break with their ties to England and to how things had been when they left. Maurice returned, pleased that he had gone, but happy to be back. It had been odd being back in England, he told Vera. He felt a bit of a stranger there, realising that he would not be able to easily slip back into his old life He was more at home in America and decided that as soon as he could, one more year, he would apply for U.S. citizenship.

Maurice was becoming discouraged with building. The housing market was in a bit of a slump, and he decided that a secure job with a salary would be best at that time. He answered a job posting for a manager of a paint and wallpaper store, one of a chain of stores in the area, and got the position. It was the perfect job for him. He interacted with a lot of people he knew from the building trade, he had an assistant to help with wallpaper customers and ordering, he kept track of inventory, mixed specialised colours, kept records and reports, and enjoyed a steady salary. He also was able to pick up occasional wallpapering jobs. This was a happy time for Vera without all the stresses and problems that came along with building and selling and waiting for closings to collect the proceeds of the sale.

Later that year, Frances went to a freshman mixer at Fairfield University with some of her high school friends. One of her friends was meeting a student she had met there at a previous dance, and he had brought along one of his classmates to meet the girls. They were waiting in the parking lot when the car arrived. The friend was introduced to all five young ladies and Frances found herself walking beside him into the student centre. His name was Joe, and they spent the evening together, dancing to the 60s music of a live band. When they took a break for a soda in the student cafe, they chatted, learning a little about each other. Joe was immediately attracted to Frances, who wore her hair pulled back on the sides and long and loose down her back, and was captivated by her English accent. Frances felt unusually comfortable and at ease with Joe, so handsome with his wool, tweed jacket, white shirt, plaid tie, slim build and head of sandy brown, wavy hair. He was an avid tennis player, a member of the varsity team as a freshman. They danced the evening away and when it was time to leave, Joe offered to drive her home. Ordinarily, Frances would decline but she felt so relaxed and safe in his company that she accepted without hesitation. After informing the friend who had brought her, the young couple headed for the parking lot where Joe directed her to a baby blue Ford Torino with a sporty white "C" stripe along the sides, and a hood scoop. It was a lovely sporty car, obviously new, and when Joe opened the passenger side door for her, she slid in rather impressed. On the drive back to her house, he asked for her phone number.

"Can you write it down for me?" he asked. "There's a pen and paper in the glove compartment."

"Yes, alright." Frances was happy to comply. She would like to see Joe again. She directed him to her house on Weeping Willow Lane. "Well," he said. "I live only a short drive from here, in Trumbull. In fact, I went to Notre Dame high school, on Jefferson Street."

"Oh, good. I'm glad you didn't have to come far out of the way. Thank you for the ride home, Joe."

"Well, it was a pleasure. Thanks for the company."

Vera was still up when Frances came in through the porch door.

"How was the dance? Did you have a nice time?"

"Yes, I did. I met someone very nice and… oh, no!"

"What's the matter?" Frances opened her hand. She still had the piece of paper with her phone number on it. She had neglected to give it to Joe.

"Oh, dear. I met someone who drove me home. He

was so nice, so easy to talk to. He drove me home and asked me for my number. I wrote it down for him, but look, I forgot to give it to him." Vera was surprised. "I can't believe you let a strange, college boy drive you home. Was that wise?"

"Maybe I shouldn't have but I had a strong feeling that I was safe with him."

"Yes, but…"

"And I forgot to give him my number!"

"Well, now he knows where you live." Vera laughed. "You will hear from him again if he wants to see you."

Joe called the next day. He had called his friend who called the friend of Frances who had driven the girls to the mixer to get her phone number. He asked her out to the movies that evening. When Joe arrived, he came to the door to introduce himself to Frances's parents. Maurice shook his hand.

"Glad to meet you, Joe," he said.

"Hello," Vera said. "Would you mind coming in here for a moment?" She preceded him into the den where she had placed a pen and paper on top of the bar. "Would you mind just jotting down some information for me? I have prepared a few questions."

"Oh, *Muuuum*!" Frances groaned, mortified.

"Well… I'm sorry if it seems silly," she explained to Joe, "but we don't know anything about you, and I think it is only right to know something about the person taking our daughter out. She is still in high school, after all and you are a college student."

"Okay… sure," Joe responded warily. Maurice was rather uncomfortable with Vera's questionnaire. He had thought it was unnecessary. "We can trust Frances to choose wisely," he had said. But Vera was insistent. "It's not as if she has had a lot of experience with boys. She has hardly dated at all. She is still quite naïve, and we know nothing about this guy, where he lives, his parents, what he is studying in college. He is just going to drive off with her. I think this is the *least* we should do." Joe was surprised with the questionnaire. He filled in his name, address, phone number, colour, make and model of his car and the license plate number, also his parents' names, occupations, what his major was at Fairfield University and what he expected to do upon graduation.

"Thank you," she said when he had finished. "I hope you have a nice evening. What movie are you going to see?"

"*The Boston Strangler*," Joe answered.

They watched through the window as Joe opened the passenger side door for Frances and they drove off. "Well… what do you think of him, Maurice?"

"*Nice car!*" he replied.

Joe and Frances began dating steadily and exclusively, much to Vera's dismay. She would have liked her daughter to go out with a variety of boys to discover the personalities and characteristics that she preferred, who had impressive career goals, who was thoughtful, kind and generous, who was sociable, outgoing, funny. However, she was pleased that they were having fun, playing a lot of tennis, miniature golf, going to movies, hiking, and spending time with friends. Vera reminded herself that Frances would be attending Central Connecticut State College after graduation from high school. She was bound to meet more young men there.

Vera and Maurice were new to the expectation of college for a lot of high school students. Fairfield was an affluent town, whose schools had a strong focus on achievement, pursuing higher education and planning for a successful career. Frances had become swept up in the movement, especially since she had performed well at school and earned good grades. It was decided by her school guidance counsellor that she should become a teacher and that CCSU would be a good choice for her. She applied and was accepted and obtained a student loan. Vera was satisfied that this decision was a sensible one and would provide Frances with a secure future.

Joseph Evan was an intelligent young man, and of good moral character. Vera's reservations about him concerned his self-confidence which she thought bordered on arrogance, his assertiveness, outspokenness, and the fact that he was overindulged by his parents. It was a clash with her own experience and the struggles she had endured as a child and young adult. Life had been easy for this young man and although she was gratified by the better life that she and Maurice were seeking for themselves and their daughters, there was residual, perhaps subconscious, resentment that the path for Joe had been so straight and smooth. He was there a lot of the time, he imposed himself on the family and took up a lot of Frances's time. He often called right at dinnertime which annoyed Vera. At times, she became quite irritated. She spoke to Yvonne about it the next morning while waiting for an electrician to arrive for a service call.

"Oh, Vera, he seems quite nice to me. I wouldn't criticise him too much if I were you. Frances will get resentful. Wait it out. She's off to college soon."

The electrician arrived to do a little work in the house updating some electrical wiring. While there, he made a call to his wife on a telephone in one of the bedrooms upstairs.

The following day, a repairman from the telephone company came out to the house to investigate a problem with the phone lines. Vera remembered that she had an extension upstairs that was "illegal." At that time, any extensions in the home cost more on the bill. So, before the technician arrived, she disconnected the phone and, on a whim, seeing Helen's plastic play phone nearby, she placed it in the spot where the illegal phone had been. After servicing the telephones and jacks, the technician asked the electrical contractor if there were any more phones in the house.

"Yes," he replied. "Follow me. There's one in the bedroom at the end of the hall." When he entered the room, the electrical contractor stood speechless staring at the toy phone. "But I made a call to my wife from here yesterday…" he said scratching his head. "Uh, huh," the telephone technician responded glancing at him sideways. "Okay, thanks… never mind."

Florrie and Ted both retired in 1968. Vera received a letter from her mother telling her that she was putting the house in Chingford up for sale. She and Ted decided that they would move to Bath, where Ted's sister, Edie, lived alone in a nice bungalow. They would stay with Edie while finding a little place of their own that they could afford comfortably on their pensions. Ted's daughter, Pearl and her family lived in Bath too and so did Florrie's sister Grace and her family. The plan seemed to suit everyone. The news, however, hit Vera hard. The house on Waverley Avenue brought back so many memories and somehow it was comforting to think of her mother still living there. This was another change, another break of another tie. However, she understood how it would be beneficial and wrote back that she was pleased with the decision and wished she were there to help with the move.

Frances graduated in June 1969. She received a massive Oxford English dictionary as a graduation present from her parents. "Every word you should ever need to look up will be in there!" Vera declared proudly. Joe had not been able to attend the ceremony since tickets were limited but he came to the house for a modest celebration afterward. Frances continued to work at the nursing home but switched to days during the summer.

Frances is very busy working during the day this summer. Vera wrote to Florrie. *Then she is out in the evenings with Joe. Weekends they are together all the time. We don't see much of her at all.*

Don't you remember your own dating days, Vera? Florrie wrote back. *You were off out at every opportunity. Especially when the war ended. You and Maurice went all over the place.*

Frances wrote to her grandmother about Joe and Florrie liked the sound of him. *Nana, he is so kind and generous to me. He is working in a foundry at a local factory, Acme Shear, during the summer. He told me that the temperature in the foundry reaches 140 degrees, and he must drink a lot of water and take salt tablets. We are able to go out to nice places for dinner and for fun day trips. We went to West Point last weekend and are going to Old Sturbridge Village in Massachusetts soon. He plays tennis on the varsity team at university, so we play a lot. I love tennis and I give him a pretty good game. It's good practice for him. His parents are very nice too. You would like them. I hope you come to visit again soon.*

Old friends from Rayleigh visited in the summer. Ted and Lil Cox made the big, exciting flight over and divided their stay between Hazel and Ray's and Vera and Maurice's homes. The three couples were united again and fell into their old, comfortable camaraderie. There was so much to talk about, so much to see and so many people to meet. There were outings, visits and several parties. Lil and Ted were amazed by it all, enjoying every minute. While with Vera and Maurice, they loved the hot weather and the days spent at the beach, packing lunches, beach chairs and the umbrella, becoming tanned and relaxed. At Ray and Hazel's, they listened to music, sang around the piano as Ray played, shopped, became friends with Harry and Renie in the first-floor apartment and enjoyed some day trips. The best times, though, were when everyone was together joking, teasing, telling stories and laughing about old times.

After Florrie and Ted had moved and were well settled in Bath, they decided that they would visit again during the summer of 1970. Vera was elated. Months before the visit, she began making plans and redecorating around the house. It was lovely for her to anticipate the time together again. Since they were coming late in the summer and staying for a couple of months, she and Maurice thought that they would be able to take them up to Massachusetts to enjoy the fall foliage before they returned home.

At the end of her freshman year, Frances got a summer job at a local bank. She became a teller and worked at a branch that had several young women about her age employed there. She enjoyed the job and her co-workers and was interested in the opportunities for advancement. As the summer wore on, she dreaded the thought of going back to university, not because she did not like the school, her new friends there, or her classes, but because she did not want to part from Joe.

Just a few weeks before Florrie's visit, Joe met with Maurice and, in the traditional fashion, asked him if he could marry his daughter. Maurice had been expecting a discussion of marriage, so he was not surprised. He gave his consent but asked if he could hold off just a little while. He thought it would be very special to make the announcement after Florrie and Ted arrived. He also told Joe that the jewellery store, a few shops down from the paint and wallpaper store, would be a good place to buy a ring. He was friendly with the owner and Joe would be sure to get a good deal. So, Joe spent all the money he had saved from his summer job, sold two tennis rackets, his golf clubs and a bicycle to buy a diamond ring.

Florrie and Ted arrived, seasoned travellers now, excited to see everyone and to enjoy another lovely, long holiday. Helen was now four years old, happy, precocious and full of energy. Florrie had seen plenty of pictures of her during the past four years but seeing her in person, listening to her chatting away, cuddling her closely, filled her heart with joy. She was amazed at how the girls had grown. They were young women, so lovely in her eyes and there was Maurice, cheeky as ever and her dear Vera. They had months stretching ahead to natter away about everyone and everything. So many cups of tea, dinners, visits with Yvonne and her family and Vera's friends. As they walked to the car at the airport, Florrie whispered to Frances. "I can't wait to meet my Joe."

Vera was delighted to have her mother with them again for an extended visit. Now that Helen was more mobile, they went all over the place together. Florrie was amazed with her young granddaughter and laughed heartily at her antics and funny conversations. They went to the park and the beach, the zoo and a local museum which exhibited dinosaur footprints, held children's activities, and also had a planetarium. They spent time at Lake Mohegan in Fairfield and visited several of Vera's friends who had young children for Helen to play with, and they watched Helen learning her ballet steps at dance class. Yvonne came over often for lunches and perhaps a drive out through woodlands to a country farm store to buy apples and pies.

Joe was often at the house also. Florrie and Joe connected instantly and became very fond of each other. He was amused with her cockney accent and some of her expressions, as well as her words of wisdom and common sense during many discussions. Florrie instinctively trusted Joe and knew he would be loyal and devoted to her granddaughter. She often defended him when Vera chided him for a minor misstep of which she disapproved. Frances and Joe returned from dinner out one evening, and Frances proudly displayed a sparkling solitaire diamond ring on her finger. There were oohs and aahs and congratulations all around. Florrie was the most pleased. "He'll always take care of you," she told her granddaughter quietly.

A difficult conversation followed between Frances and her parents.

"I don't think I will be going back to college in the fall," Frances stated.

"Oh… why not?" Maurice asked, surprised.

"Well… I really like my job at the bank and Joe and I have been talking about it. If I continue working and saving, we will have a good start when we get married after he graduates."

"Yes, but you were doing so well at college. Your grades were excellent."

"I know, Dad. But you know, I am really not committed to a particular field, and I am not sure what I really want to major in."

"Well, I think it's a great shame," Vera responded brimming with disappointment. "But far be it for *us* to persuade you to do something you don't want to do."

"Mum, I am happy at the bank. I have great new friends there and I look forward to going every day. Joe and I can see each other, and we can save for our future. I will just be miserable going back to Central." Vera sighed. "Well, that's it then. You will be working full time and living with us."

"Yes," said Maurice. "That means you will be expected to pay us a small rent for your keep."

"Oh… okay."

"I think fifteen dollars a week."

"Okay… yes Dad." Frances knew that she had disappointed her parents with the decision, so she accepted the condition without complaint. She would often think back in the future and regret leaving college and wondered why she had not considered transferring to a local school but at the time she was happy and single-minded about her plan.

Vera discussed the situation with Florrie.

"We had high hopes when Frances went to college. She always did well in school and had so much potential. We were hoping that she might meet other boys and date some more. She tied herself to Joe so quickly. We thought it would be good for her to get away and have the opportunity to get to know other young men, test her commitment, and have a comparison." Florrie could not help but chuckle.

"Think back, Vera. 'ow old were you when you committed yourself to Maurice? My advice to you is similar to 'ow I 'andled your early engagement. I asked you to wait enough years before you got married so that the relationship was well tested. Frances and Joe don't plan to marry until 'e graduates. That is two years away, enough time for them to be sure it is what they want."

"Yes, I know. It's just not what we wanted for her."

"It's 'er life, Vera. She's 'appy at work, 'appy with Joe, works 'ard. I know you 'ave your reservations with Joe, but 'e's a good, decent lad. Just let them get on with it." Vera nodded in agreement. She knew her mother was right.

Joe's parents, Geza and Elnora, invited all the family and Florrie and Ted to dinner one evening. Elnora prepared a feast including her famous veal cutlets. The dining room was not big enough to accommodate everyone, so they moved the table to the den, which was a long, wide room. There were twelve in attendance, Vera, Maurice, Frances, Joe, Ruth, Helen, Florrie, Ted, Geza, Elnora, Alan, Joe's older brother, and Lynn, Joe's younger, adopted sister. It was a pleasant gathering with lots of chatter and laughter. Helen and Lynn knew each other well because Frances and Joe often took them out together for treats and day trips, so they were happy to play together after dinner. Florrie liked the family, especially Joe's mother who was so welcoming and happy to meet her. Vera and Maurice would develop a friendship over the years with Geza and Elnora spending lots of time together at many family gatherings.

Autumn approached and the hot summer days slowly transitioned to cooler temperatures and the touches of colour on the tips of the trees began to appear. Vera and Maurice planned a trip to Massachusetts to show Florrie and Ted the beauty of New England in the fall before they returned home to England at the end of October. They took Helen with them and arranged to stay at a quaint inn for a couple of days. They drove up through the Berkshires, stopping often to view the glory of sunlit peaks, river valleys and country roads, just a golden panorama stretching in all directions. Florrie and Ted were in awe, snapping away with their camera. The colours of the foliage were so vibrant and glowing with the sunlight illuminating the various shades of yellow, gold, red, orange, rust and green. With a brilliant blue sky, the views were breathtakingly beautiful. It was a peaceful, relaxing few days with meals enjoyed in pretty country cafes along the way, and short strolls around small villages, perhaps finding a park along the way to give Helen a chance to run and play.

It was only a week after the Massachusetts get-away, when Florrie and Ted were scheduled to fly home. The days passed quickly as the date approached and Vera dreaded the separation again. She comforted herself by knowing that they would be back in two years for Frances and Joe's wedding. Although a date had not yet been set, it would most likely be in June 1972 following Joe's graduation.

It was a sad parting and then the depressing return to a quiet, seemingly empty house and the steady routine of everyday life. It was letters back and forth again. Florrie wrote that her photos had been developed and she said that everyone she showed them to believed that the autumn foliage pictures must have been enhanced somehow. They could not believe the vibrancy of the colours.

Maurice was doing well, professionally managing the store. The owners were pleased with the increase in sales and rewarded him with steady raises. He continued to take on occasional wallpapering jobs, especially hanging difficult wallpapers where he could demand a high price. He put money aside for the wedding and talked to friends about possible locations. A favourite place to stop off on a Friday after work was the Fairfield Inn, a restaurant and bar not too far from the store on the Post Road. He met James there and other friends and acquaintances. He learned about the Lions Club as he became friendly with group members who met there once a week. The club was a volunteer service organization, part of Lions Club International. The Fairfield club focused on the blind and sight impaired, which appealed to Maurice because of his fond memories of his blind friends from Vera's office in London. The club collected donations of replaced prescription eyeglasses and held events to raise funds for others charitable events in town. When Maurice was invited to join, he accepted enthusiastically, ever the one to belong to a men's club and feel important in the community. He enjoyed the camaraderie as well as the fundraising events throughout the year and the special member parties and celebrations. He bought the Lions Club ring which he proudly wore every day. The Fairfield Inn had a large banquet hall, so it became the obvious place for Frances and Joe's wedding. When the date was finally set, Maurice reserved it.

An idea was discussed amongst some of the patrons of the Fairfield Inn which began to attract interest. A club was suggested that would be made up of one hundred members in town, business owners, retail managers, realtors, insurance agents, general contractors, lawyers, bankers and others. A location was found in the lower level of a newly built mixed-use development on the Post Road. It was a large space with several large rooms. The members paid to fit it out to incorporate a bar area, lounge, kitchen, dining room and meeting rooms. Maurice did a lot of the work himself. Members then paid a monthly fee, and each had a numbered cubby where they kept their own bottles of liquor and wine. A bartender was on duty during open hours and poured drinks for the members at $1.00 each to cover the expense of mixers and his wages. The club was named "The 100 Club" and it was very successful with members happy to stop there at the end of the day or weekends to relax, chat and exchange news. Most business services were represented, and many contacts, referrals, and opportunities were passed on. It was a true collaborative network.

Between the weekly Lions club meetings at the Fairfield Inn and the availability of the 100 Club on every evening and weekend, Maurice began to spend a lot of time away from home. He justified the time at both locations as important to his status in Fairfield and to make new connections for future work endeavours. Vera was supportive at first and attended some of the special social events that were arranged but when Maurice came home later and later, she protested. Maurice was not at all apologetic explaining that it was a common practice in the business world and that she would have to "lump it." This was not the best time in their marriage. Vera made dinner every night and set his plate aside. When he came home, she heated it up and plonked it down unceremoniously on the table. There were many strained evenings of silence between them. Although they never, ever argued in front of the girls, it was obvious to them that there was a falling out.

Maurice was riding high at this time, enjoying the distinction and pride of belonging to two business groups and benefitting from the connections he made there. He was making a good income and decided that he needed a new car to complement his new, improved status. He spoke to one of the 100 club members who was a sales manager at an Oldsmobile dealership and secured a good deal on a shiny new 1972, radiant green, Oldsmobile Cutlass. It was a two-door coupe with bucket seats, a centre console, a rocket V-8 engine, a white vinyl top and a snazzy automatic shifter on the floor. It was the first brand new car that he had ever owned.

It was time to discuss wedding arrangements. Joe and his parents arrived for a wedding meeting one evening. They discussed the guest list and how large the wedding would be, the meal options, preferred dates and times, the bar arrangement and the cost. Maurice had already obtained prices depending on the number of guests and the meal choices. It was an exciting time for everyone, the first child in both families to be married. They agreed on a total of one hundred and fifty guests, an open bar, and live band. When all was decided, Geza stood up and extended his hand to Maurice.

"Well, Maurice, what do you think? Fifty-fifty?"

"Thank you mate!" Maurice replied shaking his hand gratefully. "That's very generous indeed."

Vera wrote to Florrie about the wedding plans as they progressed. *We went to a bridal shop with Ruth and Helen, and Hazel, Deborah, and Nicholas, he wanted to come along too. Frances loved the first dress she tried on. I won't describe it to you because I want it to be a surprise. She tried on a few more but when she put the first one on again, we all agreed, it was the one. I will have to shop now for my mother of the bride gown. Frances is going to go with her bridesmaids to choose dresses for them soon. She and Joe will buy the cake and flowers and they have ordered the invitations. It is really moving along now. Time for you to book your flights.*

Wedding preparations seemed to dominate in early 1972. The wedding date was set for 2nd June and the wedding party was determined; Joe's brother Alan would be best man and three of Joe's friends, Bill, Paul, and Jim would be groom's men, Ruth would be maid of honour, Deborah, Lynn (Joe's sister) and one of Frances's friends, Wendy, from the bank were bridesmaids and Helen was flower girl. There were the usual arrangements to make, invitations, photographer, wedding cake, flowers, favours, seating plan, gifts for the wedding party, rehearsal dinner, honeymoon plans. Frances and Joe had to find an apartment and Joe would be graduating just the Sunday before the wedding, which was on the following Friday, and he had to find a job. Every mealtime, the subject of the wedding and all the tasks surrounding it was raised and discussed. Maurice put his foot down one day.

"We are going to have this meal together, with no discussion of the wedding or anything wedding related," he declared.

"Okay," said Ruth. "Well, I've got something else to talk about. I've been talking to Deborah, and we thought we would like to plan a trip back to England."

"When would that be?" Vera asked.

"We were thinking in April."

"During your spring break?" Vera questioned.

"Well, yes, but we want to stay longer, maybe four or five weeks. We want to travel all over Britain, to Scotland, the Lake District, Wales…"

"Wait a minute," said Frances. "That's going to get rather close to the wedding date, isn't it?"

"Oh, we'll be sure to be back in plenty of time for that." Maurice looked puzzled. "This is your senior year. How is that going to go down with your school?"

"We are hoping to work that out. I think a letter from Mum and some extra credit work might be enough. I think it will work out."

"Why not wait until school ends to go?" Frances asked.

"We can get really cheap airfare in April."

"Well, if you can get the school to agree, it's fine with me," Maurice declared. "What a wonderful experience you will have. I expect you will do some visiting while you are there."

"Oh, yes, Nana, Auntie Julie, the Coxes, and Deborah wants to see her family too."

"Just wish it wasn't so close to the wedding," Frances fretted.

"I'll give Hazel a call and see how she feels about all this," said Vera.

It all worked out for Ruth. Vera wrote a letter to her school and asked if some accommodation could be made. Her grades were high enough that it was decided Ruth would have to do extra work in advance of the trip and write some papers when she returned. Deborah also got approval and a friend of Ruth's, Lynn, who desperately wanted to accompany them, also got permission to go. They bought open tickets so that they could return whenever they chose. Frances did not like that at all. "I'd rather you had a return date," she said. "Suppose you want to stay longer, or you lose track of time."

"I promise we will be back in time for the wedding," Ruth insisted.

As Frances was consumed with wedding preparations, her sister, with Deborah and Lynn, were happily touring around Britain. They spent time in many towns and villages in England, as well as stopping at famous landmarks along the way, Stonehenge, the Roman Baths, castles, and all the historic places, monuments and tourist spots in London. They also spent a few days with Florrie and Ted in Bath, Auntie Julie in Southend-on-Sea and with the Coxes in Rayleigh. It was very nostalgic in Rayleigh, especially staying with the Coxes on the very street where Ruth and Deborah had spent their childhood years. Ruth sent postcards back home as she travelled and finally wrote, *Mum, tell Frances that we have booked our flights home. We will be back ten days before the wedding!*

Florrie and Ted arrived a week before the wedding. Auntie Julie had travelled with them. It was a big adventure for her, first time flying at seventy-two years old, and she was the only representative of Maurice's family. "Now remember," Maurice had warned his family. "Auntie Julie lives a very quiet and respectable life. She is very reserved and proper. Let's try not to shock her with too much noise or words and behaviour that she might find improper."

"Oh, yes, Ruth replied. She ticked us off while we were staying with her for chatting too loudly outside her flat with some young guys we had met."

"She would consider that very improper!" Vera chuckled. "Whatever would the neighbours think!"

The first evening, when they all sat down to dinner together, Maurice poured wine. "Would you like a glass, Auntie Julie?" he asked tentatively.

"Yes, please," she replied immediately. She actually enjoyed two glasses, absolutely amazing her nephew, who could not recall ever having seen her drinking alcohol in his life. He did not ask her anymore; he just poured her a glass at every meal and left the bottle on the table.

The big day approached. Florrie had shopped with Vera and bought Frances and Joe a set of Farberware pots and pans for a wedding present and a wooden bookcase with sliding glass doors (the bookcase lasted many years until it was broken during a move. The pots and pans are still in use to this day). The family looked their finest on the wedding day. Vera wore a full length, turquoise blue gown with long, sheer sleeves, Maurice was handsome in a white tuxedo jacket over black pants, Florrie wore a knee length, mauve dress with a matching striped jacket, Auntie Julie wore a blue dress with an overlay and Ted wore his best suit. The bridesmaids wore yellow, floral dresses and wide-brimmed hats, except for Lynn and Helen who had flowers in their hair. Frances came downstairs in her gown to a dazzled Florrie. She wore an all lace, hooped gown with a sweetheart bodice, long lace sleeves and the skirt falling in tiered layers. On her head she wore a Juliette cap with a waist-length veil. Florrie had never seen anything like it and said over and over again, "Isn't it beautiful? Isn't she a picture!" The photographer arrived to take group photos and the usual staged pre-wedding shots.

The wedding was held in the chapel at Fairfield University, officiated by Father McInnes who was the President of the University. Joe had become quite friendly with Father McInnes during his years at the University, maintaining the private tennis court and Japanese Gardens near the clergy house. Ray drove the bridesmaids, Vera drove Florrie, Ted and Auntie Julie and Maurice and Frances were the last to leave. The road leading to the university was lined with dogwoods. The petals were falling in the breeze as everyone arrived. It was a glorious day, after four years, Frances and Joe were finally married. The reception was lively and fun with a live band playing recent hits, old favourites and taking requests. Vera was so happy that all had gone so well and that her mother had enjoyed the event. Florrie felt so blessed to be amongst so many people she loved and to witness the spectacle of a wedding such as she had never seen.

After the wedding, Vera took Florrie, Ted, and Auntie Julie all over the place on short day trips. They enjoyed lunches out, shopping trips, visits, sitting in the sunshine, long, chatty dinners in the evenings and weekend jaunts with Maurice. Julie was so happy to see where Maurice and his family lived and to appreciate another part of the world. She was enjoying a once in a lifetime trip and only wished that her sister Charlotte could have been there. When Frances and Joe returned from their honeymoon trip to North Carolina, Frances invited them to lunch in her apartment. She had another week off from her work at the bank to get settled but Joe started work immediately when they returned as an accountant for Consumers Petroleum, a gasoline and heating oil distributor. It had been a wild time for Joe. He had graduated, married, honeymooned, and started a job all within nine days.

Three weeks passed quickly, and another visit came to an end. It had been exciting, beautiful, and memorable. Florrie would have many photographs to show around to family and friends at home. Vera and Maurice took them back to the airport for another sad parting. Vera returned yet again to her house, empty again of one she held so dear. She did not know it then, but it would be the last visit for Florrie and Ted to America.

Excerpt from letter from Walter to Vera – sometime shortly after Charlotte's death

Dear Vera

Just a line to say I am not too well. I have got trouble with my tummy losing blood. I went to the doctor last week. Julie is okay. I hope Helen got the card I sent. Tell Frances I got the letters and

thank her very much, the garden is lovely. I hope Maurice is still doing well and saving money. Well, dear, I won't be coming to the U.S.A. as I am not all that good. It's a long time to go twelve hours with my tummy. Give my love to the girls. All my love to you and Maurice.
Dad XXXXX

Excerpts from diary kept by Florrie during a visit in 1970
Sept. 5
Joe's Mum and Dad came round for engagement and official introduction. Very pleasant evening.
Sept. 16
My birthday – I was awakened by Vera with a cuppa, then soon after my family followed into the bedroom with cards and presents from Vera, Maurice, Frances, Ruth, and gorgeous Helen. We had fun. This awakening will live in my heart. God bless them all.
Sept. 21
Yvonne paid us a visit and brought my birthday present. We had lunch and a good laugh.

Sept. 24
Vera woke us up with a nice cuppa. Went to beach for the day. In evening went to Yvonne and Bob's for film.

Sept. 27
Hazel and Ray came. Hazel's birthday. Then more friends came in the evening. Lovely day. Bed at 1:30 a.m.

Sept. 30
Bud Porter invited us over to see his films. I played the organ. Yvonne, Bob and Debbie were there.

Oct. 4
Left house at 10:00 a.m. and arrived at Rutland at 12:30.

Marvellous lunch. Spent the rest of the day there. Listened to folk songs in Mountainside Hotel. Fantastic guitarist and singer.

Oct. 5

Up at 7:30 a.m. Good breakfast. Took snaps then we went five miles to another mountainside. Stopped at Santa Land. Helen was bewildered. Had chat with Santa. Laughed at his monkey. Went on a train ride.

Oct. 11

Went to Massachusetts to Quabbin Reservoir. Colours were magnificent! Went back to Ray and Hazel's for supper.

Excerpt from letter from Florrie to Frances – November 20, 1969

Now when I left Evelyn on that Sunday morning tour, when I was flying back home in the late evening, she asked me to write to her. I think I will do so. Think she must have changed a little as I would have been ironed out by now for not writing. Anyhow, I will let you know when she writes back, and what she says. Do feel sorry for her here and there, although I can't forgive her for insulting your Mum and when she did that, she insulted me, in a way. Don't try to find out now as it's all passed, but one day you may be told.

Excerpt from a letter from Florrie to Vera – 1969

During last week I visited a solicitor and made my Will. I intended to do this before my last visit but didn't get down to it. However, I have enclosed a card in reference to such, for your convenience when the time arrives for action. Three cheers for the red, white, and blue. Over the top boys!

CHAPTER TWENTY-ONE

A few months after the wedding, Maurice asked Joe for help with a remodelling project on his own house. He and Vera decided to knock down the wall between Frances's old bedroom and the guest room and convert it into a large master bedroom. Joe helped with the demolition and the sheetrock patching, sanding and painting. When it was finished, wallpapered with grass cloth and new carpet installed, it was a spacious, luxurious room. Frances remembered a discussion with her parents prior to the wedding when Maurice told her that she should not expect to move back in if the marriage did not work out. Well, this remodel was a rather definitive statement reinforcing the point.

The family dynamic was changing. Frances was gone and Ruth had decided to attend a community college with Deborah in New Haven. She took classes there with the idea of working toward a degree in early childhood education. It made sense for her to move in with Hazel and Ray while she was at school. It was a nice year for her although she gained several pounds eating the meals that Hazel prepared. Vera disliked cooking but Hazel enjoyed it. She made delicious meals and baked a wide variety of cakes, pies, pastries, sausage rolls, everything that Ruth loved to eat. Ray and Deborah were both picky eaters and Nicholas was not a big eater either, so Hazel finally had someone in the house who really appreciated her efforts. Ruth also made new friends in Deborah's circle. One of these was Mike Roop, whose company she enjoyed. Ruth stayed with Hazel and Ray for a year but then decided not to continue, especially when Frances encouraged her to apply for a job at the bank where she worked. So, Ruth returned to the old farmhouse and her old bedroom, got a job at one of the bank branches and bought herself her first car, a 1973, yellow Datsun stick shift. Although Ruth had only had a few lessons on Frances's Chevrolet Vega to learn how to operate a stick shift, she wanted to drive it home herself from the dealership. Frances and Joe followed all the way home in case she ran into difficulties. It was stressful but she got home without incident. Mike Roop visited often and seemed to be an easy going, fun-loving fellow whom everyone liked. He was very tall, blond, lean and hardworking. When he came to call, there was no questionnaire waiting for *him* to fill out.

Later in the year, 1973, Vera and Maurice decided to make a trip back to England. They wanted to take Helen to see and learn about England and know something about her heritage. She was seven years old and was of an age so that hopefully, it would be a memorable adventure. Vera contacted Helen's school and explained that she would be gone for six weeks but that she would be enrolled in a primary school in Bath for two weeks during that time. The school was very supportive and asked if Helen would give a little report to her class about the school in England upon her return. Letters flew back and forth across the Atlantic again as dates, plans and arrangements were made. Vera wrote to Florrie.

Maurice can only take two weeks off from work so we thought Helen and I would fly over first and stay with you in Bath for a couple of weeks, then I want her to see some of London. Uncle Bob will take us around. He knows it so well and will be a great guide. Then Maurice will fly over and meet us in Southend-on-Sea. We'll spend a couple days with Julie and then go to the Coxes in Rayleigh. Maurice will rent a car, so we'll be able to get around all right. We'll drive down to Devon to see Eileen and Ray and Wole and then we'll come back to Bath. Maurice will stay a few days and then drive back to the airport to fly home. Helen and I will stay on for another couple of weeks. How does that all sound?

Florrie responded. *That sounds just wonderful! What a nice visit that will be. Now don't you worry about bringing a lot of money with you while you are with us. I have set plenty aside that you can use just as you like. I have it all set up for Helen to spend a couple of weeks at the primary school nearby. The headmaster was very nice and is looking forward to meeting Helen. He said he has had situations like this before and it has always been so educational for the visiting child and the primary school children. I am counting down the weeks now. I can hardly wait!*

Frances stopped at the house after work the day before Vera and Helen were to leave. She sat on the end of her mother's bed as Vera packed a few last things in a suitcase which was open wide on top of the bed and loaded to the limit. "I am so jealous," she said. "Wish I was going too."

"Oh, well… you and Joe can go soon. I expect you will want to show him around the country."

"Yes, definitely. We are thinking of going next year."

"Well, that will be lovely. Now, let me see… maybe my white cardigan." Vera added the item to her suitcase. "Hope you can lift that when you're done," Frances chuckled.

"That's it, I think. Helen's little case is closed. I've got our passports and the tickets in my handbag. I think I'm all set."

"Have a wonderful time, Mum. Give everyone my love."

Florrie and Ted were waiting at Heathrow when the flight arrived at 8:00 a.m. on 4th October. They had left early in the morning for the two-hour drive, allowing themselves plenty of extra time. It was another joyous reunion, with Vera so happy to be back in England at last and Helen chattering away about the flight. Vera thought the bungalow in Bath was lovely. "Frances Lodge" was on a quiet road, nicely landscaped, pretty, and welcoming. Ted's sister, Edie, was happy to meet Vera and Helen, having heard so much about them. There was a nice garden in the back where Helen could play, and Florrie had bought her a skipping rope, bubbles, a ring toss game, colouring books, crayons and paints and reading books. The next day Ted drove them into Bath where they did some shopping and had a look around the city. There was so much to see, Helen's head was swivelling this way and that, taking it all in, pointing and asking questions. "This is just a first look," said Florrie. "We'll be back again to see some of the big attractions." In the afternoon, Vera walked with Helen to the quaint, brick primary school to register Helen for her two-week enrolment. Mr. Thomas, the headmaster, was very pleasant and asked Helen some questions about her school back in Connecticut. "I hope you enjoy your time with us, Helen. I know the pupils here will be happy to get to know you and learn about your life in America." She would start school in a few days on Monday.

On Thursday, Ted drove them to Dorset, where Auntie Lylie lived in Weymouth. She lived in a pretty apartment, having moved from the farm when her husband, Will, died. Lylie had prepared a delicious lunch with lots of cups of tea. They talked a mile a minute, trying to fit everything in and bursting into laughter with the fun of it all. It was a lovely day, mild and sunny, so they headed out for a walk along the seafront. Helen immediately descended the steps to the beach to explore and search for pretty shells. The sea breeze was exhilarating, and the views of the bay were beautiful.

On Friday, they went back into Bath, this time to see the famous Roman Baths and the Abbey. Helen was amazed to learn about the hot springs feeding the famous structure and to see the architecture of the Romans who transformed it into the greatest spa of the ancient world. Very close by was Bath Abbey which was glorious. Vera remembered the beautiful, fanned ceiling and stained-glass windows from here childhood visit there. Helen had never seen anything like it and felt dwarfed by its height and magnificence.

Helen started school, quite happy to be occupied and with children her own age. It was a bit of an adjustment for her, since there were strict rules to follow in the classroom, but she enjoyed being the centre of a lot of attention and found a nice little group of girls to spend time with on the playground. Vera and Florrie were able to spend a lot of time together, just the two of them, with Helen in school. There was a bus stop nearby which they took into the city. It was a gorgeous route, descending from quite a height into Bath, displaying panoramic views along the way. They were able to browse, have lunch, walk in the gardens, and just relax in each other's company.

The days slipped by in steady succession with a visit to Pearl and Eric's house where Helen played with their children, a drive to the top of Brass Knocker Hill and tour of the Wye Valley, a beautifully dramatic landscape of hills and dales, dotted with hamlets and villages, which borders England and Wales. Soon it was time for Vera and Helen to travel up to Walthamstow to spend a few days with Het and Bob. Then, Maurice would be meeting them for two weeks.

They would all end up back in Bath where Maurice would leave for the airport and Vera and Helen would stay for two more weeks.

What a grand tour of London they had! Bob knew London so well, having travelled to work there every day before he retired. His blindness did not slow him down or limit him one bit. He gave a running narration on the landmarks they visited even warning them of an uneven piece of paving they needed to avoid along the way. They took the Underground back and forth into the city three consecutive days to see all the sites including the Tower of London, St. Paul's Cathedral, Trafalgar Square, Westminster Abbey, Big Ben and Parliament. They walked through St. James's Park to Buckingham Palace, saw the Horse Guard's Parade, 10 Downing Street, and Piccadilly Circus lit up at night.

Vera and Helen travelled from Walthamstow to Southend-on-Sea by minicab where Maurice met them. He had rented a car at Heathrow and driven straight there. They all spent two days with Auntie Julie in her lovely flat with views of the sea. Auntie Julie was thrilled to have them visit and to see Southend again through a child's eyes. They enjoyed a lovely lunch of delicious fish and chips, the best they had ever had, and walked along the seafront. Southend-on-Sea was a seaside destination with lots of attractions. Helen loved riding on the train which took them to the end of the famous mile-long pier, the longest pleasure pier in the world. There was a penny arcade at the end, a cafeteria, and large pole-mounted, coin-operated binoculars to enjoy the views as well as carnival-like booths with fun things to marvel. They rode the train back and ended the day at Peter Pan's Playground, where Helen enjoyed lots of rides; the Helter-Skelter, The Switchback Railway, Noah's Ark, The Whip and laughed her way through the Crooked House. It was a nostalgic day for Vera and Maurice bringing back so many memories of Frances and Ruth, who always enjoyed a day out at Southend-on-Sea, not really so many years ago. It was a lovely day for Julie too. Watching Helen skipping along, so full of life and fun, made her feel young again and remember when life was exciting and carefree. It was a difficult farewell. She was so fond of them all, especially her dear nephew. Maurice kissed his aunt goodbye wondering if he would ever see her again.

It was exciting and surreal for Vera and Maurice pulling up in front of the Coxes' house on Woodlands Avenue. "Seems strange, doesn't it Vera, being back here again?"

"It sure does. I don't remember the street being so narrow, do you?"

"No... guess it's because we are used to wider streets now, back home." *Home* thought Vera. Isn't *this* home? The front door of the Coxes' house flew open, and the Ted and Lil stood on the doorstep grinning broadly. "Come on in, you Yanks!" Ted called. "Kettle's on!" Lil told them.

It was a wonderful welcome and a very happy visit for Vera and Maurice. Ted told them emphatically, "Now while you are with us, *our 'ouse is your 'ouse*! You make yourselves comfortable and do just as you like!" Lil and Ted had contacted a lot of old friends and neighbours and a big party had been planned. Maurice wore his fashionable green, plaid pants for the occasion, flamboyant and confident, showing off his successful lifestyle to the group. There was so much to catch up on, so much teasing back and forth, so many questions about America. Vera and

Maurice were the centre of attention, and they revelled in it. Helen was also a novelty to the partiers. A little American girl who would have looked exactly the same had she been born in England. But she had an American accent and used American expressions. She was a big hit with everyone especially since she was so outgoing and precocious.

Vera took Helen a few doors down to stand in front of number 25. "This is where we lived for many years when we lived in Rayleigh."

"Did Frances and Ruth play here? In the garden and on the street?"

"Yes. They had lots of fun here. Our house had the same setup as Aunt Lil and Uncle Ted's so you can imagine us living in that same space."

"And the same size back yard too?"

"Yes. And they had a tortoise, named Crusty. He used to roam around the back garden and show himself once in a while. When they saw him, they would rush into the kitchen to get some lettuce or carrots for him." Vera smiled at the memory. She had not thought about Crusty in a very long time.

They strolled around Rayleigh centre, popping into a few shops, the café, a pub. It had not changed too much but seemed a lot busier and congested with cars. It had only been nine years since they had left but long enough that there was a sense of not belonging for Vera and Maurice, of no longer being part of this different life, of enjoying the nostalgia but feeling out of place, coming from a different time. Life had moved on in Rayleigh. Lil and Ted had even installed central heating in their home.

Maurice drove them down to Devon to visit with Walter, Eileen and Ray and the family. Helen was excited to meet her grandfather, having heard a lot about him from her sisters. He had made them a playhouse, made them stilts, let them count his takings from the shop on the white, fuzzy rug in front of the fire, and sang them silly songs. It was a great disappointment when he looked at her with no great interest, patted her on the top of her head and said that she was a pretty little girl. There was no connection, and he made no effort to make one. Helen did enjoy her stay in Devon, however. Uncle Ray took her down to the kennels to see the Pekinese dogs they were raising and breeding and entering in dog shows. They had several champions. Uncle Ray told her to pick one of the dogs that would be hers to take care of during her visit. Auntie Eileen chatted with her, asking lots of questions and asking how she liked England. Rosalind, her youngest cousin, took her on a ramble on the property, across fields and along country lanes. It was a pleasant visit but again, it was a realisation of just how separated they had become. The girls had grown up, married, and moved away, except for Rosalind, who was a teenager. They lived a country life, rather isolated, yet content with the quiet, steady pace of their days. Ray and Eileen owned a large hardware store in a nearby town where Walter worked some hours each week. Eileen confided to Maurice that he used the money he earned to gamble, never having been able to overcome the addiction. She was disappointed and angry with their father. She and Ray suspected that he was taking cash from the till also, they could never get their accounts to balance at the end of the day.

From Devon, Maurice drove Vera and Helen back to Bath, staying for a few days before he drove back to the airport to fly home. Vera and Helen spent two weeks more in Bath with Florrie and Ted. The days were easy, comfortable, and precious. It was hard not to count down to the day of departure. Both Florrie and Vera dreaded it. Helen, however, was becoming anxious to go home, to her own school, friends, and family in Connecticut. As Ted drove them back to the airport, they spoke intermittently, all absorbed in their own thoughts. At the airport, Vera thanked Ted and her mother for the wonderful time and promised she would write soon and send photographs. The parting was quick. Ted pulled up in front of the terminal and took the suitcases out of the boot. There were hugs goodbye and Vera and Helen walked through the doors heading for the check-in line. When Vera turned to look back, the car had already pulled away. She did not know at the time, that she would never see her mother again.

In fact, there were several others so dear to her that she would never see again, Ted, her mother's companion of so many years, Walter, Auntie Julie, Auntie Lylie, Uncle Bob and Ted Cox.

CHAPTER TWENTY-TWO

As Vera settled back into her life in the old farmhouse, she could not help but think ahead and wonder when her mother and Ted could visit again. In a little over a year, it would be her 25th wedding anniversary. Perhaps that would be a good time. However, it would be January, not the best time to come for a holiday to Connecticut. Maybe the summer of that year, 1975, would be a good idea. Meanwhile her life was comfortable and easy. Frances and Ruth were grown, Helen was in school, and she had lots of time for herself. She happily filled her days with spending time with Yvonne, browsing the shelves in the library for some good books, working in the yard, visiting friends and neighbours and shopping. Everything was right in her world… and then it was not.

On the date of their 24th anniversary, Maurice called from the paint and wallpaper store.
"Vera. You need to come down to the store… now."
"Why? What's the matter? Are you okay?"
"I'm okay. Just come right away."
Vera's heart skipped a beat. Maurice's voice had sounded urgent and flat. It definitely was not good news. Whatever could have happened? She grabbed her coat and dug shakily in her handbag for her keys. As she drove across town to the store, she was on edge, confused and apprehensive. There was a sign on the glass door which informed customers that the store was temporarily closed and would reopen later. She tapped and waved with a weak smile. There were a group of men standing at the counter with Maurice. She recognised the owner's son, but she did not know the others. They turned toward the door with

grim expressions as one of them unlocked the door for her to enter.

"What is it? What's going on?" she asked.

The explanation was dreadful. Vera felt like it could not possibly be happening. It was a bad dream... a nightmare. Maurice had been confronted that morning with his boss, a lawyer, and a detective. He was accused of fraud, embezzlement, and theft. Apparently, he had let a lot of products leave the shop with nothing more than a wave as contractors picked up their supplies. So many patrons of the store were well-known to Maurice, some were friends. He kept tabs in a rather casual, haphazard manner but he knew they would all settle up what they owed. He was sympathetic to the builders and painters, after all, he had been in their position and was aware that full payment for the job was often withheld until completion. However, a recent inventory showed a significant discrepancy. Maurice had been threatened with arrest and prosecution but there had also been a proposed financial settlement far exceeding the amount of the loss, that he could make instead. Maurice had tried to explain that he would be able to collect on the amounts owed by contractors and that he had been keeping a record. His explanation was dismissed. He would have to sign a document right then promising to pay the demanded amount or face charges. The amount demanded would require the sale of the house to release the equity, and other assets which were in both Vera and Maurice's names, therefore, Vera would have to sign also.

Maurice was completely defeated and intimidated with the grim, determined faces that surrounded him. He knew he had done wrong. Since he had mostly been self-employed in his life, running his own businesses, he thought of the store more and more as his own business and made decisions that he should not have. He really did expect that he would eventually receive payment from his friends for the supplies they had taken, but there had been excuses when he reminded them of their balances. "Oh, I haven't collected from that job yet," or "I need a little more time, Maurice. You know I'm good for it." The total owing had grown too large, Maurice knew that but nowhere near the amount that was stated on the document. However, he had no choice. He signed the document which was then turned toward Vera for her signature. With a shaky hand, she signed. "I don't really understand what I am signing," she said weakly.

They arrived home devastated, deflated and in a state of disbelief. Vera made a cup of tea and they sat at the kitchen table while Maurice tried desperately to explain the extraordinary turn of events. Tears began to roll down Vera's face as the full impact of what they had lost became real. Maurice no longer had a job; they would have to sell the house and lose any equity that had accumulated over the years. Maurice's new car would be claimed as part of the deal, as well as their savings. All the years they had spent in America, all the work they had done, all the assets, comfort, and prosperity they had gained was gone.

Frances received a call at work to stop at the house before going home. She knew it must be unwelcome news and braced herself as she balanced out and drove over. The situation was explained as she stood in utter dismay and disbelief. "How could you be so foolish!" she said to her father. It was the only admonition that would be directed at him. Joe arrived and reacted with anger, not at Maurice but at the "ambush" of the owners. "It's all about bleeding you for money," he said. "It's an opportunity for them to rob you blind. I think you should fight it!"

"No, I *hurt* that man," Maurice replied, referring to the owner of the company. "He hired me, was generous with me and trusted me. I let him down."

"Yes, but..."

"I cannot face criminal charges, Joe. How will I work again? How will my family manage?"

Ruth came in from work surprised to see everyone there looking so sombre. She was holding a cake. "Happy Anniversary!" she said flatly. "What's going on?" When it was explained to her, she burst into tears and ran upstairs to her bedroom. "Will you go upstairs, Frances and calm her down?" Vera asked. Ruth was lying on her bed, sobbing into her pillow. Frances sat on the edge of the bed and took a deep breath. "Ruth, Dad has made a big mistake. He is going to pay dearly for it. We are going to have to be supportive and helpful as he and Mum work through it and make plans for the future."

"*Poor Dad!*" Ruth cried. "*Poor Mum!*" replied Frances.

The lovely old farmhouse went up for sale, Maurice's prized car was forfeited, savings accounts were depleted, and once again, it was time to start over. Vera struggled with so many emotions during this time, shock and disappointment at the forefront. She suppressed her deep resentment for Maurice's carelessness and the liberties he took in his position as manager. She understood how it had evolved with his history of running his own businesses, but the consequences were shattering. It was yet another significant setback in their life, the worst yet, coming at a time when Vera really believed that they were secure and settled. Vera sometimes looked at her husband, baffled that he would put so much at risk, but other times she felt deep sympathy for his loss of pride and status for which he had worked so hard. Ultimately, she decided that she needed to be supportive and encouraging yet again. Maurice worked again for Benway, helping with construction jobs, and hanging wallpaper in the evenings and on weekends. Vera would look for a job also.

Ruth moved in with Frances and Joe who had bought a three-bedroom house a year after their marriage. She brought her bedroom furniture and all her possessions so that they were out of the way for the impending move. The house sold quickly, being in such a desirable area and appealing as a historical house with a pretty setting. Maurice, Vera, and Helen moved into a rented house in the centre of town. It was adequate for their needs but quite a comedown from the lovely home they had left behind. There was a factory which manufactured car batteries within walking distance, where Vera applied for a job. She started work there soon after moving in. It was monotonous, dull labour and she disliked every minute of it. Helen transferred to another school, entering third grade. She disliked her teacher who, in turn, seemed to dislike her, and she missed her old school and the lively, personality of her teacher there. Ruth eventually moved back in with the family, and life settled into a new rhythm. Maurice still had friends and contacts in the construction business, and he decided again, to strike out on his own. A banking friend told him about a property in Fairfield that was for sale. He said that he would pull some strings so that Maurice could buy it. The bonus with the property was that it had an adjoining piece of land that could be subdivided and built on. It would give Maurice a great opportunity and a jumpstart into the construction business again. When the one-year lease was up on the rental home, Maurice bought the property. The house was quite old, rather quaint, and quirky with an odd layout. There were only two bedrooms upstairs, the second bedroom accessed through the master bedroom, but the rooms downstairs were spacious and attractive. It would suit them well enough especially since Maurice planned to build right next door. The subdivision was approved, and Maurice was working at full tilt again, working on construction projects, wallpapering, and starting his new build. Vera left the job at the factory and was happy to get a job in the Fairfield school system as a teacher's aide in a special needs classroom. It was a wonderful position because her schedule would be the same as Helen's who had changed schools yet again due to the latest move and was now in fourth grade.

During the tumultuous year following the sale of the farmhouse, Frances, Ruth and Joe planned a surprise 25th wedding anniversary celebration for Vera and Maurice. It came at a time when it was much needed to boost spirits and bring fun and excitement back into their lives. Frances wrote to Florrie asking her if she would be able to fly over and surprise them. She thought it would be such a wonderful surprise for Vera and would make the celebration complete. The letter she received back was disappointing and a little worrying.

There is nothing more I would like, than to be with you all for the silver anniversary. But I am afraid I am just not up to it at the moment. I am a bit under the weather, and I feel the cold in my bones. I will have to wait until the warmer weather. It pains me to have to disappoint you. Yes, your plan to have me stay with you for a few days before the event would have been marvellous. I would have loved to surprise your mum and dad and see the expression on their faces. Would you buy a present from me for them? I will send you the money. You probably know what they may need after their move.

The surprise was well thought out. Frances and Ruth told their parents that they were taking them out for a fancy dinner, so they needed to dress up a bit. They had rented a hall which they decorated, invited a lengthy list of family and friends, hired a live band, set up a bar with Joe's friend, Bill, as bartender, ordered all kinds of food, buffet style, and bought a huge anniversary cake. It was a wonderful evening of celebration, dancing and fun. Frances and Ruth had arranged for a framed portrait of their three daughters as their gift and Frances had selected an ornate, gold-framed mirror as the gift from Florrie and Ted. It was a gift that would be hung and seen every day.

Vera wrote to her mother after the event including photos and giving a full description of the evening. There was also news from Frances.

I have just discovered that I am going to have a baby. I hope you don't mind me making you a great grandmother! We are very excited and hoping for a boy.

Florrie wrote back. *I am thrilled with your news. I was talking about it with Het and Bob and they said that I would be the first in the family to make it to great grandmother. What a blessing!*

Ruth also wrote to her grandmother. She and Mike were getting married later in the year, in August. She hoped that Florrie and Ted could make it over. *Maybe plan on staying a couple of months since Frances is due in early September.*

As Frances grew larger and Ruth became wrapped up in wedding arrangements, Vera became concerned about Florrie. Fewer letters were arriving from her, and she mentioned that she had seen the doctor a few times with aches and pains, weakness and fatigue. When she received a letter from Ted explaining that her mother had not been well but that she was managing a little better with the use of a cane, Vera called Frances wondering what she should do. Frances suggested that she telephone Pearl and Eric to determine the seriousness of the situation. Eric told Vera that he thought Florrie was quite ill and that, yes, she should probably plan a trip over. Vera arranged for some leave from her job and booked a flight. Before she left, however, she received a call from Eric. Het and Bob had arrived just the day before to see Florrie. Hettie had gently whispered to her sister that she would be going into the hospital the next morning so that they could run some tests and make her feel better. Hettie sat on the side of the bed into the evening, holding her sister's hand. Florrie was so weak, had no energy to even talk, had a pale pallor, and slept. Hettie had never seen her like that. Where was her dear sister, her laugh, her sense of humour, her wittiness, her rosy cheeks and twinkling eyes? She was worried! She was anxious for the morning when Florrie would be admitted to hospital and receive care and treatment. However, during that night, Florrie died.

Vera was devastated. She should have gone back earlier. How could she have not realised that the situation was dire? When she stopped receiving letters, she should have responded immediately. She should have been there at her mother's side through her last days. She finished packing distractedly, stopping to sob, consumed with guilt and grief. Maurice tried his best to console her. He had loved Florrie very much and was so sad at her rapid decline. *What had been wrong with her?*, he wondered. Ruth too was heartbroken. She had expected to see her grandmother again for her wedding. She helped her mother pack, ran out to buy things she needed for the trip, made her tea, and took care of dinner. Frances and Joe arrived to spend time with the family. They had discussed the possibility of

Frances accompanying her mother back to England. Vera would not hear of it. Frances was five months pregnant, and she did not want her to take any risk for an event that would be difficult and joyless. And so, Maurice drove Vera to the airport the next day and watched his wife disappear into the terminal, forlorn and alone to say her final farewell to Florrie.

Florrie, a unique, strong, resilient woman who had faced so many challenges and hardships in her life yet had retained a sense of humour throughout. She was no-nonsense, bold, courageous, caring and faced difficulties in her life head on. She was fun-loving, sensible and grateful for happy times while suffering heartbreak and disappointment quietly and privately. What wonderful memories she left behind and what a powerful example of a life well lived.

Vera spent several weeks in Bath. The funeral was held in the little chapel at the cemetery. There were many people in attendance; friends and acquaintances as well as Het and Bob, Grace and her husband, Colin, Edie, Pearl and Eric, Ted's brother, George, and wife, Renie, and an assortment of nieces, nephews, cousins and friends. Ted was in a daze throughout the service. He could not contemplate life without Florrie and the long, lonely, empty days ahead. Vera had to meet with the solicitor who oversaw Florrie's will. Almost everything was left to Vera, of course. He would settle the estate and send the inheritance to her. She had to go through Florrie's things, a very difficult task especially when it came to photographs and letters. She quickly took the photos out of albums and put them in a large envelope to take home and sort through later. She gave many to Ted for him to keep or distribute to other family members. There were personal items she wanted for herself and the girls and a few pieces of clothing she could wear. When she was finished, she was not ready to leave. She needed time to stay where her mother had been, to shop in Bath as they had together during her visit, to walk in her shadow and footsteps a while longer, to come to terms with her loss. One day as she looked out of the front window, Vera saw the minister who had officiated at Florrie's funeral approach the front door. He had come to see how Vera was doing and to offer her comfort and private prayer. The gesture touched her and soothed her aching heart. After that visit, she felt ready to go home. Florrie had left Ted a modest bequest and Vera told him to sell the piano and keep the proceeds for himself. He would continue to live at "Frances Lodge" with his sister, Edie but it was sad to watch him in the house. He wandered aimlessly, peering into the rooms almost like he expected to see Florrie sitting there writing a letter. Vera received a copy of the autopsy report showing that her mother had died of liver cancer.

When Vera returned home, fortunately she had two big events looming to focus on: first, Ruth's wedding and then the arrival of her first grandchild. The church was reserved for the wedding and a hall was rented for the reception. It would be a catered, buffet-style party with a disc jockey providing music and entertainment. The wedding date was in early August with the temperature reaching 104°. The hall was not adequately air-conditioned, causing guests to strip off their jackets, roll up their sleeves and kick off shoes. Hairstyles wilted and food melted, but an enjoyable time was had by all. There was a piano in the hall and Ray played a few favourites later in the evening. Many guests joined in the singing or watched and listened, laughing at the lyrics of old pub songs. Joe's dad, Geza, had been stationed for a while in Bath during World War II and had enjoyed the pubs while he was there. He knew a lot of the songs and sang them with gusto, especially his favourite, "*I've Got Sixpence*," which he asked Ray to play twice.

The next month, on 3rd September, Vera's grandson was born, Peter Joseph Evan. It was a period when she could spend time with the baby and give Frances a hand. She was still working but was able to stop on her way home, one or twice a week and spend time there on the weekends. A baby boy was a novelty for her. It had been all girls in the family up until then. When Maurice completed the house next door on the sub-divided property, he and Vera decided that they would move into it and sell the little house they had been living in instead. It sold quickly, since houses were in great demand in Fairfield, even though it was quite small and unusual. Vera, Maurice and Helen moved into the new colonial that Maurice had built. It was an attractive, three-bedroom house with a large kitchen, spacious living room and dining room, and a small but private back yard. The front of the house had a small garden edged with hedges facing a very busy main road. Vera quite liked the house and the fact that it was new, up-to-date, and convenient to shops, schools and businesses, but the constant traffic noise and the activity on the road bothered her. She managed to overlook it a lot of the time, but in the spring and summer when she opened the windows for fresh air, the underlying droning of car engines and the constant rushing sound of car tires on asphalt caused her to yearn for the old farmhouse on Weeping Willow Lane.

The next few years were years of many changes in the

family. The economy was unstable during the 1970s. Ruth's husband, Mike, worked at Bullards in Bridgeport where he learned some skills becoming a machine lathe operator. Ruth became pregnant and gave birth to her son, Adam on 9th February 1977. When Bullards went out of business, an unexpected opportunity came along. Joe was managing a gasoline station and carwash and knew of another location that was available to manage. Maurice and Mike decided to work together and run the business. Maurice was having trouble securing enough construction work and he was looking for a new opportunity. However, it was hard and frustrating work. On a warm, sunny day it was quite pleasant being outside, pumping gas, chatting with customers and guiding the cars through the carwash. He employed a couple of teenage boys to help out part time and was able to leave Mike in charge if he had a small, private construction project going. It worked well for a while. The winter was the busiest time for the carwash, with cars lined up after a snowstorm when they had become coated with salt and grime. Inevitably at these times, the carwash chain which moved the cars through, would break, the pit which collected the sand and debris would fill up and need clearing out, parts froze, clothing froze and customers became impatient. Many a time, Maurice would have to walk along the line of waiting cars to inform the drivers that the carwash was under repair. It was demoralising, hard labour and it soon became obvious that the working relationship with Mike was not going to work out. Mike was not invested in the business financially or driven to make it a success, in fact, Maurice often found him lounging around, playing cards and gambling with the other workers. Some deposits that Mike should have taken to the night drop at the bank, never got there so Mike was encouraged to find other employment. He got a job at

Avco Lycoming in Stratford, a gas turbine engine manufacturer for the U.S. military and for commercial use. Maurice continued on managing the carwash operation by himself.

Ruth's marriage was floundering. She realised that Mike was involved in some extracurricular activities which kept him out late many evenings. Ruth suspected that he had been gambling, since she heard his end of some phone conversations that were rather alarming. Finally, she picked up an extension during one of the calls to listen in. She was horrified to hear that Mike owed some gambling debts and that threats were made about "roughing up" his family. She abruptly packed a couple of bags and left their rented apartment to seek refuge with her parents on Black Tock Turnpike. It was a desperate, necessary action leaving her feeling angry, hurt and so wretched at having to impose upon her parents.

"Are you going to get a divorce from Mike?" Maurice asked.

"I don't know right now, Dad. I need time to think and decide what I want to do."

"What are you going to do about money?"

"I'm going to get a job, probably go back to the bank and I'll demand some support from Mike for his son."

"I'm afraid this is not a good time for us," Maurice said. "But we'll all muddle along together as best we can."

"We'll manage," Vera added.

A friend of Ruth's with a truck had helped her move. She brought very little with her: the crib, baby necessities and a few boxes that she packed with household items she wanted to keep. Adam's crib was put in the third bedroom upstairs which Maurice had been using as an office and

Ruth shared Helen's bedroom, even sleeping with her in her double bed for a while until a twin bed was added to the room. Helen, at twelve years old, was ruffled at having to give up her privacy at the time when she was happy to have her own space to listen to music and just escape from her ever-watchful parents for a while. But she understood that the situation was serious, and she felt sorry for her sister. Adam was lively and entertaining, especially as he was mobile, crawling and pulling himself up. Vera helped a lot with him, especially when Ruth got a job at a bank branch in Fairfield. Vera still worked. She and Maurice needed her income, but she was home by 3:00 p.m. Ruth found a day-care nearby and dropped Adam off on her way to work and Vera picked him up on her way home. It was a workable arrangement, although Maurice worried that Vera was becoming too attached to the baby, and Helen, although, she loved the baby and his activities and antics, could not help but be resentful of no longer being the centre of attention at home.

The carwash kept Maurice going for a few years, but Vera worried about the physical exertion that it required, especially in the winter. He came home some days, completely worn out, wearing wet coveralls and smelling of soap, oil and gasoline. Finally, he decided he had struggled with it long enough and he put the business up for sale. Vera was pleased, although it meant that Maurice would get back into construction again which came with its own problems and frustrations. Vera knew that her husband was becoming demoralised, weary, and desperate.

Meanwhile, Frances discovered that she was pregnant again and she and Joe decided to sell their house in Bridgeport and move to Middlebury which was an hour's car ride away. It was closer for Joe to his work managing the carwash and gasoline station but soon after moving he decided to pursue his MBA at Sacred Heart University in Bridgeport so, he was driving an hour for evening classes three times a week. Luckily, his parents lived near the university so that when winter weather made travel difficult, he was able to spend the night with them. Frances enjoyed Middlebury. It was a small town, rural and pretty with a lovely lake and beach for residents' use. However, she felt rather cut off from her family. She was just far enough away so that short, pop-in visits were impossible, and everyone was busy with work, school, and children. The winter of 1978-1979 was especially snowy and no one wanted to make the trek north. Frances's old college roommate, Elyse, had a friend in Middlebury so when she heard that Frances moved there, she recommended that they get together. Frances and Sue got to know each other and became lifelong friends. It was a godsend for Frances during the four years she lived there. She gave birth to her second son, Thomas, on 1st February 1979. Sue had two boys almost the same ages as Peter and Thomas. It was a friendship made in heaven for Frances and Sue and would continue through the years! Vera and Maurice visited in the hospital, excited to meet their third grandson, but it was a week or two later before Vera was able to drive up to help her daughter for a day. Soon after she arrived, it started to snow, so she drove home again leaving a dejected daughter behind.

Ruth saved as much as she could while working at the bank and was able to move into a second-floor apartment in Bridgeport within a year of moving in with her parents. She continued to drop Adam off at day-care and Vera picked him up after work, so often Ruth would stay for dinner when she went round to pick Adam up. It was better for all, though, that she now had her own place. Soon after moving into the apartment, Ruth received a desperate phone call from Mike's mother. He had been badly hurt in an automobile accident and was in serious condition in the hospital. When she visited him, he was apologetic about his previous behaviour, promising Ruth that he would change his ways, vowing that the accident had made him realise all that he had lost. He was so contrite, full of remorse and assurances, that Ruth began to feel optimistic that they could try married life again. Vera was not so sure.

"Ruth, be very careful," she said one evening when Ruth returned from a hospital visit. "You feel very sympathetic right now and may make a wrong decision."

"I know, Mum, but he is so determined to make up for his mistakes and be a family again. I really think this accident has made him think about his actions and the consequences."

"Perhaps so. I hope so but give it some time before you rush into anything. He has let you down before. Remember, just before your wedding, he disappeared for a week. You had no idea where he was or even if he wanted to go through with the wedding."

"Yes, I know. But that was just the cold feet thing. He needed time away from the constant wedding plans and talk."

"Hmmm…"

"Don't worry, Mum. I'll be careful."

Ruth had been debating starting a free nursing program that was offered due to the need for more nurses nationwide. It was an intensive, condensed, accelerated course that would provide her with a new career and higher income. She had always been interested in the medical field, so she filled out an application and was accepted. She changed her hours at the bank, working the walk-up window in the afternoons so that she could attend classes in the mornings. But it became a very heavy load, dropping Adam at day-care, attending classes, going to work, picking Adam up from her mother at 6:00 p.m., then feeding him, playing with him, putting him to bed and spending the evening hours studying. Mike was now working 3:00 to 11:00 at Sikorsky Aircraft, an aircraft manufacturer based in Stratford, and was trying his best to ingratiate himself with Ruth so she realised that it would make so much sense for him to help out by watching Adam during the day, saving the day-care expense. He offered to take care of the rent and expenses so that she could quit her job and concentrate on the nursing program. It was too good an offer to pass up, so Mike moved in.

Vera suspected that Ruth and Mike had reunited. When she visited Ruth at her apartment, she saw things belonging to Mike lying around. Adam pointed to a pair of sneakers on the floor and said in his little voice, "Daddy's shoes." She did not say anything to her daughter. It was her decision to make but she was concerned and worried that circumstances and convenience had forced her hand.

It was not long after this that Ruth called Frances telling her she was coming up to Middlebury with Adam for a visit. Frances was pleased. Peter would enjoy playing with his cousin and baby Tom would be happily entertained. She made a nice lunch and set out a variety of toys.

"Well," said Ruth after a nice cup of tea. "I have some news."

"Oh?" Frances replied.

"Mike has moved into the apartment with me."

"Oh... well, I'm not really too surprised. I thought you might be seeing him again after the accident."

"He really is trying hard. He's working nights and helps out during the day when I'm at school."

"That must be quite a relief for you."

"Yes, but you know, the nursing program is really a struggle. It takes up so much of my time. I don't have much time to spend with Adam and now, with Mike, I feel like I need to focus on our marriage to give it the best chance to work."

"Uh huh. So, are you thinking of quitting the program?"

"Well... yes... especially since... well, I'm pregnant."

"Oh! Oh, wow! Really?" Frances had not been expecting this news. It took her a moment to process. "Well, that's great... isn't it? Are you happy about it?"

"Yes... I am. I want another child, but I haven't told Mum and Dad yet. I'm worried about their reaction."

"Hmmm... yes. Not sure about that. But, you know, it's your life and your decision. They will be surprised and maybe a bit worried, but they will be glad that you will be more financially secure again. They will accept it, I'm sure."

"Yes, I guess so. I'll tell them tonight."

"Shame about the nursing program though. You would have been a good nurse."

"I know. I do regret that but maybe I'll get back into it later."

That evening, Ruth visited Vera and Maurice. As she expected, the initial reaction was one of stunned dismay.

"What!" Maurice burst out. "Well, my girl, you've done it now. He's back in your life well and truly!"

"Oh dear... oh dear... Ruth... is this really what you want?" Vera asked wringing her hands.

"Well... yes. I think it will be better now. Mike has a

steady job at Sikorsky, and he really wants to prove himself again."

"I should think so!" Vera declared.

"I know you both have your doubts and you're worried… but I am really quite optimistic… and I am actually excited about having another baby," Ruth announced with a catch in her throat, close to tears.

"Oh, now, Ruth," said Maurice, "Of course, we are happy about another grandchild, but you can't deny that Mike has not had a great track record. We can't help but be concerned."

"I know, I know, Dad."

"Well, it's done now," said Vera in a more conciliatory tone. "Let's have a cup of tea and we can talk about the baby and when it is due."

"I love my three grandsons," said Maurice with a chuckle, "But I think I will hope for a girl this time."

Later, while getting ready for bed, Vera could not help but share her concerns with her husband.

"What do you think about all this, Maurice?"

"I don't know… I like Mike but, as we know, he is unreliable and even dishonest. He is just not steady, and I worry that Ruth is going to get hurt again."

"But Ruth is so certain that he is a changed man."

"Well, dear, we can only hope for the best."

Ruth was very relieved at how well her parents had dealt with the news. She understood completely their misgivings, after all, she had imposed on them for almost a year to sort out her life and make a new start. However, she had never initiated divorce proceedings. Deep down, she realised, she was not ready to make the separation permanent. Vera and Maurice were cordial as Mike joined them for dinners and family occasions again. Maurice had always liked Mike, enjoying his easy-going nature and sense of humour. He often called him "mate" or "matey" which Mike reciprocated. Ruth was content with her new life and as her pregnancy progressed, she looked to the future with happiness and optimism.

Excerpt from letter from Florrie to Frances – December 15, 1974
I'm glad you received the calendar. Thought you would like that one. Never thought you would love it so much. Will have to make sure you get one every year while I'm breathing. Speaking of breathing, my breath has been a bit troublesome of late. Have had to swallow some of those airships (big pills.) Well, they have made quite an improvement with the grumbling and rumbling that's been going on down below. I think that's owing to not being able to go out, it not being warm enough. I can't get any movement much in my body to help my digestion. Anyway, my dear, the way I feel now at times, I'm glad I've cancelled my visit. It wanted some doing, I can tell you, and I shall feel the effects for some time. It's the first time I have ever refused to do anything which would put me with you all.

Now Frances, the mirrors. I'm afraid I've no liking for the two small ones. Comparing the two designs, I much prefer the big one with the scrollwork. I won't forget to send the anniversary card to you. Do enjoy yourselves. I shall be thinking of you. Now, I'm going to the bank in the morning to see if I can get this cheque off to you but remember, don't get a cheap one 'cause they don't last. Oh, yes, while I think about it, I think your four-some present to your Mum and Dad is just great. I've been thinking about it day in and day out. It's very nice of you to write and tell me all about it. Thank you, Darling.

Excerpt from a letter from Florrie to Vera and Maurice – January 19, 1975
Well now, my dears, now our secrets have been released, I hope you and everyone enjoyed your Silver Day. Can just imagine Helen enjoying all the preparations and the coverings up. Fran and Joe have

been full of it. They have been writing to me, as you know, quite a lot while this has been going on keeping me informed. Anyhow, hope all went well to give you something to remember as you ramble along the next twenty-five years. I sincerely hope that will be much more prosperous than the past twenty-five, although you have done extremely well, both of you. You have had many ups and down one way and another which needed much pluck to start from the beginning. I think you have enjoyed doing all this and you have had some lovely times in so doing.

Excerpt from a letter from Florrie to Frances and Joe – March 5, 1975

Thank you for your tidings of great joy I received from you both. How wonderful. You are going to be a Mum and Joe, a dear ole Dad. What about me then? A Great Grandma. Never thought that I would reach that stardom. Thanks a million! Hope you keep in the best all the way. Sorry I have been so long writing, Fran. My back and ribs have been so sore, I could hardly touch them and as I walked about the least jolt made me shout. I've never had my back as bad as this. I'm sure it's a chill I caught about two weeks or more ago when the weather changed all of a sudden to showers of snow. It was summer-like just before that. Well, I had to dash out in the garden to get my washing in when I must have got it then, because I felt that cold wind go right through me. At night on the same day, I couldn't undress myself. I had pains all over and it just won't go. I feel as though I have been bashed about on concrete.

I had a letter from Bob and Auntie Het, yes, of course I told them. Bob starts off, Dear Great Grandmama, do you know you are the first member of your family to have reached this distinction and lived?

I hope you get your wish and it's a boy. I guess everybody is very excited about the coming event. Joe's Mum and Dad are, I know. Wish I was you, Fran. It is so wonderful.

Excerpt from a letter from Ted to Vera and Maurice – April 17, 1975

Just a few lines in case you are wondering why Mum has not written. The truth is that she has been feeling very poorly of late and has not felt in the mood. A little while ago, say a couple of months, I noticed that she was slowing down quite a bit and I asked her to see the doctor but she kept putting it off until she complained of pain in her ribs and stomach and so I took her to see the doctor who gave her some tablets and told her to make an appointment for the following week and told her, as I understood her to say, that she was suffering from rheumatism. Well, I made the appointment, but the pain became worse and quite suddenly she found that she could not walk unless supported with an aid. I called the doctor, and he was very surprised at the sudden turn of events. As things are, I will try and drop you a line each week with a progress report. So do not worry too much as everything possible is being done and thank goodness, she is quite cheerful, considering, although a little confused at times.

Excerpts from a letter from Vera to Frances and Joe – May 5, 1975

At last, I'm writing to you. There has been so much to do and people to talk to. Well, the awful ordeal is now over, which I have always dreaded, but it seemed to come too soon. It didn't seem fair. Anyhow, Nana is at rest now and peaceful. Uncle Ted is not too bad, and Edie is looking better. It has been a very worrying time for them. I do hope you are keeping well. I expect I'll see a difference in you. I'm sitting in Bath City writing this to you. Hope you are coping, and that dad is all right. How is Helen? Is she still in one piece? Tell her I'll bring some goodies back.

I have been to the solicitor, and he is handling everything for me. I'm leaving for London, Het and Bob's, on the ninth. I have spoken to Eileen and told her the sad news. She passed on the message to Grandad, Gill and Rob and they all sent some lovely flowers. I will book my return flight in London and then drop a line to Dad to tell him when I'm returning. Thank you for everything you and Joe did to get me on my way and thanks a lot for helping with Helen. Please let Ruth read this and tell her thanks for her help and that it won't be long now, and I'll be back.

CHAPTER TWENTY-THREE

Everything was going wrong for Maurice. He ran into problems with his jobs; clients and customers found reasons not to pay him the full amount of his estimates, he ran into time delays, expensive problems, sub-contractors that let him down, changed orders that had not been properly documented and signed. Among Maurice's failings during his work life was the business end of his projects, his lack of getting everything in writing, doing extra work when requested with just a casual verbal discussion, trusting everyone too much, not drawing up a formal contract and sometimes working with little more than a handshake. Although he did not want to leave the family, it seemed that all was fine now. Frances and Joe were doing well, and Ruth was back with Mike and appeared to be quite happy. They would visit back and forth. His priority was making a living, putting himself in a position and situation where he could be successful again. He had been hearing that Florida was booming, so many people were relocating there, and the building trade was prospering. The more he heard about the sunshine state, the more convinced he was that they should move there.

1980 became another milestone year for Vera and the whole family. In the spring of that year, Maurice first mentioned the idea of relocating again with Vera, this time to Florida. He had never really bounced back from the big loss in 1974 and he was becoming disillusioned with Connecticut. It was just too much of a struggle to make a living and he had lost the spark to keep trying. He knew that Florida was a desirable location with so many attractions, an easier lifestyle and a building boom. He became convinced that it was the place to go. He knew it would be a hard sell to persuade Vera to go along with the idea, so he only mentioned it casually at first, but he followed up by reading articles to her - anything good he found about Florida and related conversations to her that he had had with people who had been there and seen the huge growth. Vera became alarmed, knowing where all his talk was leading. She could not possibly bear to move away from her family again! She just could not.

Vera was terribly conflicted. She knew what was coming. Maurice would soon talk to her seriously about moving. It would absolutely crush her. She would be leaving all her family behind... again! How could she handle that? *What about Helen? It would happen all over again.* Just like when she left England. Only this time she would not be leaving the older generation, it would be the younger generation, her daughters and her grandchildren, with one more on the way. It was unthinkable. And yet, how could she refuse? How could she insist that Maurice continue to struggle and find work in the area when he felt so utterly dejected? He would be revitalised with the move, a new place, a fresh start, where his skills and hard work and tenacity would be in demand. She knew him so well. He would charge forward as if he were going into battle, drive down to Florida with stars in his eyes, full of energy and optimism, ready to start a new life. Could she support him in this? Should she?

It took several days of conversations, many sessions of persuasive arguments on Maurice's part, and angry tears and bitterness on Vera's. "I'm fifty-one, Vera. I have a little bit of time left to work in construction but not here, not in Fairfield County. In Florida I will have a lot of work and won't have to worry about the slow winters here in

Connecticut. I'm sure I will have more projects and opportunities there. Don't you see? We can build ourselves up again. I want to get to the point where we have no debt and a paid off mortgage so that we can have a comfortable retirement."

"Yes. I understand. It all makes good sense. It's just that it will be so hard to leave."

"I know... I know. But Helen will be with us, of course, and Frances and Ruth are married women now with their own families to raise. It's not as if we won't see them. We will all make trips back and forth."

Vera thought that if she absolutely refused to move, Maurice would defer to her and continue to lump along as best he could in Connecticut, but she was just not willing to accept that responsibility and suffer the resentment that he would feel toward her. So, in the end, Vera agreed. She would again, support her husband.

Helen had to be told, and Frances and Ruth. Helen was incredulous. "Oh, no! Please, let's not do this. I'm starting high school in the Fall, Andrew Warde, where Frances and Ruth went. I want to go there... with my friends."

"Yes, I know, Helen," Maurice replied. "But we will try to time it so that you start out the new school year in a high school in Florida. That won't be so bad."

"Dad! It *will* be bad! I don't want to go. Why can't we just stay here?"

"It's work, Helen. I have to find work. Florida is the place to go. I'm sure you will like it down there."

"But... we will be leaving everyone up here. Mum, how can we do that?"

"They will visit, dear. That will be nice, won't it? We'll have fun showing them around." Vera said weakly.

"But... I'll miss them, I'll miss all of them..." Helen

was crying now, and Vera struggled to maintain her composure. "Dad is going to fly down in a few weeks and scout out the area. Let's wait until he comes back before we talk about it anymore… okay?"

Frances and Ruth and their families were told during a weekend visit. The sisters were stunned and disbelieving. "*No! You're not!*" gasped Ruth.

"I can't believe it! *Not again!*" Frances declared. "Have you tried getting a different kind of job, Dad? What about sales, maybe at a building supply company, or real estate…?"

"Construction is what I know, Fran. And Florida is the place for that. It is also easier living down there. I won't have to earn as much as I need to live up here."

"But, Dad, how can you even think…" Joe interrupted his wife, realising that Frances was getting worked up.

"Where in Florida are you thinking of going?" he asked.

"Well, Tallahassee is the capital, so I thought I'd fly down and look there. Mike, your grandparents live there, don't they? Maybe they wouldn't mind showing me around a bit."

"Yeah, sure. I think they would be happy to."

"But when are you thinking of going? I mean… will you be here when the baby is born?" Ruth was close to tears.

"Oh, yes, of course. We won't put the house up for sale until I've been down there and feel confident that it's a good prospect."

"And, even if Dad goes before me, I'll stay until after the baby is born and can give you a hand for a while," Vera assured her.

Frances desperately checked her local newspaper's

classified section for any jobs that would be suitable for Maurice. She read them to him on the phone and he even drove up once to interview for a maintenance position at a senior living facility, but she soon realised that he had made up his mind about Florida and was eager to start again there. She would just have to accept it, just as she had when the decision was made to leave England and come to America.

Ruth gave birth to her daughter, Tiphanie, on 30th August 1980. Everyone was thrilled to have a little girl in the family. Vera spent as much time as she could at Ruth's apartment, knowing that her time was limited. Maurice had flown down to Tallahassee, looked around, talked to some contractors and home remodelling businesses, and made several contacts who would later become lifelong friends. He liked the city, discovering that, although it was the capital of the state, away from the city centre where all the municipal and government offices were located, it felt very much like an ordinary town. He looked around at some home rentals while he was there also and spoke to some rental agents. He came back extremely optimistic and gung-ho. It was decided. Just as he had done when leaving England, Maurice left the final details to Vera, filled up a van rental with furniture and boxes, kissed everyone goodbye and started the long drive to Florida. Bruce Benway, a long-time friend with whom he had worked on and off since arriving in Connecticut, drove down with him, sharing the driving hours. Bruce was in need of a break from his business and considered it a bit of an adventure. Maurice had arranged to rent a condominium in a very nice area of town so upon arrival, he and Bruce unloaded, rented a car and spent a couple of days looking around. Bruce flew back home and Maurice, with his usual enthusiasm, visited his contacts and began to find work. He started with wallpapering work again, as he had so often in the past. The manager of a home decorating business became a good friend and passed on many jobs. Soon he discovered the *Salty Dog*, a local bar which was frequented by a lot of local construction workers, especially on a Friday night. Maurice's ever popular personality led to friendly camaraderie, more contacts and work. He was soon able to buy a used pickup truck and he was on his way again.

Meanwhile the house went up for sale and Vera and Helen moved in with Ruth while they waited. Vera continued to work at the special needs classroom and Helen began the school year, her first year in high school, at Andrew Warde, where her two sisters had gone. She enjoyed it, attending football games and social events, making new friends but knowing all along that she would soon be leaving. Vera was glad to see that Ruth and Mike were doing well and that Ruth was able to stay home with the baby. She was dreading leaving but was curious to see her new home and be with her husband again. The roles were reversed and now she felt that she and Helen were imposing on Ruth, but she knew her help was appreciated. They stayed for six weeks until the closing on the Black Rock Turnpike house was finalised and then they drove up to Middlebury to spend a few days with Frances before starting the long drive south. Vera dreaded the long drive on highways and unfamiliar roads. She would take a few days, stopping at hotels along the way but she was definitely out of her comfort zone. Frances was also worried about how well her mother would cope. She had never driven very far before and although Helen would help her navigate her way, Vera would not have a relief driver. Frances had mentioned her concerns to her in-laws and so when Vera came down with a very bad cold and thought she would have to postpone her journey, Geza and Elnora came to the rescue. Geza was a truck driver, having logged millions of miles during his working life. He was happy driving and liked the idea of seeing a new place and helping Vera out. They arranged to drive Vera and Helen down to Florida in Vera's car and fly home. Perhaps they would pop down to Disney World for a couple of days too.

Vera was feeling miserable on the morning of departure. Her head was stuffed, her throat was sore and she ached all over. She only managed to eat a couple of mouthfuls of the big breakfast that Joe had prepared. When Geza and Elnora arrived, Frances bundled her in the backseat with pillows, blankets, throat lozenges and juice drinks and Helen was well supplied with snacks, books, a portable radio and earphones. Frances waved them off, bravely fighting back the tears that she would shed later. She could not help but remember a similar time in her life when another car drove away from two loved ones standing at the garden gate waving sorrowfully. Vera could not turn to wave back. Her head was throbbing, so she laid it against the pillows and closed her eyes, miserably aware that a new chapter of her life was beginning.

Excerpts from letter from Vera to Frances – December 6, 1980

Thank you so much for your lovely letter. I know all you write is correct and you have a very logical reasoning about our situation. Everything you say, I agree with, but then comes my emotions and I am not able to think straight – nothing can change all those miles between us.

Dad has got a steady flow of work and earns good money when it is available. Each week seems to bring new customers. He works for the Interior Decorators, some other decorators and a builder.

Excerpts from letter from Helen to Frances – December 6, 1980

Hi, how are ya? I'm doing pretty good, probably better than Mum is. I'm finding school is getting a little better but I'm still looking forward to coming back "home" again. I don't like Lincoln as much as Warde and I don't think I ever will. But I guess I'll have to live with it. I really miss everyone a real lot.

Mum and I will never understand how Dad could have just up and left without looking back and expected us to do the same. We try to keep ourselves busy so as to not get too depressed.

CHAPTER TWENTY-FOUR

Vera slept during much of the first day of the journey south. She was suffering in body and in spirit. Geza drove a steady pace, stopping at rest stops for necessary breaks and for lunch and dinner and made it to North Carolina before stopping for the night at a motel just off the highway. After a good night's sleep Vera felt a little better, managing to eat a little at breakfast. She nodded on and off during the second day's ride but chatted more and took an interest in the scenery outside the car window. The thick woods lining the highway caught her attention, big tree branches hanging with Spanish moss and palm trees interspersed among them. So much of the land was rural, farms, pastures and open fields, and she noticed a great diversity of dwellings - beautiful, sprawling homesteads as well as dilapidated shacks and hovels. She read the billboards along the way advertising establishments she had not heard of before, Waffle House, Stuckeys, Bojangles, Piggly Wiggly, numerous South of the Border signs and religious messages and quotes from the bible. When they passed the "Welcome to Florida" sign Vera actually felt a flutter of excitement. So, this was her new home.

"Helen, look. We've just crossed the border from Georgia into Florida."

"Hmmm." Helen replied lifting her head from her book and looking out the side window. "Huh, doesn't look much different from the last few hundred miles," she said.

Geza took I-295 which fed into I-10, the highway which ran across the Florida panhandle to Tallahassee and continued far beyond, passing through Alabama, Mississippi, Louisiana, Texas, New Mexico, Arizona, and

California, ending at Santa Monica, California. I-10 was straight and rather uninteresting, but it was the last leg of the journey and both Vera and Helen watched now for signs showing the number of miles to Tallahassee. When Geza took the exit number listed on the directions that Maurice had provided, they were in the northeast section of the city making their way to Killearn Estates. Vera's first impression was quite favourable. The area was nicely landscaped with numerous developments and attractive shopping areas, golf course, lakes, parks, schools and churches. They found the condo complex and drove slowly around until they found the apartment number. Maurice had been keeping watch, expecting them to arrive that evening, so he threw the door open wide and dashed outside to welcome his wife and daughter with loving bear hugs. He hugged Elnora and shook hands with Geza expressing his deep gratitude for taking some vacation time to drive his family down. It was getting dark as they unloaded the car. "Let me quickly show you the condo and then I thought we could all go out for a nice dinner. There's a great restaurant not far from here. Are you hungry?"

"Always," laughed Geza, patting his stomach.

The condo was a townhouse style unit with two bedrooms and a bathroom upstairs and a living room, kitchen, dining area and half bath downstairs. It was well equipped with up-to-date appliances, laundry closet, and neutral carpeting, flooring, and paint colours. Maurice had everything looking neat and tidy and welcoming. Geza and Elnora would sleep in Helen's room for the night, so Maurice carried their bags upstairs. Helen would stretch out on the couch.

"Everything looks so nice, Maurice," Elnora remarked. "I hope you will all be very happy here."

"Thanks, El. Vera? What do you think?"

"Oh, I think it's very nice. It has everything we need, and the area looks lovely too." *If only the rest of my family wasn't so far away,* she thought.

"Helen, does it suit you too?"

"Sure, Dad. It's nice."

"Well then, let's make tracks for the restaurant, shall we? Bet you could do with a beer or two, eh Geza?"

"I won't say no to that, Maurice!"

This was a special friendship. Two quite different couples who remained steady, faithful friends. Geza was a large man, with a booming voice and a hearty laugh. He was American through and through, had served during World War II as part of the 12th Armoured Division, the Hellcats, and fought bravely as the allies battled their way through Europe to Germany. In one fierce battle in January 1945 in the town of Herrlisheim, his unit took heavy enemy fire and was overwhelmed. He and two others from his squad avoided capture by swimming across the Rhine River. He drove General Patch around for a period of time and was used as an interpreter at the end of the war since he could speak fluent Hungarian. He did not speak much about the war years although he stayed in touch with several of his army buddies, visited them, and attended several organised reunions. One time when Vera was visiting Connecticut, he brought his footlocker up from the cellar and let her look through it. She was very honoured and excited to examine the contents. He had a few K-rations, the tins rather rusty and the pouches limp and stained. There were German uniform patches, pins and campaign badges, swastikas, newspapers, German currency which had been stamped over, increasing the value as inflation ran rampant during Germany's defeat. There were maps, letters, and photographs of Geza himself, posing with his buddies or goofing around during a pause in the action. Maurice admired him greatly and appreciated his kindness and generosity. In turn, Geza admired Maurice's adventurous spirit, cheerful personality, and love of sport. They enjoyed many a football game or baseball game together with a few beers.

Elnora and Vera also enjoyed each other's company. They were always on the go during their visits, shopping, visiting, attending church, preparing meals together. Elnora was happy to help in the kitchen, watching Vera prepare some English favourites and making some of her own. They laughed at their differences, English expressions, stories of their upbringings and early lives. They had, of course, grandchildren in common, Peter and Tom, which meant they always had a lot to talk and laugh about.

The day after they arrived, Vera spent time checking the kitchen cabinets, drawers, and closets to see where things were. Maurice had bought all the food essentials, so she cooked up a breakfast of eggs, bacon, and toast for everyone. Maurice took them on a driving tour of the area and through the city centre.

"Wow, there sure are plenty of restaurants on this road," Geza remarked.

"Yep. This is Monroe Street. Lots of choices for meals here, shopping too, a big mall, strip malls, and all kinds of businesses, as you can see." When they returned to Killearn, Maurice took them to Maclay Gardens, where they enjoyed a stroll along neat brick walkways, around ornamental flower beds, into a secret garden, past a reflecting pool and enjoyed hundreds of blooming plants and flowers.

Back at the condo, Maurice had a surprise for Helen. "It

is so close to Thanksgiving, that Mum and I have decided not to enrol you in school until after the holiday. That will give you time to get acclimated and settled, but… tomorrow, we are all going to Disney World for a couple of days. We had this all arranged with Joe's mom and dad. They will fly home from Orlando. What do you think of that!"

"Well… cool," Helen responded. "That will be fun." Helen smiled brightly but inwardly squirmed a little. Disney World with her parents and Mr. and Mrs. Evan! She would have rather just stayed at the condominium, maybe walked around a bit, check out her new school, come to terms with her new surroundings, but she knew her parents were doing this as a kind of compensation for uprooting her, thinking it would be a fun way to start off her life in Florida. *Well*, she thought, *it would be exciting to see Disney World and not worry about school right away.*

They spent two days at the Magic Kingdom, enjoying the incredible rides and shows and the fireworks the first night. It was a unique opportunity to throw off all cares and worries and remember the joys of childhood and marvel at the colourful sights and sounds. It was a whirlwind adventure and so good to have a chance to relax and laugh, but the time passed quickly and soon it was back to reality and adjustment to life in the south.

Thanksgiving was the first difficult holiday with just the three of them around the table. Vera made a nice dinner, a modest version of the typical big turkey feast, and Maurice watched football with Helen. Following the long weekend, it was time for Helen to start school, a day she had been dreading. Maurice drove her to Lincoln High School on her first day. It was a sprawling, five-year old school, with a population of students that had already outgrown the building, so there were temporary classroom buildings also. The day was as bad as she had expected, finding her way around, struggling with the heavy southern accents of students and teachers and adjusting to the rules and structure of the school day. At lunch she found a table off to the side in a corner but was soon sent on her way by a group of boys who looked at her as if she had committed a major offence. It was hard to understand their vernacular, but she got the gist, that she had intruded on *their* space and sat at *their* table. At the end of the day, she searched for the bus with the number that she was told would go to Killearn. A girl approached her.

"You look lost," she said.

"Yeah, I'm trying to find my bus. Wow, there are so many."

"Where do you need to go?"

"Killearn… Donovan Drive."

"Oh, come with me on my bus. It goes very near there."

"That's great. Thank you." Helen had made her first friend, Paulette. She walked every morning fifteen minutes to Paulette's bus stop to ride the bus with her and home again every afternoon. Helen was naturally outgoing and liked to have fun and perhaps a little bit of mischief, so she soon had several new schoolmates to hang with. She was surprised when she suggested to an African American student in one of her classes that they should go somewhere together that he responded very vehemently. "Oh, no girl! We can't do that!"

"Why not?"

"No, no… it wouldn't be good. Believe me."

"I don't understand."

"It's just the way it is here. Trust me!"

It was rather a shock and an eye-opener for Helen. She had a lot to learn about the culture and customs that existed in the south in 1980.

As Helen slowly forged her way, Vera was also expanding her territory a little bit at a time. Tallahassee was quite spread out and some parts were very confusing and busy, but she wanted to get the lay of the land and discover all that it had to offer. Also, she would soon be looking for a job. There was a friendly young woman living in the condo complex with whom Vera chatted quite often. She was helpful to Vera, telling her where to find things that she needed, shortcuts to places, doctors, dentists etc. She became a good friend for a few years before she married and moved away.

Maurice was making more connections in the building trade and learned about Florida's building codes and requirements. He worked on many worksites on a variety of house structures and styles in many different areas. He got to know sub-contractors, filing away a lot of business cards as he felt increasingly confident about striking out on his own. After a year, Maurice was approved for a construction loan, bought a piece of property, and set about building a house as a speculative venture, or "spec house." It was quite a large floor plan, but he was lucky to have help and guidance on his first project from his new friend, Gene Pagel. There were a few bumps along the way, inspectors who required changes and adjustments, contractors who did not finish on schedule, cabinets that had been measured inaccurately, but in the end, he made a respectable profit. Maurice was quite satisfied and ready for his next build. This one was to be built under contract for a couple who had already purchased property and had pre-approved floor plans for an expansive home. All went well at first, but the property owners changed their minds often about doors, windows, finishes, and they added extras as the project progressed. When the final payment was due, there was a dispute. Maurice, again, had not properly had the changes and upgrades signed off and his extra charges were denied. His compensation was significantly reduced by the costs of all the changes to the original agreement. The old bitter feelings of being cheated and taken advantage of reared up again and he decided that would be the last time he would build under contract. From that point on, he would build only to put the house up for sale upon completion.

Vera found a job at Montgomery Ward working at the jewellery counter. She enjoyed the customer interaction but could not get comfortable with the cash register and the credit card imprinter. She became too stressed and felt that this was not the job for her, so she soon gave it up and looked for a job in the school system working with special needs students again. She applied for a position and was hired. She was happy with the work, comfortable with the students but found that the staff was not particularly friendly, not like the pleasant camaraderie she had had at the school in Fairfield. She was not included in their groups at lunch time, and no one seemed to be interested in chatting with her, so she went about her day being cordial and professional, thinking about the modest salary she was able to contribute to the household.

During the first year in Florida, Frances, Joe and the boys visited and so did Ruth, Mike, Adam and Tiphanie. It helped Vera to see the family but when they left, she became melancholy. All the holidays and birthdays were especially hard, reminding her of regrets from long ago when she missed so many holidays and celebrations with her mother after moving from England. It seemed that her life was always about parting from loved ones, beginning with the loss of her father so long ago, leaving her family and friends in England, and leaving Fairfield, her two daughters, her grandchildren and good friends. It was bad timing for relocating to Florida because Vera had also entered menopause. Her sadness was magnified with the changes naturally occurring in her own body. She became depressed, lethargic and unmotivated. She dwelt on the past, loved ones she had lost, places she had left and memories of happier times. Maurice was concerned and did all he could to cheer her up. He invited new friends to visit for an evening, he took Vera out for nice meals, they went to St. George Island to sit on the beach, they walked around the historic town of Apalachicola discovering the quaint shops, galleries, and restaurants, and visited the unique small town of Havana just north of Tallahassee with many specialty shops, historic buildings, homes and inviting cafés. Vera appreciated Maurice's efforts and enjoyed her outings but would soon slide again into her dark place. Maurice suggested that she see a doctor to get some help and for a time she was prescribed hormone replacement therapy which gave her relief from some of her symptoms. He hoped that with time, she would return to her old self and settle into her new life.

There was a problem that shook Vera and made her realise that she had been too self-focused and, if not neglecting, certainly not focused on her daughter, Helen's activities. Late one night when Vera could not sleep, she got out of bed and descended the stairs in the townhouse to make herself a warm drink. She read a little before climbing the stairs again. Helen's bedroom door was ajar, and she peeked in to see if she had organised the new desk and bookcase that she and Maurice had bought her. She was alarmed to see that Helen was not in her bed. *The room was empty.* Vera checked the bathroom and returned downstairs to check the half bath just in case she was in there. Had she missed her asleep on the couch? Helen was not there. She was not in the house. Vera ran upstairs to rouse Maurice.

"Maurice, Helen is not here! She's not in her bed and she's nowhere in the house."

"Huh?" Maurice questioned opening his eyes. "What's the matter, dear?"

"It's Helen. She is not in the house!"

"Really! Right then. Come on, let's go downstairs."

"What are we going to do, Maurice?"

"We are going to wait for her to sneak back in. Don't put any lights on, Vera. We'll just sit and wait."

"*She snuck out!* I just don't believe it."

"Why don't we have a cup of tea, dear. It may be a while."

"The little devil!" Vera exclaimed.

Vera and Maurice sat together in the dark for several hours waiting for their fifteen-year-old daughter to return home. They sat side by side on the couch glancing from time to time at the clock watching the minutes and hours tick by. Finally, they heard a key slowly inserted into the lock and the door handle gently turning. Helen stepped lightly inside and closed the front door with hardly a sound. Then she turned and gasped as two figures rose from the couch in the darkness.

"Well… about time you came home, don't you think?" Maurice declared.

"Just where have you been all this time? Do you know

it's almost five o'clock in the morning?" Vera asked.

"Oh… you scared me!" Helen panted. "Er, I've just been chilling with some friends."

"*Oh, is that all!*" Maurice responded. "Sneaking out of the house and chilling with friends… until five o'clock in the morning. Could it be that you snuck out because you thought we would not approve?"

"Well… I didn't think… I mean… I just wanted to have a little fun."

"Do you think we have been having *fun*? Sitting here, waiting for you to decide to come home?" Vera asked.

"No, but I didn't expect that you would wake up."

"Well, *I did wake up,* Helen. I haven't been sleeping well lately. It was a nasty shock to discover that you were not here."

"Well, I'm sorry guys. I didn't mean to upset you." Helen said as she walked toward the staircase.

"Where do you think you are going, my girl?" Maurice asked.

"Up to bed."

"*Oh, no you're not!*" Vera responded. "We have missed a night's sleep and so will you. "There's a lot I need done around here. You can start by vacuuming the floors, all of them, downstairs and upstairs, then you can dust every surface and wash the kitchen floor."

"But…"

"No buts!" said Maurice. "Get to work."

It was a long Saturday. Maurice went out after breakfast to his jobsite to check on the work crew and Vera supervised Helen who moved from task to task, snivelling and sniffing. Vera knew the punishment was deserved but she also recognised that her daughter was desperate to make new friends and may be making bad decisions and choices. She needed to spend more time interacting with Helen, guiding and supporting her as she made her own new life in Tallahassee.

"Alright," Vera said after they had eaten dinner. "You can go up to your room now. We'll talk more tomorrow. I want to hear about these new friends of yours."

Helen was placed on "restrictions" for one month following her offence. Maurice was deeply offended with his daughter's behaviour and disobedience of his rules. She was restricted to the house with limited telephone use and television time. This was punishment indeed for Helen who was striving to make new friends and establish herself as a "cool" person with whom to hang out. She went to school and back and moped around the house, counting off the days.

When a friend told her that a band, Cheap Trick, was actually going to play in concert at Doak Campbell Stadium on Florida State University campus the following week, Helen was beside herself with frustration that she would still be restricted and would not be able to attend. She decided to approach her mother and plead her case. Vera was of two minds as she listened to her daughter's appeal. She wanted to be firm, support Maurice's punishment, and prove to Helen that there would be consequences for bad behaviour, but she was also rather pleased that her daughter was excited about an event, something special, that she wanted to enjoy with her friends, two boys and another girl. Helen assured her mother that it was not a date, they were all just going to enjoy the concert as friends. Vera decided that enabling Helen's social life and having her feel happier about the move to Florida, outweighed the terms of the restriction. She took Helen to buy her ticket with babysitting money that she had saved.

"I will talk to Dad. But, Helen, please do not deceive us

again."

"No… Mum… no, I won't. Thank you, thank you!"

Vera made her points with Maurice and asked him to relent for this one occasion. He did not approve, discipline was so important raising children in his mind, but he softened to please his wife and perhaps make her feel better and allow Helen to become a little more invested in her life in Tallahassee.

Not only did Vera advocate for Helen to attend the concert, but she also drove the girls to the venue and picked them up when they called her from a specific gas station in the dead of night when the concert was over.

Maurice's next build went more smoothly. Upon completion, he put the house up for sale and sold it quickly making a nice profit. He had also been able to do some well-paying wallpapering jobs referred to him buy one of his home improvements contacts. He now looked around for property on which to build their own home. Vera wanted to be more in town. Killearn was lovely but it was just a little too quiet for her taste. Maurice took her to Dellwood Drive to see a beautiful lot and that is where they decided to build for themselves. Two years after moving down to Florida, they moved into their new home, a large ranch-style house with three bedrooms and two full bathrooms. It had a large kitchen looking out to the backyard and opening onto a deck. A formal dining area was off the kitchen, leading to a spacious living room with a brick fireplace. Helen had been recruited to help with painting the interior and Vera had set about seeding the lawn and planting shrubs and flowers. It was a joyful day when the three of them moved in. Vera felt more settled and was excited to meet her new neighbours and explore the area and all the conveniences close by. The only downside was that Helen would have to change schools again. She would attend Leon High School, an older, brick building where she would transfer as a junior. However, the new school suited her, she made lots of new friends easily, enjoyed her classes and liked her teachers. It seemed that the family had finally found their permanent home in Florida.

Frances, Joe, and the boys drove down for a Christmas visit a few months later. It was an exciting time for Vera, making sleeping arrangements, shopping for Christmas dinner and gifts and treats for Peter and Tom. She had forgotten the activity that two young boys brought to a household, so she took them all around to see interesting places in Tallahassee, parks, the Junior Museum, her favourite, Maclay Gardens, they went to malls, beaches, roller skating. Helen spent a lot of time with the boys, playing ball in the back yard and board games in the evening. It was great fun, but Vera was exhausted when they drove away on their journey back to Connecticut. It was the first of many drives south over the years for Frances and Joe. Ruth and Mike visited sometime later and visited Mike's grandparents too while they were there. One of Mike's aunts lived very near Dellwood Drive and she had an in-ground pool, so they were able to swim and play there a few times during their stay.

Vera and Maurice had other visitors also while at Dellwood. Geza and Elnora drove down a couple of times. Vera enjoyed taking Elnora around. She was an easy guest, game for anything, and the two were good friends. Geza was happy to watch sports on television with Maurice or go for a beer at the "Salty Dog" just round the corner. Hazel and Ray flew down. What a lively time that was. The four of them fell immediately back into their comfortable old friendship, teasing, joking, laughing, and singing. Some of Vera and Maurice's new friends came round to meet their old friends and hear some of the funny stories they shared, and it became just like the old parties of times gone by. Yvonne and Bob flew down also. Bob was an avid golfer, so Maurice, using his connections in the building trade, arranged a foursome to play on the local course. Bob was amazed when he discovered that the course, Golden Eagle Golf & Country Club, was a PGA championship course. He looked around with interest, since the house prices and cost of living would make it a possible choice for retirement in the future, especially when he noticed houses for sale that overlooked the golf course. Vera loved her time with Yvonne. They had plenty of time to catch up on all the family news and to go out together to shop, see the town, and visit some of Vera's friends. These visits lifted Vera's spirits and helped her realise that flying back and forth to Connecticut was really quite easy and routine.

By 1982, Helen was becoming quite acclimated to her new home. She was adapting a southern accent, intonation and expressions, determined to fit in. Her circle of friends was growing and at sixteen, she was dating Bret, the son of one of Maurice's interior decorator contacts. During the months the couple was together, Maurice bought tickets for 30th December for the two youngsters and himself to attend the Gator Bowl in Jacksonville which pitted the Florida State Seminoles against the West Virginia Mountaineers. Unfortunately, the couple broke up prior to the game but decided that they would still attend the game as friends. The weather was miserable, cold and rainy. They arrived in Jacksonville in plenty of time and dropped Helen off at a friend's house who had recently relocated there. She would visit for a while and get dropped off at the stadium at game time. Meanwhile, Maurice and Bret had lunch and got settled in their seats to enjoy all the pre-game activities. As the afternoon wore on and the game began, there was no sign of Helen. Maurice became worried and angry as the first quarter ended and then the second quarter began. The Florida State Seminoles were dominating the game, but Maurice could not relax and enjoy it as he was constantly swivelling around, scanning the aisles for his daughter. It was not until the third quarter that Helen showed up. Maurice was furious.

"*Where have you been?* You have missed half the game!" he growled.

"Sorry guys," she responded casually. "I lost track of time. We were catching up and having such a fun time."

"How nice for you! I have been very worried. Didn't you think about that?"

"Come on, Dad. No big deal! I'm here now. Good game! Looks like Bobby Bowden's got this one."

Bret scowled in disgust and Maurice sat quietly fuming in the cold and rain. At the end of the third quarter, he suggested that they leave early. All three had had enough.

Ruth and Mike had bought a house in Stratford, Connecticut in 1983 and the following year Frances and Joe moved there also. Frances was thrilled that the two families would be close by. The cousins got along well and there were many happy times together. The boys all played in Little League so there were many exciting games to watch. One year all three boys played on the Stoneybrook A's together. Ruth wanted a deck on the back of her house and Maurice offered to build it for her. He and Vera drove north, staying at Ruth's while he built it, and then with Frances for a while, also spending time with Ray and Hazel,

Yvonne and Bob, Geza and Elnora, and several other friends in the area.

There was a surprise visit in 1984. Frances telephoned Vera to tell her that she should arrange to stay home on her birthday, 12th March, because there would be a delivery coming from both families in Connecticut. Vera wondered what they could have bought her. She stayed home that day looking out of the front window from time to time to watch for a delivery van. When there was a knock at the door, she opened it to find Frances, Ruth and her four grandchildren standing there. What a shock it was! They had driven down in Ruth's station wagon, Ruth and Frances sharing the driving for the twenty-hour journey. After the initial excitement, exclamations of surprise, hugs and laughs, in came sleeping bags, pillows and suitcases. The surprise continued when Helen and Maurice came home, and a noisy week followed, full of activity and fun times.

In November 1985, Hurricane Kate formed northeast of Puerto Rico and moved west into the Gulf of Mexico, intensifying to a category 2 storm. It slammed into the Florida panhandle causing an eleven-foot storm surge with 120 mph winds passing directly over Tallahassee. The house on Dellwood Drive took a hard blow, trees were twisted and uprooted, slamming down onto the roof, the deck, gutters and siding, causing huge damage and destruction to the property. Vera was traumatised, huddled with Maurice in the hallway, waiting it out. It was reminiscent of the war years when she spent hours and entire nights in the air-raid shelter while bombs rained down all around her. All the terrors of those nights rose up again. When an explosive crash hit the roof, causing the house to shake and scatter debris, Vera could not help but cry out in panic. "I CAN'T STAND IT MAURICE," she shouted. "I CAN'T BELIEVE THIS IS HAPPENING. IT'S JUST LIKE IT WAS WAITING IT OUT IN THE AIR RAID SHELTER ALL OVER AGAIN!"

"It's all right dear. We lived through it then, didn't we? And that went on for years! This will be over soon. Just hold on." Maurice stood up. "I'm just going to see what that big crash was all about." He walked cautiously to the end of the hallway and peered around the corner looking beyond the kitchen to the dining room. A tree had crashed through the roof creating a large, jagged hole through which branches spread wide across the room, reaching down to cover the dining room table. He stood for a moment taking in the destruction and debris. The dining room table had been a vintage set with six chairs that he and Vera had bought at an estate sale years ago when they first moved to Connecticut, paying $50 for it. They had recovered the chairs, sanded and stained the table and coated the tabletop with many coats of polyurethane and had been very proud and happy with the results. Many holidays, family dinners, parties and games had been enjoyed around it. It looked to Maurice upon his brief, distanced inspection that it may have survived the impact, that the heaviest part of the tree had not fallen on it. He squared his shoulders and returned to squat at Vera's side. "Bit of a hole in the ceiling of the dining room," he said. "But I don't think there is any significant damage to the table or chairs." He squeezed her arm encouragingly and then poured them each a splash of brandy. "Cheers!" he said, clinking her glass. "Here's to Kate's visit coming to a speedy end!"

When the storm passed, they ventured outside and stood in disbelief at the mess all around them. Their own house was so badly damaged, and the backyard was strewn with fallen trees, branches, and littered with all kinds of debris that had been blown there. The street was impassable since trees, power lines and poles were lying across the road. All the neighbours were out assessing the damage and commiserating with each other. When a news crew from the local television station arrived, they could see the tree which had broken through the dining room roof of Maurice and Vera's house, and they asked if they could take some footage for the evening news. It took weeks to repair the damage and to clear the yard, but Maurice was lucky to have contacts who could help him quickly. Neighbours helped each other as much as they could, sharing food, offering the use of their grills and gas stoves for cooking, exchanging news of places that were open to buy supplies. It was a real coming together during a time of inconvenience and need. Vera again was reminded of her youth, during the war when kindness and compassion dominated. When the people looked out for each other, helped each other, stood together, pooled resources and overcame hardship When the power was restored and the road was cleared, it was a great relief, but even so, Vera missed the chats and gatherings.

Then, at the end of 1985, Ruth visited Frances while the children were all in school.
"We have to sell the house," she declared.
"What? Why?"
"You know it has been rough for us lately. Since Mike got laid off from Sikorsky it has been a struggle paying our bills."
"But he got the job with UPS."
"It doesn't pay as well, and it is probably only seasonal. After Christmas he could be out of a job again."

"But where will you go? Will you rent again?"

"No. Actually, we think we will go down to Florida." Frances was speechless as she let that thought sink in. Old emotions and resentment flared. The last of her family moving away from her. A big move. A big change. The cousins would be separated. "I bet Mum and Dad are happy!" she said bitterly.

"They are. We really have to do this, Frances. This winter I have kept the thermostat turned down as low as we can stand. Gas heat is very expensive. I even bought an oil heater for the living room to make it bearable. Our ARM mortgage will soon be adjusted. The fixed rate period will expire, and we won't be able to afford the new monthly payment. We have no choice."

"Can't you go back to the bank?"

"Maybe, but it will still be hard. I am tired of scrimping and worrying. It will be easier for us down south."

"I didn't know it was that bad."

"I've had a realtor round. He said we should do a few cosmetic things to make it a little easier to sell."

"Like what?"

"Change the kitchen cabinet doors or paint them, put down a new kitchen floor, paint a few walls, that kind of thing."

"I can give you a hand with some of that," Frances said with a sigh.

Early in 1986, Ruth, Mike, Adam and Tiphanie left Connecticut and moved to Tallahassee into a small house rental for six months. Mike got a job as a driver for Coca Cola and sometimes worked at special events around town providing an adequate supply. Maurice guided the couple through the process of buying some land and building a house. Ruth and Mike worked on the project as much as they could, picking up supplies, cleaning and painting until the house was finished. It was a large, beautiful ranch in the prestigious Killearn Acres area. Ruth was thrilled with her new home and optimistic for a bright new future. Vera, Maurice and Helen were overjoyed that they now had family nearby. Vera finally felt rooted in Florida and spent a lot of time with Ruth and the children. She had missed so much of their young years. Adam was now nine years old and Tiphanie, six. Holidays, birthdays and other celebrations were special and fun again, helping with the "empty nest" situation that Vera was facing. Helen had recently moved out after deciding not to go to college, getting a job and sharing a rental with friends.

For two years or so, life was reasonably stable for Vera. She was happier in mind and spirit and her circle of friends grew. Marie was her next-door neighbour with whom she chatted often. She and her husband owned a shoe store, so they were busy during the week but when Marie stopped working, they became especially close. Maurice met a fellow on one of his jobsites who made kitchen cabinets. He had a British wife, Barbara, and so Maurice invited them over for dinner one evening. Vera and Barbara became good friends from that evening on. Gail from the condos visited on occasion and there was Everett from the remodelling showroom and his wife, Sarah, Gerri, and Wayne from the Unitarian Universalist church Vera attended from time to time, Sue, the minister at the church, Gaia, the vet whose boys Vera had cared for after school. Vera was not very religious, but she enjoyed the feeling of belonging and many of the activities at church as well as the opportunity to meet and interact with a variety of people. When she met someone that she liked, and was interested to know them better, she never hesitated to invite them for lunch or dinner. Maurice was always happy and interested to meet new people, so he was welcoming and sociable when he met Vera's guests.

Tag sales became a new, fun activity for Vera. She enjoyed driving around on the weekends and stopping to peruse the items on display for sale on tables in driveways or garages. She found it very satisfying in several ways; meeting and chatting with so many different people, looking for bargains and unusual items, and cleaning them up, making them shine, restoring them to their original condition. Maurice could not help but be interested in her finds when she returned home with bulging bags. Vera dove into them bringing everything out one by one to show Maurice and declare victoriously what a pittance she had paid for each item. She went "tagging" sometimes with Marie or Sylvia and had a nice lunch out as part of the excursion. Vera would never get tired of this activity. Finding a bargain, fixing, mending, reusing, making do, had been ingrained in her psyche since the war years.

Vera had left the job in the special needs classroom when they had moved from Killearn to Dellwood Drive and had helped Maurice on his wallpaper jobs pasting up. She had also developed a little party business for children. She dressed something like an older Mary Poppins and arrived at the party with a big basket of party games, trinkets and prizes. She had researched children's party games as well as recalling old favourites from her childhood, made up flyers and spread the word to all her friends and acquaintances. She called herself, "Nana," which was the name her grandchildren called her and soon began to book appointments. This little venture lasted a couple of years until there was another disappointment and shakeup to her stable and comfortable life.

Excerpt from letter from Vera to Frances and Joe – November 18, 1980

My old Plymouth purred down to Florida like a princess – she really showed us she is not finished yet. She was dragging her tail with the load, but Joe's dad was aware of the strain and kept her rolling beautifully. I don't know what I would have done without your parents, Joe, it really saved my bacon. We had a wonderful time in Disney World and Helen loved it. Dad didn't appreciate Space Mountain and alighted looking grey. I didn't go near it.

Excerpts from letter from Vera to Frances – January 12, 1981, May 5, 1981

I cannot think or talk about our relocating to Florida without I splash buckets of tears at a fantastic volume pouring down my face and have no control over this. I have not been as bad as this before. It must be my age and change of life – a very bad time to move away like we have.

I sometimes think I am being punished for emigrating from England and leaving Nana when I knew she hated it, and now I have done the same to you girls and this is depressing me. All I have kept doing is deserting my family through the years. I know I should have been firm and refused to leave the area, but how could I have lived with Dad and known that I was keeping him from getting away and relieving himself of some of the pressures that he had building up. He was very frustrated, and everything seemed to be souring on him, his so-called buddies were letting him down, plus the fact we have to earn a living, which I know you understand.

History repeats itself so much in a lifetime. I can remember thinking I would see Nana come round the corner of Weeping Willow house by the kitchen window at any minute, which was impossible at that time. However, then Auntie Yvonne would come marching round the corner looking just like Nana. Last week I imagined you and Joe with Peter and Tom burst in my front door, which was also impossible at that particular time, and then lo and behold, you made the trip to see us. So sometimes premonitions and imaginations do come true.

I'm feeling very well and in good spirits since I've been on the medication. It's such a treat not to feel tired and achy. I'm not depressed any more – in fact, I'm a new me. I can't believe it. I wish I'd gone to him before (the doctor.)

Memory from Helen in her own words. Dellwood Drive -1986

Mum woke me up one rainy morning saying, "Helen, get up… I want to show you something!"

"Well, what is it? Can't you just tell me? Do I have to get dressed?"

"Yes, put some shoes on at least, and here, take this umbrella."

"Mum… really? What the heck!" Mum's sly grin and enthusiasm piqued my curiosity though, so I sleepily got up and joined Mum at the back door, umbrella in hand.

"Right," she said. "Come see…"

We plodded down the mushy back garden to what looked like a rock sitting under a tree. As we got closer it became apparent that it wasn't a rock at all. It was a tortoise. No! It was two tortoises… and they were… mating! slowly, as tortoises tend to do. Mum clapped her hands, laughing a bit wickedly and said, "Isn't it marvellous?!" I stood there for a minute or so, looking back and forth from my giddy-with-laughter mother, and the now very self-conscious tortoises who carried on with their business little by little, and I had to laugh myself a bit before telling Mum, "Marvellous indeed! I'm going back to bed."

CHAPTER TWENTY-FIVE

Maurice had run into a patch of bad luck building again. There had been some significant problems with his latest house. He had building supplies stolen from the property several times and ended up camping out at night in a tent on the property. He pitched it out of sight and armed with little more than an air gun and baseball bat, he hoped to drive the thieves away. During one of his camping nights, he heard rustling sounds coming from the shrubbery on the edge of the building lot. He jumped up and out of the tent switching on his flashlight. The light reflected off several pairs of eyes low to the ground. They were alligators that had come up out of the river onto the riverbank that bordered the property. It was quite a shock for Maurice who promptly took down the tent and waited the rest of the night in his truck. He also decided to add an alligator fence to the landscaping plans. Fortunately, the new house construction was closed in and secured in just a few more days. Delays followed: unreliable sub-contractors and problems with inspections that required additional work. The finished house took longer than usual to sell as did his following build and Maurice was in a bind. He needed to raise funds to pay off his construction loans and the only way he could do so was to sell Dellwood. Vera was devastated yet again.

"Maurice, isn't there any other way?"

"I'm afraid not, dear. I'll need the equity in the house to get straight again."

"But this was to be our last house, our final home."

"Yes… it was. I'm sorry, dear. I know you are disappointed, but we have no choice. I need to be able to build again and pay off my debts to qualify for another construction loan."

"Where will we go?"

"Oh, we'll find a nice place to rent for a while and then we'll build ourselves another home when I'm on my feet again."

"I really love it here…" her voice broke and she sat down heavily with her head in her hands.

"Come on, dear. It will be alright. We always work it out, don't we? We're a team, aren't we? Just think of it as a new adventure."

"I don't need any more adventures, Maurice. I've had enough!"

The lovely home on Dellwood Drive went up for sale. But even that house did not sell quickly. It was a sluggish market and months passed with not much interest. When a couple finally wanted to make an offer, however, it was not straightforward. They explained that they had a condominium which they had not been able to sell and would like to make an offer contingent upon its sale. Maurice was becoming desperate and needed funds quickly. He asked the potential buyers if he and Vera could take a look at the condo. It was not very far away, just across town in a complex off a busy road, more industrial than their area near Dellwood. The condo itself was acceptable though Vera found it rather dark and gloomy. There was a communal swimming pool which would be nice. The deal was made, and attorneys worked out the details of an exchange of properties. Since the value of Dellwood was more than the condo, Vera and Maurice would receive a cash settlement and Maurice could build again.

Helen made arrangements to move in with friends after the closing on Dellwood but prior to moving out she took a short vacation. She had been working for a few years at a local television station in the production department. It was a job she enjoyed, producing commercials for local companies and businesses. She left Vera and Maurice in the throes of packing boxes, tossing unwanted items and organising the move. When she arrived home, she found her items had been packed up also, into boxes, bags and containers, all neatly labelled and stacked.

"Here you are, Helen. All ready to go!" Vera stated.

"Oh… wow! I didn't expect that I would be moving out as soon as I got back."

"Well, we couldn't wait for you!" Maurice explained. "The closing is in a couple of days. We have to be out!" He picked up one of the boxes. "Here, I'll help you put these in your car. Looks like you may have to make a couple of trips."

"But… I thought…" Helen began, disappointed that she could not have a cup of tea, sit down and tell her parents all about her trip.

"Sorry, dear, we've got lots more to do. Good luck to you in your new place."

Helen would move from place to place rather a lot during her young adulthood. She moved from job to job also. Always a diligent worker, creative and enthusiastic, she sought new challenges and opportunities much like her father did in his young life. She was a risk-taker and party girl, intent on enjoying both aspects of her life, work and play. One Halloween, she met Maurice at the Salty Dog for a drink. "Here comes my *Wild Child*," he boldly announced to his group of friends. Helen knew he was proud of her spirit, and she rather liked the distinction of being so named.

Moving from Dellwood was another heart-wrenching move for Vera. She so loved the house and the street where she lived. She was comfortable with the area and had her favourite shops and stores. The condo did not feel like home at all. She was uprooted again and even though she was still in the same city, it felt so different. The main road that the condos opened onto was busy all the time with fast-moving traffic. She had to navigate her way around and avoid being out on the road at rush hour at all costs. Vera desperately missed her house on Dellwood, the one they had designed and built to suit their needs, the one they had planned for their retirement, the one with the quiet backyard and the beautiful camellia bushes she had planted. She could not help but drive down the street sometimes to check on the house and see if the shrubs were in bloom. She made the best of the condominium hoping that they would not be there long and enjoying it when Ruth brought the children over to play in the pool.

Maurice was able to shrug off the loss of Dellwood and look forward with optimism and enthusiasm, as he always had done. He did not spend much time looking back, lamenting or pining. He was excited about the next opportunity and was as gregarious and cheerful as ever. He chatted with the occupants of neighbouring condo units, with the staff and groundskeepers and it was not long before he was approached to join the homeowner's association. He was flattered at the invitation and accepted willingly. His ego had been stroked, causing him to feel important and somewhat higher in status. He attended meetings and contributed to the discussion especially when repairs, upkeep and maintenance issues were brought up. His experience as a builder was appreciated and soon he found himself offered the president position. Maurice was proud to accept and take on the leadership role and effect some beneficial changes for the residents. His spirits and optimism were high again since he had also been able to secure a new construction loan and had found a property near where Ruth lived in Killearn Acres. He was back in business again.

Ruth was beginning to have concerns about Mike. He had left his job with Coca-Cola for a better opportunity with Miller Beer driving a delivery truck but progressed to a sales position earning a good salary and was given a company car. Management really liked him as did the customers he serviced. However, he began drinking again, spending a lot of evenings out with a variety of feeble excuses, and coming home drunk. The drinking affected him in a negative way. His usual amenable, easy-going nature became angry, short-tempered and mean. Ruth confronted him numerous times following disturbing episodes and he was always apologetic, full of promises that it would not happen again. However, after a period of calm and family focus, he would slip back again into his bad habits. Ruth could not understand it. Their life was so much easier now. They lived in a beautiful new home, Mike brought in a good salary, the children were settled. Why would he put all of that at risk? She grew angry and suspicious of his activities, especially when she discovered discrepancies in Mike's records and reports that he kept for Miller Beer. Ruth was far superior in recordkeeping, mathematics and accounting to Mike, so she helped him by keeping the accounts and balancing the books. Many times, she found a significant imbalance.

"Hey Mike, something is way off here. These figures don't make sense."

"Oh, don't worry about it. I'll fix it. I must have more paperwork in the car."

"Are you sure? Why don't you go check and bring it in?"

"Ruth don't worry. I'll take care of it."

Ruth's suspicions grew when Adam discovered his baseball card collection was missing. He had been saving cards for several years and it would have had some value. She suspected that Mike had debts to pay, perhaps gambling debts, drinking expenses and maybe worse. When he came home drunk one afternoon and was disruptive to the household and mean to the children, Ruth had reached her limit. He would have to leave. While he flopped on the sofa and fell asleep, she packed a couple of bags throwing in as much of his clothing and essentials as possible and dropped them on the floor by the front door. When he woke late that evening and while the children were in bed, she told him to leave.

"But Ruth…" he slurred.

"But nothing. I have had it! You are not going to change, and I am not going to live another day with your drinking, lies, stealing and whatever else you are up to!"

"But Ruth, I promise I won't…"

"Get out! No more promises. *Just get out!*"

Ruth had made her decision. She would not relent again. It was over. She was done with Mike for good. However, she was scared. Where would she go from here? She did not want to count on Mike for anything anymore. She would have to be the breadwinner from now on. She called her parents the next morning asking them to come over to the house. Vera knew it was bad news.

"Mike's gone," Ruth announced without preamble. "I threw him out last night. I'm done! I've given him chance after chance…" She continued on, pouring out all her grievances; the drinking, the lying, the staying out late, the stealing and all her suspicions. "I think it's even worse than I know." There were no tears. She was more angry than anything else. Angry, disgusted, embarrassed, but also resolved.

"Where are the children?" Vera asked.

"Don't worry, they are not in the house. They are playing next door."

"Do they know about this?" Maurice asked.

"Not yet. I'll tell them soon."

"Well, now… what are you going to do?" Maurice sat down with a groan. "What a stupid man!" Maurice sighed shaking his head. "Losing his family like this."

"Oh dear… oh dear," Vera worried. "How are you going to manage?"

"I need a little time to think about what I want to do. I guess I need to see a lawyer and I will have to get a job. I'm glad that I made the decision last year to start back at college. I've got to be able to take care of myself and the kids. Can't count on *him* for anything!"

Ruth moved forward quickly. She engaged an attorney to initiate divorce proceedings and found a job with Florida State University working in the department that oversaw summer programmes at Oxford University in England. She found the job exciting and interesting and was definitely in the right place to pursue completing her undergraduate degree. She finished her core courses at Tallahassee Community College and transferred to Florida State for her last two years. But what to major in? The career centre had books to help her. She perused them with an open mind to find something that she could get excited about, finally settling on Medical Technologist. It appealed to her because she thought she would like to work in a lab, working with specimens, discovering the cause of an infection, determining the antibiotic that would work well, being a medical detective of a sort. Already working for

FSU gave her a decided advantage when registering for courses, and the staff was flexible with her schedule so that she had no problem attending classes. However, she knew that it would not be easy. She had several years ahead balancing children, work, college classes and studying. And when Mike called her soon after moving out to tell her that he had been fired from Miller Beer and that his company car was repossessed, she knew that the child support he had been ordered to pay preliminary to the divorce, would not be reliable, if sent at all!

Vera worried about Ruth and the children and did what she could to help out. There were times when she drove to the house to be there when they arrived home from school if Ruth was delayed at work or in class. Sometimes they went to a neighbour who had children of a similar age until Ruth returned home. Sometimes they had to let themselves in alone after school. Adam was almost thirteen and Tiphanie was ten, so they were able to get themselves a snack and play a game or start their homework. Vera was concerned that Ruth had bitten off more than she could chew but was quite amazed at her determination. She had set her course and was steadfast to it. Vera hoped that Ruth could finish her education and still manage to keep the new house that she and Mike had been so excited to build, but she had her doubts.

Vera had worries of her own. Maurice had bought land on Gallant Fox Road which was quite near to Ruth's house and built a "spec house" there. It was an attractive, modern plan, very open and airy. However, it did not sell. Maurice became agitated and concerned again, especially since the construction loan interest was accruing which would affect his profit. He came up with an idea.

"Vera, what if we sell this condo and move into the new house?"

"Huh?"

"Well, it makes sense, doesn't it? The condo should be easier to sell since it is a much less expensive property, and we would move into the new house with a mortgage to cover the building costs. Think about it. We will be right near Ruth and the kids, back in Killearn, and I will use the profit from the condo for the next build."

"Oh, but Maurice. Move again! Will we be able to afford the mortgage? It was never our intention to move into it ourselves."

"I know that, of course, but it seems the sensible thing to do."

The condominium was sold. Vera was not unhappy about that, but it was the idea of moving again. How many times in her life had she packed up to move to another home? One day she would have to sit down and count. This move, though, was easier to take. She would be moving into a lovely new house and be within a short walk of Ruth's house. She would love that! It was just that she did not think it would last.

The summer of 1989 was a time of turmoil for Frances and Joe. There were rumours that there would be widespread layoffs at Textron Lycoming following the purchase of Avco Corporation by Textron where Joe had worked for eight years. He was worried about the impact on his working career and thought he might need to make a drastic decision.

"This might be the time we should think about relocating to Florida," he told Frances.

"Oh, really? You have been thinking about Florida?"

"Well, yes. It seems to make sense. We have family there, the cost of living is so much less than here, and we should have a good amount of equity in this house."

"Yes… but, oh wow! That will be a big move. I think it will be hard for us to leave our friends and our lives up here. What about the boys? Oh gosh! Peter will be the same age that I was when I left England for America. You know how much I hated being uprooted like that."

"I know… I know, but government contracts are expiring at work and positions will be eliminated. My job could well be at risk."

"But even if your job is cut, couldn't you find another one somewhere else up here?"

"Maybe. I would hope so… but why are you hesitant to move to Florida? I thought you would jump at the idea to be near your sisters and your parents again."

"I guess it's the idea of following after them and making such a drastic change to our lives… doing the same thing to my children that was done to me. I mean… it would be great to be near my family but, oh, I don't know. You are shaking my world and I don't like it."

"How about we go down for a week in February, during the boys' winter break from school and look around, look at houses, job opportunities and see how we feel about it?"

"Well, I guess that would be okay."

The February visit was interesting. The family stayed with Vera and Maurice at their new house on Gallant Fox. The house was lovely and quite an alluring example of a home that Frances and Joe would be able to afford. They looked around at houses for sale in the Killearn area and found one that intrigued them both. It was a large two-storey, Victorian house with a turret on one side. They had a realtor show them inside and found it to be large and luxurious and would suit their every need. Joe was satisfied with the responses he received about employment prospects and in a whirlwind few days, a contract was signed with the builder, contingent upon the sale of their house in Connecticut. Driving back to Connecticut through an ice storm, Frances and Joe began to wonder if they had been too hasty. They now had to sell their own house and prepare for a big move south. When the house sold in June, it was the perfect time to move and get settled before school started in Florida in August. The boys now had to face reality and realised that they would be leaving their schools and their friends and all their activities. They did not complain but they spent a lot of time with their best friends in the weeks leading up to departure. It tugged at Frances's heart and conscience to witness the friendships that were deeper that she had thought and the sadness in her sons' faces as they anticipated the parting. It was also difficult leaving Geza and Elnora who were so unhappy that their family was moving so far away. Joe's brother, Alan lived with his family in Maine which was a five-hour drive. They would now have no close family living near them. They were heartbroken.

    The long drive down to Florida was not what it should have been. There was no happy excitement of anticipation. The boys played games and chatted together but there were prolonged periods of silence too when all four in the car pondered the future and thought about all that they were leaving behind. Joe had not yet given notice at Textron, wanting to wait until the closing on the Stratford house took place. He took a vacation week and was going to fly back to Connecticut, give his notice, work two weeks, and then drive the second car down. The day after they arrived in Tallahassee, Frances and Joe went with the boys to inspect the new house prior to the closing. It was not ready. The house was a mess with building materials lying around and dust coating the floors, woodwork and counters. Nothing had been cleaned. The property outside had not been cleared of debris or mowed. The realtor assured them that all would be in order before the closing but as Frances and Joe moved through the rooms, it left them cold.

That night when everyone had gone to bed, Frances and Joe sat up in bed talking.

"How do you feel about all this, Fran?" Joe asked.

"What do you mean?"

"It doesn't feel right to me. I would rather we all go back home."

"We don't have a home in Stratford anymore."

"I mean... I would rather go back to Connecticut. But, if you want to stay here, if you think this is the right thing to do, I will make it work."

"Oh, Joe! *I can't believe this.* Why do you suddenly want to change your mind? You are the one who started this whole thing."

"So, you feel good about it? You want to stay?"

Frances sighed deeply. "I feel like we are at a big crossroads in our life. Our decision will change our lives drastically. How ever would we explain ourselves? What about the boys?"

"The boys will be fine whatever we decide. You have to tell me how you feel. We can still stop this. Do you want to go ahead?"

"I don't know. I would feel bad about it either way. My family will be so upset if we went back but if we stay here, I will feel responsible for making you live where you don't want to."

"If one of us is excited about staying here, that will be

enough. I will be happy if you are happy."

"I suppose I would rather go back. But, Joe, what about the contract we have signed on the new house?"

"That can all be worked out. Look, tomorrow morning I will call the moving company and see where the van is and if it has left yet."

"We had better talk to the boys. After all, this is their life too. We need to find out how they would feel about going back."

"Come on. Let's wake them up and talk to them now."

"*Now*? Really?"

"Yes. Come on, let's see what they say."

Frances threw on her robe and she and Joe quietly walked through the living room to the other wing of the house where Peter and Tom were sleeping. Gently they nudged them awake and chatted with them about the possibility of a change of plans. The boys listened yawning and nodding with understanding as their parents attempted to explain themselves.

"So how do you feel about going back guys?" Frances asked. "Would you be terribly disappointed?"

"No," said Peter. "Whatever you both decide is okay with us. Right Tom?"

"Yes, it's okay. Do you think we can go back to our old schools?"

"We will be sure to live somewhere in the old neighbourhood so that you will be near your friends and go back to your schools… if we go back."

"Okay," Tom replied rubbing his eyes and yawning. "Night."

Frances's eyes filled up with grateful tears. She would remember this night and the sweet and generous response of her two boys always.

The following morning Frances and Joe has the difficult task of explaining their change of heart to Vera and Maurice. "I am going to call the moving company to see where the moving van is before we decide for sure," Joe said. "If it is almost here, we will probably go ahead with the closing and move into the new house."

"*Well!*" Maurice replied. "It certainly seems strange to me that the whereabouts of the moving van is going to determine your future."

"I know Dad," Frances agreed. "But it is kind of one of those things that fate has a hand in. It will help us make sense of our decision."

"Well, I think you should go back." Vera stated suddenly and unexpectedly. Frances had expected her to be teary and deeply hurt but she was calm and accepting.

"It probably is not right for you here. When Ruth came down three years ago with the family, they were excited, giddy, and itching to get their lives stared. It has been totally different with you and Joe. From the moment you arrived I noticed your lack of enthusiasm. You have been lacklustre and glum. I suspected that you were having regrets."

"Yes, Mum. It's not that we wouldn't like to be near you all again. It's just that it feels wrong… at least right now."

Joe called the moving company and fate played its hand. The moving van had not begun the route because of a mechanical problem, and it was still at the facility. He called his father to explain the change of plans and asked if he would mind storing the furniture in his double garage. Geza was surprised but pleased with the news that the family was coming back. He cleared out the garage and all the furniture and boxes were piled up inside waiting for Frances and Joe to return. The rest of the time in Florida was mostly dealing with the realtor, and Maurice's attorney who represented them with the breach of contract regarding the contract to buy the new house in Tallahassee. It was going to be costly for Frances and Joe compensating the builder for all his costs and losses until the house sold again, but they agreed willingly and responsibly for the trouble they had caused.

There were regrets all around when the day arrived for the return drive to Connecticut. It had been a difficult week for Frances, a time when she had felt shaken, guilty, and so unsettled.

"Well, that's that then!" Maurice said with finality as the car pulled out of the driveway and headed down the road.

"Yes," Vera replied. "But I think it's for the best." As she watched the car drive away, she could not help but wonder to herself if she should have had the fortitude to negate one or two of Maurice's pursuits and grand ideas. Perhaps that would have been for the best too.

Ruth put her house up for sale later in the year and when her divorce became final, the judge awarded Mike $5000 from the sale. The rest of the equity went to Ruth along with a child support judgement. Ruth had presented several bounced checks as evidence to the judge that Mike had not met his obligation, and the judge realised that she would need the proceeds of the sale to support herself and the children since Mike was so unreliable. She continued at Florida State University to finish her degree living on her small wages, proceeds from the house sale, and student loan funds. She was very lucky to find a house on Gallant Fox Trail that had an assumable, non-qualifying mortgage with reasonable payments, and she chugged along, managing as best she could with so many responsibilities on her shoulders. She worried about her situation and whether or not her finances would stretch all the way through to her graduation and internship.

Late in 1990, arrangements were made for a special Christmas reunion with Vera and Maurice, Ruth and Frances and Joe for the families to meet half the distance between them and spend Christmas together, sharing the expense of a large condominium in North Carolina, on Emerald Island, on the beach. It was fun planning and anticipating the Christmas gathering. The condo was on the sixth floor with wonderful views of the beach and the ocean. However, within a month of Christmas, while out for a walk with Vera, Maurice stepped onto an uneven piece of roadway and lost his balance. He tried to correct his imbalance by taking several quick steps down the road which was descending in a steep incline. He gained speed by doing so and when he eventually fell on his side, it was with a hard impact. He found that he could not move and was in severe pain. He had broken his hip. Surgery was required involving a plate, rods and screws, followed by rehabilitation. Maurice was frantic about the planned Christmas holiday. He had been looking forward to it and did not want to disappoint the family. The doctor advised against it since it had only been a few weeks since surgery but said that if he was intent on going, he would have to get out of the car every hour and walk around to prevent blood clots. Ruth was the driver and so everyone's bags, gifts, food supplies and Maurice's walker were packed into the back of her station wagon. Maurice sat in the passenger seat and Vera, Adam and Tiphanie were in the back seat. Helen was not going since she could not get the time off work. It was a long journey, made longer with all the stops along the way for Maurice to stretch and walk. By the time they arrived at the condominium complex it was late and very dark. Frances had been worrying and wondering how they were doing. The complex was huge. She had imagined that it would be one building but it was many high-rise structures stretching along the seafront and she did not know how Ruth would know which building was which in the dark. So, she wrote a note on the bulletin board located at the entrance to the complex with directions to the correct building. She could walk out of the condo to a railing that overlooked the car park of their building to watch for the car, which she did throughout the evening. When Ruth pulled into the complex, exhausted, stressed and frustrated, she drove past the entrance, unaware of the note on the bulletin board, pulled into the parking lot, opened the door of the car, and called out loudly and desperately, *"FRANCES!!!"* Vera was immediately transported back in time to the years they had lived in Aveley when the girls were so young, and Ruth would call out "SARSEE!!" to get her sister's attention. Frances was approaching the railing to check again for their arrival when she heard her sister's wail. "Yes, Ruth. I'm up here. We'll be right down." Maurice was standing with his walker when everyone reached the ground floor. He took one look up to the sixth floor and shook his head. "I'll never make it all the way up there!"

"Don't worry, Dad," Frances reassured him with a chuckle. "There's an elevator."

It was a happy time bringing up all the supplies, gifts and bags. Frances had a thick stew simmering on the stove and loaves of Italian bread for dinner. Wine was opened and soon everyone began to relax. Peter, Tom, Adam and Tiphanie were excited to be together and were soon immersed in their own activities and games. An artificial

Christmas tree was set up and decorated with lights and ornaments and brightly wrapped gifts were arranged around it. The Christmas celebration had begun.

The next day, Joe did not feel well and remained in bed. He had a fever and chills and vomited throughout the day. It was obvious that he had come down with a virus or perhaps the flu. Frances checked on him and tended to his needs throughout the day, splitting her time between him and the family. At the same time, Vera realised that she was coming down with a urinary tract infection which meant that a run had to be made to a grocery store for some cranberry juice to hopefully ward it off. Joe felt better the next day as did Vera. The weather was mild enough to sit outside on the veranda, where Maurice held crackers out to hovering seagulls right below the PLEASE DO NOT FEED THE SEAGULLS sign that was posted on the wall. They watched the children playing on the beach below, where they wrote MERRY CHRISTMAS in huge letters in the sand. Despite the long drive, the broken hip, sickness and infection, everyone agreed it was all well worth it. It had been a very special Christmas.

Maurice slowly recovered from his broken hip, but he walked stiffly with a bit of a limp from then on. He knew it was time to give up building and, as always, he fell back on his wallpapering skills. He was offered a big job, papering a few walls in each unit of a large new condominiums complex on St. George Island. He was offered a unit to stay in while he was there, so Vera went with him to "paste up" and keep him company. It was a refreshing change for them both with evening strolls along the beach, the soothing sound of the waves at night, and many meals out at the local cafés and oceanside pubs. The time at St. George Island was stress-free and soothing. They came to know the island well, and returned often over the years, just for a day out and chance to relax. When the job was completed, Maurice decided to look for other work related to construction that would make use of his knowledge and skills but not requiring physical labour. He thought that he could be a building inspector for local banks, overseeing and reporting on the progress of construction projects. Joe helped him prepare a resume and cover letter which he mailed out. He got two responses. One bank asked him to come in for an interview and said that they had been contemplating hiring someone to do all their inspections, since they had a lot of construction going on and could not keep up with their own staff. He got the job as an independent contractor. Another bank knew him already from his own building projects. They were interested in "drive-by" inspections with photographs. The years that followed working as a building inspector were probably the most settled and secure years of Maurice's life. It satisfied his need to be involved in construction, be on the sites, interact with builders and contractors, and serve in a position of respected authority. However, the house on Gallant Fox had a mortgage that was too high, and he worried that his reduced earnings would not sustain it. Then, a turn of events provided an opportunity. Unfortunately, Mike's grandfather died after a short illness, and Mike's mother, Larrie, came to Tallahassee to dispose of the contents of the house, put it up for sale, and take her mother back to Connecticut to live with her. Ruth suggested to her parents that they might want to consider buying the house. They knew it well, having visited from time to time. It was located in the northern section of Tallahassee on a long street, Longview Drive, near Lake Jackson. It was small and needed some updating, decorating, and remodelling but nothing that Maurice could not handle. Larrie was delighted that he and Vera wanted the house and offered it at quite a reduced price. The deal was made. This was a move that Vera did not dread. They would be able to buy the house in cash once they sold Gallant Fox. For the first time in their lives, they would be mortgage-free. Their house sold quickly and painlessly since it was in such a desirable area, and they moved into the small ranch-style house ready to renovate and make it their own. Maurice immediately set about knocking down a wall in the living room and incorporating the garage into living space. He added a new bay window to the front of the house, wallpapered the new enlarged living/dining room, painted all the walls, added a walk-in closet to their master bedroom, screened in the back porch, installed new carpeting, and replaced the exterior siding which was a combination of brick and siding and painted it a shade of colonial blue. Vera tidied the yard and planted some shrubs and flowers. There was a two-car detached garage which was ideal for Maurice's tools and equipment, and he built a nice long workbench along one side. The house looked refreshed, bright, and more spacious when they were done. It would suit them perfectly at this time of their lives. Vera settled in happily with a real sense of permanence at last. They would soon be collecting their social security checks as well as a half pension from Britain. With the additional earnings from the inspection jobs, they would be financially secure and able to enjoy life more. Vera was relaxed and content in a way that she had rarely felt before. She set about expanding her social life, joining the Senior Center and a British Club and also took on some volunteer work with a hospice group for a while. She often accompanied Maurice on his inspections, after which they enjoyed a nice lunch out at one of their favourite places. She visited with friends and often had people round the house for dinner and a game of cards. Finally, she could take a deep breath and anticipate a peaceful, sociable, happy time ahead.

Poem by Vera – April 11, 1987

He's only an old paperhanger with workmanship so very fine
When his stripes and his verticals stand all correct
The leaves and the flowers divine
He smooths it all out to make it perfect
The seams hang in perfect align
But when sometimes it isn't just so
He shouts and he raves, jumping up and about
This perfectionist fellow named Moe
His single-edged blades get thrown to the floor
The sponge tossed off in disgust
He mumbles and groans and prepares to cut more
To be finished by noon is a must
He rehangs the strips and smooths them all out
His face getting pinker with rage
A stiff upper lip but the lower a pout
A writer would just turn the page
Not Moe, his life is a game
Down the hill and up the slope
With trials forever to tame
Surely now is the end of his rope
Bright dreams of retirement in view
Happy visions of life on the way
Enjoyable chosen jobs to do
It'll surely be a wonderful day

CHAPTER TWENTY-SIX

Vera's contentment grew during the next few years. She was very active at the Senior Center, participating in many events, interesting talks and discussions, classes, holiday celebrations, and she joined the choir. Maurice had always loved singing and had an amazing voice, so he soon accompanied Vera to one or two practices, where he received much praise and many compliments. This resulted in him joining the choir also. The choir performed at assisted living facilities, nursing homes and for the community at various events throughout the year. They both loved it. Vera also joined a drama group, "Acting Up," which gave her a lot of pleasure. She became fully absorbed in the entire process from being assigned a part, reading the scripts, preparing her wardrobe for her scenes, learning her lines, and performing on stage. It was a wonderful new venture for her, and she found that she was rather a natural at it. She revelled in the entire experience and the special fellowship of the cast as well as the many laughs along the way. Performances brought the expected jitters and nervous flutters as well as a satisfying sense of accomplishment.

In 1992, Frances suggested to Vera that the two of them take a trip back to England. Vera's cousin, Dorothy, and husband, Derek, had visited the U.S. several times and had spent time staying with Frances and with Vera and Maurice and there was an open invitation to stay with them in Chingford. Vera wrote to Dorothy who was delighted that she and Frances were coming. Dorothy had very little family, one son, Barrie, and four siblings, two siblings still living, but she was the only one with a child. Dorothy had one remaining aunt, Hettie, and a cousin she saw occasionally, so she was excited to have some extended family come to stay. Vera flew up to Connecticut and Joe saw them off in style to the airport in a hired limousine. Dorothy and Derek were waiting at London, Heathrow airport when they arrived.

Dorothy had a lovely home at the bottom of Chingford Mount with plenty of room to accommodate visitors. She drove Frances and Vera all around town, stopping several times when Vera wanted to get out and walk around a particular place. Memories came flooding back and she enjoyed telling Frances and Dorothy about the various locations and why they were so important to her. So much looked the same, buildings, houses, streets, shopping centres, but so much had changed; the Odeon cinema was gone, shops and stores had changed, the town was congested with cars, so many people had paved over their front gardens to make parking spaces, and there was a diverse population from many parts of the world wearing a variety of ethnic dress. They went to Waverley Avenue and walked along the pavement as Vera had so many times in her youth, stopping at number 21. Vera stood for a long time, staring at the façade of the house, allowing her mind to wander back to her childhood. The outside of the house had changed very little. There was a new front door and a different arrangement of flowerbeds in the front garden but otherwise it looked much the same. She thought that even the garden gate might have been the original although surely that would have needed to be replaced at some point. She could almost lift the latch and walk up to the front door, expecting to see the welcoming fire in the living room fireplace through the front window and her mother and father sitting in their easy chairs beside it. It was an unsettling feeling. It was so familiar, so real, and yet, now it existed in a different time. Vera turned away abruptly as emotions stirred and threatened to overwhelm her. They crossed the street and walked on to number 22 which was located where the road curved to the left. The numbering on the street did not follow as it should. At some point, the road must have been extended and numbering resumed out of order. Number 22 had changed quite a bit. Frances too remembered this house well. There was a glass foyer added to the front entry and the entire front garden was paved with a car parked on it. The house had a more modern look to it.

"I had a word with the woman who lives here last week," said Dorothy. "I told her about you and that you lived here as a girl. She said she would be home this afternoon and that she would be happy to let you come inside."

"Oh, Dorothy, really? She wouldn't mind? That is very good of her."

"Let me go and knock and see if this is a suitable time."

A woman answered the door, exchanged a few words with Dorothy and then waved Vera and Frances an invitation to come to the door.

"Hello," said Vera. "This is awfully good of you. I hope we are not intruding."

"No, no, not at all. My husband is asleep in the chair in the living room, but he sleeps soundly. Probably won't wake up at all. Come on through. I expect you will see some changes since you lived here. We bought the house from Mrs. Middleton in 1968. We've done quite a lot to it since then."

The house was completely renovated inside. The wall between the front bedroom and the living room was gone creating a long, spacious room, bright and airy with a large bow window in the front and all glass in the back. The conservatory had been updated and enlarged with pretty views of the back garden. A gentleman gently snored in an armchair, so Vera kept her voice low remarking on the lovely remodelling and how different the interior looked. The kitchen was completely modernised with new fitted cabinets and appliances, new sink, floors, everything bright, clean, and new. Frances tried hard to remember the way it had looked the last time she saw it in 1964 but found it difficult to remember the details. The staircase was still in the same place however and she could remember old Ag peering down at her and Ruth when they came to visit. They went through to the back yard and here it looked more familiar. The old blackcurrant bushes were still there along the back wall, the large stone birdbath still stood in its place as well as some of the paved pathways edging the lawn. Ted's workshop was also still there. Frances took one photograph during the brief tour, of Vera standing by the birdbath in the garden. It was a heavy cement one that had been bought and placed there by Florrie countless years ago. The experience had been disturbing for Vera and unsettling in a way that she had not expected. It was almost a betrayal of her own memories, a disappointment that things were not just as she had left them. How could she be in that same place, in that same very space that had been so very dear, and not be there with her mother, making dinner, setting the table, lighting a fire in the fireplace?

The following day, Frances rented a car to drive to Rayleigh. They had maps and directions from Derek and set off in an automatic, leather-seated, Ford Scorpio. Frances did quite well driving on the left side of the road and navigating her way, but Vera was tense in the passenger seat, so afraid as Frances drove along narrow roads and around roundabouts which required careful manoeuvring and concentration.

"You're awfully close to these cars parked along the side of the road," Vera stated with alarm. "Ooh, I don't know how you missed that one!"

"Guess my spacing is a little off on that side. Don't worry, I will allow more room. I'll get acclimated."

"Hope so," Vera replied, squeezing her body tight and leaning to the right as they passed more parked cars.

Frances parked in a parking lot in Rayleigh centre. The high street that ran through the centre of town had become a one-way street, so she had to follow the public parking signs to the lot. She did not know about the parking machines "Pay and Display" which created a voucher to display on the dashboard in order to park without penalty, so there was a ticket on the car when she returned. Vera and Frances walked along the high street, amazed at the number of new shops and stores and the supermarkets, restaurants and heavy, non-stop traffic. The old horse trough and war memorial still stood in their old spot and most of the old pubs that Ray and Maurice had enjoyed years ago were still there and of course, the beautiful old, Saxon church still stood at the top of the hill, an unchanged landmark which had watched over the town for centuries. They had lunch in a café, sitting at a table by the window to watch the passers-by and all the activity in their old town before returning to the car.

"Oh, dear," said Frances. "A ticket. I suppose I should have paid better attention to the signs. Looks like I was supposed to pay for a permit at one of those machines."

"Never mind," Vera laughed. "We will be back home before the fine is due. They will never be able to track you down." Frances smiled but folded the ticket and put it in her bag.

Frances drove on to Woodlands Avenue, where she parked at the side of the quiet little road. They walked along the pavement down the street to the cul-de-sac at the end, around it and back again on the other side of the road. They came to a stop in front of number 25. Both stood silently looking at the house. It represented so many happy memories for each of them. This house too had been remodelled. A formal front porch had been added and a dormer on the roof had opened up another room upstairs. A new garage had been attached to the left side of the house but the brick wall and gate bordering the front garden, the pathway to the front door and the flowerbeds on each side of the path were all still there. The Lundbechs' house next door was similar, with a few updates and the Coxes' next to them looked much the same. Sadly, there was no one to visit on Woodlands Avenue. All their old friends and neighbours had moved away. It was another example of same street, same house, same place but a different time. There is no truer adage than, "You can never go home again!"

The next stop was to old friends of Vera and Maurice, Betty and Frank, who had coincidentally moved to Rayleigh a few years before Vera and Maurice emigrated. Vera had not told them she would be stopping by, so it was a shock for them to see her on the doorstep. It was a fun few hours for Vera, catching up with old friends and reminiscing about happy times in the past. Frank hurried out of the room and came back with an old photograph album, and they laughed at photos of the four of them on the beach, doing handstands, playing leapfrog and striking funny poses. Frances was keeping an eye on the clock. They had one more call to make and she wanted to get back to Dorothy's before it got dark, so she announced that it was time to leave, and they drove to Benfleet to a long street with small, one-storey, semi-detached bungalows. It was Lil Cox's new home. Dear Ted had died ten years earlier and Lil had sold the house on Woodlands Avenue for a smaller, more manageable home. This visit was a surprise also and Lil was thrilled to find Vera and Frances at the front door. Another happy reunion followed with cups of tea and sandwiches and nonstop chatter. The sun was low in the sky when they set out for Chingford and the roads were busy with traffic commuting home at the end of the day. Frances pulled into Dorothy's driveway just as it was getting quite dark. Vera breathed a sigh of relief that there had been no mishaps along the way and Dorothy too was relieved that they had arrived back safely. She had been getting concerned as the evening wore on.

The next day, Frances returned the rental car and Dorothy drove them out to Romford, to Hamlet Road. Vera looked around in amazement. The street had not changed at all. A few more houses had been built on the last of the empty lots, so the street was complete but their lovely, bungalow looked just the same from the front as they day she had left it. A small extension had been added to the back and the landscaping had changed a little, but she stared at it with such a stirring of emotions. She peered down the road almost expecting to see their old, converted bus appearing round the corner on its way home. Frances took a photograph of the house before they left, noticing that her mother was holding back tears.

They drove to see Auntie Het at her tiny apartment at an assisted living facility. Uncle Bob had died a few years ago and Hettie was Florrie's last surviving sibling; the last of the brood of thirteen. Hettie looked at Vera so intently. "Oh, I do wish I knew who you were!" she wondered. Vera was taken aback, and Frances attempted to explain. "Auntie Hettie, this is Vera. Remember Vera? She is your sister, Florrie's daughter."

"Mmmm…" Hettie responded. Dorothy looked at her aunt with a puzzled expression.

"Don't you remember, Auntie Het? I told you last week that I would be bringing Vera and Frances to see you."

"Oh…" She stared at Vera again for a long moment. "You look so familiar," she finally responded. "I do wish I knew who you were."

Dorothy's brother, Vera's cousin, Stan, came to dinner that evening. He and Vera had been good friends growing up and she was so happy to see him. Stan had been a tall, handsome fellow but at age twenty-one, had been diagnosed with schizophrenia. The treatment he had received as a young man had been harsh, including electroconvulsive therapy and a lobotomy and he was forever changed. Vera had always thought it was a terrible shame, that he had so much potential, was intelligent, quick witted and kind. Treatment had left him timid, passive and so limited in life, unable to drive or hold a job other than something menial and repetitive. Still, Vera and Stan sat next to each other on the couch, chatting quietly together and enjoying each other's company once again.

It was on to Bath the next day. Dorothy drove Vera and Frances to visit Pearl and her family. It was quite an adventure for Dorothy, who had not driven long distances herself before. They stayed a night in "Frances Lodge." It had been fifteen years since Vera was last there when Florrie died. Edie had since died also, and Pearl had inherited the cottage which she and her husband had remodelled and modernised. Vera coped well because the house looked so different from when she had stayed there years ago with Helen and the house was lively when Pearl's children and grandchildren stopped by to visit.

Then it was on to Ilminster, in Devon, to see Eileen and Ray. A lot of the family gathered and put on a lovely spread of salads, casseroles, sandwiches, cakes and pies. Frances was excited to see her cousins, Christine, Gillian and Rosalind and some of their children. Their lives deep in the countryside of Devon was so different from hers and she loved discussing the differences with them all. Another cousin, Rosemary, lived in Wales and was not able to be there. Vera could not have known that she and Maurice would see her several years hence under disturbing circumstances.

Finally, back in Chingford, Derek had planned a special treat for Vera and Frances. He and Dorothy took them to a medieval banquet in the Great Hall at Hampton Court. The banquet was based (loosely) on medieval fare presented in authentic style with entertainment presided over by Queen Elizabeth I, who was seated on her throne on a raised dais. It was a grand occasion, such a thrill, and a memorable ending to their nostalgic holiday.

Back in Florida, Vera resumed her activities but reflected often of her time in England. It had been nice to see people again but so sad not to be able to see those who had passed on. The trip had made her rather depressed and aware that she no longer fitted in or belonged there. That feeling bothered her and lingered for some time. She thought perhaps she would not go back again.

And Frances paid the parking ticket.

From Vera's diary of nostalgic trip to England with Frances

Friday – Hired car (Ford Scorpio) with leather seats for trip to Rayleigh. List price of this car is £20,000 which we discovered later that day. Frances enjoyed the challenge of driving on the wrong side although it took its toll on our nervous systems. We received a ticket for incorrectly parking because we neglected to read the directions on a giant-sized notice board about inserting cash into the parking machine. It cost £6 to be paid within ten days – a minor summons. The library furnished us with maps and we xeroxed copies to trace our way to friends in the area. It was great fun paying surprise visits to Betty and Frank and Lil Cox. We arrived home by the skin of our teeth just before dark, with much relief because London in the rush hour is no picnic.

Saturday – Dorothy dropped us off at Chingford Mount for shopping. Took photographs of numbers 12 and 49 Hurst Avenue. We walked back to Dorothy's and took pictures of New Road Primary School. In the evening we went with Dorothy and Derek to Flora's house (Dorothy's sister-in-law) for cocktails before proceeding to Hatfield House for an Elizabethan Banquet and entertainment. We returned to Flora's for a nightcap arriving home at 1:00 a.m.

CHAPTER TWENTY-SEVEN

Christmas 1992, another family Christmas was planned. Dorothy and Derek and their son, Barrie, would be flying over from England, Frances, Joe and the boys would drive down and the whole family would travel in a convoy, two-and one-half hours, to St. George Island to spend the holiday in a large, rented house on the beach. Vera had been planning, packing and making lists for weeks. Helen, who was dating Johnny, a rock musician, would meet everyone there for a day during the holidays. She could not get much time off since she was working at a radio station in Tallahassee, a job she loved.

Fortunately, everyone was healthy for this Christmas gathering, unlike the last one in North Carolina, and it was wonderful. Once the bedrooms had been sorted out and everything had been unloaded from the cars and put away, it was amazing to look around and get the lay of the land, to step outside onto the beach and relax in the sun, take a walk, or sit around the fire with a cup of tea or glass of wine. The children were growing up, ranging in age from twelve to seventeen and entertained themselves, appearing at mealtimes and for games and to join in walks along the beach. Mealtimes were fun with all the women working together, organising the tasks, laughing, and joking while they created a sumptuous feast. There was a volleyball court outside on the beach and the group was divided into two teams. The technique and the rules had to be explained to Dorothy, Derek and Barrie, who had never played, or even seen volleyball before. It became quite the match, with everyone playing, six to a side. Competition was fierce with many a nosedive into the sand, spikes, lobs and impassioned discussions of whether the ball had landed "in" or "out." The game ended when Joe attempted to save a point by backpedalling for the ball. He staggered and fell hard into the sand on his back. When everyone rushed over to see if he was okay and to help him up, he moaned resignedly, "just let me lie here!" When Helen and Johnny arrived, everyone gathered around to sing some Christmas carols as Johnny strummed his guitar.

Maurice had insisted on bringing a Christmas tree, lights and decorations and on Christmas Eve, everyone arranged their presents around it. There was quite a pile. He always loved Christmas, especially Christmas Eve, his favourite day of the year. He had all his special Christmas food, treats and his Christmas pudding to make it complete. His voice was raised in song whenever a favourite carol came on the radio and that evening, there was dancing in the large living room reflected in the windows that looked out onto the ocean while a crackling fire burned in the fireplace.

"This is the nicest Christmas I have ever had," said Dorothy sipping her wine. "I will never forget it. It is just perfect."

"Hear, hear!" Maurice agreed.

"A Christmas toast," Derek suggested. "Everyone got a drink? Here's to a very merry Christmas and a happy new year for us all!"

The new year included Peter's graduation from high school. Vera and Maurice travelled to Connecticut for a big backyard picnic and party to celebrate and to also wish Peter good luck as he would leave soon for basic training with the army. He had decided to enlist and become a Chaplain's Assistant. Peter had met Cheri during the time between enlisting and leaving for basic training. It was a happy romance for them both, but Frances thought that it would probably fizzle out once Peter became immersed in army life. She was wrong. It was a happy visit and a chance for Maurice and Vera to enjoy time with Frances, Joe, Pete and Tom as well as Yvonne and Bob, Hazel and Ray and Geza and Elnora.

There was another dramatic turn of events later in the year. Maurice had another good idea and discussed it with a couple of his long-time associates that he had made throughout his building years in Florida. The small group would create a fund to make loans to customers who needed financing to complete building projects, renovations and the like and who were having difficulty getting approval for loans with established banks. They worked up contracts and repayment terms and thought they were providing a much-needed service as well as receiving a good return on their money. One afternoon there was loud banging on the front door and a demanding voice of authority from law enforcement to *"OPEN UP!"* Maurice and Vera were stunned. Whatever could have happened? When they opened the door, a badge was thrust in Maurice's face and then an arrest warrant and a search warrant were presented.

"What is going on? I don't understand," Maurice exclaimed.

"You are under arrest for charges of usury. We will be confiscating any records, files, computers that we find in the house. You and your wife will sit quietly with this officer until we are finished."

"Usury?" Vera questioned. "What exactly is that?"

"Please sit down, madam, while we go about our business." Vera could not believe this was happening. She waited in a state of confused horror as grim-faced men poked around all the rooms and then settled in the office.

Vera had always kept accurate, well-labelled files and records. She had made it easy for them. Everything was swept up and placed in boxes and carried out to cars outside. The computer was removed too and finally Maurice was escorted from the house in handcuffs to be arraigned at the city court. Vera watched him go in shock and despair. She collapsed on the couch and buried her face in her shaking hands. What trouble were they in now?

The inquest into all the records revealed that this money lending operation was a small operation and obviously a terrible mistaken business opportunity. One of the "customers" had turned the group in while others did not want their payments returned to them as was ordered by the judge. They had been happy with the arrangement. The judge realised the big blunder that this group had made and that it was not the bigtime criminal setup that law enforcement thought it to be. He penalised them heavily, however. *Ignorance of the law is no excuse.* They were ordered to pay back all loan payments, forgive the loans, and pay interest and penalties. Maurice was also embarrassed and humiliated because the local television station covered the story and Helen worked there as director of the news. The whole episode affected him deeply. He had been brought down to a new low. His lawyer was incredulous. "If I had only known what you were doing, Moe! Why didn't you discuss this with me?"

"I just didn't think it was a big deal. We have a cousin in England who has had a business like the one we set up for years."

"That is England!" the lawyer replied. "Laws are different here. Moe, believe me, you got off easy on this!"

Maurice had become "Moe" sometime after moving to

Florida. He quite liked the nickname and had embraced it. It was on all his letterheads and business cards. He was grateful that the relationship with the banks was not affected. His contacts there never mentioned anything to him about the unfortunate incident or perhaps they had missed the story on the news, but in any event, Maurice continued with his inspections with no interruption. It was about this time that he was diagnosed with diabetes. He was told to change his eating habits, take regular blood sugar readings by pricking his finger and using the meter, and he was given pills to take. These made him feel ill, so he was soon prescribed insulin and had to give himself daily injections. This new situation with his ailment caused him to assess his physical health. He realised that he was getting older, less vigorous, and more limited with his activities. He had always prided himself on being strong, hardworking, energetic and resilient. It was hard for him to accept his new reality. The whole nasty affair with the usury charges lingered with him for some time. It had cost him a significant amount financially but had also taken its toll on his body and soul. He had been physically shaken up and his feeling of good standing in the community, which had always been important to him, had suffered. It took a while for Maurice to recover some of his natural exuberance and optimism. His joy of life was suppressed.

Maurice had to call in a loan that he had advanced to Ruth during the tough years working toward her degree. She had not had enough money to manage and was working her apprenticeship for her final year with only a small stipend. Ruth had to sell her house to repay the loan and move in for several months with her parents until the apprenticeship was complete and she was able to get a full-time job in a lab. Vera fretted for them all. She worried about Maurice, his health, and low spirits. She worried about Ruth and her situation, and Tiphanie who had been unsettled with an absent father and now the loss of a home, and Adam who had moved in with a friend rather than cause more disruption for his grandparents.

Mike had disappeared from his children's life. For a brief time after the divorce, he had picked them up for visits but had driven to a bar, leaving them outside in his car. Ruth had been outraged when she heard this and had not allowed him to take them again. He had not pressed the issue, obviously following a downward path, drinking and becoming involved with drugs. He eventually returned to Connecticut to live with his parents, bringing a questionable young woman with him who soon moved on. Mike's parents helped him get a job and a car, but he was an addict, desperate for cash to pay for his drug supply. It was a speedy, downhill slope eventually leading to jail time, rehabilitation, recovery and relapse.

Although it was sometimes difficult for Vera to share her home with Ruth and Tiphanie, it also helped her - and Maurice - recover from their latest setback. The house was busier and livelier than it had been in a long time. They had more activity, a changed schedule and lots to talk about. For Ruth, it actually became a time of relief from all her pressures and worries and she could focus on completing her internship and looking forward to her future employment.

Ruth completed her internship and was offered a job at Tallahassee Memorial Hospital in the lab where she had worked her apprenticeship. She moved out of Longview Drive and into a small, rented house with Tiphanie and Adam. Vera and Maurice had a quiet house again… too quiet. They decided to adopt a rescue dog, Pepper, who became a happy member of the household and a spoiled companion for them both. Life had settled down again for Vera. She was happy.

The next few years were exciting, with significant family events spaced nicely apart. Peter and Cheri's wedding in April 1995 was a wonderful celebration. As with most big weddings, the planning had been going on for over a year. Peter was a young bridegroom, which would have worried Frances, but for the fact that she thought he and Cheri were so well matched. They had met at church, both were very active there and had generous, outgoing and caring personalities. Peter was stationed at Hunter Army Airfield, and they would live in a small apartment near the base in Savannah, Georgia. All the Florida family would be attending (Tiphanie was a bridesmaid) and Dorothy and Derek would be coming over from England. Frances was able to accommodate everyone with some shuffling around and bed rentals, so it was a busy but gloriously happy time. Tom was his brother's best man at only sixteen, Adam was a groomsman as well as Peter's lifelong friend, George. The reception was held at a venue located on the shores of Long Island Sound. It was idyllic with a gathering of such beloved friends and family. Vera was thrilled to enjoy the company again of Yvonne and Bob, Hazel and Ray, Geza and Elnora. Ruth and Helen had to head back to Florida and work a few days later but Vera, Maurice, Dorothy, and Derek stayed longer, spending more time with Yvonne and Bob, who would soon be relocating to Seattle, Washington, and with Hazel and Ray in New Haven, and enjoying a big family dinner hosted by Geza and Elnora.

The following year was Yvonne and Bob's 50th wedding anniversary, which would be celebrated in Seattle. Vera and Maurice decided to attend, flew to the west coast, rented a car and drove along part of the Pacific Coast Highway. It was a much harder drive than they had thought, amazingly beautiful, but Vera was worried about Maurice. He was tense, white knuckled, and obviously feeling the strain. Vera later told Frances that some of the curves and drop-offs had been frightening and perilous. They were both relieved to arrive in Seattle and relax in Yvonne and Bob's new home. The anniversary party, hosted by their children, Barbara, Gary and Debbie, was held and catered at a venue with a live band that would play a variety of music including golden oldies and songs popular during World War II. Evelyn would be in attendance with her (third) husband, Douglas, daughter, Janet and her daughters, and son Kevin. Vera had been corresponding with Evelyn occasionally, so the estrangement had thawed a little over the last few years, but she was rather apprehensive about how meeting up again would go. Maurice approached Evelyn early in the evening. "What do you say, Evelyn?" he said, cheerily. "Shall be bury the hatchet?" Evelyn readily agreed and introduced Douglas, who was a retired British military officer. The two couples enjoyed an interesting conversation, resulting in an invitation to visit for lunch before they returned home to Florida.

Evelyn and Douglas lived on an island accessed by ferry from Seattle, so it was a full day out to visit. The weather was perfect, and the ferry ride was smooth. Maurice was grateful since he was not a very good sailor. Evelyn put on a lovely lunch for them all. Everyone was careful not to touch on sensitive topics but reminisced about happy days and humorous memories. Vera could not help but wonder when the last time was that she had been in the company of her two cousins at the same time. It had been a long time ago, before Helen was born, perhaps 1965? Yvonne did not see Evelyn too often, it was better that way, but at this meeting, around this table, she was laughing and revelling in the company. It was an occasion that she had thought would never happen and she was so happy that old resentments and grudges had been cast aside. It was especially meaningful in retrospect since Vera and Evelyn would never meet again.

And then 2nd June 1997, was Frances and Joe's 25th wedding anniversary. Peter and Cheri had just returned from a one-year deployment in South Korea. Cheri had accompanied Peter there and worked in a school near the base, teaching English. They managed to quickly arrange a party complete with decorations, food and cake at Frances and Joe's house. Vera and Maurice drove up from Florida with their gift. Maurice had recently taken up furniture making as a hobby, building bookcases, small tables, magazine racks and clocks. He made a wall clock with a pendulum and chimes for Frances and Joe. It included a small brass plaque engraved:

> Happy Silver Anniversary
> Frances and Joe
> Love, Mum and Dad
> June 2, 1997

It was Maurice's 70th birthday in 1998, so Frances and Joe drove down to Florida again to celebrate. Cheri and Peter were also able to attend. They were now stationed at Fort Benning in Georgia, and it was only a three-hour drive to Tallahassee. Cheri was heavily pregnant with their first child. The baby would be Vera and Maurice's first great grandchild. The birthday dinner was held in a private room at a local restaurant. Maurice was flattered to see so much of his family in attendance and of the fuss made for his birthday. Frances thought that both he and Vera looked well.

A letter came from Florida State University later in the year which interested Vera and Maurice greatly. The University decided to create an archive of personal accounts of individuals who had lived through World War II. They found a wonderful resource at the Senior Center and sent out mailings to determine who would be interested in sharing their experiences. Vera and Maurice felt honoured and excited to have been contacted and responded that they would be happy to be participate. The University discovered that there were two other seniors who had lived in Britain during the war as children, so a panel of four was created at an open forum where each senior would give an overview of their experiences and then answer questions. The entire event would be video recorded and added to the archive. Maurice and Vera were a little nervous on the day of the forum, especially when they saw the considerable number of people attending. Maurice started off telling his story of evacuation, deciding to return home to be with his family, the bombs, the dogfights, the devastation, his participation in the cadets determined and anxious to reach an age to be able to serve and fight. He told about being issued a rifle, to learn to load it, shoot it, clean it and keep it at home, ready to meet the invasion if necessary. "I felt like the cat's whiskers!" he exclaimed. He told of his duty to help find and remove bodies from bomb-damaged homes and buildings and he spoke about the powerful V-1 and V-2 rockets and how the morale of the British people sank facing the new terror. He spoke about his schooling and how it had become interrupted, diminished, and just not a priority during the war years, crucial years for him. He was eleven years old when war started and seventeen at its end. The war had affected him in so many ways and limited his options for a prosperous career substantially. Lastly, he spoke about

Winston Churchill, his hero, and how he had continued to rally the people, assure them of ultimate victory and encouraged them to be strong and resolute.

Vera related her experiences, focusing on dealing with rationing, gas masks, identification cards, youth groups, air raid shelters, the bombing of London Docks, how families had become closer, how people still found ways to have fun, the Underground and the songs and entertainment during a bombing raid to keep spirits up. "It was a time of great patriotism. We were all in it together. People were kind, generous, and compassionate. We learned to get by on much less, we learned to fix, mend and make do, we grew our own food. Nothing went to waste. We were stoic! Mr. Hitler raged about that. He could not understand why the nation did not despair, capitulate and surrender."

A hearty round of applause followed and a question-and-answer period. Vera and Maurice both felt gratified to have been able to share their war years on the British home front. Their life experiences would be available to teachers and students at the University and would help them to understand that challenging time in history and its aftermath a little better.

Later in the year, Ruth received news that her ex-husband, Mike had died of a drug overdose. She was shaken and worried about how the children would cope with the news. Tiphanie accepted it sadly but not with surprise, but Adam was full of emotion, anger, resentment, disgust and bitterness that he was now robbed of the opportunity to prove to his father that he could succeed, live a better life, and prosper *in spite* of him. He was determined not to be like his father in any way.

It was Vera's 70th birthday in 1999 and she and Maurice decided that a trip back to England to mark the occasion would be very special. They planned the trip determining their own itinerary, who they would visit and what places they wanted to see. For some reason, Maurice wanted to see Chester in northwest England near the border with Wales. He wrote to the chamber of commerce and received a packet with lots of information and places of interest and an invitation to have lunch with the mayor during one of his weekly "meet and greets." They were rather excited about this. They planned to fly to Heathrow, travel to Paddington to take the train to Bath and visit Pearl, then take the train to Taunton in Somerset where Eileen and Ray would pick them up, then on to Chester, then to Wales to visit Rosemary and enjoy the countryside and then to Rayleigh where Betty and Frank were planning a gathering of old friends from their youth. They would end up at Dorothy and Derek's before flying home. The itinerary sounded rather hectic to Frances and Ruth who tried to encourage them to start at Dorothy's where they could be picked up from the airport and spend a couple of days to rest and get over the jetlag before setting out on their tour. However, they were happy with their plan, had it all worked out, and were excited to go. What should have been a happy time, full of meaningful reunions, reconnections, and exploration, became a time of disappointment and a life-altering event.

Notation in one of Vera's notebooks
Houses built by Moe (18 houses)
Hamlet Road, Romford, Essex, U.K. – our first home
Black Rock Turnpike, Fairfield, CT – for sale
Beach Road, Fairfield, CT – for sale
Dellwood Drive, Tallahassee, FL – our first home in

Florida

    Tim Tam, Tallahassee, FL – for sale

    Kingman Trail, Tallahassee, FL – for Ruth and Mike (with their help)

    Gallant Fox, Tallahassee, FL – for ourselves

    Gallant Fox, Tallahassee, Fl – for sale

    Kingman Trail, Tallahassee, FL – for sale

    Native Dancer, Tallahassee, FL – for sale

    Lucky Debonair, Tallahassee, Fl (2 houses) – for sale

    Whirlaway, Tallahassee, FL (2 houses) – for sale

    Man of War, Tallahassee, FL – for sale

    Majestic Prince, Tallahassee, FL – for sale

    Killearn Lakes, Tallahassee, FL – for sale (miserable lady)

    Killearn Lakes, Tallahassee, FL – for sale

CHAPTER TWENTY-EIGHT

If Vera had been able to look ahead, she would never have considered a trip back to England. But she and Maurice had been excited about planning a trip that would be an opportunity to visit dear family and friends and travel around to see unfamiliar places in their home country. It would not be purely a nostalgic trip. They would, of course enjoy some visiting but it would be a trip of exploration. They had always so enjoyed travelling around in their youth and they wanted to recapture the joys of discovery together. They realised it would probably be their last trip back, so they wanted it to be special.

It was April when they left. They had dreams of seeing springtime in England again, hoping to see carpets of bluebells, a host of daffodils, trees in blossom and the emerald green of the landscape. They flew from Tallahassee to Orlando and from Orlando to London, leaving in the evening, which would put them in London the next day around midday. The flight, unfortunately, was delayed landing in London due to unsuitable landing conditions. The eight-hour flight from Orlando became more than eleven hours after circling for three hours prior to landing. When they cleared immigration and customs, retrieved their bags and boarded the train to Paddington, they were stressed and exhausted. It was bustling at Paddington as they navigated their way to the ticket counter. People was striding with purpose about the terminal, many dragging suitcases, as Vera and Maurice were. A woman darted in front of Maurice unexpectedly and he tripped on the bag she was pulling behind her. He went down hard on the cement surface of the terminal.

"Are you alright?" the woman asked. "So sorry." And then she was gone, hurrying to her gate to catch her train. A porter rushed over to help Maurice to his feet. Vera thanked him and took hold of her husband's arm. "Look, there's a bench over there. Let's sit down for a while. Do you feel okay? Are you hurt?"

"I think I'm okay. Just a bit shaky." Vera guided him to the bench, concerned with the way Maurice looked. He was white in the face and a little wobbly on his feet. They sat for a while watching all the activity. People were moving in all directions, businessmen and women, family groups, students, porters and many travellers with their suitcases. Many stopped in front of the huge lit up information board displaying destinations, times and gate numbers. "Stay here, dear," said Vera. "I will get our tickets."

When they boarded their train, they stowed their luggage in the racks at the end of the car and found seats. Vera breathed a sigh of relief. It was only about ninety minutes to Bath station. Maurice leaned his head back and closed his eyes. *Good,* thought Vera. *"Perhaps he will doze a little.* He had a little more colour in his face. She thought he looked better. As the train approached the platform at Bath, they rose and headed to the luggage racks. Their bags were buried under a pile of heavy suitcases that had been stacked on top of them. Maurice had to lift and move several to get to theirs. By the time he was able to pull them out, the train had started moving again. They had missed their stop. Maurice was exasperated. "Well, I never!" he complained bitterly. "Things have changed a lot since we last travelled by train. Do you remember this many bags? We'll have to get off at the next station, cross the platform and come back. What a bother!"

"Well, I expect people travel more these days… all over

the world," Vera replied. "Let's just stand here with the luggage so that we can get off easily." At the next station, they rolled the bags off onto the platform and looked for the way to cross the tracks. They would have to climb many steps to cross the bridge over the tracks and descend the steps on the other side. Maurice stared in dismay as he rolled his case toward the bridge. "Just a minute," said Vera noticing a young man in a railway uniform. She approached him and asked for his help. "Certainly, madam, no problem at all." He took a suitcase in each hand and climbed the steps with ease.

At Bath station, Vera and Maurice climbed into a taxi which took them to "Frances Lodge." Pearl and Eric hurried out to help them. "I was waiting for your phone call to come and pick you up," said Eric.

"We had such a terrible journey," Vera answered, "that we jumped into the first taxi we saw, just to sit down and get here all the sooner."

"Oh, dear," Pearl replied. "Come on. I'll put the kettle on. Do you want anything to eat?"

"No, thank you, Pearl," said Maurice. "Just a cup of tea and a bit of a lie down, if you don't mind."

They spent two nights in Bath, just relaxing, catching up on all the family news, walking around the garden, and enjoying Pearl's good cooking. They telephoned Eileen to tell them the time of the train they would be taking to Taunton train station so that they could be waiting for them there. This time, Vera and Maurice were prepared to remove their luggage well before arriving at the station but there were only a few bags on the train anyway, so it was not a problem. It was only a little over an hour train ride, so they arrived much calmer and more rested. Eileen and Ray were waiting and were so pleased to see them. They lived alone now. All their daughters had married and moved out, but they would be coming for a visit the next day, all except for Rosemary who lived in Wales. Vera and Maurice planned to see her in Wales later during their holiday. Eileen and Ray had moved years ago to another large, beautiful home in Somerset. It was not far from their last one, but Vera and Maurice had not seen it. They had to leave the narrow country road to Dowlish Wake and follow a dirt track which went on for half a mile until they arrived at the house which stood all alone amongst the hills and dales of the beautiful countryside. They had a wonderful time together. Years and distance had separated Maurice and Eileen, but the powerful sibling bond was still there. They teased each other, laughed at each other's stories and remembered times gone by. The property was quite large and seemed to go on forever, since it bordered farmland. Ray took Maurice for a stroll around. "See that big pond, Maurice?" he said. "There's a Sherman Tank submerged in there. It was driven in by mistake while conducting training manoeuvres when the Yanks were here during World War II. Been there ever since."

"Well, I never!" Maurice replied.

They went out for dinner that evening where Vera snapped a photo of Maurice and Ray sitting on a low stone wall in front of the lovely, old pub where they ate. She sent Eileen a copy later from the U.S. It was such a good shot of both the men, sitting relaxed together, enjoying the evening. Eileen had it framed. It was a favourite picture of her husband and her brother which she kept on prominent display.

A few days later, Vera and Maurice departed for Chester from Taunton train station. It was a long journey with a change of trains along the way. Vera noticed that Maurice looked drawn and tired and seemed rather stressed and uncomfortable. He was uncharacteristically nervous and unsettled, not talkative and rather grumpy. She thought it was because he was worried about the luggage and did not want to miss the station as before, when they could not pull it from the pile in time. They managed their bags with no problem at the station where they had to change trains and disembarked at Chester easily since they were not travelling during peak times. A taxi took them to their bed and breakfast in the centre of town where Maurice sighed with relief, stretched out on the bed and fell asleep. Vera watched him sleep with concern. This was so unlike him to be so worn out, not to want to walk around the immediate vicinity to get the lay of the land, check out the nearby restaurants and feel the pulse of the town. Perhaps he just needed a restorative nap to counter the stresses of travel. He was, after all, seventy-one years old. She would let him sleep, not disturb him until he woke up naturally and then they would get some dinner. She peered out of the window which was at street level and watched the locals going about their daily routine. Chester was a mixture of medieval buildings, Victorian and modern, as well as the remnants of Roman walls that were added to in medieval times and surrounded the town. It also boasted a magnificent cathedral dating back to the eleventh century. They were going to have lunch with the mayor the next day and then they would explore. Vera turned from the window and took in the room which was large and comfortable with a nice sitting area and low table. She noticed a tea tray with an electric kettle, cups and all the fixings, so she made herself a cup of tea, found her book and settled down to read.

The next morning Maurice seemed better although he

ate little at breakfast. "Saving my appetite for lunch with the mayor," he said when Vera questioned him about it. They strolled slowly around town, heading to the Chester Town Hall, peering in shop windows and checking out restaurants and pubs along the way. Lunch with the mayor was simple but elegant. There were several tables set with crisp, white tablecloths and a platter of assorted sandwiches, cups and saucers for tea and a tiered dessert stand with currant cakes, scones and cream buns. The mayor introduced himself and spoke for a little while about Chester and its impressive history and landmarks. He praised the people of the town and their commitment to preserving the past as well as embracing the future. Tea was then poured, and he spent time at each table chatting with the attendees. He was very interested to hear a little about Vera and Maurice's life in Florida and that they had lived through the war years in Chingford. He announced to the group, "Vera and Maurice Brown are the guests who have travelled the furthest to be here today. They have come all the way from Florida in America. They are also members of the *Greatest Generation* living in the suburbs of London as youngsters during World War II." The occupants of the hall clapped and smiled. "I do hope you enjoy your visit to our town and with your family and friends around Britain. Thank you for coming today," the mayor concluded.

It was a lovely spring day with daffodils and tulips in full bloom all around town as they exited the town hall. Vera had been looking forward to touring the cathedral, but Maurice seemed to have used up all his energy and enthusiasm at lunch with the mayor. He was visibly fatigued. "See that bench over there," he said to his wife. "I could lay down on it right now and go right off to sleep."

"Oh, dear. We had better go back to our room so that you can rest. Must be all the excitement of the trip affecting you," Vera responded, but she was worried. Maurice was not right at all. He looked pale and weary and had lost his natural enthusiasm and exuberance. Tomorrow they were leaving for Wales to visit Rosemary and her family. She hoped he would feel better there.

Wales was lovely. They had always enjoyed their holidays there during courting days. They watched the rolling hills, rivers and streams, and the emerald green grass of the fields and meadows pass by through the train window. Rosemary picked them up at Newport station and drove them along narrow country lanes to her home, which was located at the end of a long, dirt track, all by itself amid a glorious landscape of sweeping open grassland, distant hills and woods covered in a carpet of bluebells. Rosemary's husband was a veterinarian, so they had horses, dogs and cats, as well as two children. Rosemary prepared a roast dinner while they chatted. Vera produced some photographs of the family to share, and they reminisced about times gone by. They remembered Charlotte who had been gone for so long and Walter and Julie who had both died in the early 1980s. Maurice had no appetite at dinner even though the food was so delicious and included all his favourites, roast beef, mashed potatoes, Yorkshire pudding, Brussels sprouts, parsnips, carrots and rich, thick gravy. He apologised, explaining that he had been feeling unusually tired and unwell. "I am rather worried," admitted Vera. "I feel we ought to see a doctor. What do you think, Mervin?" she asked, turning to Rosemary's husband.

"Well, if you want my opinion, I think you should see a doctor quite soon. Rosemary, why don't you give Doctor Thomas a call. Perhaps if you explain the situation, she could see him at the end of the day."

"Yes, yes. I'll telephone now."

"I don't want to put you to any trouble," Maurice stated. "You've made this lovely dinner. Perhaps we can go tomorrow."

"Let's ask if she can see you today," Mervin replied.

The doctor's office was a half-hour drive away. The doctor agreed to see Maurice after her last patient, and they had to head out almost right away. Maurice closed his eyes in the passenger seat as Rosemary navigated the turns and curves of the country road. He felt awful physically but also felt horrible to be such a bother to his niece and her family. Vera sat in the back seat, chatting nervously about the scenery, pretty cottages and gardens along the way, trying to lighten the mood, but she was fearful of the change of events. Rosemary had to stop twice on the way so that Maurice could exit the car to vomit.

The doctor listened to Maurice's situation, questioned him about his symptoms and examined him. She then asked Rosemary and Vera to join them in her office.

"Mr. Brown," she said. "I believe you have suffered a heart attack."

"Oh, *dear*!" Vera exclaimed. "Surely not!"

"Yes, I think perhaps you are right," Maurice acknowledged grimly.

"I would like you to go directly to the hospital in Newport. I will telephone and let them know the circumstances and that you are on your way."

"Oh, my goodness, oh dear," Vera fretted.

"Don't worry, Auntie Vera. I will drive you there right now," Rosemary stated.

"Thank you for seeing me, doctor," Maurice said gratefully, extending his hand.

"Not at all. They will take good care of you. You should feel better soon."

Maurice stayed in the hospital for a week. He was in a large room with three other patients with whom he enjoyed chatting. One was there to get his diabetes stabilised, another was recovering from surgery and the third had black lung disease from his years working in the mines. During his torturous coughing fits, Maurice rubbed his back and comforted him as best he could. The men shared humorous stories, life experiences and their hopes and fears. The men in the hospital room with Maurice were very interested in hearing all about America and Florida. He was happy to tell them all about it. They listened in awe, hearing about the hot climate, the heavy rainfalls, Hurricane Kate, palm trees, beaches, Disney World and the southern culture and lifestyle. Outside the big window, the view was magnificent; a patchwork quilt of fields, grazing animals and a mountain in the distance. It was soothing just to gaze upon it. The doctors ordered tests and monitors to determine the condition of Maurice's heart and the appropriate treatment. He began to feel better although he still tired easily. Vera was encouraged because his face lost its grey, pasty colour and looked normal again. She had telephoned back to the U.S. to inform the girls of the situation. Frances made arrangements with Virgin Atlantic to fly over immediately. The airline was most accommodating, extending an emergency ticket price and booking her the next day. It was a long day's journey all the way to Newport and Frances was glad to see Rosemary and her mother waiting at the railroad station. She promptly rented a car and followed Rosemary to the hospital. She was glad to relieve Rosemary of the trips back and forth and would take over the transportation for the duration of her father's hospital stay.

"Well Dad," she said after giving him a hug. "You are looking quite well. How do you feel?"

"Better, dear. The doctor said I should be discharged in a few days."

"Oh, good!" Vera exclaimed.

"Yes, but I will not be released to fly for three weeks. That is going to be a huge nuisance. I don't want to impose on Rosemary all that time and I want to be closer to London and the airport."

"Okay, Dad, don't worry about it. I'll make some calls. Mum and I will work it out. You just keep getting better and stronger."

Back at Rosemary's, Vera's first thought was Dorothy. "You call her, Frances. I'm in a bit of a state. I still can't believe all this is happening. This was supposed to be such a happy trip. Poor Dad! It has all been too much for him."

"Dad's in good hands, Mum. We just have to make sure he follows doctor's orders."

There was no answer at Dorothy's, although Frances called well into the evening. "They must be away," said Frances. "They do travel a lot. I'll try again in a few days. Shall I call Lil Cox in the meantime?"

"Oh, yes. Lil now lives alone in that little bungalow, but she has a spare bedroom. Perhaps she wouldn't mind having some company."

There was no answer at Lil's either, so Frances telephoned her daughter, Gill.

"Oh, Frances! I am so sorry to hear about your father and I hope he has a fast recovery. Mum is visiting her sister, Grace, at the moment, but let me give her a call. I'm sure she will come back home when he is released."

And so, in a strange turn of events, Frances, Vera and Maurice found themselves together on a train from Newport to Paddington, a taxi ride to Liverpool Street station and another train to Rayleigh.

"My word!" Maurice declared. "How strange, us three traveling to Rayleigh again! I expect we will see such a change. Seems unbelievable, doesn't it?" Vera nodded, feeling so many emotions. How different life would have been if they had only remained there! Would life have become easier in time? Would they have been more settled? Happier? Would Maurice have done well at Jacob's Crackers and prospered there?

Frances led them to a taxi and gave the driver Lil's address and they were driving up Crown Hill to High Street. All three were craning their heads looking around at their old hometown. It had changed. There were many new buildings, signs and storefronts, and the afternoon traffic was congested in the centre of town.

"Mmmm… amazing…" Maurice mused. "Not our Rayleigh, is it?"

"No," Vera responded. *But it would have been if we had stayed,* she thought. *We would have seen the town gradually change and grow slowly over the years. We still would have belonged here.*

The taxi pulled up in front of a small bungalow on a fairly busy road in Benfleet, just a few miles from Rayleigh. Lil had said if they beat her home, they should go next door to the neighbour, who would have a key. Frances knocked on the door of the house number Lil had given, and an elderly gentleman answered.

"You must be the Americans," he said.

"Yes. So sorry to bother you."

"No bother at all! Let me get the key and I'll let you in. Lil said to tell you to make yourselves comfortable. She should be along soon."

"Thank you."

"Have a good journey, did you?"

"Yes, thank you. But we are all a bit hungry. Is there a fish and chip shop nearby?"

"Oh, yes. Not far at all. I'll show you."

"Thank you but I really don't want to put you to any more trouble."

"No trouble at all. I'll probably pick something up for me and my wife while I'm there."

Frances let her parents into the little bungalow and went along with the helpful neighbour to get some dinner. They were just settling down at the kitchen table to eat when Lil arrived.

"Well, hello!" she laughed. "I'm so happy to see you both. Sorry about the circumstances, Maurice. How are you feeling? Let me put the kettle on. Have you got everything you need? Did you find the utensils? Ah, good."

"Come on Lil. Sit down with us. Help yourself. There's plenty," said Vera. "Thank you so much for letting us descend on you like this. Sorry to interrupt your visit with your sister."

"Not at all! I can go there anytime."

The old friends sat and ate talking about the situation that had brought them together again so unexpectedly. They talked about their families and remembered old times together. Then, Lil shared the sad news that she was dealing with bladder cancer.

"Oh, no!" Vera exclaimed. "And here we are imposing on you!"

"No, no… I'm all right… really. I am doing quite well right now. And it is not bothering me. It's actually nice to have a happy distraction."

"Well, aren't we a couple of old crocks!" Maurice laughed.

Maurice retired early to bed after Lil and Vera changed the sheets. Lil would sleep in the spare bedroom and Frances would have to stretch out on the couch. The women made more tea, chatted for a few hours, and discussed the plans for the rest of the time they would have to stay in England before Maurice would be able to fly home.

"I am afraid that I will have to fly home in a few days," said Frances. "I have a medical procedure scheduled, nothing serious but I need to get home for it. Mum and Dad will go to Dorothy's when we get in touch with them. I'll try to reach her again tomorrow. They can stay there in Chingford until their flight home and I'm sure Derek will drive them to the airport."

The next day, all was arranged. When Frances telephoned, Dorothy answered. They were back from a one-week cruise. At the end of the week, Lil's sister and brother-in-law would pick up Lil, Vera and Maurice, and take them to Dorothy and Derek's in Chingford. They would all have lunch there and then Lil would go back to her sister and brother-in-law's house which was not far away, to continue her visit. Frances breathed a sigh of relief. She could go home knowing that her parents were in good hands. She spoke to Ruth on the phone also about the plans and Ruth managed to get the same reasonable emergency airfare from Virgin Atlantic and would travel to Chingford to stay for a while to help and then fly home with her mother and father. Maurice was doing his best to be cheerful throughout, but he was uncomfortable being dependent on his friends and family. He appreciated all the effort and extra work that was necessary due to his poor health, but he only wanted to get home where he could properly rest and recuperate. He was not used to being weak, limited and fatigued. He certainly hoped that he would soon recover because he would absolutely not want to live this way.

In Chingford at Dorothy and Derek's, Maurice relaxed a little more. The house was bigger, and he was in his familiar childhood hometown. He had felt terrible when he learned of Lil's health situation, although her daughter, Gill, had assured him that her mother had really enjoyed the visit and coming to the rescue. "It did her a lot of good," she said. When Ruth arrived, she took over caring for her father, monitoring his medication, getting him up to walk a little, making sure he ate and drank appropriately. Dorothy was a very good cook, so Maurice ate some familiar old meals, although only managing small servings. He enjoyed steak and kidney pie, leg of lamb, kippers, bangers and mash, rice pudding and trifle as well as other special treats. The days passed quietly and pleasantly until it was finally time to fly home. Maurice managed the flight well enough and was met with a wheelchair in Orlando but there was a long delay for their connecting flight and by then he was dragging visibly. He was impatient and irritable, waiting for the plane to arrive at the gate. "Just try to relax, Dad," Ruth instructed. "There's nothing we can do about it. No use getting all worked up. I'll get you a cold drink. Do you want anything to eat?"

"No… no. Nothing to eat, thanks."

"Okay. I'll be back in a minute. It won't be long now. Mum, I'll get a drink for you too."

When the plane arrived and was ready for boarding, they were directed to the gate and found that the small jet was to be boarded by climbing portable steep stairs. Maurice looked at them with dismay.

"I'll never be able to get up those!" he moaned. An

attendant hurried over.

"It's all right sir. We have a lift at the back of the plane. The attendant wheeled him away while Vera and Ruth ascended the stairs. The small jet was small and tight, but it was only a one- hour flight to Tallahassee and all three breathed a deep sigh of relief when it landed.

"I am so glad to be home!" Maurice declared.

Excerpt from letter from Lil Cox to Frances – April 28, 1999

Fran, you don't have any reason to thank me, I think you were very brave, with your news at the back of your mind, travelling alone to Wales not knowing for sure what you would find, then the train journeys, watching and taking care of your dad, making sure he was comfortable, plus your mum and the luggage, Whew! I think you're a hero.

CHAPTER TWENTY-NINE

Maurice felt better after a few days' rest at home and was anxious to resume his building inspections for the two banks. He had been away over a month, and he knew that there would be a backlog of work to do. He contacted both banks to get updated and set about visiting the building sites to make his reports. He knew that he should visit a cardiologist soon and discuss the file that the doctor in Wales had given him with information about his care and test results, but he was busy catching up and he put it off for a while. Vera nagged him about it, but he would wave her off with assurances that he would make an appointment soon.

A month passed and then two. And then Vera went to see her doctor about a health issue of her own. She had noticed a swelling in her stomach. Not a lump but a general swelling or bloating that had become too prominent to ignore. When the doctor examined her, he became alarmed and sent her for X-rays which revealed a very large cyst on the liver. She was referred to a surgeon who decided that the cyst was too large to be removed and the potential damage to the liver would be dangerous so, she was referred again, this time to Dr. Ginaldi, a radiologist. His treatment consisted of draining the cyst and then filling the sac with ethanol to destroy the cells of the inner lining. This procedure was done twice, during which Vera was rolled around on the table so that the ethanol would touch the entire area. Following the treatments, she felt the effects of the ethanol which caused her to behave as if she were quite drunk. It was very entertaining for Ruth who was there with her mother following the procedure and for Dr. Ginaldi who had enjoyed Vera's personality from their first meeting and would chat and joke with her during doctor visits and treatments, which continued for several months. Following the ethanol, a drain was inserted into the sac to drain off any residual fluid that continued to collect. It would need to remain there for an extended period of time. Vera was miserable with this situation, since she was instructed to stay at home to prevent infection. The drain and bag were necessary for several months and she was so limited in her mobility and activities. Maurice had to step up and take over many tasks, shopping, vacuuming, driving his wife to doctor appointments and performing the more strenuous cleaning chores. After a few months, Vera developed a serious infection, MRSA, which resulted in her having to be admitted to an extended care facility. It was necessary to treat her with vancomycin, the drug of choice to combat the resistant bacteria and she needed a PICC line inserted into a large vein to accommodate the long-term intravenous medication. She was placed in a large, comfortable room at the end of a hall and was told that she should not leave it during her stay. She could be contagious and a risk to other patients. Also, visitors were limited to family only. Vera was desperately unhappy, lonely and bored. For her, a sociable, active, outgoing individual, it felt like prison. Ruth and Maurice brought her books, magazines, puzzles, music, notebooks for writing stories and letters, which she always enjoyed doing, and anything else they could think of to help her pass the time. Once or twice, she emerged from her room to walk to the nurse's station, and she was promptly escorted back with a gentle reprimand to remember the rules. She telephoned her friends and family, lamenting her situation, crying and making everyone feel so helpless and sad.

As Thanksgiving approached, Frances and Joe planned

to visit. Maurice spoke to the doctor who approved a few hours home visit so that Vera could enjoy Thanksgiving dinner with her family. Vera was thrilled when she was told.

"Now, you have to understand," Maurice instructed, "that you must go back to the care facility after four hours. Will you promise to do that? If you think it will be too hard to go back, perhaps you should not come home and we can visit you there instead."

"No, no. I promise I will go back," Vera responded.

It was a nice afternoon. Frances, Ruth and Helen prepared the big turkey and all the trimmings so that it was ready as Maurice pulled up with Vera. They sat around the table for hours, filling themselves up to capacity. It was the usual pleasant, chatty, occasion which felt quite normal to Vera although she felt a bit like a guest at her own table. Pies and tea followed the dinner after a brief respite and before they knew it, the allotted time for Vera had passed. Maurice guided her to the front door, where with tears in her eyes, she waved goodbye. Frances, Joe, Ruth, and Helen were able to talk about Vera and Maurice's approaching 50th wedding anniversary in January, while they were gone.

"Well, I think we have to have a plan A and a plan B," said Frances. "If Mum still has the drain but no longer has MRSA, we will have to plan something here at the house. If the drain is removed by then, we can plan something out somewhere."

"Oh, she should be over the MRSA by then." Ruth responded. "The anniversary is two months away. I don't know about the drain, though. So, plan A will be to have a catered gathering here at the house. And plan B… at a hall or restaurant?"

"Yes," said Joe, "but at what point do we decide? Maybe see how things are looking after Christmas before we reserve a location?"

"I will call around and get an idea of availability. January 21st is on a Friday. Would it be better to have the party on the next day, Saturday?" Ruth asked.

"Saturday would be better for me," said Helen. "I will be driving up from Tampa."

"Us too," Joe agreed. "We will probably drive down from Connecticut."

"Maybe we need a plan C also," Frances added. "Which would be to postpone the event if Mum is still in extended care."

"Oh goodness!" Ruth exclaimed. "Let's hope that is not the case!"

It was plan A. Vera was home from extended care by Christmas but still had the drain. Ruth sent invitations out for a celebration at the house and the catering choices were made as well as some home-made dishes. Ruth used the bakery that could create images on cakes from photographs and so she arranged to have one made from one of her parent's wedding photos. Frances, Joe, Ruth and Helen decided to share the cost of a computer as their joint anniversary gift.

The day before the event, the visiting nurse told Vera that she had been authorised to remove the drain. It was such a relief for everyone that she had recovered from the unpleasant episode. She would have to go for follow up CT scans to ensure that the cyst did not recur, but otherwise, she was back to normal.

"Just in time," Frances declared. "We have a bit of a party planned here at the house, and you are not to lift a finger. We have it all sorted out."

Saturday was busy. Food was picked up, dishes were

made, a bar was stocked, decorations were hung, seating was arranged, music was selected, and the magnificent anniversary cake with a gorgeous rendition of a wedding photograph was displayed prominently for all to see. The entire family was in attendance. Frances and Joe, Ruth, Helen, Peter and Cheri and baby Josephine who had driven from Georgia, where Peter was stationed at Fort Benning, Tom who had flown from Connecticut, Adam and Tiphanie. A group photo was taken to commemorate the happy occasion with everyone dressed in their finery. Guests began to arrive and soon the house was bustling with good friends, activity, congratulatory wishes, funny stories and music which had been carefully selected to include oldies and favourites of the anniversary couple. Vera and Maurice danced to *"You Make Me Feel So Young"* followed by toasts and speeches. It was a wonderful evening and the last happy family event in Maurice's life.

The following day, Vera told Frances that she was worried about Maurice.

"That dance last night," she said, "Dad could barely manage to get through it."

"Really? He seemed to be okay to me."

"I know. He does a good job of hiding his condition. I watch him walk to the mailbox… just the short distance down the driveway to the street. He has to stop on his way back and lean against the fence or the car to rest before coming back to the house."

"Oh dear. I didn't realise he was so weak. Has he been to the cardiologist?"

"No, he procrastinated when we first got back from England and then he was busy getting back to his inspections and with me and my health problems."

"He was told to follow up right away with a cardiologist by the doctor at the hospital in Wales."

"Yes, I know. But every time I mentioned it, he got irritable and told me that he would soon."

"He is going to have to go, Mum. Now that you are better. There is no excuse."

"I know. But you know how he is. He must be perceived as strong, active and in control. He doesn't want to admit to weakness or limitations of any kind."

"Well, I think it's time for all of us to gang up on him and insist that he makes that appointment."

Maurice finally capitulated and made an appointment in February. He met with a cardiologist who examined him and immediately scheduled a stress test. When he failed the test, he had a heart catheterisation procedure in the hospital which revealed five blocked arteries. He was admitted to the hospital and would have open-heart bypass surgery after the weekend, on Monday 14th February, Valentine's Day. The family was stunned by the suddenness of the surgery. The doctor advised them that Maurice was in bad shape and could have had another serious heart attack at any time. It was the outcome that Maurice had anticipated and dreaded. He knew that he was declining and tried to be optimistic about the outcome but deep down, he felt rather apprehensive and fatalistic. Ruth worked in the lab at the hospital and one of her co-workers brought the morning newspaper to Maurice over the weekend. Maurice confided in him the feelings that he would not reveal to his family.

"Thanks for the newspaper, mate," he said as the lab tech sat to chat for a few minutes. "I'm glad to have a diversion while I am waiting for Monday. "I can't stop thinking about the surgery and how serious it is. I just have a bad feeling about it all."

Ruth and Vera waited together at the hospital during the

surgery. Vera was restless and anxious as they waited to hear from the doctor. When he appeared after several hours, he reported that the surgery was complete but that one of the new blood vessels was spasming and would cause a heart attack if not replaced. He needed authorisation to operate again.

"*GO, go, go!*" Ruth responded. So, Maurice was taken into surgery again while his wife and daughter waited, wondered and worried. Ruth called Helen and Frances to update them on the situation and they waited too, trying to keep positive thoughts, and hoping for good news. The doctor appeared again to inform that the second surgery had gone well and that all should be fine. There was relief all around. He told Vera and Ruth that he had done three bypasses since one was not as bad as they had thought, and another was so bad that they decided not to touch it at all.

As Maurice recovered, he suffered adverse effects from the anaesthesia, causing him to be extremely nauseated, vomiting and unable to eat. A series of events followed which affected Maurice's recovery. A week later, while still in the hospital, he was passing blood due to stress ulcers which meant that the blood thinner medication had to be stopped. He developed a problem with his swallowing mechanism and, though the specialists could detect no visual damage or cause, this particular condition never did improve. He could eat very little and, in fact, had no interest in food at all. Then, one leg became swollen and hot to the touch, and it was determined that he had developed blood clots which were traveling to his lungs making his breathing strained. He was rushed into surgery to install a "cage" into a main artery to catch any traveling blood clots so that they could not cause a stroke or heart attack. When the clots dissipated and the swelling went down, he was finally released to a rehabilitation hospital where he spent two weeks. Vera began to hope that the worst was behind them and that he would now recover, gain strength and return home. The rehabilitation hospital did manage to get him up and walking albeit small, slow steps and he too became encouraged. He still could not manage to eat very much however, since the swallowing mechanism was impaired somehow. He was given speech therapy to help correct it. Vera encouraged him to attempt to eat and drink as much as he could, but if he was pushed too much, he would vomit.

Vera tried to explain to the doctor that he was not eating enough, hardly anything, but the doctor only chuckled and told her that he should not get fat anyway. She consoled herself with the fact that he would be coming home soon, and she could prepare his favourite meals which he would be sure to eat. However, Maurice's appetite just did not return at home. He declined slowly and steadily. Vera was in an absolute frenzy, trying to entice him to eat. She tried all sorts of recipes, special nutritional drinks, soft food, all his old favourites, anything she could think of, but he would turn his nose up at anything she brought him. She felt dejected and helpless and was reduced to tears when her husband often got very annoyed and nasty to her when she tried to coax him to take a bite of something. He just did not want to eat at all. Vera told the doctor that he was eating less than a mouse could live on but was told not to worry and that as he got stronger, his appetite would improve. He did not get stronger. He got weaker and one day he did not even have the strength to get out of bed.

Ruth called the doctor and insisted that her father be put back in the hospital so that something could be done about giving him nutrients. "How is he supposed to recover and get stronger if he is eating half a teaspoon of food every day?" she demanded. So back in the hospital Maurice went and a huge intravenous contraption (a swan) was put into a vein in his neck so that finally, he was getting the nutrients that he needed. It was later decided that he would be better with a feeding tube directly in his stomach. While he was waiting to be taken to surgery, he had another critical episode. Vera and Ruth noticed a change in him. His breathing became laboured, and his pallor was awful. Ruth asked the attending nurse to call the doctor to take a look at him, but she insisted that there was no problem with his vital signs and would not call him. He passed out shortly after and was rushed to intensive care with a condition called "acidosis" which is an imbalance of the blood gases. It caused his blood pressure to bottom out and a resuscitation team had to work on him for four hours to get him stabilised again. They had to pump his body full of fluid to get his blood pressure up. The doctor came to tell Vera and Ruth that she doubted he would make it. Ruth called Frances who booked a flight immediately. Maurice was revived although he was terribly weak and found that he had now lost control of his bladder and bowels. This bothered him more than any of the rest of the horrors he had been through. He could not stand it! After another week in intensive care, he had the stomach tube installed and a week later, Frances returned home, worried, and distraught having seen her father as she had never seen him before, hopeless, noncommunicative, staring into space, distancing himself from his loved ones. He was discharged to the rehabilitation hospital again. He was miserable there. The staff did their best to get him on his feet again, but he only managed a few tottering steps with the aid of a walker. He was in the rehab hospital when his second great grandchild was born. Nicholas Peter arrived on June 22. At two weeks old, Peter and Cheri took him to visit his great grandfather. He was placed in Maurice's arms where he reclined in his bed, gaunt and frail but amazed at the wonder of the tiny new-born. One branch of the family tree in decline and another just beginning!

The attending doctor requested a conference with Vera and Ruth to tell them that Maurice would not be getting better, that his body had been through just too much. He suggested taking him home and getting hospice involved to help with his home care. Vera was devastated. It seemed so unfair that he had battled so hard and so long only for it to end this way. Maurice was told. He was quite accepting. He had kept his thoughts to himself during the last two months or so, but he had known long before everyone else that he was not going to make it. In his own mind, he had determined that he was unwilling to live with tubes, catheters and with such a reduced quality of life. The hospice nurse said that the withdrawal was typical of the behaviour of someone anticipating death.

Maurice returned home and opted to have the feeding tube removed after asking permission of his family. Frances and Helen received a very difficult phone call from their father. "I just want to know that you are alright with it," he said to Frances. "I don't want to go on like this. Do you understand? Do I have your approval?"

"I will support your decision, Dad," she answered. "We all want what you want. You have been through enough. Yes, I understand." She collapsed into her husband's arms when she hung up the phone. Both Frances and Helen had been making regular trips to Tallahassee during the months following his surgery and they prepared to make a last visit to be with their father until the end. They arrived on a Tuesday in July. On Wednesday, he wanted his wife and daughters to listen with him to a tape he had made of his life during his recovery from his broken hip some years ago. He called it his memoirs. It was interesting and funny. He talked about his childhood, family, the war years, meeting Vera, his three daughters, his work, emigrating to the United States and his life and work in Florida. He had only got as far as 1975 and he asked his daughters to finish it for him. That evening he started getting restless with pain in his joints. He said that his chest hurt him and that he ached all over. He kept asking for the "knockout man." Frances wondered if he was flashing back to his boxing days in his youth or whether the "knockout man" to him was God. She asked him if he would like to go to sleep and not know any more and he answered, "Yes!" Hospice prescribed some medications which Ruth put into his stomach tube every few hours and from then on, he was asleep. Joe had just started a new job after months of searching, so he was not able to take any time off. He had to attend a meeting in New Jersey on Friday and managed to get an afternoon flight to Orlando followed by a four-hour drive to Tallahassee. But he made it in time to be with his father-in-law at the last. Maurice's breathing was very erratic those last days. It would stop and start and was very raspy and congested. At three in the morning of Saturday, July 29th Vera, who was sleeping on the floor in the living room alongside his hospital bed, heard a marked change in the breathing sound and she woke Ruth to administer more medicine. Frances heard her and got up also and roused Helen. Vera and her three daughters were around the bed as Maurice's breathing slowed and his heart stopped. In the last minute he opened his eyes and was staring directly at Vera. She was telling him that she loved him and that it was okay for him to go. It was his dear wife's face that he saw as he died.

CHAPTER THIRTY

It was 6:00 in the morning when the funeral home arrived to take Maurice's body away. Vera and Frances had dressed him in a casual collar shirt and shorts, perhaps as he would have been dressed to pop down to the Salty Dog. The family group then sat at the kitchen table in melancholy togetherness, processing the fact that Maurice was gone. Vera asked Joe to disassemble the hospital bed in the living room and put it in the garage until it could be picked up. Joe was glad to be busy. He soon had it removed and out of sight and then he made trips to pick up lunch and dinner and came back with wine to lead the group in a toast, "To a life well lived!" he announced.

Maurice had always said that he did not want any fuss made at his passing. He and Vera had long since visited the funeral home to arrange their cremations and pay for them with a monthly payment book. There would be no formal wake or funeral, but his daughters convinced Vera that a gathering of his friends and family for a celebration of life should be the very least that they do. It would have to be soon since Frances would have to return to Connecticut and back to work. She had already been in Tallahassee for almost a week prior to her father's death. Helen also had to get back to Tampa, so it was decided to hold the gathering on Monday. Vera was given the task of listing the people and telephone numbers of those she would like to invite and to dig through photograph albums for photos to display. This helped to settle her. She was not yet in the throes of grief, she had company in the house and things to do but she was flustered and full of nervous energy, staring into space and periodically returning to the living room where the hospital bed had been, seemingly to remind herself that Maurice was really gone. She also felt an immediate sense of relief which was difficult to process and made her feel uncomfortable. Was it relief for Maurice or relief for herself that she felt? How could he have gone on the way he was, she thought? He was unwilling to live so weak and infirm. But was there more that could have been done? Should she have tried harder? For months following his death, Vera would rehash all that had happened since the bypass surgery over and over again. "I hope that when I die, I just go *Poof!*" She told her daughters.

Monday evening was determined to be the time for the celebration of life gathering. Joe could not be there. He left Sunday afternoon to drive back to Orlando and fly home. He was unable to take time off from his new job. Tom also was not able to attend. He had made a very difficult, emotional last telephone call to his grandfather during the previous week. Frances, Ruth and Helen planned the food, arranged the seating and set up displays depicting portraits of Maurice at various times of his life, family groups and happy times. When the guests arrived, it was almost exactly the same group who had attended the fiftieth anniversary party just six months before. It all felt very strange. Everyone stood around uncomfortably, but Vera managed to circulate, chatting and pointing to some of the photos and explaining when and where they were taken. Peter led the group in a prayer and stories and memories were shared which eased the tension. Some people drifted away early in the evening and others stayed quite late. For Vera, the occasion helped her get through the first days following her loss but soon long, lonely days would follow.

Frances phoned Hazel when she returned home to ask her if she would be willing to visit Vera and help sort through Maurice's things. Hazel was happy to contribute in some way and visited for two weeks. This was another immense help to Vera. Hazel was a good, devoted friend and their old camaraderie was a great comfort. Vera wanted Maurice's things sorted out and disposed of swiftly. She did not want to see his clothing hanging in the closet, so they were sorted out, thrown away or put in bags to take to a charitable organisation. They threw out his toiletries, books, eyeglasses and any articles pertaining to his health and care, medications, protein drinks, syringes, protective bed pads. It was important for Vera to have his things gone but there were still forgotten items. For quite some time after his passing, she would open a drawer or a cupboard or a closet and find something of his that would cause her to freeze, and then lose her stoicism and strength. She would fall to her knees and sob her heart out.

When Vera and Hazel had completed their task, Vera took her out and about and they visited several of Vera's close friends in Tallahassee. There was Marie, Sylvia, Barbara and Patsy and more people she wanted her to meet at the Senior Center. The two weeks were busy with activities and lunches and brief social visits. Hazel was glad to meet everyone and was happy to discover that Vera had such a nice, extensive circle of friends to support her. The last errand that Hazel completed with Vera was to pick up Maurice's ashes from the funeral home. They drove home in silence and Vera placed them on her bedside table where they remained for several years. When Hazel returned home to Connecticut, Vera stood in the living room on the spot where Maurice had died with tears rolling down her cheeks. She was living alone now, the house would be empty when she came back from activities, shopping, visiting. Frances lived in Connecticut, Helen in Tampa; only Ruth lived nearby. There would no longer be a husband, a centre to her life, someone with who she had shared life, shared a common history, someone who understood her likes and dislikes, her moods, her needs and who would love her in the most deep and intimate way. How empty her life would be and how sad that his familiar, lively, gregarious personality was lost to the world.

Vera dealt with her grief by keeping very active and busy. She went out every day to break up the prolonged periods of feeling lonely and bored. She had never been a big fan of the television, but now she had it on most of the time for noise in the house, voices speaking, news to watch. She visited her friends, spent a lot of time at the Senior Center and popped in on Ruth rather often. She needed to talk about all that had happened in the preceding months, go over the details of her husband's decline, second guess decisions that were made about his treatment and care and wonder why he was unable to get stronger and recover.

"What if we had not gone to England for my birthday?" she suggested to Ruth. "Maybe he would not have had the heart attack."

"Maybe not, Mum, maybe not then, but it would have happened at another time."

"Why didn't he get to the cardiologist sooner?"

"Well… he must have felt there was no urgency, and he was taking care of you at the time."

"Oh, dear! That awful cyst. I think it worried him and he had to run about more doing things for me."

"Mum, it's what married couples do. They take care of each other."

"Yes, but it was an awful strain on him. Oh, and he just wouldn't eat. He *couldn't* eat. Why was that? I don't understand what happened." Ruth sighed. They had been over and over this so many times. Her mother just could not accept and process the failure of all the efforts of the medical profession and could not come to terms with the defeat that she saw in her husband. He had never given up before. Throughout his life, he had recovered from his mistakes, disappointments, and bad luck. With determination and renewed energy, he fought back, found another path, and forged on.

"It was a consequence of all the complications that he had, Mum," she said gently. "He tried but I think he decided and knew at some point that it was hopeless, and he was just unwilling to live in such a weakened state."

"Oh, yes, I suppose so," Vera acknowledged wiping her eyes. "He would have been miserable."

Frances asked Vera to come to Connecticut for a month in September. She thought it would provide a change for her and a chance to visit the family, see dear old friends, especially Ray and Hazel and Geza and Elnora.

"A month?" Vera questioned.

"Yes, come for a nice, long visit. Ruth will fly up with you for a week, but she will have to get back to work. We will take you back to the airport when you leave, all the way to the gate and Ruth will pick you up at the other end."

The month passed swiftly. Frances kept Vera busy visiting, shopping, eating out and sitting on the deck with countless cups of tea and long conversations. Maurice was the main topic of the conversations and Frances recognised that it was important for her mother to understand and come to terms with the sequence of events that had led to his death. She needed to satisfy her deep resentment on so many levels, but it was difficult continuously going over the same ground. One day she asked Frances to drive her around Fairfield. They drove through the centre of town. "How it has changed!" Vera said. They drove past Evelyn and James's former home on the way to the beach and so many landmarks, Fairfield University, Fairfield Woods Junior High, Fairfield Woods library, where Vera had spent so much time with young Helen, Yvonne and Bob's home of so many years before they left for Seattle, Andrew Warde High School where all three girls had attended (Helen only for a few months before the move to Florida) Black Rock Turnpike, Lake Mohegan and finally, Weeping Willow Lane to see the magnificent home where they had lived so happily. Vera sat quietly for a long time staring up the long driveway at the house sitting on a slight rise. She was amazed at the trees that she had planted on the front lawn. They had grown so tall. She remembered when her neighbour, Peter Hope-Ross had commented with a shake of his head as she was planting them. "They will never take, you know." So many memories flashed through her mind: parties, picnics, Christmases, visitors, Florrie and Ted, Hazel and Ray. She remembered the waterfall, gone now, but the wonder of it frozen in the winter, the girls ice skating on the pond above, Helen born there, playing as a little girl, running around the property, blonde ponytail swinging. The house had an addition on the left side, but the façade looked much the same. She felt that she could drive up the driveway as she had so many times and enter through the porch to the side door into the large informal den with the bar that Maurice had built. The one with the mural behind it of a mountain, trees, and a lake. Charlotte had written soon after they moved in when they had sent back photographs, *what a lovely view you have from your window.* Frances always felt sad and resentful when she thought about the old farmhouse and she could see that her mother was becoming teary, so she turned the car and headed home. "Time for a nice cup of tea, don't you think?"

When Vera returned to Florida, she spent time almost

every day at the Senior Center. She participated in anything and everything that appealed to her. She continued singing with the choir, attended discussion groups, played ping-pong, went on bus trips, participated in exercise sessions, and decided to learn how to play pool. It was there, at the pool table that she met Ed. Ed was a widower of several years with three sons who all lived far away. He helped Vera with her technique and strategy at the pool table and they played many games together. He enjoyed Vera's sense of humour as well as her energy and interest in so many of the activities at the centre. They began to attend events together and then they went out for coffee, lunch, becoming more comfortable with each other and appreciating the companionship.

Ed was eight years older than Vera, almost eighty, but he was smart, spry and keen to learn, discover and travel. He was comfortable in his retirement, having worked for many decades for American Airlines, first as a mechanic and then in a managerial, supervisory position, rising to Vice President of Operations for his region. He had served in the army during World War II in the Pacific. Vera was most interested in his years of duty and his experiences. The two shared their war stories, so different, yet so compelling and they became constant companions enjoying their time together and quickly developing a strong fondness for each other. Ed was so different from Maurice. He was doting, always concerned with Vera's comfort and happiness. He was kind and generous, a touch possessive, eager to please and to indulge her by taking her where she wanted to go or visiting someone she wanted to see. He was a take charge person but always had Vera's best interests at heart. Ed often took her out to eat, so happy for the companionship which he had missed for so long. He had spent several years nursing his wife at the end of her life and had been so lonely after her death. The new relationship with Vera was invigorating, comforting and provided so many social opportunities. She was outgoing and drew him out more, widening his social circle and activities. It was around Christmas time that Ruth was visiting Vera at home when she noticed something new on display.

"Oh! This is nice," she said. "Where did you get it?"

"My boyfriend bought it for me," Vera responded. Ruth froze for a moment wondering if her mother was kidding her.

"Your *boyfriend*?"

"Yes, Ed. We have been seeing each other for a couple of months now," she answered matter-of-factly. Ruth was appalled. Was her mother serious? *How could she possibly have a boyfriend so soon after her husband had died?*

"But… Mum, don't you think it is a bit too soon to have a relationship? I mean, it hasn't even been six months since dad died."

"I know, but Ed is wonderful. You will like him, I'm sure," she replied brightly. Then, in a sombre tone, "I can't stand it, Ruth. This house, coming home to the quiet, emptiness. I found myself calling out for Moe, looking in all the rooms for him. I had to get out. I had to make another life for myself. I couldn't bear it."

"But you need time to properly grieve."

"I've been grieving since February when he could not recover from the bypass surgery."

Ruth telephoned Frances later that day to give her the news. She poured out all her misgivings, disapproval and outrage. "Oh, dear!" Frances responded. "Yes, it is too soon."

"And she's behaving like a teenager. All giggly and silly

talking about him. He held her hand soon after they met when they went out for coffee. She told me she has been dancing around the living room ever since!"

"Well, I remember a conversation years ago when Mum and Dad were discussing how they would deal with being alone. Dad said that he would have to meet someone quickly, that he would hate to be alone and come home to an empty house. Perhaps Mum always had that thought in the back of her mind too and she was just ready after Dad's lengthy illness to move on quickly."

"It just seems so disrespectful… after all that they have been through together. I don't know, seems like she would need some time to adjust, mourn and settle into a new life."

"Well, they say that everyone grieves differently. Dad was Mum's centre. She revolved around him all her married life, following him, supporting him. He was her world. I think she is lost without that centre. She recognises her need. Let's hope she has chosen wisely. We will just have to watch out for her and make sure she is happy and safe and not manipulated in any way."

"I suppose that I will meet him soon. So, we shall see."

Vera had another reason to focus on a happier future following Maurice's death. Helen discovered that she was expecting and announced the happy news to Vera just months after her father's passing.

"I had hoped to get pregnant while Dad was alive to be able to tell him of another grandchild on the way," Helen lamented.

"Oh… I don't know if that would have made him happy or sad that he would never see his youngest grandchild." Vera thought about it for a long time after Helen's call. Life could be so unfair at times. *What a shame!* Maurice would have been so tickled to have another baby in the family. Their youngest grandchild, Tiphanie, was now twenty years old. He would have been pleased that Helen and Johnny were starting a family. But she believed that it would have caused him deep regret as he lay dying, to know he would be missing out on such a happy occasion. Vera realised that she would be seventy-two years old when the baby was born. She would be an older grandmother to this child. She had been quite a young grandmother for her other grandchildren. Since Helen and Johnny lived in Tampa, she would not be in close proximity either. She would have to make the most of her time with the child during visits back and forth.

Ruth met Ed and was not too impressed at first. He was polite and happy to meet her, but he did not have the natural ease and charm that her father possessed. He was rather to the point and on the brusque side. She noticed that he watched Vera quite closely and protectively, making sure she did not hurt herself. "Be careful with that knife." "Don't trip over that mat." "Don't jump up so fast. Take your time, Vera." He would say. He was so different from her father. However, as time went by, Ruth appreciated him for his care and concern, for the companionship he provided, for the activities they shared together and for his generosity. He could not understand how Vera managed living on her social security check and her small pension from the United Kingdom, so he helped her financially in so many ways.

The couple lived a few miles apart, but they decided early on that each would maintain their own home and keep their finances separate and secure as their established inheritance for their children. They visited back and forth and "stayed over" quite often. Within a year, Ed had met all the family, Frances and Joe, Helen and Johnny, Peter and Cheri, Josephine and Nicholas, Tom, Adam and Tiphanie. He enjoyed them all, thinking of them as his second family, and was interested to hear about their lives and activities. The first big event was the birth of Helen's child in May 2001. Helen had a little girl and named her Marissa as a tribute to her late father. Ed drove with Vera to visit the baby in Tampa. Helen may have felt significant regret that her father was not there with Vera, that Ed had filled his place so swiftly, but she was glad to see her mother content and enjoying life with her new companion. Vera was thrilled to meet her new granddaughter who was little blonde-haired baby, reminding Vera so much of Helen as a child. She wished that she could see her more often.

Ed took Vera to Long Island that summer. He had been born and raised in New York and lived on Long Island for many years while working for American Airlines. He showed her around all his old haunts, introduced her to a brother and son who still lived there and took the ferry over to Connecticut, where they visited another son in Hartford and then Frances in Stratford. He did not want to stay with anyone, so he and Vera stayed a couple of nights in a nearby hotel while in Connecticut. Frances was disappointed with the brief visit but realised that things would be different now that her mother had a new partner. How strange it sometimes felt.

For Marissa's first birthday, Helen organised a large party in Tampa and all the family managed to attend. It was the first time that Ed was introduced to Peter and his family, Tom, and Adam. He had already met Tiphanie and her boyfriend, Cliff. He was quite amazed at the family for making the effort to be together for the occasion and was happy to get to know everyone. Unfortunately, Helen and Johnny were separated by this time. Johnny's musician lifestyle had not been conducive to a happy marriage. He was at the party, but the relationship was obviously strained. Helen had moved out into an apartment in an attractive complex where she was able to rent the community room for the event. During the next year, Helen drove often to Tallahassee to spend time with her family and one evening at a friend's party, she met Matt and her life changed for the better.

Later that year, Frances flew to Columbus, Georgia, to visit Peter, Cheri and the family and Ruth drove up from Tallahassee with Vera and Ed. Ruth stayed at the house, but Ed opted again for a hotel. Giggling, Vera told them of an incident that occurred at their hotel when they returned one night. They discovered that their key card did not work in the lock. The tried many times but the door would not open. Finally, they went to the desk and complained. An employee led them back to their room, placed the card in the slot and opened the door. "I couldn't believe it," Vera cried, doubling over with laughter. "We couldn't understand what we had been doing wrong. It was not until the next morning that we realised we had been trying to access a room on the wrong floor!" It was a pleasant visit, even though it was a bit reminiscent in some ways of the eventful North Carolina Christmas years ago. Frances came down with a stomach virus later in the day and Ruth developed a urinary tract infection. It became so severe that she had to be taken to the emergency room at the local hospital. By the evening, however, all was well, and they were all playing a trivia game around the dining room table, moving it to the living room so that Frances could play while lying on the couch.

It was during this visit that Vera first told Frances and Ruth something that they would wonder about ever after. The three of them were in Cheri's kitchen washing and drying dishes when Vera told them suddenly and out of the blue, that she had a secret which she would take to her grave. Frances and Ruth stared at her in stunned surprise.

"A secret?" Ruth wondered. "About what, Mum?"

"Oh, I'll never tell you."

"Then why bring it up?" Frances asked.

"I don't know. I shouldn't have. It just popped out."

"But, Mum, now that you have said it you must tell us," Ruth told her.

"No. I can't. I won't," Vera responded and then turned on her heels and left the room.

"What could that be all about?" Frances wondered.

"I don't know… an attention getter, do you think?"

"Oh, dear. What a thing to say! We will be wondering and imagining all sorts of things."

"Best to let it drop for now. I'll ask her about it at another time. Maybe when it is just the two of us having a cup of tea."

Ruth brought up the mysterious secret several times with her mother. But Vera shook her head and looked away. "I'll never tell you!" she declared.

Every year, there was a reunion for American Airline retirees that Ed enjoyed attending. He had missed a few while his wife was ill and a few others when he did not want to go alone. With Vera in his life, he was anxious to enjoy the experience again. The reunions were held at different, exciting locations and venues each year. Vera was thrilled to go. They travelled to Las Vegas, where they enjoyed all the sights, the bright lights and shows, lavish meals and the big reunion banquet, complete with dinner and dancing to a live band. There were introductions to many old friends and co-workers of Ed. Everyone was happy to reminisce and laugh at funny times and memories. Vera chatted happily, took group photographs around the table, and loved every minute of it. They went on an open-top night bus tour of the city to view the neon lights, illuminations, fountains and erupting volcanoes, pirate ships, pyramids and more. They enjoyed a desert tour, and a visit to the magnificent Hoover Dam. Vera was dazzled with it all. She had never dreamed that she would ever go to Vegas, and in such style.

Another reunion was in San Antonio, where Vera was amazed with the history and heritage of the city. She found it very beautiful strolling along the river walk with all the interesting shops and restaurants along the way. They toured the Alamo and learned about its history and significance during the Texas Revolution. Vera could not help but think how much Maurice would have enjoyed seeing it. *Why had they never gone*? There was also a reunion in St. Louis where Vera and Ed rode the tram to the observation deck at the top of the Gateway Arch, took a tour of Civil War battle sites, the Anheuser-Busch brewery tour, and took a boat ride on the Mississippi River. All the reunions were great adventures for Vera and especially enjoyable as she came to know many of the couples who attended and looked forward to seeing them again.

Vera was having the time of her life thanks to Ed. She could not help but compare him with Maurice at times. He was not as naturally outgoing or charming, but he was more eager to please her, worry about her and take care of her. With Maurice there was more of a partnership, taking on life together, overcoming obstacles and carrying on. He was caring but not demonstrative. He was very much a product of a disciplined, "stiff upper lip" upbringing. Showing emotion, coddling, pampering and displays of affection were just not part of his makeup. He was determined to be strong, bold and resilient throughout his life. He was a risk taker. Ed was not. Ed had worked steadily for one company most of his life. He saved, advanced in his career, was careful, thoughtful and logical in his decision-making, providing comfort and security for his family. Vera appreciated both men for their differences. She had loved Maurice deeply throughout their marriage but this time with Ed was so different that it did not take away from her previous life with Maurice at all. It was a new chapter. The previous chapters were intact and appreciated and remembered lovingly, but she was living a new, more carefree and a less stressful, easy life with Ed.

During another visit to Long Island and Connecticut, Vera took a bad fall which resulted in a broken wrist. Ed took her to an ER near where they were staying, and she was put into a temporary brace and sling to immobilise the arm. They cut the visit short, returning to Tallahassee to see an orthopaedic specialist. It was determined that the break was quite serious, involving several bones and it required surgery, rods and pins. During her recovery, Vera stayed at Ed's, where he took very good care of her, helping her with everyday tasks, dressing, bathing, shopping, making meals. One of the pills that Vera had to take was large and difficult for her to swallow. Ed placed it on a spoon with yogurt which helped it go down easier. Ruth was visiting during one of these events and watched in amazement. Vera caught her eye and laughed. Both were thinking how different it would have been with Maurice. "Oh, for goodness' sake, Vera," he would have said. "Just swallow it down!"

After many months of driving back and forth to be with Matt, Helen decided to relocate back to Tallahassee and the romance blossomed. Matt worked for the state of Florida, owned his own home, loved music, concerts, parties, the beach and the two discovered that they were very compatible. Matt was divorced with two daughters. He loved children and Marissa soon became his beloved third daughter. They married in December 2007 on the beach at St. George Island. Matt proved to be a loving, attentive husband and an adoring father to Marissa. He was the one who carried her around on his shoulders, taught her how to ride a bicycle, read to her, played with her, swam with her in their pool, helped her with homework, cuddled her when she was sick, hurt or unhappy, took her on vacations, attended all the school functions. Helen held no grudge against Johnny and was very diligent about making sure her daughter spent time with her father quite regularly. She and Matt drove her to Tampa and visited friends for the weekend while Marissa stayed with her father, who now was in a new relationship and would produce four more daughters. Sometimes they would drive down one weekend to leave her for a week and drive back the following weekend to pick her up. Marissa was a remarkable little girl. She welcomed and loved all the little girls in Johnny's new family as well as Matt's two daughters. She grew up happy, loved, secure and well-adjusted.

Vera was very happy when Helen lived in Tallahassee again and she could see more of Marissa. She was an older grandmother now, well into her seventies when Marissa was born, but she babysat for her, read to her, told her stories and played games. When Helen sometimes called her daughter "little Moe," Vera found herself thinking again of her husband and all that he had missed in the family. Apart from Marissa, he had missed a third great-grandchild. Leah had been born to Peter and Cheri in 2002, Frances succeeded in publishing a book of historical fiction, *The Forgotten Flag*, in 2003, Frances's son Tom was accepted by Oxford University in England to their MBA program. How proud he would have been. Frances gave Tom her father's cuff links and tie clip which had been given to him by Charlotte, his mother, before he emigrated to the United States. They depicted knights holding shields of mother of pearl and the tie clip was an axe with a mother of pearl blade. Maurice had cherished them. "Just wear them to a formal function while you are there," Frances suggested to Tom. "It is just symbolic of course, but something of your grandfathers with you on your way." Peter left the army after two tours of duty during which he had serving in Egypt, Cuba and a year in South Korea. They moved back to Connecticut after Peter began civilian life. He had studied computer programming during his enlistment and began a successful career in that field.

Tiphanie married Cliff in 2005. The family came together again for the festivities. Adam gave his sister away to the strains of a harp at an outside garden venue at a lovely community estate with a banqueting hall. The couple would have a daughter, Kendall, in 2007. Vera was thrilled to have another baby in the family and one who lived so close by. She was amazed at all the new equipment available then for babies and often exclaimed, "Well… I wish I had *that* when I had my babies!" She was impressed with how well Tiphanie coped and managed her baby daughter and she and Ed saw her often, enjoying watching her grow.

All this, Vera thought sadly, Maurice had missed. The family, grew, chose their paths, carried on his spirit of adventure, worked hard and prospered. He would have been proud. One morning, she stood for a long time looking at the box on her bedside table containing her husband's ashes. It was time to dispose of them. She carried the box outside to the back garden to one of the rose bushes that Maurice had planted long ago. She tipped the box and scattered the ashes around the base of the bush without ceremony. "I remember the day you planted this bush," she said. "I think you would have liked to be scattered here, my love."

Excerpt from one of Vera's notebooks

I keep busy as much as I can. I have several very good friends, one especially, Marie. Two of my three daughters living here in Tallahassee, also two granddaughters and one great granddaughter. I'm grateful for that. My oldest daughter, Frances, I don't get to see a lot of the time, but I look forward to seeing her once or twice a year, with her growing family.

Last but NOT least – there is Ed, whom I met at the Senior Center while trying to learn how to play pool. I never did master the skills needed to play on the billiard table but was compensated with a lasting, happy relationship with Ed who is now my everlasting companion, since 2001. We prop each other up during our surviving years! We care for each other through our declining days enjoying the remaining time we have left.

CHAPTER THIRTY-ONE

In 2009, as Vera's eightieth birthday approached, Frances, Ruth and Helen put their heads together to plan a surprise party. They decided on a similar venue to the one where Tiphanie was married. They rented rooms at Dorothy Oven Park, decided to have some catered dishes, and would make some of Vera's favourites themselves. They decided on a guest list which would include fifty people and were able to obtain addresses rather furtively by snagging Vera's address book for a couple of days. Ed was told about the plans and the date of the party when his task would be to take Vera out on a pretence and drive her to Dorothy Oven Park at the designated time instead. Keeping the secret was definitely out of Ed's comfort zone. He had to be careful not to spill the beans when talking with Vera. Frances, Joe and Peter. Cheri and the children arrived a few days before the event to help with the preparations and on the big day, they helped set up, put up decorations and carry food and drinks inside. A large cake with a picture of Vera as a young woman was displayed at the centre of the buffet table.

The rooms in the large house were ideal. There were several comfortable conversation areas, lots of tables for eating and a large open space for dancing, as well as pretty gardens outside. When Ed finally arrived with Vera, who had been puzzled when he pulled into the park, she gasped in shock when the room erupted as she entered with shouts of "Surprise!" and "Happy Birthday, Vera." Ed collapsed into a chair with relief. "Oh," he sighed wiping his brow. "This has been so stressful. It was so hard to keep the secret!"

"You did a good job, Ed," Joe chuckled. "Now relax

and I'll get you a drink."

Vera was giddy with excitement. She could not believe the number of guests and all her favourite people gathered together to celebrate. She suddenly found it funny to have all eyes on her and she laughed, bending over double in her delight. Everyone laughed along with her. This was their Vera, so exuberant, so social, so happy to be with friends and family, so interested in their lives, always there to listen if they needed a sympathetic ear and a cheerful participant in so many activities. Apart from family, there were guests from so many aspects of her life, friends she had made soon after moving to Florida, neighbours, friends from the choir, the British Club ladies, Senior Center favourites, some of Maurice's cronies who had become her friends too. She was appreciated for her enthusiasm, her stories, and her love of learning something new. There were hugs all around as Vera made her way through the group, exclaiming and bursting with glee.

The party was fun for young and old. Vera enjoyed being the centre of attention and moved from table to table, group to group, wanting to catch up with everyone, introducing her family to those who had not met and chuckling while she commented on photographs on display from various times and events in her life. She danced with Ed to some "oldies but goodies" and soon the place was hopping with an assortment of music and dancers. It was a happy birthday indeed.

Vera and Ed continued to enjoy their time at the Senior Center. They became infatuated with ping-pong, playing often and participating in some friendly competition. Vera was quite the player and enjoyed the feeling of victory. Ed told her more than once to remember that it was just a game and not to reach and dive so much for the ball. He was afraid that she would strain herself. And sure enough, when she reached too far to try to return a ball one day, she fell hard on the floor. She grabbed her shoulder after the impact and felt a searing pain immediately. "There you are!" said Ed as he helped her to her feet. "Didn't I warn you? You just have to let some of those shots go by." A visit to the ER determined that the shoulder was broken and would require surgery, so yet again, Vera was in a sling and dependent on Ed's help and care.

On 21st January 2011, Ed turned ninety years old, and Vera organised a small gathering in a private dining room at Longhorn's Steakhouse, one of Ed's favourite restaurants. There were about fifteen people attending, including Ed's friends, Frank and Carol, mutual friends, Sylvia and Marie, Helen and Matt, Ruth and her recent boyfriend, Stefan, and Stephen, Ed's youngest son who was able to make it from Long Island. Ed was touched to see the group around the table and thanked everyone for coming. There had not been many occasions in his life when a special fuss or commemoration for him had occurred. Ruth remembered having her mother and Ed over for dinner in years past, when she brought out a birthday cake glowing with candles to mark one of Ed's birthdays. He had been rather overcome, actually tearing up. "This is the first time anyone has ever had a birthday dinner and cake for me," he said.

Soon after the party, Vera noticed a change in Ed. He slowed down rapidly, lost his appetite, began to lose weight and became weak. It was a marked decline which concerned her. She insisted that he see the doctor who arranged for him to go to the hospital for tests. Tests showed that Ed was dehydrated, deficient in sodium and his electrolytes were out of balance. Back home, Vera took care of him, encouraging him to eat but he could not manage much at all. Vera was worried. She had seen this before! She spoke to Ed's son Stephen about his condition and her concern that Ed was not strong enough to rally from this decline. Early in June, his three sons, their wives and a grandson, Patrick, arrived to help with his care. The two older sons were cool towards Vera, considering her an intruder and encouraged her to go back home, but Ed wanted her there, so she stayed to comfort him. Stephen was kinder, and more understanding of the caring relationship and the long time together. But Vera felt uncomfortable and out of place as the family took over. Ruth and Stefan arrived one afternoon to visit. One of Ed's sons answered the door and attempted to turn them away, telling them that he was not up to a visit, but Ed heard Ruth's voice. "Is that Ruth out there?" he called. "Let her in. I want to see her." So, Ruth and Stefan sat with Ed for a while. They had brought a balloon and flowers to brighten up the room and they chatted for a while, telling him about the family and asking if there was anything he needed or anything they could do. "Just take care of your mother," he answered.

Later that evening Ed's family sat around the bed forming a symbolic wall around him, keeping Vera out. She looked at their backs sadly and thought she should leave for the day and give them private time alone. Ed was looking for her, asking for her, wondering why he could not see her. The wall had to break so that she could approach the bed. "Goodnight, my dear," she said. "I'm going to catch a few hours' sleep at my home. I'll be back in the morning." Ed grasped her hand as she bent to kiss him gently on the cheek. "I love you," he whispered.

Vera slept soundly that night. She was exhausted from long days and nights caring for Ed and worrying. She was woken up by the telephone ringing. One of the family was calling to tell her not to bother coming back over, that Ed had died in the night. She collapsed in a chair, heartbroken, feeling the loss and emptiness immediately, feeling guilty that she had not been at his side when he died. She sobbed knowing that she would miss him so, miss his loving presence in her life, his care and concern for her and the security it afforded her. She telephoned Ruth who came to the house to be with her mother. She was appalled at the way Vera had been told of Ed's passing.

"I think I want to go over there," Vera stated. "I would like to see Ed one more time. I had told him that I would be back this morning. I feel that I should go."

"Okay," Ruth agreed. "Let's go."

Unfortunately, Ed's body had been removed by the funeral home by the time Vera arrived. She was not welcome there and an unpleasant exchange ensued between Ruth and Ed's middle son. Vera had not realised the depth of the resentment against her, and she wept shakily. She turned and walked away from Ed's home which had been so familiar, such a comfortable space where they had spent so many happy times. She would never come here again. It was over. She did not attend the funeral service. She knew that she was not wanted there. She felt shunned, treated as if she was a gold-digging opportunist. It was obvious to her what the resentment was all about. They had not witnessed the loving care she and Ed had for each other, the shared lives, ten years together. She was deeply hurt that it ended this way. And then, a few days later, Stephen knocked on the door with a box of her belongings from the house. He also handed Vera an envelope. "Dad wanted you to have this," he said. "He knew it would be a help to you."

"Oh, my goodness. I did not expect this!" Vera declared as she gazed at the generous check written out to her. "Thank you, Stephen for bringing it to me."

"Thank you, Vera, for bringing Dad so many years of happiness and companionship."

Stephen's visit soothed her soul. She welcomed the small legacy that Ed had left her, it would certainly provide some financial security, but it was also the gesture and words of kindness from this son that gave her comfort and some closure.

Vera contemplated her remaining years ahead. She was now eighty-two years old and in reasonably good health. The liver cyst had not returned, her broken bones had healed and she still had sufficient energy. However, she noticed that she was becoming more forgetful and took to writing notes and taping them up around the house to help her remember important dates and events. She kept a notebook by the phone to jot down information, names and telephone numbers. She dreaded long, lonely days and got out of the house as much as possible. She called on friends, spent time at the Senior Center, and spent a long-time shopping choosing her groceries. She often popped in on Ruth, becoming dependent on her for help with her finances, medications, repairs and maintenance of the car and the home, and poured out her worries and concerns. The office in her home began to become a fixation. It had been such a hub during her life with Maurice. It was filled with files dating back decades. There was also a bookcase filled with photograph albums that Vera had kept organised and labelled. The photographs inside were captioned with places, names and events. She had kept medical files, tax files, bank statements, insurance policies, service and repair records, utility bills, receipts, letters and documents dating back to their move to Florida and beyond. On the shelf in the closet, she had box upon box stacked up with Maurice's business records and contracts from building days, wallpapering agreements, bank inspection paperwork, as well as business cards and letterheads from his businesses. She was overwhelmed whenever she attempted to sort through it all and she would become depressed. Usually, she ended up paperclipping notes to papers and envelopes and put them right back in the file. Frances often received a phone call with Vera upset and weepy having found a bill or statement that she did not understand or thought she had forgotten to pay. She was also very nervous about her taxes. Someone had told her that if she missed a tax payment, the town could take her house. No matter how many times Frances and Ruth assured her that this would never happen, she had that fear in her mind continually. Ruth decided it was time for her to take over the bills for her mother. She was already jointly on Vera's accounts, so she set up online banking on her computer. Vera often visited the tax office, even so, to check that she was not delinquent.

Cheerful news arrived from Dorothy in England. She would be coming to the United States and would like to visit with Ian. Her husband, Derek, had died a few years ago in 2007, and she had met Ian on a cruise. The two had stayed connected and had visited back and forth. Ian, a widower, lived in Liverpool, quite a distance away, so after a time, he sold his house and moved in with Dorothy in Chingford. He was almost ten years younger than Dorothy, but they were both retired, well off financially, and had many interests in common, especially travelling. Vera was happy to have them come and stay. She craved company and would enjoy taking them around and showing them all the places of interest. It was an enjoyable visit. Ian was happy to meet the Florida family, and everyone liked him. But Dorothy noticed a substantial change in her cousin.

"Isn't she fretful?" she remarked to Frances when they flew up to spend a few days in Connecticut. "She repeats things over and over and forgets where she puts things all the time. Then she gets herself all worked up."

"Yes, I know. It is becoming a bit of a worry."

"I don't want to tell tales," Ian added, "but we had a few scary moments when she was driving us around. She turned at an intersection and was on the wrong side of the road for a while."

"Oh, dear. I will have to speak to Ruth about that."

After the visit, Vera called Frances telling her that she was finding toothbrushes and pencils all around the house. "I think Dorothy left them for me," she said.

Ruth, Frances and Helen began to have three-way calls at this time. They were all concerned with Vera's mental state. Frances told them the information Ian had given her about their mother's driving. "Is it time to take the keys away, do you think?"

"Oh dear!" Ruth groaned. "That is going to be so hard for her. Getting out and about and being able to visit her friends is her life right now."

"She will be miserable not being able to drive," Helen agreed.

"Well, I think the time is approaching. We had better be prepared."

The time came quite soon. Vera began to have hallucinations. At first, the girls thought that she was having vivid dreams and was unable to discern dreams from reality upon wakening. But she insisted that Maurice was coming into the house at night with a woman and a little boy. Vera was indignant at the nerve of them. According to her, they left ashtrays about with cigarette stubs, and they left glasses and dishes where they had helped themselves to her food. The little boy ran up and down the hallway. She was angry and upset. She insisted that the woman lived down the road and that she would often stop in front of the house in her car. She would call all three daughters to complain of the behaviour. The girls were worried. Was it a change of medication? Was she sleeping too deeply? Too lightly?

"Oh, you are just dreaming, Mum," said Frances.

"No, I'm not! There are ashtrays and dishes in the living room when I wake up."

"You are imagining them," said Helen.

"Well, I should think I would know when someone has been in the house!" Vera said indignantly. "The cheek of it all!" She often called distressed and crying. "Dad and the woman came again last night. I'm fed up with it. Why are they doing this to me?"

She dreamed of her mother, Florrie too, insisting that she and Ted had come to visit but had left without saying goodbye, just leaving a note.

"Mum, Nana and Uncle Ted have been dead for years," Ruth reminded her.

"Well, they left me a note."

"Where is the note?"

"Well, I don't know what I did with it."

Frances, Ruth, and Helen decided something had to be done. Ruth got a referral to a neurologist from Vera's doctor. The neurologist listened to Ruth's concerns, tested Vera's memory, cognitive skills, and chatted with her at length. "Now that you have told me about these issues," he said. "I'm afraid that I must recommend that you not drive anymore, Mrs. Brown. With these symptoms on your record, if you were to cause an accident that seriously hurt someone, you could be completely wiped out financially."

This was the news that they all had been dreading. It was time for Vera to give up the keys. She was deeply dismayed and depressed.

"I also think you are lonely," the doctor continued. "May I recommend that you get a dog?"

CHAPTER THIRTY-TWO

Vera's daughters decided that a young rescue dog would be best for their mother. A puppy would be too active and need too much training. Ruth discovered through a friend that there was a program in effect in Florida that partnered a rescue dog with a prison inmate as part of a rehabilitation program. After several months of training and living together, the dogs were available for adoption. There was a website with pictures of the next group of dogs who were soon graduating from the program. Ruth and Helen showed the pictures to Vera, read about each dog and she selected a four-year-old male beagle, named Austin. There was a form to fill out with questions about the home set up location etc. to determine that the living situation would properly accommodate a dog. Vera was accepted and was invited to go to the prison to meet Austin. Ruth and Stefan drove her there. The prison was located a two-hour drive away from Tallahassee, east toward Jacksonville. The dog was brought out on a leash so that Vera could spend some time with him and walk him. The two were very comfortable with each other. It was a good match. Vera returned to claim Austin a few weeks later when she was informed of the graduation date at the prison. This time it was Helen and Ruth accompanying her and they were surprised to actually be admitted to the prison for a formal graduation ceremony. It was a unique experience. In a large hall, the adopting individuals and families waited until the inmates entered one by one leading the dogs on a leash. Each inmate introduced their dog and demonstrated some behaviours and obedience training that had been taught. An official adoption certificate was awarded to each inmate which they would turn over to the adopting owner. There was a large cake and coffee for all to enjoy and a chance to chat with the inmate who had trained their dog. Austin's trainer was a burly, tattooed young man. He told Vera that he had lived with Austin in his cell for three months. He had been responsible for the total care of the dog, feeding, walking, grooming, training, as well as providing praise, comfort and affection. When it was time for the inmates to take their leave, it was quite an emotional parting. These unfortunate convicted men who had been found guilty of serious crimes against society, were reduced to tearful lads, bereft and heartbroken, but hopefully the better for the experience.

Austin and Vera sat in the back seat of Ruth's car during the ride home. The dog sat obediently while Vera stroked his head and spoke to him about his new home and all the people he would meet in the days ahead. After a while, Austin laid down on the seat and put his head in Vera's lap. He remained there for the rest of the ride. A bond had formed immediately and would continue for many years.

Austin joined Vera at Longview Drive in 2013. The two became devoted to each other. Austin was the new male in Vera's life and was a faithful companion. Vera talked to him constantly and swore that he understood most of what she said. She fussed over him, walked him, and took him to the vet for regular check-ups. She fed him well and offered him treats a little too often. He became rather chunky over the years.

For some time, the hallucinations that Vera experienced, became infrequent and she seemed to be coping well. She missed driving her little car (the one that Ed had bought her when he had damaged hers in a minor accident years ago) and the freedom and independence that it had afforded her. She relied on Ruth and Helen to take her shopping and to appointments and visits. The car sat in the driveway, a constant reminder of how her life had changed. She managed alone in the house but became increasingly forgetful. She recognised this problem in herself and coped by posting more and more notes and keeping more notebooks with information for her to refer to. She began labelling items with notes about where it was purchased or who bought it for her and when. She tucked notes in her jewellery box about particular items of special value or sentiment. She constantly fretted about her finances, checking her bank statements often to remind herself of the balance. She misplaced things regularly, her house keys, her wallet, her bag, her medication, a letter, her glasses. She got frustrated with herself and sometimes was reduced to tears. She would call one of her daughters in distress, her voice clearly shaken and tearful.

"I've lost my wallet! I've looked everywhere. It's not here. I think it has been stolen."

"Oh, Mum, I'm sure it hasn't been stolen. Take a break from looking. It will turn up soon." Frances said.

"No, it won't! I tell you; it's gone."

"Have you looked in all your drawers? Maybe you tucked it away for safe keeping. What about the office? Maybe you put it away in there?"

"I've checked everywhere!"

"Now Mum, try not to worry, worst case scenario, we will have to replace the cards you kept in it."

"Oh, I'm fed up! Why does this keep happening to me?"

"I expect Ruth will come over after work to help you find it. Just relax."

Ruth would inevitably find the lost wallet tucked

between the cushions of the couch or hidden on the shelf of the closet.

One day Ruth popped in to have a cup of tea with Vera and there was a packed suitcase waiting beside the front door. "What is this suitcase doing here, Mum? Going somewhere?" She said with a chuckle.
"Yes. I am waiting for the young men to come. They are taking me to Disney World."
"*What*? What young men? Who are they?"
"I don't know. I was just told to be packed and ready early this morning. They haven't come yet though. They're late."
"Mum… I think you had a vivid dream last night. You are not going to Disney World."
"I'm sure I am."
"No Mum. I think your dream must have seemed very real. But think about it, why would young men who you don't know be coming to take you to Disney World?"
"Well, I… don't know… but they said to be ready."
"Come on, Mum. Let's unpack this bag and then we'll have a nice cup of tea."

During another consultation with her sisters, it was decided that Vera needed a daily caretaker. They were concerned about their mother's mental state and wanted her to be safe. Ruth suggested that she call *Visiting Angels* to set up a schedule for someone to provide help and care. Several different women came but Vera was resentful and angry. "*I don't need them here! I don't know them, and I don't want someone in my house every day.*"
"But Mum, they are there to help you. They will stop you worrying and getting confused. They will take you places, shop with you and help prepare meals," Ruth

reasoned. "Won't that be nice?"

"*No.* I don't trust them. I am fine on my own!"

Ruth sighed with frustration and reported back to her sisters, with whom she discussed an alternate plan. Vera had a wonderful neighbour, Tanya, who had lived next door with her family for many years. Tanya was very fond of Vera and took to taking breakfast over to her in the morning and often a small meal in the evening. Vera would call her for help when she could not reach one of her daughters and she came to the rescue on many occasions. She would search the house from top to bottom with Vera to find a missing item. The elusive wallet was found in many unusual places, on the porch under a seat cushion, in a coat pocket hanging in the closet, tucked behind a book in the bookcase. When the girls discovered just how much Tanya was helping Vera, taking her shopping, to church services from time to time, to the pharmacy and calling Ruth when she noticed a problem or when Vera was especially distressed, they insisted that Tanya accept some compensation. Tanya refused, "I want to do this out of the goodness of my heart," she said.

"We want you to accept out of the goodness of ours," Frances responded. "It gives us such peace of mind to know that you are keeping an eye on Mum and helping in so many ways." And so, an arrangement was made, and the girls breathed easier.

In May 2014, Ruth and Stefan got married. The couple had been together for three years and Ruth's life had become fuller and easier with a loving, caring partner who shared the living expenses of the home. They enjoyed life together, eating out, going on trips and becoming part of each other's families. Stefan was twice divorced and had a grown son and daughter, Chris and Nicole. His children visited often and Ruth enjoyed their company. Stefan attended Ruth's family's gatherings as well as grilling for them when they came for a visit at home with Ruth. The wedding was on St. George Island, which was a favourite place for all the family. They rented a large house with many bedrooms which accommodated a number of their guests. Stefan's brothers and their families rented beach cottages close by. Vera, Tiphanie (now pregnant with the twins), Cliff and Kendall, Adam, Frances and Joe, Stefan's son Chris and his girlfriend, Christina, and Nicole all stayed in the big beach house. Helen, Matt, Marissa and Matt's daughter, Courtney, stayed at a hotel on the island. Cliff was the justice of the peace who performed the ceremony, and it was a relaxed, happy long weekend enjoyed by all. Ruth and Stefan had brought plenty of food and drinks and everyone pitched in with preparing meal and cleaning up. There was a pool, fishing pier and kayaks available, and there was plenty of time to just sit and chat and enjoy the sunrise and sunset. Vera was happy to see Ruth settle down with Stefan. Ruth had been alone for a long time, and she deserved a happy relationship. But Vera was a little unsettled in the big house, having trouble finding her bedroom, opening doors unexpectedly, startling other family members. In the past, she had been at the centre of parties and celebrations, moving easily from group to group joining in the conversations. Her laugh often rang out as she told a funny story or found something humorous. But, at the big house, she was overwhelmed, seemingly not quite sure where she was and what was going on, sometimes wandering aimlessly trying to get her bearings.

The following year, Tiphanie and her family, which now included twins Samantha and Cyrus born in December 2014, moved from Tallahassee to Crawfordville, a forty-five-minute drive away. Crawfordville was a quiet, growing town, very rural with neat, new developments sprouting up on so much available land. Ruth and Stefan had been planning some renovations to Ruth's small home in Tallahassee. They had contractors come to give suggestions and prices to open the house up, knock down walls, modernise the kitchen, but ultimately, they decided that they liked Crawfordville too, and contracted with a builder to build a house there in a new development. Vera was interested when they took her out to see the site periodically to see the progress on the construction. "Wouldn't Dad have liked to see this being built?" she mused. "I can just see him giving it a thorough inspection."

Ruth and Stefan moved into their new home in May 2015. They were thrilled with its open kitchen, living room and dining room. They had a large master bedroom suite and two other bedrooms. The backyard was fenced in, they added a pergola over the patio and enjoyed planting flowerbeds, trees and palms. There was a screened-in porch with a perfect view of dramatic sunsets, where they could sit with a drink in the evenings. The only drawback for Ruth was the distance she would now have to travel to visit her mother and to take care of her. Helen was still nearby, however, and there was Tanya next door. Ruth sometimes picked Vera up to spend the weekend with her in Crawfordville. However, her mother seemed a bit lost, out of her comfort zone, up at night wandering around. She would get confused when she saw Stefan's dog, Lance. "But where is my dog? Where is Austin?" She would inquire.

"He's fine, Mum. Tanya is taking care of him while you are here visiting."

Vera had also become incontinent and had frequent accidents. She did not like to wear the protective underwear, or she would forget and then become so upset when she lost control. During a visit to Connecticut, Frances collaborated with her, reminding her to use the undergarments and pack extra when they were going out. "Wear them, Mum. It will put your mind at ease." Vera was happy to see Yvonne again during that trip. Yvonne and Barbara had moved back to Connecticut in 2006. Both were now widows. Barbara's husband David had died too early of pancreatic cancer and Yvonne's dear Bob had died following a stroke in 2003. Vera and Yvonne always dropped back into their natural ease and comfort with each other. They loved to reminisce about old times, family members long gone, and repeat the often-told funny stories from the past. Inevitably, the two would be bent over double at a humorous memory, wiping tears from their eyes. This was Vera's comfort zone. Talking about the distant past, reliving the war years and the hardships of that time brought her a feeling of pride, accomplishment and satisfaction. She recalled details perfectly, telling Frances and Barbara about her life back then and the sacrifices that had to be made. But she revelled in it. It was part of her life that had always been with her. It had influenced her thinking, her attitudes and her strength. It was amazing that she remembered those years in perfect detail but could not remember what she had eaten for breakfast or what day it was.

Sad news came on New Year's Day in 2016. Christmas in Connecticut had been its usual, busy, happy holiday. Frances had a Christmas Eve bash and Cheri hosted Christmas Day. All the family was there including Barbara and Yvonne. And then Barbara called to tell Frances that

Yvonne had fallen ill. A blood clot had suddenly developed in her bowel and was causing her great pain. At Yale New Haven Hospital, the doctor said it was life-threatening and must be operated on immediately. Yvonne survived the surgery but died soon after in the early hours of New Year's Day. Barbara was heartbroken and Frances was shocked. Even though Yvonne was eighty-eight years old, she was still a lovely looking woman, gentle, caring and dignified. She had looked the picture of health at Christmas. How could this have happened so suddenly? She had to break the news to her mother. She and Yvonne had always remained so close even though they lived so far apart. It was a dreaded call to make.

"Mum, I am afraid I have some sad news to tell you."

"Oh, dear! What is it?"

"It's Auntie Yvonne. I'm sorry to say, she died yesterday." There was a long silence and then almost in a whisper, "What happened? How did she die?"

"It was a sudden blood clot, Mum. She was in hospital. They tried to save her with surgery, but she was not strong enough to handle it."

"Oh… poor Yvonne." Another long silence. "How old was she?"

"Eighty-eight, Mum."

"That's right, she is just a little bit older than me." Her voice quavered. "Oh dear, she was the closest relative that I had left."

"Not true. What about us?"

"Well, you know what I mean… from years ago, from my mother and father, from England."

"Yes, I know what you mean." This gentle, loving, devoted woman and cousin to Vera, lifelong friend, and confidante, was gone from her life.

Tanya began calling Ruth more often as she was concerned with Vera's failing memory and anxiety. The hallucinations were back, mostly the nighttime visits by Maurice, the woman and the little boy. The girls decided that there must be an unresolved issue, either in Vera's conscious or subconscious mind which brought on this repeated dream.

"Could it have something to do with the secret that she will take to the grave?" Frances wondered.

"Could be," Ruth answered. "Or it could be something that her imagination created for one reason or another."

"Guess we'll never know."

Tanya noticed the lights on in Vera's house very late at night and then one night, at midnight, she saw Vera wandering around the front yard in her nightgown. She brought her back inside and made sure she was back in bed before she left. The next morning, Tanya called Ruth about the episode. She was worried for Vera's safety.

There was a long, difficult conference call between the three sisters discussing the situation and deciding what had to be done. They shared concerns, debating whether *that* time had come. Had Vera reached the point where she would need more care? In home help? Perhaps live in with one of the three of them? They had several calls attempting to resolve the issue. Helen thought that perhaps Vera could live with her, Matt and Marissa. Ruth knew that her mother would not be comfortable at her home in Crawfordville and Frances thought that a permanent move to Connecticut would cause a huge disruption for her mother. Everything would be so different and strange, and she would not see her friends and Florida family. They struggled with the dilemma, each wondering if their mother would be happy in their homes and what could be done to make it work.

They discussed assisted living. Ruth and Helen would investigate places in and around Tallahassee to determine if that was the best option.

Frances wanted Vera to come up to Connecticut for Thanksgiving. It would most likely be the last time she would visit and see all the family up north. She discussed it with her sisters who decided that they could make it work. Helen would take her mother to Jacksonville so that the flight would be direct to Hartford. They were able to get gate passes so that Helen could see Vera safely to the boarding gate and Frances would be waiting at the gate when she disembarked at the other end. They also arranged for a wheelchair escort on and off the plane. Ruth helped her pack everything she would need for cooler weather, and all went well with the transportation plan. The visit, which was for ten days, proved to be overwhelming for Vera. She became muddled often, not knowing where she was and why she was there. She enjoyed seeing the family but forgot the names of her great grandchildren. She would forget that she was in Connecticut, the layout of the house, where they were going and where they had been. Frances realised that her mother was quite anxious and unsettled during the visit and tried hard to keep her calm so that she could enjoy her time with them all. On Thanksgiving Day, a traditional dinner was served with the family in attendance. There were twelve around the table, including Barbara, who was pleased to see Vera again. During the Thanksgiving visit Vera asked Barbara more than once, "Well, where's your mother? Why isn't she here? Where's Yvonne."

Several times when Frances came downstairs in the morning, she would find Vera sitting fully dressed on her bed with her suitcase packed waiting to go home. Frances had to remind her mother that the visit was not yet over. She put a whiteboard in the room with the day's date and the date she would be leaving, to help her understand and keep track. However, it did not help. Vera was not able to retain the information. The bag would be packed again the next morning. Frances did her best to keep her distracted with short trips out and conversations that she knew would engage her mother. World War II was a safe topic. Vera could recall everything about that time in her life and although Frances had heard the stories and memories many times, she listened again and again. Vera also enjoyed talking about her childhood and family in England, the happy times, the funny incidents, the loss of her father, Maurice's eventful working life. These conversations with a nice cup of tea or lunch salvaged a difficult time for Frances. She knew her mother would never visit again. It was too difficult, but she wanted to cherish their time together and prayed that her mother's mind would not deteriorate to the extent that she would not know her or any of the family in the future.

When Frances took Vera to the airport for her journey home, she had a gate pass and wheeled her mother to the gate. "Your mother is going home?" an airline employee asked. "Did you have a nice visit?" he asked Vera.

"Oh, yes, thank you very much."

"Wonderful! How nice that you were able to come. God bless you." Then quietly he said to Frances, "You are lucky to still have her. I lost my mother recently and I miss her terribly." It was a long, sad, tearful drive for Frances as she drove home alone from the airport.

Ruth found Pacifica, an assisted living facility, on Monroe Street, three miles from Vera's home. She arranged to take a tour of the facility with her mother in early December. They saw two available nice-sized rooms which included a refrigerator, microwave and private bathroom. They took a look at the communal spaces, dining room, music room and gardens, and learned about the bus which took residents to locations around town. There were organised bus trips and outings and various activities offered during the week. There were exercise sessions, discussion groups, arts and crafts, worship services, holiday parties, social hours, games and quizzes, health and wellness presentations and much more. The residents brought their own furnishings for their room to make it comfortable and familiar. Vera knew about Pacifica, having passed it countless times on Monroe Street during her life in Tallahassee. The director who took them around was charming and the staff and residents greeted her warmly and cheerfully. Everyone was so welcoming and friendly that Vera found herself chatting away with the staff and residents quite comfortably and easily. The whole episode reminded Ruth of a movie she had seen years ago, *Funny Farm,* starring Chevy Chase, where he decides the country life is not for him and puts his house up for sale. The townsfolk help him find a buyer by providing Currier and Ives scenes of Christmas cheer, neighbours waving and delivering fresh-baked pies, children skating on a frozen pond, the mail carrier chatting like an old friend on his rounds, a perfectly happy place full of kind and caring and cheerful people.

Vera liked the atmosphere and the fact that it was not as she had imagined with residents all in wheelchairs staring listlessly into space. She could choose the activities in which she would participate, or she could stay in her room if she wanted private, quiet time to herself. She was very happy that a minibus was available every day to take residents shopping. She had disliked being dependent on friends and family to get out and about.

"Well, what do you think, Mum?" Ruth asked when they had a private moment.

"I think it is very nice."

"Shall we go to the director's office and tell her we will take one of the rooms she showed us? Which one did you like better?"

"Yes, I think we should. I liked the corner room best. There were two windows, one in the living room and one in the bathroom. I like a lot of light."

"Alright then. Let's go." Ruth was so relieved. How nice it was going to be to have her mother settled and safe. They signed up for the corner room that day. Vera would take occupancy on 1st January 2017.

When Ruth described the establishment to her sisters, they discussed the cost and decided it was a good choice. She had funds to cover the cost for over a year and during that time the house could be sold which would pay for many more years.

"What about Austin?" Helen asked.

"She can have Austin with her, if she wants," Ruth answered. "But she will be responsible to walk him, pick up after him, feed him…"

"I don't know if she will be able to manage that," said Frances.

"Well, there *are* residents who have their dogs with them, but yes, I don't know how she will handle that. She will have to take him down in the elevator to the doggie area several times a day. She won't be able to let him out the front door into a fenced-in yard like she does at home."

"Yeah… it will be tough during the winter and on rainy days," Helen interjected. "What if I take him? I already have Jack. Austin knows us and my house and Mum will be able to see him when she comes to visit."

"That's nice of you," Ruth responded happily.

"Guess we will have to talk it through with Mum and see what she wants to do," Frances said.

Vera struggled with the decision for a while. She would be so sad to part from Austin after so many years. The two were very close and devoted, but she thought he would be happier with Helen, and she recognised that caring for him in the assisted living was beyond her capability. The decision was made. Vera would spend her last Christmas in her home with Austin and would move on to Pacifica in the new year.

CHAPTER THIRTY-THREE

After Christmas, Ruth and Stefan moved the bigger items using Stefan's truck into Vera's new room at Pacifica. They did a bed swap with Helen, who took Vera's queen-sized bed for her guest bedroom and gave her mother a quite new single bed that had belonged to Marissa before she moved up to a double size. They moved Vera's favourite recliner chair, a side table, chest of drawers and her free-standing dining cabinet into the room. Ruth was then able to move the smaller items herself in numerous trips back and forth from Longview Drive to Pacifica. She bought a small table and two chairs, an area rug and a low bookcase which also served as a stand for the television. She also brought some pictures and photographs for the walls and new bedding including a colourful comforter for the bed and pretty throw cushions. She brought a few plates, cups, and some silverware, as well as towels, toiletries, books, some carefully selected photograph albums and a box of cherished letters that Vera had kept over the years. She debated about bringing those, thinking it might make her mother sad to read them, but she could not deny her such beloved treasures. When Ruth surveyed the finished room, she was very satisfied. It looked neat, bright, cheerful, and welcoming.

On 1st January 2017, Ruth took Vera to her new home. There were decorations still up from the holidays and celebration of the New Year. Vera was very happy with the room, oohing at her familiar items as well as the new bed. "It all fits in here very well, doesn't it?" Ruth showed her where everything had been placed. "Look, Mum. Your chest of drawers is here in your closet. I have put your underwear and socks in the top drawers, but the bottom ones are empty for you to put what you want in them." She opened the refrigerator to show her mother that she had stocked it with yogurt, fruit, milk, juice, butter and cheese. "You will have your meals in the dining room but here are some things for snacks and milk for tea. Tea bags and sugar are on the hutch, and I got you a Hot Shot to make hot water."

"Oh, thank you. You will have to show me how it works."

"Yes, it's very easy. Watch me, I'll show you." Ruth went through the process several times and then showed Vera her telephone. "I have pre-set the phone with my phone number, as well as Frances' and Helen's. All you do is pick up the receiver, push the button with the name of who you would like to call, and it will go through. I arranged for you to have the same phone number that you had at home so everyone will be able to reach you too." Vera nodded. "And here is your call button on the wall beside your bed. If you ever need help or do not feel well, just push it and a member of the staff will come to help you."

"Oh! Really? That's very nice."

"Well, let's go down to the dining room now and have lunch and then we'll come back up and put away the things in the bags we brought with you today."

Residents were arriving in the dining room as Vera and Ruth entered. They made their way to an empty table and sat down.

"You can't sit there!" a woman announced gruffly.

"Everyone has assigned seats in here," another woman added haughtily.

"Oh, well this is our first day," Ruth replied rather put

out. "We don't know all the procedures yet."

A lady sitting at a corner table waved them over. "Sit with me," she said. "I'm Isabelle, a sort of ambassador here at Pacifica. You must be Vera. Welcome. Never mind those two, they can get a bit bossy at times. You will be at my table, Vera, with Carol and Ann. They are very nice. They will be down soon. Now look, here is the menu for today. Put your name at the top and circle the items you would like for lunch." Vera smiled. "Oh, how nice she said." Ruth breathed a sigh of relief. She was afraid that the unfriendly ladies might have upset and rattled her mother. This first day was going to be difficult enough without dealing with nasty attitudes.

Back in the room, Ruth helped Vera unload her bags and showed her again where everything was kept. Then it was time for her to go. "I've got some errands to run before I go home, I will call you later and see how you are doing," she said cheerily. On her way out she found Isabelle, the ambassador.

"Would you mind keeping an eye on my mother?" she asked. "It may take her a while to learn her way around and if she forgets to come down for dinner, would you be able to go to her room to remind her?"

"Yes... yes, of course. Now don't you worry. She will soon feel right at home. I will watch out for her and help her. That's what I do here."

"Thank you... thank you."

Ruth drove home full of worry, regret, guilt, and sorrow with tears sliding down her cheeks. She could not help but think that she had incarcerated her mother in a way, placed her in the care of strangers where she would live the rest of her days. Were they doing the right thing? She so hoped that her mother would settle in. It reminded her of the first day she had dropped her children off at kindergarten and all the sadness that came along with it as they entered another phase of their lives.

Vera did adjust after a while. She soon discovered residents who would make good companions and those whose company she enjoyed. She also latched onto Don, a portly gentleman who she referred to as "her boyfriend." She looked for him all the time and sat with him as much as possible. Ruth called Frances about it.

"Well, that's Mum, isn't it? Seems like she has to have a man at the centre of her life."

Don, though, did not last long. He transferred to another assisted living facility, a more expensive, deluxe residence. She then discovered James, an African American man, quiet, calm and lonely. The two were good for each other, Vera brought James out of his shell more and encouraged him to join in more activities. James helped Vera feel at home and not fret or worry so much. They began to spend more and more time together.

Vera was given a walker that had a seat and storage container in which she placed her handbag. In the handbag she always had a wad of napkins, sugar packets, the activities schedule and some of her cherished letters. She carried her key on a lanyard around her neck, sometimes not returning to her room until she was tired and ready for bed. Frances often tried calling her mother at various times of the day, not reaching her until well into the evening. "I've been trying to get you all day," Frances would say.

"Oh, I've been so busy today. I went to exercise. We all sat in a circle and threw the ball to each other. It was going all over the place, and we would laugh and laugh. We had such a good time. We had a trivia game in the afternoon. I enjoyed that. Got quite a few of the of the answers too."

There were activities every day. Vera joined in most of them, even arts and crafts, which she disliked. But she laughed at her poor effort when it was done. There were presentations about health, history and music. There were weekly worship services and bible study classes. There were holiday celebrations and birthday parties. There were visiting choirs when they could join in with the singing. Bus excursions took them to view gardens, shows, concerts and interesting landmarks. There was a social once a week when the residents could enjoy a glass of wine or beer, mingle and chat. The courtyard had a pagoda, chairs, tables, flowers and birdfeeders. James taught Vera how to play checkers and although she was not a strong opponent, James was very patient with her. "Now, Vera. You can't move onto that square, can you? Remember the rules." They watched television together in the evenings, sometimes in the big, communal living room where a popcorn machine always had fresh popcorn bagged and there for the taking, or in each other's rooms.

Sometimes, however, Vera became confused and resentful. She would call Ruth to complain.

"How long do I have to stay here in this hospital? I feel much better now. I think I can go home."

"Mum, you are not in a hospital, you are in assisted living."

"Well, when can I go home?"

"You are home, Mum. Pacifica is where you live now."

"You mean I have to live here for the *rest of my life*!"

"Well... you like it there, don't you? It's a very nice place."

"Yes, but I didn't think I had to stay here forever!"

There were conversations with Frances also, often about her mother, Florrie. "I haven't seen my mother in ages," she complained.

"Mum, Nana has been gone a long time. She died in 1975. You went back for the funeral, remember?"

"I did?" she responded incredulously.

Frances spoke to Ruth about their mother's confusion. "She is carrying Nana's letters around with her all the time. I think she reads them and thinks they are recent and that is why she thinks her mother is still alive. Nana's letters are so full of her personality, newsy, and funny. I think mum is transported back in time when she reads them and is reading them as if they just arrived."

"Yes, I think so. Oh dear, I had wondered whether or not to leave them with her. Maybe I should remove them from her room."

"Oh, I don't know. She saved them all these years and reading them must make her feel very close to her mother again. It seems a shame to take that away."

One day when Ruth was visiting, Vera seemed agitated.

"I've been looking everywhere for my baby. Where's my baby? I can't find her."

"Mum, you don't have a baby."

"Oh, yes, I do! It's a little blond girl."

"Do you mean Helen? Helen is all grown up, Mum. She has a daughter, a teenager of her own, Marissa. You remember Marissa."

"Oh... yeeess... I do," she replied haltingly and not convincingly in the least.

Ruth called Helen. "Can you pop in to see Mum sometime today. She is looking for you and thinks you are still a baby. It would probably help if she saw you to bring her back to the present."

"Oh, dear. Yes. I'll stop in after work today."

Only rarely now did Vera have dreams (or visions) of Maurice, but when she did it was always disturbing and upsetting for her as she described him to be cold and distant towards her. "Dad was here last night. He wouldn't even look at me. He had that woman and the little boy with him. I don't know why he bothers to come."

"It was only a dream, Mum," Frances assured her. "Your imagination has got the better of you. Try not to think about it."

In February, Frances and Joe took time off from work and drove to Florida to help get the contents of the house sorted out so that it could be prepared for sale. Vera had enough funds for a year or so at Pacifica, but the house would have to be sold to sustain her beyond that. Ruth and Helen would hold an estate sale but first they went through the house to remove items that family members wanted. They spread out many items on the dining room table and sent pictures to Frances so that she could select some things that she would like to keep. Along with the queen-sized bed, Helen took the sewing machine in the wooden cabinet, a recliner, an antique cabinet, the gold mirror that had been the twenty-fifth wedding anniversary gift from Florrie, a coffee table, a painting and vacuum cleaner. Ruth took some paintings, the daybed and trundle, an antique credenza (sideboard) and Persian rug given to Vera by Ed, and Maurice's tool bench. Frances took a Victorian copper pitcher, some of the artwork she had created for her parents over the years, silver decorative plates which had been given to Maurice and Vera as a wedding gift, and Maurice's prized chess set and chess table. They all took some little trinkets and mementoes too, things they remembered Vera wearing, a piece of jewellery, a favourite tool that Maurice used, a glass bowl, an antique toasting fork, a pen, a figurine, a watch, a teapot.

On the day of the estate sale, Ruth and Helen watched

as so many of their parents' belongings left the house forever. The couch and loveseat went quickly; the couch, where so many family pictures were taken at so many family occasions and holidays. Maurice's bar which he had enjoyed when entertaining, the kitchen table and chairs, the side tables, lamps, books, Maurice's desk chair, the bedroom dresser, and the dining room table and chairs, the set that Maurice had bought so long ago in Connecticut, restored, and moved from house to house. How many dinners, parties, Christmases, celebrations, card games had been enjoyed round that table? It had been in the family from the early days in Fairfield with the Lundbechs; parties, lunches with Yvonne, dinners with Florrie and Ted during their visits, adding chairs for the girls' spouses, then grandchildren and great grandchildren, and finally, Ed.

Ruth arranged to have a dumpster in the driveway the day before Frances and Joe arrived in February. Then, it was "all hands on deck." Helen and Matt, Frances and Joe and Ruth and Stefan all worked to clear out the house. Decisions had to be made along the way: toss, donate or keep if someone decided they wanted a particular item. Joe took on the office. He went through each file, only keeping important or sentimental personal documents. Everything else he ripped up or put through the shredder. He went through drawer after drawer, file after file, box after box. Finally, he tackled Maurice's business records which had been stored on the shelf in the office closet. It all ended up shredded. Joe watched it reduced to a tangle of paper strips with overwhelming sorrow. It represented a lifetime of work, struggle, determination, success and failure. It represented a livelihood and Maurice's enduring optimism of the next project. He was shredding it all.

Cliff sorted through the garage. A few more things were kept but almost everything ended up in the dumpster.

Within a couple of days, the house was empty. The family looked around and felt the strangeness of it. The house echoed, the bareness of it was so unfamiliar. The personality of the house had disappeared. It had no heart. They talked about putting the house up for sale. Should it be sold "as is" or would some updates significantly increase the price? Ruth suggested that she contact the realtor who had handled the sale of her house almost two years ago to see what he thought would be best.

The realtor informed Ruth that some improvements would indeed increase the price enough to make it worthwhile and would speed up the sale also. It fell to Ruth to coordinate the renovation. She contacted a roofing company to install a new roof, a siding contractor to make some repairs to the outside, a flooring installer, painter, electrician to install some new switches and fixtures and a plumber to install a new sink and faucet in the hall bathroom. It meant a lot of driving back and forth from Crawfordville to Tallahassee for Ruth. Fortunately, she had recently retired from her work at Tallahassee Memorial Hospital where she had worked as a laboratory technologist for twenty years and had the time to devote to the renovations. It also provided her with a sense of duty and accomplishment. She was thrilled as each step was completed and the house became modernised, brighter and fresher. It was satisfying for her to witness the transformation and discover the full potential of the house. She sent pictures to Frances of the rooms as they were finished. New vinyl, woodgrain planking was laid in the kitchen, living room and down the hall and new carpeting was installed in the bedrooms. All the walls were painted a soft off-white, the hall bathroom was updated with a vinyl floor, a new vanity, sink and faucet, new overhead fans and light fixtures were installed and undercabinet lighting in the kitchen. It was ready for sale.

While the house was on the market, Ruth took it upon herself to attend some Alzheimer's meetings in her hometown. They were extremely helpful. During a three-way conference call with her sisters, she discussed what she had learned.

"We have been doing it all wrong," she said.

"We should not be trying to correct Mum all the time. It only distresses her."

"Yes, I can see that," Frances admitted. "It's as if she has to relive losing her mother or dad all over again."

"What do we do then?" Helen asked.

"We deflect. We give her an answer that puts her mind at rest. For example, if she asks why her mother has not been to visit, we say that she has been busy. Perhaps she will come next week."

"So that timeline I made her so that she could refer to it to remember when people had died, babies were born etc. is really of no value," Frances sighed.

"No, she cannot process or retain the information. It just frustrates her. We should just give her gentle answers and change the subject."

"Okay," said Helen. "I can do that."

"I think we will all be happier... most of all, Mum," Ruth concluded.

Vera often mixed up the time of day. She had been up at all times of the night at home before moving to Pacifica. She continued to wake at night and would rummage through the closet, her drawers, and boxes. Often, she would sit with one of her photograph albums on her lap, slowly turning the pages as tears filled her eyes and blurred the faces. Sometimes she left the room and wandered the halls. The staff gently took her back to her room, reminding her that it was the middle of the night, and she should stay in her room. One time, the night nurse had her sit with her at the nurse's station for a while before she was able to leave her work and return Vera to her room. The next day Vera called Ruth complaining that she had been locked up all night in an office. "I feel like I am in prison!" she complained, "When can I go home?"

Ruth wondered if it would be helpful for Vera to see her house renovated. She knew her mother would be interested to see it in its new state, but would it make her terribly sad? She discussed it with Frances.

"Oh, I don't know," Frances said. "She may want to move back in," she said with a chuckle.

"It just looks so nice. I'd love to show it to her. I think she will be so impressed and pleased to see it looking so new. And I thought maybe it might make her realise that she has moved on and won't be going back there again."

"Hmmm... it's a tough call. Maybe ask her. When she is having a good day, tell her the house is now for sale and has been renovated. Would she like to see it before it is sold?"

"Yes, perhaps that is the approach. I'll try it."

So, Ruth asked her mother during her next visit. Vera was bubbly and laughing about the previous day when they had played a group game with a giant ball. "It was so funny! You should have seen us!"

"I'm sure it was amusing," Ruth smiled. "I stopped in to see if you were interested in seeing the house on Longview. It is up for sale now and it looks so good."

"Oh? Longview? My old house?"

"Uh huh."

"Oh, well yes. I'd like to see it."

"Great. And I'll take you out to lunch afterwards."

"Ooh, that will be nice. Just a minute. Let me tell James

that I will be gone for a while." Vera was never far from James. The two of them had become so close that everyone knew they were a couple, attending most of the activities together, sitting together in the lounge, the courtyard or in each other's rooms. She looked for him first thing in the morning and parted from him last thing at night. She often had trouble remembering his name, though. "I was showing some pictures in my photograph album to... oh, what is his name? Why can I never remember it?"

"James?" Ruth would ask.

"Yes, James! That's right... *James!*" And she would bend over laughing at herself, reaching out to grasp Ruth's arm to steady herself.

When Ruth pulled up to the house, Vera studied it with a slightly puzzled look. The outside had not changed at all, but it still seemed that she was struggling to remember it.

"Yes... it does look familiar," she said wonderingly. Ruth was amazed. This house had been her mother's home for almost thirty years. She had pulled into the driveway countless times to the same view. Surely the colonial blue of the siding, the brick facing below the windows, the bay window in the living room would jog her memory. Vera followed Ruth up to the front door. When she stepped inside, she looked around appraisingly. "I do like these floors. This is a nice size room."

"Look, Mum. The floor continues all the way into the kitchen and down the hall too."

"Oh, yes. Very nice."

"There's new carpet in the bedrooms. Doesn't it look nice?"

"Yes, it does. This will make a very nice home for somebody."

"Look in the bathroom. A new sink and vanity.

"Do you like the light fixtures? This one pulls down over where the kitchen table used to be."

"Oh, I don't remember. I had a kitchen table here?"

Ruth noticed her mother looking out through the French doors to the porch. "Oh look, a nice screened-in porch. Oh, I would like that! She opened the doors and stepped out. "Very nice." Vera walked through the porch and out the side door, into the back yard. "Rose bushes! Maurice loved rose bushes," she said. She stared down at one of the bushes for a long time. Ruth wondered if she remembered that she had scattered her husband's ashes there. Gently she touched her mother's arm. "Let's go for lunch now," she said.

Later, when she phoned Frances, Ruth recounted the episode to her.

"I don't think she fully understood where she was. Some things looked familiar to her, but it was different enough that she could not relate to the house much at all."

"Was she sad?"

"No, not at all. She looked around the house and commented as if she was a potential buyer. I was the one who was sad at her loss of memory of it."

"Well, at least it didn't make her miserable and depressed and you were able to show it off to her. Maybe, we just don't mention it again."

"Yes, I think you're right."

When Vera returned to Pacifica, it was truly home. She knew the routine, all the communal spaces, where the music room was, where the worship services were held, the beauty salon where she got her hair cut once a month, the sign-up sheet for bus trips, when to go to the dining room, where to sit, where she could get the sheet of activities for the week, where to put her clothing that needed laundering, whose company she enjoyed, who she avoided. Helen picked her up from time to time to take her home for dinner and a visit with Austin. She always remembered him, as he did her.

"Here's my dog," she would say. "Here's my Austin. Have you been a good boy?" Austin would lay at her feet during the entire visit while Vera chatted to him and petted him lovingly. Vera's life was quite full, busy and happy at Pacifica. Her three daughters were relieved and grateful for the care she received. The staff all loved her. They joked and laughed with her, listened to her stories and words of wisdom and helped her with particular tasks. Fortunately, Vera was always able to dress herself and care for herself in many ways. She kept her room neat and tidy and made the bed every day. Her medications were brought to her in the morning and at night. She did not have to think about it at all. She had been very anxious about taking them when she was at home, keeping many charts and notes to keep them organised. And she had James. James was at the centre of her life. The three sisters often talked about it. They wondered at this need of their mother's to always have a male central figure. Did it go all the way back to her childhood when she had lost her father so suddenly? Was she always searching to fill that loss, that hole in her life? Vera and James spent almost all day together. James told Vera that he had property and was planning to build a house. He said that he and Vera would live there together when it was built. Vera loved the idea. She told her daughters about it.

"Of course, James and I plan to leave here one day, you know. He has a lot of property and has plans already drawn up for a house that he is going to build on it."

"Oh, really?" Frances would say, remembering the Alzheimer's instruction, "well that will certainly be very nice for you both."

During another visit, Ruth noticed a big sign on the reception desk. "THE REMOTE FOR THE TV IN THE LOUNGE IS MISSING. IF YOU FIND IT, PLEASE RETURN IT. THANK YOU. She smiled to herself as she continued up to Vera's room thinking it could be anywhere. Someone inadvertently must have walked off with it. She chatted with Vera for a while and then made them both a cup of tea using the Hot Shot that she had bought her. She did not think her mother ever used it herself, or watched her own television, even the phone had become daunting for her. Operating anything electronic, anything that had buttons, was too complicated. No matter how many times Ruth explained and showed her the process, she could not retain the information. She would still answer the phone but calls out were becoming rare. Ruth seemed to be the only one she would call occasionally. After their tea, Ruth washed the cups and put them back on the hutch. She opened the drawer to put the spoons away and there lying alongside the silverware tray, was a television remote, not Vera's, which was black, this one was beige and had a label across the bottom of it that said, "Lounge TV Remote."

"Oh, Mum, what is this doing here?" she asked, holding the remote up to show her mother.

"I don't know. What is it?"

"It's the TV remote for the flatscreen in the lounge downstairs. There is a sign on the reception desk saying that it is missing."

"Well… I don't know how it got in here."

"Oh, dear. Well, never mind. I'll put it back when we go down for lunch."

Ruth furtively placed the remote on one of the side tables as she passed through the lounge on the way to the dining room.

The updated, remodelled house on Longview Drive sold quickly for a good price, as the realtor had assured Ruth it would. Since it was empty, the closing took place early in June. It was with relief and sorrow that Ruth signed the paperwork in the attorney's office and handed over the keys. She had left a pretty china cup and saucer and a box of teabags on the large windowsill of the bay window with a note: *Please accept this little gift. There have been many happy times in this house, parties, celebrations and family gatherings. We have enjoyed countless cups of tea together over the years. We wish you good luck and much happiness in your new home.*

CHAPTER THIRTY-FOUR

Ruth told Vera about the sale of the house, but her mother showed little interest. "It fetched a good price, Mum. You will have no financial worries now at all."

"Oh, good," she responded. "I really should get downstairs now, my boyfriend, er... oh!" she giggled. "What's his name... oh dear, why can't I remember?"

"James," Ruth reminded her.

"Yes! James. He will be looking for me." Just then there was a tap on the door. Vera darted across the room to open it. There was James. "Oh, sorry," he said. "I didn't mean to interrupt."

"No problem," Ruth replied. "I was just going. I'll see you again soon," she added as she kissed Vera's cheek.

The year wore on. Frances made several trips down to Florida to visit. She spent a little time at Pacifica, having lunch, sitting in the courtyard, meeting some of the residents. Vera introduced her as "daughter number one." The people she met were all very pleasant and told Frances how much they loved Vera. "She is so funny." "I love talking to her, she is so interesting." "She helps me tidy my room sometimes when my back is bad." "She knows so much about World War II. She had told me so much that I never knew." "She is so good with our trivia quizzes. She often wins, you know."

Sometimes, Frances and Ruth took Vera out to lunch and shopping. Other times, they took her over to Helen's when she got home from work, bringing some take-out for dinner. Vera would sit with Austin, talking away to him as he gazed up her lovingly. They took her to Ruth's house in

Crawfordville, where the family would gather for dinner: Matt, Helen and Marissa, Tiphanie and Cliff, Kendall, Samantha and Cyrus, the twins, who Vera loved to watch, always amazed at how fast they were growing. She sometimes would play simple games with them, giggling when she was corrected by one of the twins for not playing by the rules. Stefan would cook on the grill, Ruth would bring out salads, garlic bread, wine and beer and there would be a luscious dessert of some kind, and of course, tea. Vera spoke often of James, wondering what he was doing, wondering if he missed her and asking when she would be going back. She was increasingly uncomfortable away from her surroundings at Pacifica and felt so far away. She would always comment on the ride to Crawfordville, "It is such a long drive, isn't it?"

The Fourth of July was observed at Pacifica with flags, red, white and blue decorations, holiday arts and crafts made by the residents on display, and patriotic music. There was a "monster mash" Halloween party, and Veteran's Day observances and tributes to residents who had served in the military. For Thanksgiving, the lounge was converted to a huge dining room so that family members could join the residents in a Thanksgiving dinner, and then came Christmas. A large Christmas tree was sparkling in the lounge, decorations hung everywhere, carollers came to entertain, Santa Claus came to visit with a big sack of goodies. Vera enjoyed it all. There was dancing one evening to slow, ballroom style music. James and Vera danced together, James softly singing some of the lyrics to her. A staff member took some video of the event to post on their website and it resulted in some lovely footage of the couple enjoying a tender moment.

Early in 2018, Helen became concerned about Austin.

"He has become very lethargic and won't eat," she told her sisters.

"Okay," said Frances. "Better get him to the vet."

"Mum set some money aside for Austin's care so let's see find out what the problem is," Ruth added.

"And… let's not mention it to Mum. I hope it's nothing serious," Frances groaned.

The vet's diagnosis after some tests and a biopsy was not good. Poor little Austin had cancer. "He will only get worse according to the vet," Helen reported. "He has some medication to help with the discomfort for a while, but it's only a matter of time."

"Oh, no!" said Ruth. "Mum will be devastated."

"Don't tell her," Frances suggested. "She only sees him periodically now. He is not part of her daily routine."

"What if she asks to see him?" Helen asked.

"We'll cross that bridge when we come to it," Frances replied.

In February, at Pacifica, there was Mardi Gras. The staff made it a happy event for the residents. They decorated carts, trolleys and wheelchairs with brightly coloured streamers and balloons and organised a parade. In front of the building the residents sat wearing colourful beads, hats and sunglasses as the staff rolled along in front of them dressed in outlandish costumes, waving and laughing as they went by. They tossed handfuls of candy into the laps of the spectators who clapped and cheered while a selection of jazzy music played. The event was covered briefly on the local evening news. There were Vera and James, front and centre, holding hands.

Frances and Joe decided to make a trip down to Florida to celebrate Vera's eighty-ninth birthday. It would not be a huge party but a gathering of family at Ruth's house. A couple of special gifts were planned: a photobook of Vera's life and a special audio player, similar to a radio, into which selected music and audio could be downloaded. Both gifts required a lot of work and collaboration on the part of the three sisters. All the photographs to be included in the book were scanned, enhanced and uploaded to an online site to be included in the book. The photographs were captioned with names, dates and events. It was a labour of love for Vera's daughters, who were on the phone to each other constantly during the process. The result was amazing. They knew their mother would love it. The music was easy to find and upload to the audio player once the songs had been selected - big band music, wartime songs, favourite old pub songs, classical selections, funny little ditties, and the hits of popular crooners. They also included some excerpts from Winston Churchill's wartime speeches as well as speeches by King George VI and Queen Elizabeth II. Ruth had a decorative blanket made for Vera's bed with photographs of the family. She was careful to include everyone.

It was a happy event. Ruth's house was full, with all the Florida family and Frances and Joe in attendance. Stefan was cooking on the grill, as usual, while Frances and Ruth prepared several sides and ordered a special cake. The children played outside as the adults looked on enjoying some beer and wine together. When the photobook was presented, Vera was thrilled.

"Oh, look at this!" she exclaimed. "A book all about me." She pointed excitedly as she turned each page. "Look at me as a baby!" she laughed. "Wasn't I scruffy...? *I ask you!* Oh, I look a bit neater as a young girl. This picture was taken on one of our camping trips. I loved that checked skirt and jacket I am wearing, with the hat too. I remember feeling very grown up in it. Oh, here's my dad. He looks young and healthy here... I didn't have him very long though," she added softly. She continued on, turning the pages of her life with a full commentary as she went. Her family stood around, listening to stories and family events from long ago that they had heard many times before but enjoying them again one more time. It was a special day gathered around the dining room table together, watching Vera relive her past and remembering more recent photographs and events along with her.

The audio player was then presented, and Vera listened to several old favourites that transported her back to another place and time. She grasped Matt's hand and swayed with him to the music. Matt smiled indulgently, touched that she wanted to share a dance. The audio played on for the rest of the day into the evening. Intermittently, a speech popped up and Vera stood stock still. "Listen... listen," she announced to the group. "It's Churchill... oh, listen to this." Everyone stopped what they were doing and listened. "Oh, yes," she said at the conclusion, "I remember it like it was yesterday." She gazed unseeing for a moment, drawn back to those days that were always with her in a way, and always brought so easily to mind. They were years of terror which induced strength in the population, rationing which created challenge and ingenuity, low morale which ultimately blossomed into newfound pride and patriotism. After living through the war, she could tackle anything. All struggles after those years paled in comparison.

Helen, Matt, and Marissa drove Vera back to Pacifica that night. She had her new blanket over her knees. "Put it on your bed when you get home, Mum," Ruth said. "Then every night, your family with be with you to keep you warm."

Easter followed soon after the birthday party. Pacifica organised an Easter Egg hunt for the grandchildren and great grandchildren of the residents. Ruth and Tiphanie took Samantha and Cyrus to enjoy the event. It was held in the courtyard and was fun for all. The residents and staff looked on with smiles as the children scurried around filling their baskets. There were refreshments and a chance for residents to introduce their families, grandchildren and great-grandchildren to each other. Photos were taken of the generations gathered together. A precious opportunity.

Early in April, Deborah Lundbech, who now lived in Vermont with her family, made arrangements with Ruth to make a visit to Florida. Frances and Ruth had spent some time in Vermont a year or two earlier and Deborah wanted to see Ruth and Stefan's new house and see the Florida family, including her "Auntie" Vera. A day or two after arriving, Deborah and Ruth went to Pacific to bring Vera back to Crawfordville for the day. When they arrived and exited the elevator on Vera's floor, Vera was walking down the hallway pushing her walker towards her room. Deborah and Ruth were behind her, so she did not know they were there. "Hello, Auntie Vera!" Deborah called. Vera stopped in her tracks. That voice was so familiar. She had heard it before so many times but could not place it. She turned and smiled but there was no recognition in her expression. "It's me, Deborah."

"Oh…" Vera said uncertainly.

"Deborah… Lundbech. Hazel and Ray's daughter. You've known me for so many years."

"Hazel and Ray…" she said, thinking and staring.

"Oh, come on, Mum. Let's go to your room and get a few things. We are taking you to my house for the day to visit with Deborah. You'll remember soon when we get to talking and reminiscing."

It was another happy day. Sure enough, as the day went on, Vera's memory was jogged, and she laughed heartily at some of Deborah's stories and memories. Deborah brought her up to date on her family in Vermont, her four boys and her grandchildren and her mother and father, Hazel and Ray.

"I think you last visited when you came up with Frances about four or five years ago. My mother's eyesight has deteriorated even more, I'm afraid, but she manages quite well even so. We take her shopping once a week and to doctor's visits. Dad is in a nursing home. He had a bad fall and needs full time care now. Mum is just not able to handle him. She will be moving in with me soon."

"Oh, dear, oh dear! What is the nursing home like? He must hate it there."

"No, actually, he is quite content. He has a radio, just like yours with all his favourite music recorded. And he has his books. We keep him well supplied. He is very realistic about things and knows he needs to be there. It is a bright and cheerful place and someone in the family pops in every day."

"I'm glad to hear that. Remember me to him, and your mother when you see them, will you?"

"Of course, they will be anxious to hear how you are doing and I'll have photos to show them too."

There were lots of cups of tea around the table, just like old times. Memories came flooding back, intermixed with current events, babies, family members, Nicholas in Arizona now with his family, Deborah's job at the library, and photos she had brought to share. Deborah played the guitar for everyone later in the evening when Helen, Matt and Marissa and Tiphanie, Cliff and the children joined them. She played an assortment of tunes that Vera knew and was able to recall every word as she sang along. The children looked on in amazement to hear the raised voices of the adults, and the words, sometimes so ridiculous and funny that everyone dissolving into giggles at the end. *Knees Up Mother Brown* was especially interesting to them as their great grandmother laughed, explaining the conga line and dance moves that would accompany the singing of the song.

A few days later after Deborah had returned home, Ruth went to Pacifica for a brief visit. She waved to her mother who was sitting with James in the lounge. "May I have your key for a moment, Mum, I am just dropping off some fruit, yogurt and cheese and crackers for your room. I'll be right back down." She put the supplies away noticing that the room was quite clean and tidy as always and was just exiting the room to head back downstairs when a gentleman came out of the door of the adjoining room. Ruth recognised the person as the son of Vera's neighbour, Nancy, who was suffering from dementia also, in a little more advanced stage than Vera. "Would you mind coming in for a moment?" he asked. "There is something in my mother's room that belongs to your mother, I believe."

Ruth popped inside and was surprised to see the blanket she had given to her mother neatly spread across Nancy's bed.

"I don't know how this ended up in here," he continued chuckling. "But I recognised some of the faces in the pictures and knew that it belonged next door."

"Oh, yes. She got this for her birthday in March. Oh, that's funny!" Ruth laughed. "Maybe she brought it in to show your mother and then forgot about it."

"Yes, and my mother forgot that it wasn't hers!"

Ruth put it back on Vera's bed and chuckled all the way down in the elevator. She returned her mother's keys and sat for a while telling her what she had brought and where she had put the food items, before leaving to take care of some errands in town. Vera nodded and thanked her before turning her attention back to James, her boyfriend, the latest man at the centre of her world.

Poor Austin's condition had deteriorated quickly to the point where the decision had to be made to put him down. Helen especially was broken-hearted. The little beagle had become part of her family for a year. He had settled in well, became friends with Jack, Helen's dog, and enjoyed the busier household. He walked several times daily with Jack, Helen and Matt, and enjoyed his occasional visits with Vera. Everyone was sad to lose him. The vet was kind and understanding, making the process as swift and peaceful as possible. Several days later, Helen received a card in the mail of Austin's pawprint made from his ashes. She sobbed when she saw it thinking how upset her mother would be. Hopefully, his memory had faded significantly, and Helen would not have her mother visit for a while. She would go there to Pacifica or take her out somewhere instead. She would keep the news from her as long as possible.

CHAPTER THIRTY-FIVE

It was early one morning, when Ruth got the call. A nurse from Pacifica asked her to come immediately.

"Why? What has happened?"

"We will explain when you get here. You must come *now!*"

It was 6:30 a.m. Ruth and Stefan hurriedly dressed and jumped in his truck. Ruth was physically shaking, and she had a sinking feeling in her stomach. Something was very wrong. She called Helen and asked her to meet them there and then she called Frances as they made their way.

"Pacifica just called. We are on our way there now. They told me to get there right away. I think something awful has happened."

"Oh... no! Oh, dear. I hope she is all right."

"I don't think so. They said *NOW*, get here now!"

"Oh, Ruth. You had better prepare yourself. It may be the worst news," Frances replied as her throat tightened. "Call me as soon as you know anything."

There were police cars in front of the building when Ruth and Stefan arrived. They entered to find Helen waiting for them in the lounge. No one else was around. The lounge was clear of residents, and no one was at the reception desk. Helen was silently weeping in a chair. They rushed over to her dreading the news they were about to hear.

"She's gone! She's dead! Helen sobbed. "I was heading up in the elevator and a cleaning lady stepped in with me. She guessed I was here about Mum, and she told me that she had died in the night. When I got to her floor, the hallway in front of her door had a lot of people standing there, cops and Pacifica staff. A policeman told me to go downstairs and wait for someone to come and speak to me. He wouldn't let me go inside."

"Oh, no!" Ruth cried out. "I just knew it would be bad!" She dropped into a chair and buried her head in her hands. Stefan sat too, shocked, and white-faced. They sat there for half an hour or so waiting, until the residents began to come down for breakfast. "We can't sit here like this," Ruth said. When a policeman appeared, she jumped up. "Is there somewhere we can sit that would be a little more private?" she asked.

"I'll get the nurse, he said.

"I'd like to go up to my mother's room."

"Oh, no. The coroner is examining her now. The nurse will be with you in a moment. Sir?" He motioned to Stefan. "May I speak to you a moment?" he asked, stepping away.

"Do not let your wife go upstairs," he said quietly. "It will only distress her. Don't let the last memory of her mother be of an unpleasant scene."

Ruth was indignant when Stefan returned. "What did he say to you? Why couldn't he speak to *me*?

"He assured me that you should not go up there. He said you would be very upset."

"I like to make my own decisions, not be told what is best for me and…"

Just then the nurse appeared.

"I'm surprised no one was here to greet us and explain things," Ruth said angrily. "This is unacceptable to leave us here like this for so long."

"I'm very sorry," she said. "An emergency like this disrupts our usual routine. Please, follow me into this office where we can be private." When they were all seated, she continued, "I am so sorry about your mother. She was very popular here and will be sorely missed."

"What happened?" Ruth asked.

"It appears that she suffered a massive heart attack sometime during the night. Her door was ajar early this morning, so a staff member poked her head inside to check on her. She was lying on the floor."

"Oh, poor Mum," cried Helen.

"It must have happened very quickly and suddenly sometime after her night pills were brought to her."

"I… I can't quite believe this," Ruth declared. "If I could just see her…"

"It's better that you don't."

"What do we do now? Helen asked.

"I suggest that you go home and contact the funeral home that you would like to officiate. They will take it from there."

"We just go home…" Ruth wondered aloud. "This just doesn't seem real!"

Helen went home to talk to Matt and Marissa and Ruth and Stefan drove back to Crawfordville. Ruth called Frances from the car as they drove. She answered after the first ring, knowing what she was going to hear. "I didn't expect it to be like this," Ruth sobbed. "So suddenly. I saw her yesterday and she was perfectly well." She related the events at Pacifica. "I was disappointed with the way they handled the situation. I don't know why they called us to come immediately. No one was there to greet us and explain things. We weren't allowed to see her so it could have been discussed on the phone."

"Probably could have… but whoever called thought you needed to be there for some reason." Frances was silent for a moment. "Remember?" she continued softly. "Mum always said that she would like to go "**POOF**" when her time came, didn't she? Well, she got her wish. How weird it is going to be without her! It will take some time to process. What do we do now?"

"I will call Bevis Funeral Home when we get home. I'll let you know after I speak to them."

The funeral home made an appointment with Ruth in the afternoon. Helen and Marissa would meet Ruth and Stefan there and Frances would join the conversation on a conference call. It was surreal for them all. The day had started with the dreadful telephone call and here they were making all the final arrangements for their mother, their beloved mother, who they would never see again. Ruth had asked the funeral director if she could see her mother before cremation and he had responded that he would have to prepare her for a viewing which would take some time to make her presentable. "She had been lying on the floor for some time," he said. When he started to explain what he would have to do, Ruth interrupted. "Oh, I understand," she said remembering what the policeman had advised Stefan. "No, that's okay. I don't want her body manipulated in any way. Just tell me please, was she dressed or was she ready for bed when she was found?"

"She was wearing her nightie," the funeral director responded gently.

The date of the funeral was set for Sunday 29th April, which would give enough time for Frances and Joe, Peter and Cheri, Tom and Adam to make arrangements to attend. The cremation had been pre-paid by Vera and Maurice years ago, but the funeral director could not pull up that information on the computer. Ruth had thought to grab the file that her mother had kept with the "paid" notice from the institution before she came. She presented it. "Oh, yes. I see that it was paid. I apologise, our mistake. We moved our location recently and some of our older records have not been updated. You have saved me time digging through old files." There would be a cost to rent the hall at the funeral home for a service or memorial and he set up a meeting for them with the representative at the cemetery that the girls had chosen. It was on Monroe Street, only a half a mile from Longview Drive. It seemed the obvious choice.

All the arrangements were made. A niche was selected, and a brass plaque was designed. It would have a heading of "Brown," a Union Jack, the names Vera and Maurice and their dates of birth and death. There were no ashes for Maurice, which was a cause of great sorrow. The casualness of their father's memorial and the disposition of his ashes had troubled them all for years. They had only discovered about Vera's decision to scatter Maurice's ashes around the rose bush by chance. One day when Ruth had noticed the box that she had kept on the bedside table was missing, she had questioned her mother about it. Vera's daughters wanted their mother's arrangements to be quite different. It would give her daughters comfort and closure and a chance to put their father's name alongside their mother's name on the plaque.

During many phone calls, the details of the funeral service were decided. Peter would be master of ceremonies and would lead the attendees in prayer. Frances would give a eulogy covering the war years, early life and the years in Connecticut, Helen would cover Vera's life in Florida. Ruth was not comfortable speaking publicly, so she declined. She had done so much for her mother over the years, she would leave this last task to her sisters. Cheri, who had a lovely singing voice, would sing a special song. There would be a display of photographs from all times and places of Vera's life and some simple refreshments would be available. The audio player, so recently given as a gift, would be playing in the foyer as the family greeted guests.

Frances and Joe arrived two days prior to the event.

Frances, Ruth and Helen spent a lot of time together making the photograph displays. Frances brought some photos with her, and Ruth and Helen had their selections. It was actually a special time together of closeness, peace, and satisfaction of working together on this last task for their mother. While they were working, a magnificent flower arrangement was delivered. It was sent, "*With all our sympathy and love*," from Hazel, Ray, Deborah and family. They could not make the trip to say goodbye to their old friend but had spoken at length with everyone. There was more work to do to prepare food and make up beds but when Peter and Cheri, Adam and Tom arrived, everything was ready.

There were a lot of people attending. Vera had touched so many lives over the years. Everyone spoke so kindly of her, telling snippets of their experiences, chuckling at some of their memories. Vera had friends of all ages. "I sang with her in the choir," "I took care of her at Pacifica," "She became my friend at church," "I knew her from the British Club," "She came to visit my grannie." The girls, of course, knew many of Vera's old friends; some were couples who were friends of Vera and Maurice for years, there were neighbours, business acquaintances, residents from Pacifica, Senior Center friends. There were friends of Helen, who knew Vera well and enjoyed her company and sense of humour, there were friends of Ruth, who knew her from when she worked at the lab, and dear friends of Frances and Joe who travelled from Jacksonville to attend.

When the formal service began, everyone was ushered into a memorial hall with pews, a dais adorned with flowers, a podium, and a decorative box containing Vera's ashes centred on an altar-like table. Two flags, a Union Jack and the Stars and Stripes represented her two beloved countries.

Peter welcomed everyone, spoke briefly about the

proceedings, and led everyone in prayer. Frances spoke about her mother's early life, telling stories of the war years, her courtship and marriage to Maurice, raising her daughters in England, the decision to emigrate and the years in Fairfield, Connecticut. She told the garbage can story and the plastic telephone incident which brought chuckles to the sad occasion. Joe spoke briefly following Frances, speaking of the difficulties dating the daughter of strict, British parents and of the questionnaire that he was asked to fill out. There were more chuckles. The atmosphere was relaxing. People were enjoying the stories of such an unusual woman. Helen then continued Vera's life starting with the move when she was a teenager from Connecticut to Florida and the culture shock that ensued. There were touching accounts of her parent's concern for her as she became more independent and a touch "on the wild side." She contrasted her upbringing with that of her sisters, referring to how much her parents had mellowed and how much more lenient they were with her. She mentioned how popular Vera was with her own friends and how much they enjoyed being in her company. She ended with some more amusing stories which drew more smiles and chuckles. It was a celebration of Vera's life. Stories and events that were memorable, a personality that made her special, loved, and unique.

Cheri sang an old favourite of Vera's, so poignant for a funeral service, "We'll Meet Again." The lyrics were in the order of service that had been handed out as people entered the hall.

We'll meet again
Don't know where
Don't know when
But I know we'll meet again some sunny day

Keep smiling through
Just like you always do
Till the blue skies drive the dark clouds far away

So will you please say hello
To the folks that I know
Tell them I won't be long
They'll be happy to know
That as you saw me go
I was singing this song

We'll meet again
Don't know where
Don't know when
But I know we'll meet again some sunny day

Then she asked everyone to join in and sing along with her, just as it might have been sung long ago, so courageously, during a perilous time, back in England, during the war, perhaps in an air raid shelter, at a dance hall or along with the radio.

It was a wonderful moment. Frances, Ruth and Helen heard so many voices raised together honouring their mother and her life, singing slowly, softly, but deliberately, remembering her as she had touched their own lives, saying goodbye in such a special way.

A sizeable group from the funeral gathered at the Salty Dog following the service. It was an opportunity to relax, have a drink to toast a life well-lived and to chat informally where Vera and Maurice had spent many a cheerful afternoon or evening. Later in the evening, the family enjoyed a quiet dinner together at a restaurant in a reserved private room, providing them the opportunity to reflect on the day, drink a toast to Vera and relax in each other's company.

Vera was interred the following day in her niche. A small group, Ruth, Frances, Helen, Joe, Matt, Tiphanie and Cliff, and Kendall, Peter and Cheri were there to see her put to rest. There were a few last words and memories, time to think and remember, or pray quietly while sitting on chairs under a canopy. Then the box was handed to a cemetery worker. On top of the box was Maurice's Lion's Club ring, his Medic Alert bracelet, a couple of old British currency coins and Austin's paw print. The group watched silently as the worker sealed the niche. It was over.

Following a last lunch together, the family dispersed. Peter and Cheri headed to the airport, Frances and Joe hopped onto I-10 which would take them to I-95 and then the long haul north to Connecticut. Ruth and Stefan, Tiphanie, Cliff and Kendall returned to Crawfordville, Helen, Matt, and Marissa went to their home in Tallahassee. All took with them their own memories, the sound of Vera's laughter, unforgettable stories, funny episodes which had become classic over the years and would be related yet again and again to the younger generation. They would remember the life of this woman, so unique in her own way, never to be forgotten, but loved, cherished and admired for the rest of their lives.

AFTERWORD

The hidden scars of war were borne by Vera throughout her life, sometimes openly and consciously, such as when she reminisced about her father who became saint-like in her memory, so beloved and revered, and also when memories of terror resurfaced during Hurricane Kate, transporting her back to the nights of bombing raids during the blitz and the horror of the V-1 and V-2 rockets. However, many of the scars were subtle and unconscious. They marked her in her behaviour, her attitude, her view and expectation of life. She never could completely dismiss her need to conserve, save, make do, carry on, and sacrifice. She found it very difficult to throw anything away that was the least bit useful. She witnessed terrible destruction, hopelessness and despair but also the powerful pride of nation, caring, generosity and compassion of her neighbours and the population. She learned to be strong, persevere and accept her life, so disrupted, unsettled and uncertain. The scars of war helped her on her journey, sustaining her during tough times, setbacks and disappointments. She had survived the worst. She could live through anything.

The secret Vera mentioned toward the end of her life was never discovered. During my research to tell Vera's story, I read through all my mothers' papers, stories, memories and letters in the hope of discovering a clue. However, nothing was revealed. The declaration of a secret has created the titillation of a family mystery and has been the subject of much speculation and wonder with her daughters. What could it be? Why did Vera mention it if she had no intention of divulging it? Vera did seem to need to be the focus of attention at times, especially later in life, so perhaps the mention of a secret was just that, a call for attention.

After her death, as time has passed by, the secret has become more of an amusement and something to bring up occasionally to chuckle about, ponder about and contemplate. I have decided that her secret was more of a perspective and appreciation of life. Vera's life was one of love, challenge, adventure, overcoming hardship, and most of all, maintaining a sense of humour. Perhaps that is the greatest secret of all.

List found in one of Vera's binders of memories of the addresses of all the residences in which she had lived during her life.

36 Cassiobury Road, Walthamstow, London E17

143 Hall Lane, Chingford, London E4

21 Waverley Avenue, Chingford, London E4

22 Waverley Avenue, Chingford, London E4

120 Riverside Road, Watford, Hertfordshire

94 Gammons Lane, Watford, Hertfordshire

587 St. Alban's Road, Garston, Watford, Hertfordshire

7 Hendon Wood Lane, Hendon, Near Barnet, Middlesex NW7 (border of London)

4 Spring Gardens, Garston, Watford, Hertfordshire

11 Fuller's Road, Watford, Hertfordshire

10 Waverley Avenue, Chingford, London, E4

22 Waverley Avenue, Chingford, London, E4

12 Hurst Avenue, Chingford, London, E4

20 Hamlet Road, Romford, Essex

7 The Parade, Hall Road, Aveley, Essex

11 Broadlands, Road, Hockley, Essex

25 Woodlands Avenue, Rayleigh, Essex

39 Brocksford Avenue, Rayleigh, Essex

124 Weeping Willow Lane, Fairfield, Connecticut

26 Overhill Road, Fairfield, Connecticut

587 Old Stratfield Road, Fairfield, Connecticut

970 Black Rock Turnpike, Fairfield, Connecticut

2430 Donovan Drive, Kilearny Way, Killearn Estates, Tallahassee, Florida

2420 Dellwood Drive, Tallahassee, Florida

124 Westwood Drive, Tallahassee, Florida

3420 Gallant Fox Trail, Killearn, Tallahassee, Florida

2024 Longview Drive, Tallahassee, Florida

About The Author

England was Frances's childhood home. She emigrated to the United States with her family as a teenager many years ago. Although she loves America, a part of her heart always remains in the country of her birth.

Frances has been a storyteller for as long as she can remember, with her first audience consisting of neighbourhood playmates sitting on the curb listening to her tall tales. More recently, she has written and told or performed her nautical themed stories for school children visiting on field trips at a local seaport association where she worked.

She has visited numerous organisations, upon request, to speak about *The Forgotten Flag*, her first published work, and continues to visit classrooms at local schools to meet students who have read the book as part of their American History curriculum.

Frances worked for many years at a high school in Connecticut in the English and Social Studies Departments, which provided the perfect environment to inspire her love of history and writing. She has self-published several books, *The Brass Bell*, *The Curse of the Shark's Tooth*, and *Oscar of the Bismarck* which are young adult stories, as well as *St. Katherine's Dock: Target Tower Bridge* adult historical fiction. While working at the school, she prepared presentations for teachers to enhance their curriculum and subject matter when it pertained to British history. These have included the Elizabethan Era to better understand the time of Shakespeare, the Victorian Era to portray the time of Charles Dickens, and World War II – the British

Homefront.

When Vera passed away some years ago, Frances decided that her story must be told. *Vera's Story: Hidden Scars of War* tells the tale of a not so ordinary woman, whose memories of war were never far below the surface.

Author's Website

www.francesyevan.com

www.blossomspringpublishing.com

Printed in Great Britain
by Amazon